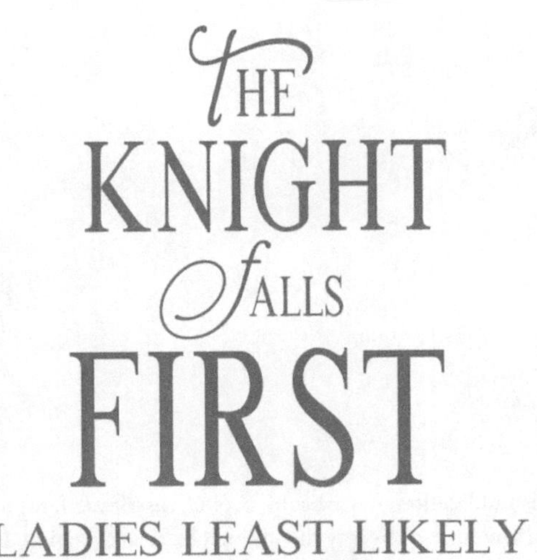

THE KNIGHT FALLS FIRST

LADIES LEAST LIKELY

MISTY URBAN

CHAPTER ONE

NEWPORT, WALES—LATE SUMMER 1799

Anne Sutton sat in the quiet pool of colored light falling through the windows of the church and watched her childhood friend—the woman Anne had once thought would be her ally for life—say her wedding vows to a man who really ought to have married Anne.

She shifted on the hard bench while the vicar expounded on the delights of marriage. Marriage, the promised future for which Anne had been preparing her entire life, and Gwen—disgraced, exiled, ruined Gwen—achieved it first.

To a *viscount*.

Anne opened her fan and studied the delicate painting on the leaf as if it could explain how her life had gone so terribly wrong.

Anne was lovelier than Gwen, always had been. Gwen had that dark red-brown hair and tended to freckle if she were not careful to stay out of the sun, and she never did stay out of the sun. Anne was the classic English rose: skin fair as porcelain, large eyes as blue as a summer sky, a prim red mouth, and hair the color of an old guinea. True, Anne's nose was too long for her face and had that bridge her mother referred to as "aristocratic," but Mrs. Sutton had always read her nose as a sign Anne ought to marry high.

A score of years ago, when the wide-eyed, motherless Gwenllian Carew had been delivered to Vine Court, Anne had sat on the tasseled cushion of fortune, in possession of every asset of birth and breeding, favored and petted and loved. And now look at her.

She watched the motes of dust twirl in the air when she swished her fan through them. Untethered, directionless, just like Anne's future. In the old abbey's lancet windows, stained-glass saints stared down on the scene. Saints didn't care how quickly, how sharply, fortune turned her wheel.

Richard Sutton, son of a successful collier in Oswestry, was once a gentleman rising in the world. His estate was the pride of the neighborhood, his wife and daughter envied, his heir adored by all. But then Gwen, his charity ward, drew the son of Vine Court into her snares, and that was the first cut, really. The first wound.

The Suttons turned her out at once, Anne's mother bitterly holding her head up above the scandal while Anne was forbidden contact with her companion of ten years. Daron's intended broke their betrothal and Daron ran wild after that, racking up debts. Then fate and a summer storm spilled Richard Sutton's last hopes into the ocean, leaving the family with only their house and their name.

And David Carew discovered veins of lead-silver, won himself a knighthood, and left all his lands and mines and money to Gwen. Who, after she had gone off alone and without a word, breaking her friendship with Anne like an old stick, found a viscount to marry her.

Anne's stomach pinched. She'd had nothing but a nibble of toast to break her fast and some tea brewed of weeds from St. Sefin's gardens. She must not let her belly rumble before Lady

Vaughn, sitting on the bench beside her. Her son Calvin might have made an ass of himself recently, but her ladyship meant to assure everyone in attendance that the Vaughns were a family to be reckoned with. In the weeks since she had come to Newport, Anne had taken real tea, China tea, with Calvin's mother and the Penrydd dowager viscountesses enough times to know that the Vaughn matriarch was born a predator. Weakness, to her, was a bone thrown to a hungry dog; she would attack.

Lord Penrydd pledged to endow Gwen with all his worldly goods, and the hot, dry taste of sand filled Anne's mouth. Gwen had broken the bounds of propriety and gentility, had lived for years on the ragged edge of respectability and poverty, and now she would be a viscountess. She would have several homes and estates, including Penrydd Castle nearby, which was as admired as Tredegar House.

Anne had peeped at grand Tredegar House in its park, home of the Morgans, when they drove the bumpy track between St. Sefin's and the Vaughn estate of Greenfield. *Anne* was meant for all these things. A husband with a distinguished family. Influence. A beautiful home furnished with expensive and tasteful items and herself, dressed in exquisite gowns.

The viscount gave his bride a wicked smirk when he said the bit about worshipping her with his body. Anne wondered if he knew that Daron had worshipped Gwen with his body first. She squeezed the ivory sticks of her fan, focusing on the prick of pain. The child would have been Anne's niece, had she lived.

Anne knew nothing about children, making or birthing or raising them, and she was four-and-twenty now. Her best child-bearing years were falling away like petals while Calvin Vaughn, who had accepted her parents' offer for Anne's hand, waited for her dowry to be restored.

There was a certain freedom in the waiting, in being admired and claimed but not yet bestowed. Yet for a young woman bred for one purpose, to preside over an elegant home and raise comely and well-behaved children, no dowry was a sentence of eternal spinsterhood. Such a girl would end up alone. Pitied. Probably poor.

At least she was not obliged to marry Calvin any longer. He'd thrown over Anne when he tried to convince Gwen to marry him. The gleam of those lead-silver mines held a powerful allure. When Daron failed to win Gwen back, Calvin made his bid, and neither of them, of course, had any chance against a viscount.

Anne didn't blame them for trying. She'd made her own pitch at Penrydd—how could she not, given she was obviously the superior choice? But he'd already lost his heart to Gwen, and Gwen had given hers to him. The vicar, a mild, genial man with spectacles and a rather endearing flop of hair over his brow, solicited Gwen's consent to the marriage, and she promptly gave it, along with an adoring gaze at her bridegroom.

What a notion. Marrying for affection instead of the usual reasons. Just one more instance of Gwen not caring about the rules.

He was an English vicar, so Anne could understand him. She had never learned the Welsh tongue, though she was born and raised in Llanfyllin, a good ten miles from the English border. Her turn of fate might taste less bitter were the ceremony held in Welsh and she couldn't understand more than the broadest outlines, Anne thought.

"Just as well they're making their vows before the babe comes." Lady Vaughn sniffed.

"Do you mean her maid of honor, Mathry?" Anne whispered behind her fan. The girl was clearly *enceinte*.

Anne had heard talk that Mathry had been employed in the Vaughn household. Of course maids weren't supposed to fall pregnant; it was a guaranteed dismissal. But the disgraced

Mathry had nevertheless caught the eye of Lord Penrydd's secretary and would be installed in Penrydd Castle as the housekeeper, so here was another girl who had given away her virtue and come out quite well on the other end of things.

"La, the viscountess herself is expecting a happy event, judging from the ripe look of her," Lady Vaughn replied. "I've had the girl harping in my house, and she's never been more than a scrawny sack of bones. How fortunate my Calvin was promised to you, dear, so that cunning baggage didn't get her hooks into him."

His mother could not think that Calvin still wanted Anne, not after all that had transpired. But Anne was not going to contradict her ladyship. She was too well-bred, for one thing, and for another, she was currently Lady Vaughn's guest at Greenfield while St. Sefin's filled with Penrydd family and friends in advance of the wedding.

And after the wedding, Anne would be blown off like dandelion fluff, with no notion of where she might land.

The vicar moved into his discussion of marital duties, placidly recommending the wife's subjugation to her husband, advising a meek and quiet spirit. Anne barely contained her snort. Gwen didn't have a single part of her frame that bent toward subjugation. Anne was the one who had been raised to obedience. She was an expert at meekness.

And look what that had achieved her. Gwen, the woman turned out in disgrace, had won the lordly husband and the title and the castles, and Anne had nothing, nothing.

What had she done *wrong*?

The crowd stood when the vicar pronounced the pair man and wife. Anne clapped politely along with the rest, but her thoughts floated everywhere, like those dust motes.

What did she do now?

Anne followed the stream of guests into the spacious, well-lit refectory where the wedding feast was laid out, her stomach a pot of boiling eels. The crumbling old priory meant enough to Gwen, and to her new husband, that they'd chosen to host their wedding festivities here and not somewhere more elegant, like a decent church in Bristol across the bay, or perhaps the cathedral at Gloucester.

Married in a cathedral: *that* was a way Anne could do well for herself. And a viscount was practically the lowest rung of English nobility, one bare step up from a baron. Anne could attach an earl and become a countess, and then she would outrank Gwen.

Too bad English lords were thin on the ground in Wales. Anne would have to go Bath, or even London, to put herself in the way of one, and how was she to manage that, without any money to fund such travel nor a dowry to tempt a lord?

She'd not find any prospects here, though Penrydd had made a public occasion of his wedding. Several of his London acquaintances and a good portion of the men he'd served with in the Navy were attending, including some who had survived whatever battle had injured Penrydd. Most of the population of Newport had also turned out, though this was a small enough number, considering Wales had nothing like a proper town— unless one considered Cardiff, which Anne didn't.

Then there was the strange community who lived at St. Sefin's, the misfits that Gwen had collected when she left the Suttons and came south. Thank goodness Prunella was here, one other young lady of birth and breeding. Prunella had married Penrydd's elder brother, the one who died trying to swim a cold Scottish loch for wager, and as a dowager viscountness, still young and pleasant looking, she, too, must be considering the options before her.

"A rather poor ceremony, didn't you think?" Anne whispered, attaching herself like a limpet to Prunella's side.

Prunella wasn't Anne's usual sort of acquaintance. For one, she was a soft, sweet dumpling of a woman, whose mother clearly had not hawkishly supervised every morsel of food Prunella put in her mouth. She also had no proper respect for London fashions. Unlike the muslin drapery which was *à la mode,* Prunella wore the native Welsh costume of a bedgown with the addition of lace at her bodice and a linen apron covering her silk petticoat. On another woman the bright red shawl and tall beaver hat would have looked a bizarre affectation, and on Prunella, it looked adorable.

"I thought it was lovely. Ooh, Gwen made her Welsh cakes." Prunella gazed with delight at the long, heavy oak table laden with dishes. "I helped pick the blackberries. Quite a few brambles around here, though I think we were on Morgan land. Went with the widows, didn't I, Mother?"

Prunella beamed at the old crone pushing her way toward the pile of golden, luscious cakes. Anne recognized her as one of the two widows who lived at St. Sefin's because they had no family and nowhere else to go. Why else would anyone live in a drafty old priory that smelled of old, wet stone and dust?

"All right for a *Saes.*" With a cackle, the crone snatched the very cake Anne had staked out for herself.

"What did she call you?" Anne whispered.

"It's what they call the English," Prunella said serenely. "It's not likely Mother Morris will ever approve of us. She has such a sad history, do you know it? Everyone here does. It was wonderful of Gwen to take them all in."

Anne shuddered, a chill dancing its way across the delicate muslin of her bodice and the lace she'd tucked around her neck. Gwen had said Anne might remain at St. Sefin's if she didn't wish to return to Vine Court and the teeth of her mother's disappointment, the trap of another arranged marriage, the humiliation of seeing her father burying himself in a bottle to avoid staring his problems in the eye and ignoring Anne, who had always been his pet.

As if she'd consider staying here, *living* in this half-ruined pile, with a motley group of outcasts and the destitute. How would she ever find a husband to support her? She'd never see the fashion plates or hear news from London. Lady Vaughn was at the center of the Newport circle. Anne would never escape the humiliation of being jilted.

She stabbed a cake and lofted it onto her plate. Of course everyone would admire Gwen for taking in outcasts. She'd been one herself, a motherless child, brought to Anne's home to be a companion, receiving the same tutoring, sharing the same table and even a bedchamber. And what had the Suttons received for their generosity?

Betrayal.

Little enough here she'd care to eat even if she could force food into her mouth, Anne thought peevishly. Half the dishes looked unpalatable. Breads too thick and heavy, several dishes with seaweed—could anything be *less* like food? What wasn't mutton or beef was cockles. At least there was a wedding cake, alongside an assortment of pies and tarts. Anne's mouth watered despite herself at the red, purple, and blue juices leaking out of the cut fillings. A proper sweet would temper the bile in her belly.

She took a tiny piece of the bilberry tart as she followed Prunella down the line. Their housekeeper at Vine Court was ever trying to show Anne how to forage from the land, and while Anne didn't care to put things in her mouth until they'd been properly washed and gone through the mysterious alchemy of the kitchen, Gwen had been an avid learner. Anne still remembered an afternoon when she and Gwen sneaked away from lessons on Greek history and lolled in an empty field full of knapweed and meadowsweet, daring each other to eat raw wimberries off the bramble and laughing at the faces the other made. They'd come home with their chins and aprons stained purplish-blue, mouths puckered in smiles that survived Mama's scolding about their errant ways.

What had they talked about in those golden rambles, those sun-blessed days? Anne plucked flowers and muttered verses over puddles of water, scrying to see the face of the man she'd marry. Gwen stopped to chat with every crofter or peasant or miner or carter whose path they crossed. Anne fussed over catching her apron or spoiling her shoes, while Gwen didn't care if her hair fell loose and snarled in the wind. Gwen was nothing but a miner's daughter; she was permitted such hoydenish ways. Anne was a gentleman's daughter and must behave like a gentlewoman at all times.

A destitute gentlewoman, on the knife edge of spinsterhood. Defiantly, Anne took another slice of pie—raspberry, she hoped —and trailed Prunella to a table. She couldn't grow fat and horsey when she needed to be married, but she could expect two days of greasy food from coaching inns when she traveled back to Llanfyllin.

Prunella's mother-in-law, the other dowager Viscountess Penrydd, took a seat down the long oak table, holding court with the Price relations. Lady Vaughn hovered near, trying to insert herself into their conversation. Prunella seated herself a safe distance away, and Anne beside her.

"So what shall you do, Miss Sutton? Now that you're not to be married after all." There was no malice in Prunella's expression, only a friendly warmth as she took a large bite of tart.

Anne put down her fork.

It was too noisy in this room, all the feasting people speaking so loudly. The scent of myrtle overpowered all, reeking from Gwen's bridal bouquet, strewn in small bowls along the table, spilling from the deep recessed windowsills. Just seeing other people put seaweed on their plate, though she would never eat it, set those eels alive in Anne's belly.

"I do not know," Anne confessed. "There is no one at home left to marry." An engagement broken, at her advanced age, and what other prospects had she? Panic clawed up her throat.

Penrydd and Gwen stood near the door of the chapel, accepting congratulations. They hadn't been showered with grain yet, but if Gwen had already caught a babe, they didn't need blessings for fertility.

Gwen was five and twenty, only a year older than Anne. All the years Gwen had spent building this place, overseeing a community, cooking and tending to travelers and providing care to the ill and needy, Anne had sat quietly in the parlor at Vine Court, embroidering pillows and darning stockings, having the same conversations and organizing the same church meals, waiting for her family to scratch up a dowry so Anne might marry at last.

Penrydd hadn't married Gwen for her mines of lead-silver.

Anne wanted to shriek her rage and grief to the high timbered ceiling of the hall, built to house ancient Welsh nuns. Her future ruined and lost, everything she'd hoped for her life out of reach, and she'd done nothing to deserve this. Had she?

"I don't suppose I shall marry again." Prunella bit into another thick slice of tart. Prunella didn't appear the type to let anything turn her off her feed.

"But you're a viscountess," Anne said. "Men will want you for your title, if nothing else."

Prunella wrinkled her nose. "But do I want them?"

Not to be married? The thought drew a great blank in Anne's mind. What did a woman become if she weren't desired by, attached to, under the protection of a man? Marriage defined a woman. It meant everything, a house, a home, a family. A spinster was an emptied-out husk, pushed about by any careless breeze.

"What will you do instead?" Anne asked.

Prunella shrugged and chewed her tart. "I'd liefer set up my own house somewhere. Lydia, that's the dowager, I'm naught but a servant in her eyes. She orders the household as she likes, and the townhouse in London is so poky, at least a hundred years old. I'd like a cottage of my own where I might order things as *I* wish."

Anne regarded her tart. Prunella would have a jointure from her husband, a comfortable income if she spent it wisely. Widows were not held in contempt.

But what could Anne do? Return to Vine Court and live quietly with her parents, an embarrassment, their unmarried daughter aging before their eyes. She would grow crotchety and eccentric and end up keeping the kind of small, nervous dog she had always detested.

Or she could go to a fashionable town and find a post as a lady's companion, fading to a long gray shadow in her looking glass, overlooked and unloved.

At the moment, either of those options appealed more than marriage to a man who didn't really want her.

"I've been looking for you two merry maids, I have. Here's wine."

Anne drew back as Mathry set a goblet before her. A pregnant and unmarried woman must be beneath Anne's notice, even if Gwen had made her, and not Anne, a bridesmaid. "Oh, I'm afraid—"

"Elderberry? I'm very partial." Prunella sniffed her goblet, then took a hearty sip.

Elderberry wine at a wedding breakfast? Anne went rigid. Not to serve proper, imported French or Portuguese wines, at least to the ladies—

"Made it meself a few days ago. Dovey showed me how." Mathry leaned against the table edge beside Prunella as if she had every right to mingle with gentlewomen, one of them a dowager viscountess. "Turned out rather fine, would you say?"

Prunella smacked her lips. "Delicious. You must give me the receipt."

Mathry fixed her gaze on Anne. "And where's that brother of yours got to, then?"

Anne put down her cup and swallowed, trying to push the bilberry down her throat. "I—I do not know."

Daron was not invited to the wedding on account of his attempt to blackmail Gwen into marrying him by bringing, with Calvin Vaughn's assistance, a suit claiming that St. Sefin's was a brothel and Gwen its madame. Penrydd, as the proper owner of St. Sefin's, had put paid to that notion. Anne had been witness to his rather splendid performance in court, and must admit it was a fine thing for a well-looking man to behave heroically.

Not one to quit when he was already behind, Daron had then attempted to negotiate with a notorious criminal who insisted Penrydd owed him money. To Anne's everlasting shame, she had delivered Gwen, the Viscountesses Penrydd, and herself into the clutches of the Black Hound to lure Penrydd and save Daron. Penrydd had managed another heroic rescue, the result being that Gwen had finally been brought to admit she loved him and Daron must never show his face around St. Sefin's again. Anne herself was only here by the grace of abject and humilating apologies to her former friend, who had been polite but distant with Anne ever since.

"My dear Miss Sutton," Lady Vaughn broke in, delivering a glare so potent that Mathry ought to have disappeared with a shriek and a puff of smoke. "I hope you will not listen to a word of gossip that evil-intentioned people may spread about my son. People," she added pointedly, "who have reason to bear a grudge against my family, though they had been deprived of their position on proper grounds."

Mathry merely lifted her brows and stared Lady Vaughn full in the face. Anne, in her position, would have shriveled into tears.

No, Anne would never be in Mathry's position, because she would cast herself into the pit of hell before she would submit to a man without marriage. Just look what it gained a woman.

Gwen, a viscountess. And Mathry, a marriage proposal from Penrydd's Scottish secretary, who, it seemed, planned to accept her despite the babe in her belly and offer her a home in a lovely Welsh castle.

Anne blinked. The wages of sin were not what she'd been taught to believe.

"I ... I suppose you are looking forward to your own wedding?" Anne ventured as Mathry showed no sign of taking her leave. "You and the father of your babe."

Mathry's normally dreamy face hardened. "Oh, the Scot didn't plant a babe in me. Want to know who did?"

The glitter in the other woman's eyes warned Anne that she did not, in fact, want to know who had fathered Mathry's babe.

"Your intended," Mathry said, cutting a look down the table at Lady Vaughn. The words splashed into Anne's stomach like a stone in an algae-covered pond. "Came at me like a midge the moment I set foot in that house, and won me, *twymffat* that I was, with promises he never meant. Then when I caught, told his mother I'd tucked meself into *his* bed, and she turned me out with no more than the clothes on my back. Calvin Vaughn," Mathry said with a sneer, "ain't fit to lick your boots, nor mine."

Anne stiffened her shoulders. A knight's second son could not be expected to acknowledge a throw he'd gotten on a serving maid. It simply wasn't done. Men had their needs, and women accommodated.

But Anne, as a gentleman's daughter, deserved at least some boot-licking, didn't she? As a consequence of her birth?

"I don't—"

Anne closed her mouth on the words. She'd been about to say she didn't believe Mathry, but that was a reflex that came from her long training not to question men, not to trouble men, not to defy men. Every aspect of Mathry's expression said she was not lying.

Anne believed her. And moreover, she knew, with the knowledge that went deeper than training, that Calvin Vaughn was exactly the type of man who would do such a thing.

"I ... I don't suppose he's attempted to make things right with you since," Anne managed, since she couldn't leave the previous words hanging, especially with the way Mathry and Prunella were staring at her.

Mathry snorted. "You're a sweet dolly, aren't you? He's too much a slubber de gullion for an innocent like you."

"I'm not a simpleton," Anne riled, though she feared she was. All she knew was how to navigate the safe, cushioned spaces she'd been born into. A place like St. Sefin's, on the edge of society, was beyond the pale to her.

No one seemed to heed the usual boundaries between lord and peasant. The maimed and idiots dined at a table with titled ladies, and Dovey, an African woman who had been born enslaved, sat beside a new viscountess, heads nearly touching, ash-brown hair tangling with black as they discussed some private and delightful business, judging from the smiles on both of their faces.

No, Anne didn't have the sophistication, if such it was, to navigate this kind of world. Praise *God* she was going back to Vine Court, where at least if she were poor, she would remain respectable about it, and the lines that ordered the world in its proper hierarchies were clearly drawn.

"Mum's right. Shouldn't be listening to nasty gossip, my sweet."

Calvin Vaughn appeared out of the crowd. Anne swallowed a gasp that felt more like a burp of those noxious fumes boiling in her belly. Calvin, for all that he looked like a spoiled prince, was another predator.

"You should not be here," Anne said in a low voice. My, but she sounded so calm and steady. Almost achieving Lady Vaughn's archness. "I am *sure* Lord Penrydd does not want to see you."

Or Gwen, given that Calvin had tried to publicly shame her. But Gwen only borrowed her power from her spouse, another advantage of having a titled husband.

"My pet." Cavlin gave her a full-toothed smile. "I am a Vaughn of Greenfield. I am the son of Sir Lambert Vaughn of Rogerstone. Everyone wants to see me."

"Knight of the Bath or of the Garter?" Prunella demanded.

Calvin blinked. "Er. Knight Bachelor. Awarded for service in the Royal Household, under the direction of the Marquess of Bute, he who—"

Prunella scoffed. "Not inducted to an order, then."

Anne would never in her life be able to deliver a man such a cool, evaluating stare as Prunella levied at Calvin Vaughn. She didn't have the temerity.

Calvin straightened his shoulders, eyes flaring. "Our family is on its way up. Hewitt was quite the hero at Acre. Honor to the name, and all that."

In her visits to Greenfield, Anne had heard the Vaughns' elder son, Hewitt, spoken of as if he were no less than a second Jesus setting foot on the Levant. Bolstering the Royal Navy as they held back the conquering forces of the French and their megalomaniac little general, Napoleon. Protecting the Holy Land as if he were a crusading knight, this time preserving it for Ottoman rule, rather than Europe's. He was likely twice as arrogant as his brother, and three times as proud.

On the surface, Calvin Vaughn appealed. His blond hair was brushed forward in the current style, his eyes the blue of the sky on a cool day in spring. His dark blue coat was expertly cut, and the clawhammer tails tapped the backs of his knees in tune with the latest fashion. But on closer appearance, his stiff neckline lent the illusion of a line to a jaw that was puffy with signs of spleen. The eye-watering stripes of his waistcoat disguised the barrel-shaped chest and stomach. The buckskin breeches, on the other hand, disguised nothing. The leather clung and dipped to every bulge in his plump thighs and—she couldn't *not* look—his crotch.

Anne averted her eyes. Calvin Vaughn appeared as slenderly endowed with virility as with good sense. Since here he was, showing up at the wedding reception as if he'd never tried to ruin Gwen, as if he'd never cozened and then rejected Mathry, who faced him with a stare as cool as Prunella's.

"I hope your lady's smarter than I was. Listen to that gossip long and hard, dearie," Mathry advised Anne. She straightened and strolled away, hips swaying.

The bride and groom took seats at their small table of honor beside a distinguished-looking gentleman with white hair, the epaulettes of an admiral on his coat, and the badge of the Knight of the Garter on his chest. Prunella whispered that he was the new Earl of St. Vincent, under whom Lord Penrydd had served when he was still a lieutenant in the Royal Navy.

An earl! Anne regarded the honored guest with new attention. Did he have children? A pleasant, robust, well-shaped son who was not prone to swimming icy waters or getting himself blown up in battle?

"Would you look at that. Penrydd giving his wife a love

spoon. How very Welsh," Calvin sneered. "Completely gone native, hasn't he?"

"A what?" Anne asked.

"A love spoon," sighed Widow Jones, taking Mathry's place at their table. Widow Jones was slightly younger than the other crone, but they were two peas in a pod when it came to running St. Sefin's and poking their noses into the business of folks about. "My Conan carved one for me, he did. One with a wheel, to signify our life going on well together. And so we did, until he went and died."

Anne froze. What was she to say that would not sound condescending or ineffectual? Losing the man she had pinned her hopes on upended a woman's world, whether it was after many years of marriage or simply a long-hoped-for betrothal.

Look at Lydia, the Dowager Viscountess Penrydd, who, having failed to catch the notice of the earl, sat with her mouth puckered as though she'd been served vinegar instead of wine. Her husband had died and she relied on a stepson to support her, and with a new viscountess who clearly had a leash around Penrydd's neck, what could the dowager do to protect her position? Look at Prunella, who despite her wishes would have to keep her brother-in-law happy to claim her jointure.

What could Anne, a gentleman's daughter, say to a peasant woman whose life had been years of childcare and endless work? They all of them were made to depend on men, fathers or lovers or husbands or brothers. And when they lost that protection, they were prey, naked as field mice. No wonder Gwen, destitute and alone, had taken shelter in this old stone abbey, trying to find some rest from the cold and the wind.

Anne might very well find herself in such a position, one day.

Calvin Vaughn scoffed. "Looks as if Penrydd carved that one himself, and not with any skill."

Gwen accepted the token, her eyes shining with a softness Anne had never seen. "What is this, milord?" she asked with laughter brimming in her voice. "A sea serpent?"

"A bird," Penrydd replied, affecting sternness. "Which anyone with proper eyes would detect. Clearly my whittling skills are far beyond your ability to decipher."

"Clearly," Gwen burbled. "I will treasure it, sir."

Anne had to turn away at the look that passed between them. Such adoration. Such *joy*. She'd never seen a man look so at a woman, with such care and feeling, as if she were the sun that bounded his world, all the light he needed to live.

"Come, Anne," Calvin said. "I've no stomach for more of this foolishness. Your brother's waiting."

Anne's last bit of courage picked up its skirts and whisked out the door like a child set free from her lessons. "I don't believe I want to see him," Anne said faintly.

But when had a man ever heeded Anne's wishes? When had anyone?

CHAPTER TWO

Daron waited at the rear of the priory, where outbuildings ranged around a spacious courtyard hemmed by a low wall separating it from the pasture beyond. The heap perched on a hill that afforded a lovely view of the River Usk and the Severn Estuary beyond, where the Bristol Channel eventually poured into the Irish Sea. Around and to the north of them, the shadowy hills of south Wales sat crowned with thick woods and seamed with coal and precious ores. The sky, studded with clouds that promised a light rain later, looked as if it might swallow the land.

Anne wished it could swallow her. Pluck her up and toss her onto the waves of cloud, carry her away like a bird. How nice it would be to fly for the first time in her caged life.

Daron looked awful. Every one of his recent sins was stamped upon his face. A healing wound above his temple marked the blow by which the moneylender had defeated Daron's foolish attempt to barter with him. His complexion was sallow and his eyes fever-bright. He had been living with the Vaughns since he couldn't set foot near St. Sefin's.

"You shouldn't be here," Anne said. A regular Cassandra,

she was, croaking of doom to her listeners, none of whom heeded her.

"Anne," Daron said. "Listen to me. You must marry Vaughn."

Calvin slid a hand inside his waistcoat and rocked on his heels, smug. "See now?"

She didn't see. "Why?"

"The money," Daron said simply.

Anne narrowed her eyes. "My dowry is gone." And how unkind of Daron to rub a fistful of salt in *that* open wound.

Once, her brother had been her protector, her hero, her knight in shining armor. There was nothing Daron did not know, nothing that could daunt or defeat him. He walked the streets of Llanfyllin like a minor god, adored, fêted, a model for all to imitate. Even after their ward had thrown out her scarf for the Sutton heir and they'd had the unpleasant business of turning her out, Daron was untouchable. He was engaged to be married to an heiress, the daughter of a man whose coal mines had earned him a gentleman's estate and a baronet's title. As the man had no son, he'd likely make Daron his heir. Daron Sutton was climbing his way up the ranks.

And then, somehow, his fortunes changed. Anne shivered and plucked at her shawl as a playful breeze swirled up from the Usk, nipping at the bare skin between her short sleeves and gloves. The baronet's daughter had run off with her dancing master, breaking the engagement. Daron brought a suit for breach of promise, and while he was within his rights to do so, the persecution had made him slip further in the eyes of his peers.

Tradesmen stopped extending him credit. Others came forward with debts of honor that Daron had accrued while gambling on the fortune that was to be his. Anne's dowry trickled away into the hands of Daron's creditors. Then her father attempted to make up the losses with investments that proved too good to be true, and—

Here they were now. She, standing in a thin gown and a cold breeze, the air blowing through her. The brother who had betrayed her on one side, the betrothed who had abandoned her on the other. Both holding up the sides of the chute meant to funnel Anne, like a reluctant calf, to the cart that would bear her to slaughter.

"It's all right, pet." Daron's eyes shifted to a point over her shoulder. He looked wary, as if he expected attack from an unseen menace. "Calvin will marry you and make everything right."

"I don't have to marry anyone," Anne lied. Of course she did; there was no other future for her. What, she was to live here at St. Sefin's like the widows and idiots, working her hands to sticks, living on scraps from the butcher? She'd—she'd trade her modesty first.

"You have to marry him, you worthless tart," Daron said, impatience edging his tone.

The breeze turned cold and plunged down Anne's spine like a sluice. Daron had *never* spoken to her like this.

"Calvin can apply for probate for his father's estate," Daron said. "The plantations. The ships. He'll own all of it. He'll say Hew is dead at Acre. No one's heard from him in months, and the siege ended in May. Calvin will gain control of the money, and he'll marry you, so you're taken care of. It's the only option you have."

Anne pointed her nose toward the sky and hugged her shawl around her trembling shoulders. "I have options aplenty."

Another lie. Her mind reeled, clawing and keening like a bird trapped in a cage. Marry Calvin Vaughn? With what she knew about him?

"What options, Nanny?" Daron sneered.

That hurt, that he would dredge up her childhood nickname now. Using their old affection against her. "I'll go home to Mother and Father. They'll arrange a new betrothal for me." There had to be *someone* left. Someone who, in the years since Anne had reached a marriageable age, they hadn't passed over or alienated in their calculations.

Gwen's betrayal and abandonment had changed Anne's fortunes, too. Once she had been the most sought-after maid in Powys. She'd been flooded by invitations from the genteel families of Oswestry, turned heads when she and her mother went to Shrewsbury for the shops. She'd had offers from young men across Wales.

She didn't quite understand what connection her father had to Sir Lambert Vaughn, or how Calvin Vaughn became the candidate of choice, but surely her father would never wish her to cast herself away on a dirty dish. She would return to Vine Court—it was a rough, bumpy journey of at least two days by coach, and that was without dumping rain—and she would begin anew.

"You can't go back to Vine Court." Daron shook his head. "Mother and Father are about to lose the place."

"What?" Anne whispered. The cold swooped and dove around her, like a great hawk that might carry her away. The talons pierced straight to her heart. "That cannot be."

"They've mortgaged the place twice over for money to live on. They'll lose it unless we can find them money to pay." Daron trained his stare on her, his eyes the exact shade of her own. Anne had always thought she could see her soul reflected in Daron's eyes.

Not anymore. She didn't know where her brother's soul had gone, but it wasn't with them.

"Marry Vaughn," Daron repeated. "He will have money. He can help save Vine Court so our parents aren't turned out into the street. But he won't have any reason to help old friends, will he? Unless he has married their daughter."

"No." Anne's heart did something strange then. It turned on itself like a small, frightened animal and dove down to her belly, seeking shelter. Her lungs bellowed for air. "I cannot marry him."

Daron shook his head sorrowfully. "Can you really be that selfish, Nanny? When Calvin could help me, our parents, and give you a place in the world—you can't do this for your family? For all of us?"

Why me? Anne wanted to shriek. Her dowry was gone. Her looks would go soon, worn down from having her future in doubt for so many months and years. She and Daron had come south with the intent of securing Daron's marriage to Gwen so her fortune, left her by her father, could restore their prospects. Clearly, a certain viscount had ruined *those* plans. Daron was nothing if not clever; she was certain he had other recourse. But *this?*

"A home," Daron whispered. "A family. Pretty curtains at the window, Welsh cakes on the table at every meal. Gowns from London. And you, alone, would be the saving grace of your family. We would all be uplifted by St. Nan."

Anne tugged at the lace around her throat, which strangled suddenly.

"Silk curtains," Daron crooned. "Silk gowns."

"The fashion is for muslin, now."

"Muslin gowns, then. All pretty and white. And you like Greenfield, don't you? Such a pleasant house. All those gardens. Such grand families here about, living in grand homes. You'd be the reigning hostess, queen of the neighborhood. Travel to Bath or London whenever you wished. Perhaps even Paris."

Paris. Anne's mind whooshed away, snared by the long-held fantasy come to life. Of course, no one wanted to go to Paris now, with the streets still running revolutionary blood, but elsewhere on the Continent—there was a whole magical world shimmering just beyond the blue waters of the Channel. Anne had dreamed of it for so long, of seeing the lands beyond her stolid Welsh hills.

"And Calvin," Daron added, "dotes on you entirely."

"Developed the most violent attachment," Calvin agreed with a grunt. He shifted his weight, and Anne's gaze flitted, against her will, to the small bulge in his groin. "Go mad if I can't have you."

The wings of the sudden dream broke, and Anne crashed back to earth. To this green hill, this cruelly chill breeze, the smell of smoke on the air—she swore she could still smell the wreck of the burning boat she'd barely escaped from. The scent of sulfur and dung had clung to her for days. Daron had led her to that trap, and he meant to trap her again.

The brother of her heart, her childhood hero and her first love, turning against her—why? The tart she'd eaten lay like bitter ash in her mouth.

"You don't want *me*," Anne said to him. "You want something you can get through me."

"Anne, don't be a—" Daron began, but Calvin cut him off, stepping closer to Anne.

"Anne, old girl, don't be a ninny," Calvin admonished. "You're not all bad. Can bear to have you in my bed, I wager. And you won't get a better offer."

That goat beneath the lean-to across the way would be a better bedmate than Calvin Vaughn, Anne knew, but the words couldn't make their way through her lips. This? This was to be the end of all her girlhood hopes, her passionate dreams? What had she done to deserve this?

Her lips were glued shut. It was as if she'd eaten that dratted seaweed and it had sealed her mouth. Her heart battered her chest, but no more than a whimper escaped her as Calvin Vaughn lifted her hand to his lips. Her gloves were silk, the thinnest barrier, and somehow his lips were not warm, but clammy.

"Bring you back to Greenfield with us," Calvin said confidently. "Mother'll be in transports. Post the banns and find you a frock. Wed within a month. All falling into place." He leered and winked. "Have a mind I'll enjoy the marital bed. Usually like my ladybirds with a bit more *here*—" He shaped hands along his own curved hips— "but s'pose I can make do, eh? Plant a babe and a girl fills out nicely, I've found."

Anne stared in disbelief, waiting for Daron to slap the man's face and call him out for speaking to her in such a degrading manner.

Daron laughed. "Name one after me," he said.

Anne turned and bolted back into the building, using the first door she could find.

CHAPTER THREE

Anne didn't know her way around this heap, though it wasn't terribly large; she simply had a regrettably poor sense of direction. Instead of taking her back to the refectory where there was food and, at the least, elderberry wine with which she could try to drown out thoughts of the grim future that awaited her, her chosen exit led into the church.

The long nave lay cool and quiet, soaring to the timbered ceiling. The tall windows, newly repaired, let in the kind of soft light that made the world seem a deceptively kind and lovely place. The saints smiled from behind the lead cames holding together panes of stained glass. Knots of flowers decorated each pew, garlands draped between like loving arms, and petals drifted along the stone floor, releasing sweet scents as Anne trod upon them.

The air after the vanished festivities was melancholy, which suited her exactly. How many human trials had these saints witnessed, uncaring? And how many human joys had they presided over, caring less still. Their function was merely to hear prayers and pass them along. They were saints, with their eyes on the holy; they cared not at all for the tides that tossed the human heart.

"I suppose you're proud of yourself," Anne said to the one with the unfurled scroll naming her St. Gwladys. Gwen's favorite.

St. Gwladys returned a self-satisfied smirk.

A bundle of myrtle, the largest on offer, sat in St. Gwladys's window, marking her special status. Anne grabbed a stalk. She always imagined she'd have myrtle at her wedding, heaps of it; every Welsh bride carried a sprig if she could. The small white flowers opened like tiny hands, innocent, trusting, bristling with delicate stamens, each topped with a tiny yellow bulb. Stupid myrtle. It didn't look like a flower—it looked like a bug.

Anne tore apart a bloom and grimaced with satisfaction as the scent released into the air, spicy and sweet. She continued until every bloom on the bough had been mutilated, then crushed the dark oval leaves beneath her shoe, releasing the smell of rosemary. She reached for another sprig.

"Do you plan the same fate for all of them? You've a great task ahead of you if so."

Anne whipped her head around at the intruding voice. A man's voice, deep and full of humor, with a raspy timbre to it that suggested his amusements were few. She located the man who had produced the voice and threw him a glare of rebuke.

He stared back. Insolent churl.

"You might warn a body of your presence," Anne snapped, feeling her heart, belatedly, knock out of its usual rhythm and start speeding as if she were a hare being chased. "Rather than creeping about like a spy."

"I knocked on the front door. No one answered."

His lips twitched. Still amused, despite her tart reply. She felt the brazen need to attack and scrub that smirk off his face. She couldn't make the saint or Calvin Vaughn or the rest of the world stop smirking at her, but condescension from an arrogant stranger she didn't know was the outside of enough.

"They're all in the back, enjoying the feast. You missed the wedding by a mile," she said with every bit of insolence she could muster.

"So it would seem." His brow creased. He had straight, dark eyebrows that arrowed toward a small scar between them that made it look as if he were scowling. Perhaps he *was* scowling. His manner seemed one of forced calm, and so did his dress.

His neckcloth was wrapped in a stiff cuff and tied in a manner that held no pretense to fashion. His coat was dark blue superfine but not cut in the clawhammer style, and the puffed shoulders and broad, deep lapels were at least two seasons out of fashion. His waistcoat was of plain gold silk and his pantaloons didn't cling, yet the shape of his clothing hinted at a frame that was strong and honed lean.

His military boots came up over his knees and dangled small tassels, nothing ostentatious, nor was the chain depending from his waistcoat at which he tugged to produce a watch. Nothing about him was overblown. On the contrary, his effect was studiously understated, as if he restrained himself with great effort. Anne, in her cross and contrary mood, found this utterly aggravating.

"Better I missed it. The wedding. As I was not invited." He snapped the case closed and tucked the watch back into his fob pocket.

"Then why are you here?"

"Curiosity, you might say."

"Do you know the groom?" Anne demanded.

He could be an acquaintance of Penrydd's. He had that military air about him, the straight back, an alertness to his posture that said he was ever on the watch. Waiting for an enemy to attack from behind, much the way Anne was ever looking over her shoulder these days. The recognition did not put her in charity with him. Penrydd's friends were, by and large, indigent second sons, inveterate gamblers and rakes, and not a one of them would make a decent husband and save her from Calvin Vaughn.

"Penrydd? I know him only by repute." His remark, delivered in an impassive tone, told her he knew of the old Penrydd, not the man he'd become. "Are you the bride?"

Anne gave in to an unaccustomed bout of spleen and tore apart a second bough of myrtle. She threw it to the floor and stomped on it for good measure. "Hardly."

"That's a relief."

An odd tone in his words made her lift her head and stare again. He looked almost as if the words had escaped against his will, yet she would swear he was a man who measured every word, thought through every action before he executed it. He had that deliberate, intensely focused air.

That intense focus was trained, for the moment, on her. In the shadow of the church, she could not detect the shade of his eyes. His sideburns were trimmed, as was his hair, exposed by the tall beaver hat tucked in his elbow. But the skin along his straight jaw and around his firm slash of a mouth looked a shade paler than his cheeks, as if he'd recently shaved a full beard. He had a pronounced groove above his upper lip and a dimple in his chin, as though a loving Creator had run a finger along his mouth before sending him out into the world.

Anne wanted to trace the exact path with her own finger.

Was she going daft?

"Why?"

She meant to make the words an accusation. They came out a whisper, as if her voice had caught on something.

"Why what?"

She cleared her throat and told herself to stop being the

nanny goat Daron had always called her. "Why are you relieved I am not the bride?"

He gestured toward the bough of myrtle in her hands. "A bride destroying her wedding decorations would suggest she discovered the holy state is not as blessed as she'd been led to believe."

Certainly not if her matrimony led to Calvin Vaughn. Anne shredded a flower of its silken petals and tossed the stamens into the air. They twirled like pixie dust before floating gently to the floor and, in some part, her gown.

"Matrimony is a hoax," Anne declared.

He cocked one straight brow. The pronounced slant made him look devilish. "Not a sacrament?"

"It's a *lie*. All our lives, we are told we are made for it." She tore one petal off a fresh, innocent flower. "Meant for it." Another petal followed the first. "Promised love and poetry, a home and *babanod*." Petals three and four parted their stem at her savage yank. The Welsh word slipped out; she didn't speak Welsh. She barely understood more than a dozen words.

"And then, once the shackle is on, we discover it's a trick. A trap designed to convenience a man at a woman's expense. Not the safety we were promised."

She tore the fifth petal free, tossed the handful of stamens into the air, and threw the sprig to the floor. The scent of juniper filled her nose, peeling back the top of her head, releasing her inhibitions. This was a feral Anne she'd never unleashed. She was beginning to frighten herself.

No doubt she had frightened the stranger as well. His mouth quirked up at one corner. Goodness, he had a riveting mouth. The thin upper lip bore a marked Cupid's bow, in a line with that groove, but his lower lip was almost too full. His face was handsome, in an unremarkable way, but that mouth snagged the eye. A blend of harsh discipline and sensuality, and a betraying hint of beauty.

Heavens, the myrtle was infecting her brain. She had no business admiring men, beautiful or otherwise. And on the whole, this one was rather shabby. He might have that mouth, and that watchful air, but he also bore the look of a man who had been accustomed to rough living. He dressed like a gentleman, but perhaps that was only to insert himself into a wedding and find food.

"So you wish not to be married?" He moved through the nave along the outside of the pews, as if he meant to protect the other windows and their burden of flowers.

"Emphatically not." Prunella had said she might not marry again. She'd hinted she would wait for a man she liked.

Anne didn't have that option. She reached for another myrtle branch to commit savagery and realized St. Gwladys's windowsill was bare.

The saint smirked.

"I can see why you are not enjoying the festivities, given your feelings about the matrimonial state," he remarked.

"The food's nothing to speak of. And the wine?" She snorted. "Elderberry. What I wouldn't give for a good Madeira right now."

"A nice rich port," he agreed. "And a haunch of mutton."

Anne sneered. "They'll have smeared it in seaweed."

"Laver sauce? How I've missed that."

She turned to face him, appalled. "You can't want to eat seaweed."

"*Bara brith*," he said. "Laverbread. Cockles with vinegar. And Welsh cakes. I've dreamed of them."

"You have strange dreams."

"Who are you, milady, to denounce a man for his dreams?"

His regard spurred strange sensations, as if he'd trailed a

hand over her bare skin and left her with gooseflesh. The hair on the back of her neck lifted in warning. The dreams he spoke of were not all about food.

She turned away, flinging out a hand. "The seaweed is that way."

"Ahem. Why don't you precede me?"

"Do you require an introduction?"

"Let us just say there are one or two people in that company who will be very glad to see me." He touched his fob pocket, as if checking for a valuable. "And one or two people who decidedly will not be overjoyed."

"Why? What have you done?"

"That depends on who you ask. Proceed, Miss—" He gestured with one hand, a rather elegant flick of his wrist. So, the manners of a gentleman, if not the birth. "You have not told me your name."

"Will you tell me yours?"

He drew in a sharp breath as a surge of voices rose suddenly, an excited babble. His gaze went to the hall leading to the refectory. "It's time for the reckoning," he said.

This ought to prove interesting. Anne, not certain she had fully vented her spleen, wanted to see the impression this stranger made. More than that, she wanted to watch him a bit longer. He grew more prepossessing the more one looked at him, more discoveries to acknowledge and appreciate. There was something not quite right in the way he moved, though she couldn't define what it was, and at any rate, as she turned toward the refectory, he was behind her. Hair prickled all over her scalp.

Why should she be so very conscious of his eyes on her, perceiving the cut of her gown, the drape of her shawl over her arms? She put a deliberate sway in her hips, a delicate, ladylike glide she'd been taught in endless grueling lessons in the

Vine Court drawing room. Let him look. She *wanted* him looking.

The noise had resulted from the long, heavy refectory tables, there since the reign of Henry II, being moved aside to make room for dancing. Everyone in the room was on their feet, circulating excitedly, while musicians set up in one corner. Someone brought in Gwen's traveling harp—Anne remembered her having it at Vine Court. She felt an imposter, an imposer on these revelries, watching from the outside but not part of the merriment.

And beside her this stranger, tall, lean, and alert, was an outsider, too.

"Oh, someone dropped a pin." Anne spotted the small stick of bronze on the floor, about to roll between two flagged stones, and picked it up.

"The pin!" Prunella shrieked. "Anne found the pin!"

"The pin!" The cry spread, leaping from mouth to mouth like the sweep of wildfire. "The pin has been found!"

Anne stood bewildered. Pins were dear, yes, especially a bronze pin like this, but such an uproar. It must belong to someone important. Her heart took up its rabbit beat once again. Perhaps Lydia, the dowager Dowager Viscountess. Perhaps she would notice Anne at last and make a pet of her. Take her to London. Introduce her to men who were as handsome as this stranger, but less alarming in their manner. Perhaps she could marry someone proper and *he* would pay to keep her parents in their home.

Dovey, the dark-skinned beauty, clapped her hands. "Bodes a wedding!" she said with a smile. "Another wedding for St. Sefin's."

Gwen slung her way through the crowd toward them. "You found my pin!" she exclaimed. "That's the custom, it is. You're next to be married, Anne *bach*. Who's the young man to be, then?" She turned to the newcomer with a frank, curious grin that faltered once she got a look at him.

A storm of wind shook through Anne's head. Calvin Vaughn, back inside, pushed toward them like a fat pike swimming upstream. The smirk on his face was ten times as smug and condescending as the saint's in the window. *Marriage.* He meant for Anne to marry him, and now this blasted pin was his opportunity to claim her.

Then he marked the man standing beside Anne, and the smile dropped off his face.

The most curious silence followed the pin clamor. It spread swift and somber, like the ripples in a pond when something precious had been dropped and lost in it. The hush reached the edges of the room, including the head table, where Penrydd stood, his eyes widening.

Beside him the Earl of St. Vincent shot to his feet, disbelief overtaking his placid features.

"You," he exclaimed.

"Me," the stranger agreed.

Lady Vaughn gave a scream like her soul had been torn from her body. Her eyes rolled back in her head and her limbs collapsed like a marionette clipped of its strings. Mr. Evans, Dovey's new husband, caught her ladyship with his one good arm before she hit the floor.

Anne turned to regard the stranger. He started forward in a halting fashion, his eyes on Lady Vaughn, every line in his body as tight and pained as a rigged sail fighting the wind. The fragments of suspicion rushed together with a snap, and she knew him.

Calvin's older brother, Lady Vaughn's revered hero, Greenfield's prodigal son and heir. Hewitt Vaughn.

Back from the dead.

CHAPTER FOUR

"Well, clearly I'm not dead," Hewitt Vaughn said. "And was at no time that I can recall. Though I did believe I'd been cast down to hell a few times."

He spoke to Anne, it seemed, though he knelt on the floor and held his mother's inert body upright. When everyone else had panicked, Hewitt, like Evans, had acted, and that was likely the only reason her ladyship hadn't split her head like a melon on the flagged stone floor. A wave of sound surged around them, like high tide coming in, yet for a moment Anne had the strangest sense that she and he stood alone together in the eye of a storm.

Calvin Vaughn bleated something in his brother's ear. He sounded exactly like a sheep that had been cut from its flock and stranded alone on the hillside.

"Get hold of yourself, man," Hewitt snapped, "and do something to revive her." Their mother was no slight woman, and a wince crossed his face as her torso sagged against his.

"Her vinaigrette." Anne glided forward. It wasn't like her to run to the assistance of those in distress—she tended to run away from, not toward, danger—but she felt pulled to his side as if a toy on a string.

Or a lure meant to draw its prey toward the jaws of a predator.

Now that was silly. He was only a man, despite the fuss being made over him. Anne knelt across from him, her skirts folding beneath her.

"It's a small silver box. She carries it on her chatelaine."

"Would you?" Hewitt gestured toward his mother's ruffled form.

Anne had admired the gown earlier. Making no attempt to look like a maidenly sylph, which was the current ideal, Lady Vaughn had instead chosen a lavish morning gown of yellow-dotted muslin, with ruffles at the hem of the full skirt and crossed bodice. Anne ran her fingers around her ladyship's waist and found the small chain and the carved silver case that held her smelling salts.

"Here." Anne wrinkled her nose at the overwhelming scent, ammonia dissolved in her ladyship's perfume, a heavy attar of roses. Cautiously, she waved the tiny casket before the older woman's face.

"Closer." Hewitt clamped his larger hand around her wrist and pulled. Anne squeaked and nearly dropped the vinaigrette.

He was strong. He'd stripped off his gloves while speaking with her in the church, and his bare flesh seared heat into the silk barely shielding her skin from his.

The smelling salts awakened Anne's own senses. Above the sharp ammonia and roses, she smelled *him*, leather and a trace of smoke, woodsy and deep. His shoulders were so broad—his coat must be padded. His hair was the color of the bark on the blackthorn that grew around his house, but there was a hint of gray above his ears. That must be a trick of the light. Hewitt Vaughn was young, not yet thirty. And his eyes were blue. Not the pale spring blue of Anne's eyes, but a deep, infinite blue, like the waters of Llyn Tegid when the clouds rolled back in deepest summer.

Those eyes bespelled her, conjuring up a cascade of memories. Family excursions to that lake, eating bread and cheese amid the cottongrass and watching butterflies land on the plum preserves. Listening to the call of the curlew and watching the spotted wings of the hen harrier glide through the air above them, its sharp eye seeking dinner. Anne searched the bogs for asphodel and cloudberry while her father and Daron cast nets for the *gwyniad*, a delicious whitefish that could only be found in that lake. Those days when she was young and the princess of her world, cherished, coddled, given all she desired.

Daron terrified her with stories of the *afanc*, part dragon, part crocodile, that crouched in the fathomless depths and surfaced to snap unsuspecting humans, preferring, Daron claimed, young maidens like Anne.

Hewitt Vaughn gave her the same impression. All calm and inviting scenery without. Something dark and dangerous lurking within.

Lady Vaughn stirred and moaned. Her eyes fluttered open, hands clasping and unclasping as if reaching for knowledge. "Can it be? Hewitt! They told me you were dead."

"Not dead, Mother," he replied.

Gwen stepped to the rim of the circle that surrounded them. "I have hartshorn—never mind. Well done, Anne *bach*."

One of Hewitt's straight eyebrows winged upwards. "Anne?"

"Sutton," Anne managed, more clumsy than usual as she snapped the silver vinaigrette case shut.

His eyes clouded, turning gray like the lake when a storm gathered. "Ah," he said. "The Suttons."

He said this as he might have said *the plague*.

"Hewitt Vaughn, in the flesh." Penrydd joined his bride and surveyed the newcomer with interest. "Survived Acre, then?"

"After a fashion." Hewitt dipped his hands beneath his mother's arms and shrugged, asking for aid. Penrydd and Evans both reached down a hand to lift her ladyship. Calvin Vaughn goggled at his brother as if he were indeed the *afanc* who had crawled from dark waters, dripping slime.

Evans left Penrydd to deal with her ladyship and reached out his arm to raise Hewitt.

"You're home now, soldier," Evans said. "It's over."

Hewitt looked into the other man's eyes, gripping his arm as if in a vise. His gaze flicked to the empty sleeve pinned against Evans's coat, the crutch under his armpit.

"It will never be over," Hewitt said quietly. A cold shiver wormed down Anne's spine.

"Captain Vaughn." The Earl of St. Vincent pushed forward.

"Admiral, sir." Hewitt snapped to attention and made his salute.

"I thought you were supposed to be in chains," St. Vincent said.

"I was, sir. But the colonel brought me home with the rest."

At the mention of prison, the other men stepped back. Almost as if Hewitt, now, were the one with the plague.

"No," Lady Vaughn moaned. "Oh, no."

Everyone fell back save for Anne, who stood alone beside the returned stranger. She'd thought him a war hero, a prodigal son. But it seemed Hewitt Vaughn was in worse trouble than she was.

～

SO THIS WAS ANNE SUTTON. Hew tried not to stare like a schoolboy as the Vaughn carriage jostled its way back to Greenfield.

The Sutton name nudged up memories. Sir Lambert Vaughn, in the days he was a servant on the fringes of the royal household, had done business throughout Wales and the west of England, and had cronies everywhere. Sutton had been one he mentioned often. Hew tried to recall the source of the Suttons wealth—lead mines? Coal? His father claimed the girl was comely and would have a staggering dowry. Told his mother they should secure her for Hew.

There was a baker's dozen of heiresses Hew's parents wanted for him, and he'd botched all their plans by earning his commission in the Royal Artillery and leaving to fight the French. It was a loud declaration that he meant to be his own man.

"So after I left for war," Hew said, "they staked you out for Calvin."

The passionate fire in her remarkable blue eyes as she decimated boughs of myrtle in the church of St. Sefin's had burned out. The delicate glow he'd seen when she administered the vinaigrette to his mother was gone. Her gaze, as she turned it from the window of the carriage to his face, was flat, cold, and hard as blue glass.

"My parents and yours came to the agreement," she said. "I had little input in the matter."

The scorn in her voice scraped his skin. What had *he* done? Besides return, seemingly from the dead, to give his mother apoplexy.

And fail, in the crucial moment, to plead his case before the Lord Admiral St. Vincent, the man he'd infiltrated a wedding to see. Standing face to face, it was clear the earl believed the story that had been given out about Hew's imprisonment. And with his mother so fragile, under the eye of every one of her friends, he couldn't bear to trot out the accusations that had been leveled against him.

They would know soon enough. And so would she. That curiosity on her face, lovely, sharp, and knowing, would turn to contempt.

His brother rode alongside the coach, along with Daron Sutton, on horses they'd borrowed from the King's Head in Newport. The angry gestures accompanying their low mutters sent a warning prickle down Hew's spine.

He'd learned to heed that warning. It had saved his life on more than one occasion.

Hew shook his head. His mind buzzed like angry bees: so much information, so much newness, coming at him all at once. St. Sefin's, a dilapidated ruin when he left, housed a community of people. Penrydd, a name he'd heard around the borders of his childhood, an estate he'd assumed a vacant ruin much like Rogerstone Castle, had a robust new lord to fill the viscountcy. A naval man, but such things could be forgiven.

There was a new viscountess, and this Anne, doing her best not to bounce on the hard seat of the coach as it rolled along the track toward Bassaleg, had some association with her. That explained why a woman with her delicate, cultivated beauty had appeared in a provincial village like Newport.

Yet Newport had doubled in size since he left, with more ships than he'd ever seen floating in the Usk or drawn up on the sands, loading and unloading cargo. There was scaffolding around the old wooden bridge that signaled a coming replacement. There were opportunities here, if a man had not ruined his future.

What was not here: his father. That gap loomed larger than anything, but no one had yet dared to bring him up. It was as if they all feared the mention of Sir Lambert might conjure him, roaring up from the pits of hell like a demon he was, or had been, to his eldest son.

Not to Calvin. Calvin, the younger, their father's favorite, had known a different set of parents than had Hew. Calvin knew his way around this world that had sprung into being while Hew was away, while Hew felt as if he'd landed on a shore as foreign as the Levant.

He hoped he wasn't staring at Anne Sutton like the lighthouse who could guide and safeguard his path. She—an utter stranger—somehow felt like the one person who could translate all this strangeness for him. Make it legible, this land he'd returned to. Put things back in their proper order, and make him believe his path wasn't lined with mines or shrapnel waiting to come at him from some hidden angle.

But she'd seen how the Earl of St. Vincent had hailed him. And so had everyone else.

"Ought I congratulate you?" Hew asked finally.

She lifted her chin. "On what?"

"Your engagement."

She turned her face toward the cloudy glass of the window. "Save your felicitations, please."

What a profile she had. *Comely* was a staggering understatement for the beauty that Anne Sutton possessed. It might be a word used of her face were she captured in a portrait or even in a cameo. But with the living spirit of the woman to animate it, that face was the stuff of legend, of epic poetry. She could launch a thousand ships and a hundred more.

That bold, straight nose would no doubt, to some, pose an argument against the full measure of beauty, at odds with the sweet slope of her brow, the delicate cheekbones, the pert chin. But Hew liked the indication of strength in that noble nose and the straight line of jaw that hinted she was clenching her teeth.

Good teeth, white teeth, cared-for teeth. With her milky skin and glorious hair and the sweetly rounded bosom tucked under a modest lace kerchief, she was the image of English womanhood, everything he was sworn to protect.

All that beauty meant for his worthless, petulant brother.

He'd found her savagely tearing apart myrtle, declaring marriage was a trap and a lie. Clearly, Anne Sutton did not anticipiate wedded bliss with Calvin. "But why?"

His mother, sitting beside Hew on the forward-facing seat, spoke for the first time. Till now she'd been staring at Hew with her mouth moving in silent expressions, of what, he didn't know. Curses? Prayers of protection?

Hew knew he wasn't the cocky, handsome lad who'd sailed away five years ago with the rank of an officer sewn on his sleeve, and he wasn't the slightly graver young man who'd been granted a brief leave a year later. The years of wear and danger had left their mark; every ugly choice he'd made, he wore on his face.

"Calvin has rather a bit to do to mend things with Miss Sutton," his mother said. "There has been a misunderstanding."

Anne raised her brows. They were chestnut brown, like her lashes, a contrast to her guinea-gold hair. Hew sensed, from her expression, that his mother had delivered a magnificently inappropriate gloss on a tricky situation.

"I should think you'd wish better for him than me, madam," Anne said flatly. "Given my father has lost all his fortune and left Daron and me with nothing."

"All his fortune?"

He was too used to the bluntness of soldiers and knew the remark was inadvisable even before she scowled. Yet he'd been under the impression that the Sutton fortune was large. One would have to approach the squandering of it with a degree of concentration, or outrageous bad luck.

"Now, now." His mother toyed with her chatelaine as if she might resort to her smelling salts once more. "Calvin esteems you for your own self, Anne."

"Does he?" Anne replied, and turned a wooden face toward the window.

She was holding something back, though with the greatest of restraint, given the way her knuckles clenched the reticule in her lap. Hew wondered what Calvin had done. He'd hoped time and years would mature his brother, bring out some hidden vein of honor. Surely with Hew gone, after their father's death, Calvin would have come to some sense of responsibility.

"You could say no." Hew's voice came out roughly, scraping like an iron chain over stone. A sound he knew well. "Refuse to marry, if you don't wish to."

"Oh, good heavens, how simple a solution. I wonder I did not think of it." She returned to the window in a huff.

Being in the army roughened a man. Acre wasn't a place where the officers dined their ladies or entertained diplomats and their wives. All Hew had known in the last few years was artillery blasts and the noise of battle, hot, dry, and filthy, and then a cold prison that stank of plague and despair. He might have become careless of the finer points of etiquette. But he was certain Anne Sutton was treating him as rudely as possible without hurling direct insults into his face.

Hew looked to his mother for an explanation.

She plucked at the ruffles about her waist, flipping them in and out of place. "Calvin has had a difficult time," she said weakly. "After the passing of your father."

"Difficult how?"

His mother's eyes flitted to Anne, who held herself stiffly, but Hew could almost see her little ears pricking.

"His behavior has ... not been as I might wish. No need to discuss it here." His mother forced a smile. "Let's get you home and settled first, shall we? The dinners and parties I must plan! All our friends will want to see you, Hew."

Home. He'd forgotten what home felt like, looked like. He'd forgotten what safety meant. For so long he'd lived with the shuddering jolts of artillery thudding into the pocked earth, long mindless stretches of time interrupted by surprise attacks, the day framed by the muezzin's ululating call to prayer.

The English countryside was so bloody pastoral. Bullfinch and pipits peeped from the leaves of the alder and wych elm climbing the slope of the old fort built before the time of the Romans. A breeze stirred shushing waves on the River Ebbw as they passed Pye Corner and Bassaleg, turning up the track toward Tregwilym.

The leather and wood creak of the coach, the clop of the horses' hooves on the roadway, was a lullaby compared to the throaty cacophony of a ship under full sail. Prison had not been silent either, not with the wails of the despairing, the screams of the tortured, the whimpers of the starving, and the dragging chains of the mad who could not keep still. The quiet here might well drive Hew out of his head.

Looking at Anne Sutton, for some reason, made the sudden tension in his muscles recede. The gathering noise in his head subsided. There was something so calming about her. She soothed his fretting like the hot milk posset his nurse used to make him at bedtime.

He couldn't deny the parts of him stirred by her beauty, but he had learned, through long deprivation, to ignore those baser urges. It was her civilized demeanor that called to him, that mixture of grace, intelligence, and fortitude, a balm on his raw and wounded edges.

He didn't deserve such soothing. He'd been a savage for far too long; there was no redeeming him now.

And Anne Sutton wasn't for him. She was trapped in this

carriage with his mother and a war-scarred, bitter soldier, and somehow, though it seemed she disliked the idea, she'd been claimed by his brother. Who, it seemed, had not improved from the sulky, arrogant boy who threw a tantrum at watching his favorite playmate go to war.

They passed the iron gates leading to Tredegar Park and its acres and acres of elegant landscaping, with the enormous red-brick house nestled at its heart like a jewel. That was the place for a woman like Anne. A stately mansion, embossed with the elegance of a past age more mannerly and courteous than this one. Greenfield, for all its grandeur, was a poky dower house compared to Tredegar. She likely knew this, and perhaps it was one reason she resented her obligation.

She was going to marry Calvin. The thought twisted Hew's gut as if a grappling hook had caught him there.

It was time to bring his mind away from Anne Sutton and back to his mission. Back to the reason he had returned to Wales, aside from the wish to quiet the roaring in his head, aside from the hope to redeem himself, which apparently was as vain as all his other dreams had become in the last few months.

"Are the Goulds in residence?" Hew asked his mother. "At Tredegar House, that is. I imagine Sir Charles, the old judge, is and always will be MP for Breconshire." Sir Charles could be a formidable ally in Hew's cause.

His mother pursed her lips. It had been one thing when Gould inherited the Morgan estate and adopted the surname as well as the house. A new knight in the area was on her footing, the knight's lady her equal. But then George III made Sir Charles a baronet so he might have a title worthy of the Morgan wealth, and that rankled.

Never mind that the family had seen their share of troubles, if Hew's memory served. One son had died young, another in action when he was barely twenty, and a daughter's first husband, a naval captain, had left her widowed a few years ago.

"And the heir, Charles," Hew added. "Where has he been kicking about, now that he cashed in his colors and retired?"

The baronet's eldest son and heir, a captain in the Coldstream Guards, had been taken prisoner at Yorktown during the fight with the American Colonies and was fortunate to return home. Hew would categorically deny that any of Charles's stories had fed his imagination about seeing new lands and peoples, even down the barrel of a gun. He had run away to enroll in the Royal Military Academy by his own lights, and not to impress his friends, a neighbor he looked up to, or a father who would not, under any circumstances, admit that his eldest son and heir would ever be worthy of his approval and commendation.

When Hew passed the difficult entrance examination and was admitted as a Gentleman Cadet, first class, all Sir Lambert was heard to remark was that of course Hewitt would not simply buy his colors, as was the done thing, but would instead choose the one segment of the army, the Regiment of Artillery, where a man had to work his way up, prove his worth, and earn his commission as an officer.

Lady Vaughn shifted on her seat, gazing out the window at the squared brick expanse of St. Basil's church in Bassaleg, home to generations of Tredegar's honored dead and, more recently, Sir Lambert Vaughn. Hew hadn't been present for his father's death or interment; he wasn't allowed leave. And he knew his mother would never forgive him for that.

"Charles is MP for Monmouthshire now," his mother said. "He'll inherit Tredegar, and his wife, Mary Magdalen, can talk of nothing else. But then she was only the daughter of a naval captain, so this is quite a step up for her."

Anne winced, and Hew wondered what accounted for the

expression that drew together her brows. Unplucked brows, with a delicate arch, giving her an innocent, vaguely surprised expression. Her lips must naturally be that coral color, since she would long ago have rubbed off any paint by the way she pressed them so tightly together. And the flush on her cheek that rose, then faded, told him she was wearing neither rouge nor lead paint.

She didn't need anything to accent her native beauty. The longer he gazed at her, the brighter she blazed, until now it almost pained him to look upon her.

His brother would escort this woman on his arm at parties and dinners, and perhaps a drawing room of the Queen's, if he took her to London to celebrate their marriage. He would behold her down the dining table from him at breakfast and dinner.

He would have the liberty of her bed.

Hew had thought, as the frigate ferried him and the last of the troops and guns away, leaving Acre nothing but a golden-brown line on the distant horizon, that the breeze over the Mediterranean might blow away the haze of acrid smoke that had filled his lungs and his head for so long. He'd been certain, as the ship passed Gibraltar and nosed into the cold Atlantic, that the worst of the torture lay behind him and in time would fade only to nightmares. He'd thought he could leave it all behind.

He'd imagined, all this time, that home in Wales, with the green hills and the dreamy valleys and the very different kind of sea, would be a refuge, a haven, a paradise after the dry, flat land of the Levant. That with British food and British songbirds and the staunch, stolid sounds of the English language in his ears, he'd forget the scars he bore and the pain in his body would fade, eased by the damp breezes and the thick sky and the thinner, gentler sun.

Now he saw that a worse fate awaited him, a torment he could never have imagined. This creature was staying in his home, belonging to his brother, and Hew would live within sight of a glory he had never thought to long for, but now would be reminded every day he could never have.

The real torture was only beginning.

CHAPTER FIVE

Anne paced the knot garden at Greenfield, waiting for Daron for return. He'd slipped away somewhere, without a word to her, when surely he knew they must talk.

Everything was changed now that Hewitt Vaughn was home. Calvin couldn't take over the property. He couldn't help the Suttons. He didn't need to marry Anne.

Her heart swelled, pressing against her short stays. She didn't need to marry at all.

She'd done everything wrong anyway. She'd been good and quiet, obedient and demure. She'd done everything her parents wanted. And for that she was promised to a man who lied, cheated, seduced housemaids, and was likely an opium eater, considering that his breath ever smelled of saffron.

She was tired of being good, if it gained her nothing.

She could wish to live at Greenfield, though, Anne thought, dawdling along a garden path as the sun shone gently upon her.

Would her parents truly lose Vine Court? It was a lovely home, a trim Georgian block nestled in its green vale like a jewel box on a lady's dressing table. It had been built by Anne's grandfather when his coal mines made him rich, then enlarged by

Anne's father when new methods of extraction made him richer.

Greenfield, a century older, felt wilder, still recalling its medieval roots as a castle built by the Kemeys family, who had come to Britain in the train of William the Conqueror and become one of the strong marcher lords shielding civilized England from the fierce Welsh. Anne had never before thought it strange that the Suttons, like the Vaughns, had lived inside Wales for most of their lives and still thought of themselves as English.

Calvin was sure to discard her now, since she could bring him nothing. But perhaps Lady Vaughn would want Anne as a companion, and she would not be a burden on her parents. Anne could fetch shawls and carry parasols. She'd already proven she could administer a vinaigrette. She was an amusing conversationalist, and she possessed all the other required accomplishments: she could recite poetry, she played the spinet, the harp, and the pianoforte, and she was often praised for her voice.

This would become her favorite walk, the Elizabethan garden with its tall hedge of holly and yew, the sky a dome as blue as sheep's bit. Gwen had been the one keen on the names of plants and the remedies they could be used in, making her a favorite with Anne's nurse Pym. But it was Anne who had learned how to supervise a kitchen, double-check the house-keeper's accounts, and barter for goods when a merchant or peddler had priced them too dear. Gwen might sprawl on the ground among the flowers; Anne learned how to arrange them in the most attractive manner, matched to the occasion and the season.

But Hewitt Vaughn was returned now, the master of the household. Lady Vaughn must have all her decisions approved by him.

Say no, he'd counseled, as if Anne had the liberty of her own desires. *Refuse to marry, if you don't wish to.*

Her steps faltered on the raked gravel path. Did he mean he did not approve? Calvin did not need his brother's permission to marry, but he would require a home. Hewitt could turn them both out if he wished. Anne sensed Hewitt Vaughn would make a formidable adversary.

A heavy step sounded on the gravel walk outside the garden, a man's tread, and Anne tensed as a flash of dark blue coat shone through a gap in the hedge. Daron had returned. He would listen to Anne's pleas. He would know what to do next, to save her.

It was Hewitt Vaughn. She had summoned him by thought, like a demon.

He strode through the hedge onto the gravel pathway of the knot garden and stopped, staring at Anne across the stone sundial. His brows drew together toward that small scar, and her shoulders tingled as hair lifted at her nape. He had learned what Anne had done, how she had risked the lives of innocent women to save her brother, and he meant to turn her out at once. There would be no position as his mother's companion, no safe shelter here. She would be turned out with nothing, like Gwen had been turned out of Vine Court all those years ago.

He hadn't changed his dress. The same coat hugged shoulders that couldn't possibly be that broad without padding, the neckcloth still looked as if he hadn't given it a single thought beyond the knotting, and the gold silk waistcoat and the pantaloons outlined an ideal masculine form, as though he were a classical statue brought to life. But his manner held an ease she hadn't seen at St. Sefin's. His hair was tousled, his mouth no longer a straight slash, and he'd unclenched his jaw at least once into a smile, judging by the grooves on either side of his mouth.

Anne supposed he couldn't help if the bones of his face

made him look as if he could be ruthless. That mouth said not everything about him was rigid.

But his demeanor changed as he regarded her. He'd come loping into the garden like a satyr enjoying his domain, until he saw her. Now his body tightened like a bow drawn to the arrow.

"I can leave, if you like," she blurted. She didn't refer only to the garden.

"Nonsense. You were here first." He dipped his head in a gentleman's acknowledgement of a lady's presence. He had better manners than her brother or his, that was certain.

A flutter set up around the edges of her chest. He'd startled her, that was the reason. "Walking," she blurted, hearing how nonsensical the words were the moment they emerged. "Only walking."

"Enjoying the space, I hope. My mother used to love this garden in particular."

He strolled one of the brushed paths beside a small flower bed outlined with a short hedge of yew. A blend of red and pink flowers flung their scent into the hair, heavy, alluring.

She'd removed her hat and gloves, like a hoyden, and left them on the wooden bench in the arbor, because she thought she was alone and there was no one to scold that she'd freckle. Let her freckle. If it were just for Calvin Vaughn, let her chase away all her beauty with a stick.

Except it was Hew who stood here, and suddenly Anne wanted her gloves, because her fingers tingled in the strangest manner, and she wanted her hat as well, because an odd warmth rising along her neck told her she must have taken too much sun. Thank goodness for the lace tucked at her bodice. Anne's mother counseled her to show more of her breasts, but Anne felt altogether naked already, with nothing but the muslin of her gown and the scented air between them, laced with the chatter and whistle of birds.

He glanced about. "You have no companion?"

At Vine Court, Anne would have a maid to accompany her out of doors, but maids were thin on the ground at Greenfield. There was a hallboy and staff enough in the kitchen, a cook and kitchen maid and someone for the scullery, but of chambermaids, Anne hadn't seen so much as the edge of a skirt disappearing down a hall. Perhaps they were trained to be invisible, as the best maids should be, but even so, they couldn't spare a girl to help Anne dress for the wedding. The housekeeper, Mrs. Harries, had come with a grim set to her lips to help fix Anne's hair and gown, and it had been all too clear she felt called away from other, more important duties.

The gooseflesh spread down her arms, not accounted for by the soft breeze that carried the smell of the river. Was Hew cast in the same mold as his brother? Anne tensed as his amble brought him to the path intersecting with hers. She was alone with him. He was a large, powerful man. And he blocked the exit.

She had the strong intuition that Hewitt Vaughn would never, in his life, use his size to impose his will on a woman. Her senses stood at high alert as she watched him look about the garden with its neat knots of flowers grouped by colors and height, the decorative elements placed here and there. But it was not fear that he roused in her.

"Greenfield is very beautiful," she said.

He nodded, glancing at the red brick of the building behind them, the tall windows in their casements catching the light. Someone could look out and see them. He wouldn't attack her in plain sight. The tangle of sensations in Anne's chest rolled tight like yarn around a spindle.

No, this strange reaction to him wasn't fear. She drew in her breath as he walked closer, but not because she was preparing for flight. She *wanted* him to draw closer.

Was she addled from the sun?

"I suppose my mother has told you all about the history. How the castle was sacked by the armies of Owain Glendŵr, then rebuilt into a manor house under the Tudors, using the same brick they made for Tredegar. The house escaped destruction during the Civil War, when Cromwell's armies razed Newport Castle. My father bought it from a man who made improvements using his profits from the slave trade, and my father built his wealth the same way." He broke off, a bitter edge entering his tone.

Anne reached for her shawl and realized she didn't have one, thus the sudden shiver. She'd never given a single thought to the slave trade or anything about it until she came face to face with Dovey, Gwen's dark-skinned friend, and learned the woman's history. Africans weren't what she had been taught to believe.

That tangled feeling roiled through her chest and downward, as if it meant to draw all her innards into a tight, writhing mess. Nothing about the world was what Anne had been raised to believe it was, and should be, and was what she deserved. And now here was this man, who'd spent years in places she couldn't locate on a map, who carried a haunted shadow in his eyes and a bronze tint to his skin cast by a faraway sun, and he seemed the most exotic and dangerous element of all.

She swallowed hard, feeling a sweet-bitter taste on the sides of her throat. That infernal elderberry wine.

"It is still very beautiful," Anne whispered, wondering if she oughtn't enjoy the elegance of the place, now.

He might think that the reason she wished to marry his brother. So she might visit Greenfield once in a while, sit in the papered parlor beneath the crystal chandelier, drink from Lady Vaughn's prized porcelain tea service, and brush her silk slippers along the expensive carpet. But it was Hewitt's lady who would preside over this place, approving the menu with the cook, supervising the chambermaids, strolling these very paths with her hand on the arm of her husband.

This man. That strong arm. Anne flushed with envy for that unknown woman.

He leaned over a bed lined with small green plants, examined one, then plucked a leaf and chewed it.

Anne stared with astonishment. She oughtn't stare. Staring made her notice the way his jaw moved as he chewed. Made her look at his mouth. And looking at his mouth pulled at that knot rolling about her innards. Perhaps she was not sun-touched, but ill.

"Feeling peckish?"

"Mint." He smiled. "Freshens the breath. Try one." He held out a leaf.

"Er—thank you." She took the leaf and examined it. Indeed, it smelled like mint, tasted like mint, that sharp, sweet tang that lifted a lid off her mind. A memory flashed up, green hills starred with daffodils, a sky that hefted its blueness to infinity. Gwen, whooping and running through meadows dotted with orchids and hoverflies rising from the rampion, skirts clenched in her fists. Anne, always more careful, half-running behind her, pausing to peer at each butterfly, eating whatever Gwen pulled from a stalk and offered to her. It was always sweet.

Hewitt Vaughn called up the same sense of wildness, of freedom, that Gwen had released in Anne. So much the opposite of the strict discipline her mother demanded, the decorum she had to observe within the beautiful painted walls of Vine Court.

He plucked a handful of leaves from another plant, deep green and spiny. "Wild lettuce," he said, crunching on one. "Good for relieving pain and inducing sleep." As Anne reached for a leaf, he gently moved her hand away. "But also known to induce hallucinations."

She pulled her hand back. His bare skin had touched hers. The place felt hot, as if she'd passed her hand near a flame. "Is that why you are eating it?"

She meant the hallucinations. She meant to be sharp. She oughtn't let a stranger jest and be familiar with her. *Certainly* not allow him to touch her bare skin with his.

Instead, her voice came out breathless, curious. And as he turned to look at the rest of the garden, she realized: he held himself like a man in pain. Like a man carrying some inner ache, some unhealed wound.

Something it would take more than plants in an herb garden to cure.

"That is all I remember," he said, his gaze ranging over the knots of beds. "But every plant here is useful in some fashion. Mrs. Harries knows all of them."

So would Gwen. Anne was already weary of comparing herself to Gwen, and finding so much lacking. She didn't want Hewitt Vaughn to see her deficiencies.

"Hellebore at the doorway will keep witches away," Anne said, grasping for what she remembered of herbal lore. Superstition, mostly. "And a sprig of ivy under the pillow ..." She caught herself. That was a charm to make a girl dream of her lover. Anne had tried it several times, to no effect. She slept as sound as a hedgehog in hibernation, always had.

He turned to face her, and every bit of Anne's customary common sense fell away as if snipped by scissors. Had she dreamed of him? She could almost see him in her imagination, lodged far back in the mists. The strong shape of his face, the clean cut of his features, the noble lift to his chin. That *mouth.* Those eyes, the dazzling blue of deepest summer, and the rest of him—she shifted her eyes so she could look at his body without seeming to, let the impression of him rise to the edges of her vision. Well-knit limbs. So tall. Yes, if she'd dreamed of anyone, she'd dreamed of him, and—

"Why are you here?" he asked.

Anne gulped. "Here? In the garden?"

"At Greenfield," he said softly. "Why are you to marry my brother?"

Every soft wisp of dreaminess left her head too, clipped away by the cold steel, following her last bit of sense. And apparently decorum.

"Why didn't *you* accept me?" she asked. "My parents offered you first."

Immediately her face burned with shame. *What* could have made her so forward of a sudden? And why did her voice hold that plaintive, wistful quality? She grabbed the nearest flower, a daisy, and plucked its petals with nervous fingers.

Hewitt's eyes narrowed, the lines about his eyes tightening, and she would swear his ears moved back on his head. She'd shocked him. She felt a delicious rush of satisfaction. Shocking, forward Anne: this was a novel creature. She might come to like her. She yanked the white florets from the flower head and let them waft to the ground, settling on her slippers. As if she were a fairy queen and only walked where flowers strewed her path.

She should not be standing here with him. She was growing fanciful. Delirious, perhaps, from the heady perfume of the enclosed garden. And the growing awareness of his presence, the solidness of him, the maleness. He was taking too long to answer.

He cleared his throat and shifted his weight. "I knew as a lad that I wanted to be a gunner," he said finally.

"A what?" Anne knew she was not going to like his answer, but she meant to force it from him anyway. She had the urge to *break* something—the urge had goaded her all the way from the church of St. Sefin's—and for some reason, this man before her, this utter stranger, seemed the proper target. He held a piece of her past and the means to her future. It was as if, by attacking him, she could somehow tear herself free.

"The Royal Artillery," he clarified, which was not much use, since Anne didn't know the first thing about the military. "I knew since I was twelve that I wanted to enter. I took the exams at fifteen. Made bombardier at eighteen, commissioned as an officer at twenty-one." He glanced around the garden again, as if growing reacquainted, and again Anne noted his strained movements.

"My mother hoped I would come home and head the militia. She was sure the Duke of Beaufort would give me a regiment—he has the charge of the Monmouthshire militia, has for years. And with the militia I would not have to leave the country, or even the county. My parents pressed hard to have me married, invest in the family business, set up a household of my own." He winced. "So I went to the West Indies to fight the French, and I've only been back once."

"No wonder your mother fainted at the sight of you," Anne murmured. "Calvin thought you were dead. He was ready to take over the estate."

Hewitt's eyes tightened again, as if he braced for a blow. "That is disappointing, but not at all a surprise."

He would assume Anne had plotted with them. She twisted the stem of the flower in her hands. "I should not be here," she said. "Your brother is the one pressing for our marriage, though he does not even like me. And my brother stands his ally."

That must all change now that Hewitt was home. Anne could be free. No prospects, no income, her parents starving in genteel poverty in their home, no dowry but her looks to try to find a husband who could save them all.

Refuse to marry, if you do not wish to.

Anne's heart inflated, straining at her ribs. She *would* refuse, if it would not mean disgrace.

But Gwen had survived disgrace. And come out, at the end of things, with a viscount who loved her.

Anne pulled the last floret from the flower as if it could foretell her future. "*Pas de tout,*" she muttered, throwing the petal to the ground. Of course the answer would be no.

Hewitt's mouth twitched. That mouth was going to be the death of her. She couldn't tear her eyes away. "Are you playing 'he loves me, loves me not?'"

"It's not." She popped off the head of yellow florets and tossed it on the ground as well. "Hardly a surprise."

Her chest constricted, as if a great dragonfly sat on her heart, beating its wings. Marriage for love. What an impossibility.

Hewitt Vaughn was handsome. Very. They talked of him as a war hero, though the Earl of St. Vincent's reception of him cast that reputation in some doubt. With his father gone, he would have control of Greenfield and the money.

Hewitt Vaughn's wife would not have a care in the world, Anne guessed. He would treat her with attentive courtesy, perhaps even gentle affection. He would smile fondly at her when she entered a room, stick his head in the parlor to greet her guests while she chattered with neighbors who had come to call. He would arrange her shawl over her shoulders when they went out to walk the gardens together. He would present her with gifts at the birth of each child, and he would never shame her by openly flaunting a mistress.

The kind of husband Anne had always supposed she'd have, one day.

But he'd already been offered her hand, and had fled the country to avoid her.

Hewitt withdrew his watch on its chain and glanced at it, then the sundial. "I would like to hear more of my brother's doings, but I've a meeting with my father's solicitor." His mouth twisted. "My solicitor, now."

Anne nodded, numb. This was his home again. He would turn out the Suttons, and good riddance.

At least she would not have to marry Calvin.

"What does it say?" Anne asked, her throat dry.

When his brows rose, she pointed to the sundial, heavy gray stone, weatherworn, with moss tracing the brass inlaid face with its etchings. It wasn't a ploy to draw out this moment. She was not trying to drink him in, as if he were the one solid thing around her, a steady rope to anchor her in the storm. Because he was not.

"*Utere, non numera*," Hewitt said after a moment. "Use, do not count, the hours."

He met her gaze and held it. He did have the most commanding manner. Anne's head grew foggy, and she felt herself sway. Good *heavens*, how strong was the sun here in south Wales?

"I will see you at dinner?" he asked.

She swallowed. Did he want her gone before then? "I expect to attend." Where else could she go?

She regarded the stem in her hands, the leaves opening like a spread hand. So much was falling away from her. What could she cling to? What could she *build*, instead of destroy?

He knelt and gathered up handfuls of the very flower Anne had decimated. "I advise you not to eat these. It's feverfew. Good for relieving pain, but do not take it unboiled."

Anne dropped the stem to the ground, her face burning. How did he know these things? And why did she, at her advanced age, still know nothing?

He rose, turning to go, and, drat it, Anne did not want him to leave. She'd thought she wanted to be left alone to brood; now she didn't want him to leave the garden, with the sun kindling the red hearts of the flowers and pulling out the heady, hazy scent of the roses and linden trees. He moved as if his back were stiff, as if he were the kind of man who never unbent from his posture, from correctness, from the rules that hemmed him in as a soldier and a gentleman and the owner, now, of an estate and all its burdens.

"Mr. Vaughn," she said impulsively.

He faced her. "Captain."

She rubbed her lips together, moistening them. "Captain Vaughn."

His gaze fell to her mouth and his face went still, as if he couldn't look away. "Yes?" He had to clear his throat to force the word out.

"Welcome home."

He inclined his head. Light gleamed off the hint of gray above his ears, and a darker shadow kindled in the blue of his eyes. "Thank you, Miss Sutton."

He left, pulling up anchor, leaving Anne adrift.

CHAPTER SIX

She would have to leave Greenfield, and she couldn't return to Vine Court. Anne needed a plan.

She needed to talk to Daron, but he was nowhere to be found. Anne walked around and through the house several times, and at last saw some sense to the labyrinth. The main block, two stories with its five bays of windows, held the reception rooms, along with the front door under its pedimented porch and the hall with its grand marble stair. She'd peeked into most of the rooms in the wing that spread out to the west, dressing rooms, bedchambers, a grand dining parlor, and a library. The servants' quarters and kitchen offices extended to the back, places Anne didn't set foot and Daron wouldn't, either.

She knew the gardens better. There was the walled Elizabethan garden, where Hewitt Vaughn had found her. There was a stately parterre, mostly roses and shrubs, a few small trees in the corners. She'd wandered through a vegetable and herb garden, property of the kitchens, and threaded through the fruit trees in the orchard. She'd ventured down to the fish pond, not close enough to peer in—she didn't care what kind of fish lived there—and she'd passed a paddock where sleek, well-fed horses raised their heads to examine her.

Perhaps Daron had walked into Rogerstone, a hamlet of not more than five hundred souls, but Anne doubted it held any amusements beyond a public house, the church, and perhaps a village green where people would stare at her if she wandered through. Greenfield lay at the foot of unfolding hills—as did most every place in Wales, even here along the fringes of the sea —but Anne was not one to set out on solitary rambles across countryside she didn't know, and who would go with her?

Daron would not have left on his own, abandoning Anne at Greenfield—would he? But with Hewitt Vaughn returned, he must know all of his and Calvin's plans were a loss.

Anne had never been alone in her life. There was always a maid, a mother, a neighbor, a friend. Family. A house guest. Someone to chaperone, someone to oversee. Gwen, for all those years, growing at her side like clematis and ivy.

She ought to be terrified at the prospect of solitude. But instead, Anne felt that stirring inside her once more. All her life she had been a dragonfly nymph, clinging to her branch, afraid to become prey. Now her skin was falling away, everything inside of her shifting, and something new was emerging. Something with wings.

Calvin Vaughn was nowhere to be found, either, but his absence was a reprieve. Lady Vaughn disappeared into the kitchens to confer with Mrs. Harries on how they might welcome Hewitt home. As it seemed she would not be turned out until after dinner, Anne dressed for it, dispensing with the need for a maid and pulling on a simple round gown of spotted muslin. She mustn't soil it, because she didn't have many.

Say no. Refuse to marry.

If she did not marry, there would be no new gowns, not for a long while. And if Calvin married her without his brother's approval, very likely his source of funds would be cut off. She would live in genteel poverty with a husband she could not like and knew his neighbors did not respect.

Not that she wanted a husband who would make it impossible to hire decent maids. What she wanted was that someone else—including Hewitt Vaughn—not settle her life for her. Anne wanted, for the first time, to decide something for herself.

Embroidery always soothed her. She loved the precision of it, the steady progress, the orderly stitches that in time came together to form something useful and beautiful. Daron was most likely roaming the park, so Anne took her embroidery to the small terrace at the back of the house where she could wait for him. The raised patio opened onto careful landscaping that had improved upon nature's choices, creating small coppices in their swales of green that sloped down to the meandering river. There, the gently sloping hills to the south grew spines and climbed to rounded mountains in the west. The prospect reminded her of Llanfyllin and the familiar features of home, and a wild loneliness pierced Anne's heart.

She'd be surrounded by people had she stayed at St. Sefin's. But would she feel less alone? Her friendship with Gwen had been broken beyond repair. The acquaintances she'd had in Llanfyllin had all, to a one, gone and married or taken up their trades. Anne had no companion left except Daron.

The rumble of a masculine voice reached her ear. Not Daron's voice; Hewitt Vaughn. The library sat beside the terrace, with a French door that opened onto the flagged stone. He must be meeting his solicitor there.

She could not escape him, wherever she went.

"—that much a loss in profits?" His low voice held concern.

Another man answered, his voice high, nasal, peeved. "—divested as you instructed," Anne heard. "I warned you to expect a significant loss."

"No wonder my mother is fretting. Still, I refuse to profit from such a shameful ..." Hewitt's voice drifted away. It sounded as if he were moving through the room.

A treacherous impulse slowed Anne's feet. Eavesdroppers never heard well of themselves, her mother always said. But even her scrupulous mother would be led to listen if she happened across the men deciding her fate.

Someone had conveniently placed a willow chair on the terrace, along with the small folding table. It was designed for gentle repose. Anne had already tossed her pride to the wind a dozen times this day. What was one more trespass?

Embroidery was the one thing she was good at, Anne reflected as she waited for the gentlemen to move back near the window. Her stitches were neat and even. She had a fine eye for color and the harmony of a design. Her creations were graceful and elegant, and hardly anyone outside her own household saw them.

Could she make a trade out of that, making and selling embroidery for fine ladies? She could design trousseaus or help with special occasions, baptismal gowns, court gowns. Dress debutantes for their come-out, brides for their weddings. Could she earn enough to support herself?

But she was a gentlewoman, and gentlewomen did not go into trade. Their work was to create a comfortable and charming home for their husbands, lay a pleasant table when hosting dinners, offer an elegant tea. A housewife used her skill at numbers to ensure the accounts were in order and they were not being robbed by merchants or servants. A gentlewoman displayed her embroidery in the altar cloths she decorated for church and chapel, for the darling clocks she stitched on stockings for herself and her children.

Anne plunged her needle into the linen cloth. That urge to break something was still upon her. Or rather, the sense as she sat in that chapel watching Gwen put her heart and life in the keeping of a man who adored her, some great overarching order to Anne's world was breaking and falling away. All her life she had followed the proper steps, and they led to an abyss.

So where did she go next? What other paths lay before her?

"—the canal?" Hewitt asked, finally coming close enough for her to hear.

"Not performing as well as expected," the other man replied. "The issue of water—" Their voices came and went. "—other investments," the solicitor finished.

"I don't expect I need to honor all of my father's commitments," Hewitt said sharply.

A silence followed. Anne expected the solicitor was as surprised by this declaration as Anne was. A gentleman always honored his commitments. She'd learned that from Daron. True, he honored his commitments to other gentlemen first, for somehow the debts accrued at a gaming table were more pressing to discharge than paying tradesmen or servants or keeping intact a sister's dowry.

Anne stabbed her linen, her heart beating in her ears. Did Hewitt mean he did not need to honor his father's promise that Calvin would marry Anne?

"—buildings," Hewitt was saying. "And a fund set aside for repairs. The household fund, of course, and pin money for my mother, along with her jointure." A beat passed. "But my brother's allowance could be less."

Anne missed the solicitor's response to this, if there was one, because of her own intake of breath. If Calvin Vaughn had no money, and Anne had no money, there was no reason to marry.

People of their station married for money, after all, affection being a convenient gloss if the couple got on well. A lord like Penrydd picking a country maid like Gwen was unheard of. Only her father's knighthood, and her inheritance of his mines, made the choice explicable. Penrydd needed to repair his fortunes, and Gwen was an heiress. Everyone wanted an heiress.

And no one wanted Anne.

The heartbeat rose behind her eyes, pounding at her head. Without a dowry, she knew what her marital options were. Spinsterhood. Really, she was a spinster already; only her engagement to Calvin Vaughn had let her hold up her head around Llanfyllin. The best her parents would find for her now would be some doddering squire who required a nurse, or a widower with a houseful of children who wanted a governess and nanny whom he would not have to pay a wage.

But she didn't *have* to marry. Prunella had said it. Hewitt Vaughn had said it.

She could choose something else. Freedom.

"—the bridge ... other investments," the solicitor said. "They're wanting ways to transport more ore to the ports. If the problems with the Monmouthshire Canal cannot be remedied—"

"They can be," Hewitt said firmly. "I am sure of it. It only needs a good engineer to look at the lay of it."

The silence following was loaded with doubt. Anne couldn't see the conversants, but an occasional shadow flickered past the door, and the wooden floor creaked under a certain window. One of them was pacing in large circles, like a big cat in a menagerie.

"If only there were," the solicitor said.

"I'll take a look. There may be improvements possible." Hewitt's voice was clearer, gaining in confidence. Or he was closer to the door, to where she sat out of sight of the window.

She hoped.

Another beat, laden with doubt. "I thought you were a gunner, Mr. Vaughn."

"Captain. And I spent my fair time with the sappers. An honorary engineer, by the end, if you can believe that."

"Very well. I can look into the construction projects you suggest. And the shipping line. But as for the rest—" The solicitor clicked his tongue. "You will need a source of capital."

Hewitt's voice went muffled, as if he were speaking into his hand. "I am aware."

"Do you have any ideas, Mr.—Captain?"

"If I can keep my rank, I can go begging to investors with hat in hand. But if this business at Acre has followed me home ..."

Anne strained her ears, but his voice moved away.

The solicitor cleared his throat. "Your mother has suggested a marriage. To a woman with a sizeable dowry."

Anne went very, very still.

"Of course she would see that ... an option."

"It *is* an option, Mis—Captain."

"Ask a woman ... share the dishonor? Would you want that for a woman you cared about, Beddoe?"

Anne wished she had antennae she could turn and point, like an ant. *What* dishonor? What had Hewitt Vaughn done among all his heroics at Acre?

"Your father—"

"Is spinning in his grave that I hold the reins, and my mother ..." There followed a diminishing of voices, as if Hewitt were on the far round of his circuit. It was a moment before he came back within hearing. "... penury ... the slave trade."

Anne flashed hot, then cold. But that tore it, for good. Anne could not look Dovey Evans in the eye knowing she had married a man whose comfortable life rested on the exploitation of a race of people whose ancestry Dovey shared. That all the pleasures of her home were built on the misery of others.

"... invest in ships carrying such cargo, either," Hew said. "There must be other opportunities. Newport—"

"Yes, canals and trackways that ferry goods out, and bring goods in," the solicitor said, his tone disapproving. "Supplies to meet the demand in growing towns. Sugar. Cotton. Opium. Tea. *Someone* will profit from them, Captain. It might as well be you."

Anne watched with astonishment as a small crimson stain bloomed on her linen. She withdrew her needle and saw, once the pain registered, that she'd pricked her finger.

Anne hadn't pricked herself with a needle since she was seven years old. She studied the spot, wondering if she could disguise it with a spray of roses or perhaps peonies. Not wanting the blood to fall on her white gown, she stuck her finger in her mouth and sucked at the wound.

A man approached over the empty back lawn. Cocky stride, cane swinging as if he owned the place. Her brother.

Drat it. He couldn't expose her *now*. The men would know she had been eavesdropping and had heard them discussing how to profit from enslavement. Anne rose and went swiftly down the shallow steps, meeting him close to a stone bench positioned so that a stroller might sit and contemplate the river, or the house, depending on which view was the more pleasant.

"Where have you been?" she hissed.

Daron raised a wheat-gold brow. Her beloved brother had gotten a bit portly about the middle, and it made his legs look spindly in the yellow pantaloons. Their family might be on the edge of poverty, but Daron was eating well.

"I've the run of the place, since m'sister's to marry a Vaughn," he drawled. "Why the pelter, pet?"

Anne straightened her shoulders. *Refuse to marry*, she reminded herself.

"I have given Mr. Vaughn's offer careful consideration, and regretfully I must decline."

Daron blinked. For a moment he looked like a fat, fluffy bird facing a predator he'd never seen. Anne herself didn't know when she'd grown teeth. Right this minute, likely.

"You can't jilt Calvin," he said flatly.

Anne raised her chin. Her finger throbbed where she'd pricked it. She hoped she wasn't bleeding further into the linen; this strip, bleached white as it was, had not been easy to obtain.

"I see no reason to move forward. There is no affection between us. No signed contract, for that matter, so he can't sue for breach of promise. I have found him to be—" She thought of Mathry, the look of disdain she'd shot Calvin Vaughn before she maneuvered her swollen belly away. Could Anne bear to marry a man she knew her acquaintances held in contempt? A man *she* held in contempt? No, she could not.

The idea, the sheer terror it inspired, gave her strength.

"He is not someone I can esteem. We do not suit," she said firmly.

Daron gripped her arm, and a surprising jolt of pain shot up her arm. Daron was *never* rough with her.

"You *have* to marry him, you witless goose."

Not if Hewitt objected, which she gathered he did. Greenfield needed capital, and Anne had no dowry.

"Let me go." She tried in vain to tug her arm free. Daron would never hurt her—save that time he had gotten her kidnapped along with the Viscountesses Penrydd, but that was just the once, surely.

Daron's eyes, normally such an innocent blue, had a hard slant to them, and the whites were clouded, as if he'd been imbibing. All at once, as if the sun had shifted to a new angle, Anne saw her brother in a strange light. It was as if he were no longer the Corinthian, the pillar of fashion who had held up her world, the Exquisite who had set all the hearts and fans of Llanfyllin aflutter. It was as if he'd become—someone else.

She blinked, and he was Daron again, giving her an ingratiating smile, though his lips were thin and strained. "It's the money," he said.

She pulled on her arm, hoping not to give anyone who might be watching from the house the impression of distress. Was Hewitt watching? Could he see her?

"There is no money. You spent my dowry. Father lost our fortune. We are destitute."

"You forget Aunt Gertrude," Daron said.

Anne stilled. She *had* forgotten Aunt Gertrude. Their eccentric relation, their father's aunt, lived in Llandrindod Wells, residing at the gracious hotel and swearing the waters of the spa town kept her youthful and vigorous. Delight swirled in Anne's chest, though there was a keen edge to it. How had she forgotten Aunt Gertrude?

Perhaps because throwing herself on her aunt's mercy was the most desperate of measures. But desperate times had arrived. Anne could be her companion. Anne would make a *perfect* companion. She would be discreet, invisible, polite, charming, fetching shawls and smelling salts as requested, and though she would live on another's charity, she would not be subject to a husband.

She would go to Aunt Gertrude. Of course.

"She's on her deathbed," Daron added.

The swirl of delight collapsed like a summer breeze gusting out.

"How do you know this?" Anne whispered.

"She wrote Father of it, peagoose. We thought at first dear old Aunt Gertie would be the saving of us all. Too tight-fisted to give Father a farthing when he needed it, but she can't take her jewels with her, can she? Only fancy." Daron's face twisted into a grin that hadn't the ghost of his usual charm. "She's written her will and had it witnessed. It's all to go to you. To her little favorite, Nanny."

Anne blinked. That wet, molting thing in her chest stirred its new wings, as if testing them. "Why me?"

"Likely because you charmed her well enough when Mum dragged us along for visits. Or she sees herself in you. Or pities you. I don't care. Because here's the fact of it."

He dragged Anne further down the groomed pathway that led in a gentle meander to the fishpond and the river beyond, all the lines of landscape smoothed to picturesque effect. The masters of Greenfield controlled the very land they looked upon. Except the mighty Welsh mountains: no one could master those.

"That money will get me out from under the hatches," Daron said, the cast of his mouth turning grim. "Our worthy sire will be able to hold up his head and his lady beside him. And you, pet, will live like the little cat you are, fat and sleek on your cushion, with nothing to bother your pretty head save ensuring your husband has his port and slippers when he returns to his loving home after a taxing day in the world. That's all you ever wanted, isn't it, Nanny? And it's all to be yours. Courtesy of Aunt Gertrude."

If Aunt Gertrude left money, Anne's parents would not lose their home. If Anne had a dowry, she would be desirable again. To more than just Calvin Vaughn. The new wings beat in her chest, gaining strength.

"What must I do? Visit her, I suppose," Anne said, her thoughts leaping forward to Llandrindod Wells, to freedom. Away from all the disappointments that Newport held.

"Here's what you'll do, pet." Daron's fingers dug little wells into the delicate skin of her arm. "The solicitor tells me our aunt, the crafty old beldame, put one or two requirements on how you can use the money. And the way around all of it is to marry Vaughn."

Anne stared. Daron could not still want Calvin for her.

Calvin Vaughn was only a second son. Hewitt controlled Greenfield now. Hewitt was the war hero, by some accounts if not all. Hewitt was the heir. Hewitt had that rugged face and an officer's bearing and that delicious line above his lip—

"Then Calvin will control the fortune," Daron said with satisfaction. "And everything will be set right."

"Calvin." Anne attempted to pry her elbow from his grip. It was like trying to peel off a leech.

"Well, of course. Can't trust the pater with an inheritance, look what he did the last time. Aunt Gertie didn't give it all to *me*, when she ought've. I owe Calvin an opportunity, and this repays all. As your husband, he'll control your fortune and can set himself up like a gentleman without his blasted brother controlling the purse strings. Everyone wins."

"Except me," Anne said.

Daron blinked in surprise, and Anne jerked her arm free. His face changed swiftly, into such a contortion of anger that Anne almost thought a demon looked out through her brother's eyes. "Now listen here, Nanny, don't you dare think you can—"

"Can what?" Anne cried. "Be the pawn who sets all right for you? What about what *I* want?"

Just as swiftly Daron's face changed again, as if an eddy had churned through the River Ebbw, and it was back to its gentle self. "Nanny!" he said, his voice hurt and surprised. "This is all for you! Thinking only of you. How you can be a fine lady. Safe. Taken care of. Pampered as you deserve."

Her mind flicked to that morning and the ceremony in the church—how had it only been that morning? Gwen standing in a shaft of colored light that fell through the stained-glass window of St. Sefin's. The mild-voiced vicar proclaiming the holy words of matrimony. Penrydd, in a tailed coat and breeches, promising to worship her with his body. Gwen would be a viscountess, and she would be fighting for her place among all the aristoctracts who saw only a miner's orphaned daughter. But she would be loved by a man who had chosen her, who had blown up a ship to stop the villain who would keep them apart.

There were other images from that morning. The heads of the two widows of St. Sefin's crowned with their black hats, faces wreathed in smiles as they sat at their table eating their plain seaweed fare. Under no one's bidding but their own.

The smile that Dovey Evans sent her husband as he used his good arm to set up and tap a cask of wine she'd made, with the first glass toasting his wife and their recent marriage. Dovey wasn't pampered with luxuries, not living in St. Sefin's, but she had a companion she trusted and admired, a solid, steady man.

Prunella, the newest dowager Viscountess Penrydd, had calmly sipped her wine and doubted she would remarry. She wanted to order her own life as she wished and no longer bend herself around a mother, a brother, a husband.

Anne hardly knew where she found the temerity for her next words. "The money does not change the fact that Calvin Vaughn and I will not suit."

As if another rock were rolling through the river, once again stirring its quiet depths to violence, rage kindled Daron's face. Anne took a step backward. She reminded herself Daron would never hurt her.

But Daron had never been thwarted as much as when they'd come south to Newport. He'd never had his native luck and charm turn against him for this long.

He smoothed his face into a strained smile and reached out a hand.

"Nanny!" he said in cajoling tones. "I'm only working so hard because this is what you want. Isn't it why we came here? So you could marry Calvin and start your life at last. Get away from Mother and that miserable tiny town of ours. Start your life in truth."

Anne faltered. Those *were* the reasons, or had been. She'd been dwelling on them only this morning. Yet her mind felt fogged, as if the scented air of this place were disordering her mind.

"But Calvin," Anne said, hating the plaintive thread in her voice.

Daron tucked Anne's hand over his arm as he turned her toward the house. "It's best for all of us, Nanny. You'll be taken care of, which is what we all want for you. Living in a near palace—better than Vine Court, isn't it? And think of it. You'll be the savior of your whole family. Giving her brother a leg up in the world, getting him back on his feet. You'll turn the tide back in my favor. The deliverance of our mother and father as well, paying them back for their devotion. You'll set things right for all of us, Saint Anne. Everything, finally, going on as it ought, because of you."

Because of Aunt Gertrude's money, Anne thought, but did not say, because the picture Daron painted tugged at her heart. She *did* owe her parents for all they had invested in her with tutors, music instructors, dancing masters. And if she paid his debts then Daron would adore her again, the way she'd always adored him.

At the cost of marrying Calvin Vaughn.

A good daughter would make that sacrifice, wouldn't she? So she'd been taught, all her life, by the example of her mother and their friends and the sermons at church. A genteel woman married for the advantage of her family, not for silly fancies of love. A high marriage was a business arrangement, and a woman needed to know her worth and negotiate for the best offer she could find.

"Of course I want to help," Anne said, her voice ringing hollow in her ears. She meant the words, didn't she? She wanted to help her family.

But Daron didn't know how Hewitt Vaughn felt about this marriage. Hewitt Vaughn might yet be the rock all his hopes and plans crashed upon, for Hewitt Vaughn was not a man to be cowed or cozened or cajoled. If he did not think Anne worthy of Calvin, he would bring an end to this, and Anne would be left battered, still jilted, but free.

Only imagine—not an hour earlier, she'd thought the man meant her doom. Now Hewitt Vaughn was Anne's last slender hope of deliverance.

CHAPTER SEVEN

Hewitt Vaughn did not look like deliverance, seated at the head of the Greenfield table. He looked like a dark angel filled with righteous wrath.

None of the important people Lady Vaughn had wanted were free to dine, all of them otherwise engaged. She could not even claim the vicar of St. Woolos, Mr. Stanley, who sent back word that he had accepted an invitation to dine at St. Sefin's, in ongoing celebration of the festivities. Instead they suffered the addition of one Mr. Rafael Darch, a friend of Calvin's, leaving Anne and her ladyship the only females to balance out the table of men.

Daron sat glowering at his plate as if he'd been informed the meal was his last. Calvin, with a sour slant to his mouth, kept shooting dark glances at his brother. Hewitt sat at the head of the table, the position Calvin had occupied up till now, and addressed his plate with steady attention, seeming not to notice any of the hostility, or curiosity, directed toward him.

Anne admired his cool head. She herself became rattled if she detected any animosity in a room, even if it wasn't directed at her. But Hewitt Vaughn had that training around heavy artillery. Likely a cannon could be shot off right next to him, and he wouldn't flinch.

What a difference from Anne, who flinched at everything. Especially every time Calvin Vaughn regarded her with a smug, satisfied smile that said, his brother aside, he saw everything he wanted within reach, and all would work out as he wished, whether he deserved it or not.

Mr. Darch was not introduced by way of profession, so Anne couldn't guess his background, but she could see the man styled himself an Exquisite. Whatever affectations of fashion Calvin and Daron had contrived, Mr. Darch took to excess. The lapels of his coat stretched nearly the breadth of his chest. His stock rested beneath his ears, obscuring his chin, and instead of a waistcoat, some stiff insert occupied the front of his chest, making him move like a wooden doll. His hair was long and dangled nearly to his shoulders. Anne detested long hair on a man; it looked sloppy. He had a habit of flicking back locks of it when he spoke, as if he meant for his hair to emphasize his conversational points, and his drawl was certainly affected.

When he was introduced, he produced a bow so deep it seemed almost mockery, twirling a hand in its thick leather glove, and Anne disliked him on the instant. She felt herself fortunate at the time to be seated at Hew's right at table, with her brother on her other side, and Calvin across from her, so Darch was left to flatter Lady Vaughn with his forced witticisms.

At least she'd never be forced to take someone like *him* for a husband.

But Calvin introduced her to Darch as his fiancée, so there was that.

"We are fortunate to see our family so enlarged," Lady Vaughn said to Darch. "Miss Sutton is about to settle our Calvin's wildness, and my dearest Hew returned home at long last." She rested her gaze on her eldest son with a smile that turned thin at the edges.

Hew had done something to displease her—what? Perhaps Lady Vaughn knew the precarious state of the Vaughn finances.

Well, Aunt Gertrude was about to remedy that, wasn't she? She would bequeath her fortune to Anne, and Calvin, as Anne's husband, would control every shilling and pound. He would shore up Anne's family and his own, and Aunt Gertrude could look down from her heavenly abode to see that Anne had sold her soul for a secure home. For a set of new gowns and gloves and a lovely manor house to sleep in, and Calvin would no doubt spend his portion on garish neckcloths and cravat pins.

Unless Hewitt Vaughn could step in and save her.

Anne didn't need her mother's advice to daintily pick at her food; she had no appetite. A sultry heat had followed the sun of the afternoon, and though Lady Vaughn kept the tall windows of the parlor tightly closed, the many-paned windows framed in their green velvet draperies looked out on a landscape blurred with falling dusk. Wax candles sputtered from the chandelier that dangled crystal droplets low over the table, and the line of candles dividing the long oak dining table, in addition to the sconces on the wall, raised the temperature to the level of a brick oven.

"You need a new coach, Mother," Calvin said, as if he were spending Aunt Gertrude's fortune already. "Your darling Hew ought to deck you out in a new vehicle, don't you think? You've been racketing about in that old relic far too long. A smart new phaeton, that's what a good son would set you up in."

"As finances allow, of course," Hew said, refusing to be needled.

Only Hewitt did not seem made snappish by the heat. He'd changed to a long, gray tailed coat, one that might have once been perfectly tailored but now hung loose. His cravat was tied in a simple twist, his waistcoat had only a single row of bronze buttons and no collar at all, and his hair had been trimmed. He must have taken advantage of Calvin's valet, if not his wardrobe; his brother was fuller in the chest and belly, though Hewitt was taller. He wore no gloves, and for some reason Anne found the flex of his fingers utterly distracting. Why, she couldn't say, save her disobedient mind kept flashing to that light-drenched moment in the garden when she'd watched him strip a green plant, then pop it into his mouth, exactly as if he were some god of the wood.

That thought made her go hot in the belly, as if she were hungry. But not for the lamb chops fricassee that sat before her.

She wouldn't call Hew a satyr, one of those bestial men given over purely to lechery and revelry. That described her would-be husband, Calvin Vaughn. Hewitt Vaughn was a different creature entirely. Steady. Solid. He would look almost humorless to some, yet Anne remembered the lines that creased his lean cheeks when he'd smiled at her, and—

Marrying Calvin Vaughn would save her family. Anne sawed at her new potatoes in onion sauce. She would prop up her parents in their advancing age and repay all they had invested in educating and polishing her. She and she alone could release Daron from debt, free him to marry well once Vine Court was restored.

And she would be married. No longer Miss Anne Sutton, inching down the barren road to spinsterhood. She would be Mrs. Calvin Vaughn, mistress of—well, nothing. Not her own household. Not this house. She would go from living under her parents' direction to living under a husband's thumb.

"I would very much like to put up new paper in the Pineapple Parlor," Lady Vaughn said. "The whole place could use a refurbishing. The last few years have left us very drab."

"But investing in canals, Mother!" Calvin said heartily.

"The canals will pour out money, once the iron ore and coal start flowing. So your darling Hew says."

Hewitt's jaw tightened. Did Anne only notice because she was watching him so closely? "The canals will bear out the investment we've put into them," he said, his voice full of forced calm. "It may take a few years, but they will."

"Need water in the canals to cart your narrow boats. Horses can't do all the work themselves. And when the ore's at the seaside, it needs a way to get aboard ship, aye?"

Darch swirled his wine in his glass. He imbibed heartily, matching Calvin drink for drink. Daron tried to keep up, yet Anne noticed whenever he met the stranger's dark gaze, Daron flushed and looked away.

Anne pushed a piece of turnip through its butter sauce. She couldn't fret over Daron's discomfiture when she was so caught up in her own. Mathry, the former maid, danced in her head, pushing out her pregnant belly.

Your intended, she'd told Anne, the indignant hurt showing through her sneer. *Came at me the minute I set foot in that house. Like a midge. Wouldn't let me be.*

He'd never shown the least bit of adoration for Anne. Not that she wanted him to.

But she wanted him not to be one of *those* men. The kind that would see any female as laced mutton—a phrase she'd heard Daron use once, and here it seemed to fit. She didn't want the man she married to be a man who put his lusts above honor.

She didn't want to marry a dirty dish. She wanted a clean dish, one with nice-smelling, minty breath. A man who was selective about his pleasure and didn't follow everything in a skirt.

"Well, once your shares in the canal start producing income, I can put my lady in a new frock or two." Calvin leered across the table at Anne. "Looking a bit peaky, my

Nan. Not the glow of a maid about to be wedded and bedded."

Hewitt, poised above the loin of mutton, froze with the carving knife gripped in his hand.

Anne glared across the table at her intended. He didn't get to call her Nan or Nanny. Not ever.

"I am as giddy at the thought of our nuptials as you are, sir," she said icily.

Darch guffawed. Daron squirmed in his chair. "Now, Nanny—"

"Nay, Sutton, let the kitten show her claws. I like my fluff to have a bit of bite. No fun when the gel just lies there and takes it."

The silence in the room hung heavy, rippled with the growl of distant thunder. The heat felt like a hand wrapped around her neck.

"Calvin, my darling, do not tease your bride," Lady Vaughn said. "Allow the child her last days of innocence."

Calvin smirked. "You forget, our Anne's not much on the young side, Mum. Don't doubt she's near fainting with impatience to relieve herself of her maidenhead." His grin widened, revealing stained teeth. "Or p'raps she'll teach me a thing or three, eh?"

Darch chuckled at this, topping off his laugh with a noisy slurp of wine. Daron, who should have been her champion, shifted in his chair and scooped collops onto his plate, following with a large ladle of lobster sauce. They ate well at Vine Court, but the Greenfield cook was truly gifted. Too bad Anne's throat couldn't admit anything larger than a pea.

"Calvin." Hew's voice from the head of the table was quiet but firm, and there was a deep current in it, like the thunder grumbling beyond the hills, rolling in from the sea. "You will show respect for any lady at this table."

Calvin's smirk shifted into a sneer as he faced his brother. "Would expect an army man to appreciate the sentiment," he said. "Imagine it's been a long while for you, old man. Maybe you've forgotten how you apply your tool?" The sneer flattened. "Or maybe you were happier with your merry band of brothers and—"

Hewitt slammed his fist on the table. "Enough. I won't have An—Miss Sutton be subject to such talk. From you, or anyone."

Calvin fell silent for a moment. The entire table did. Perhaps because Hewitt, clenching the carving knife, had pointed it at his brother. Anne felt a thrill of—terror, it must be terror that winged its way up her back and fluttered along her arms. Because he looked so formidable in that moment. Like a man who would put his body in the way of an injustice, and stop it.

That strange heat in her middle shifted, dropped lower. Almost as if she needed to visit the necessary. But no, that wasn't the urge. The sight of Hewitt Vaughn, his muscles clenched and bunched beneath that handsome coat, his mouth a firm line, his eyes hard and brilliant—no, the thrill was not terror, or not terror alone. He was a powerful man, but he was protecting her.

"'Pears I'll have to watch my property," Calvin said finally. "Brother wants m'things for his own, wouldn't it seem?"

Darch guffawed at this, as he was meant to. Daron blinked blearily at Calvin, then Hew, as if gauging which fighter he meant to place his money on.

The fine hairs rose on the back of Anne's neck. She wasn't Calvin's *property*.

"You may not respect my decisions." Hewitt spoke softly, holding his brother's gaze, one the watery blue of turned milk, the other the deep blue of a stormy sea. "But you *will* abide by them."

Calvin gripped his hand around his fork as if he thought to use it as a weapon. His thin lips trembled as he searched for a retort, but his mother swept in.

"I know my boys would not quarrel at my table when I have contrived a celebration," she said, her voice cool and cutting. "Calvin, you won't spoil all our appetites, will you? When I have specially requested Cook bring out a roasted leveret for you in the second course."

Calvin relaxed his grip on his implement. "Of course not, darling Mumsy."

Hewitt applied the carving knife to its designated task, and Anne let out her breath. It came out uneven, much to her surprise. Her insides jumped about like crickets as she watched Hewitt carve the meat, his movements swift and precise. Such control in the man. Such leashed strength. Calvin Vaughn was a soft pudding wrapped up in superfine and brocade. Hewitt was all lean sinew and hard, smooth muscle.

Saliva pooled in her mouth as the loin fell into neat slices beneath his knife. He extended one to her, and Anne fumbled as she held out her plate.

His eyes met hers. She couldn't read the dark emotion in their depths, and she blinked rapidly, fearing it might be anger. At her, for causing discord at the table when this was supposed to be his welcome-home dinner.

He watched her eyelids flutter. Then his gaze dropped to her lips.

Anne's hand shook as she set her plate before her, the choicest cut of loin nestled next to her stewed cauliflower. That wasn't anger in his eyes. It was—something else.

She stared at the slice of mutton, still pink in the center, like a heart.

The thought came as if it had been loitering a long while at the back of her mind and finally saw the space to step forward.

If the money was to come to Anne, why must she hand it over to a man straightaway?

Prunella could set up her own household because Prunella had money. What if Anne needn't be under anyone's thumb, but could take Aunt Gertrude's fortune and set up a household of her own?

"—have one or two business ventures you might invest in," Darch was saying when Anne blinked to clear her head.

The thought sat there still, solid and formed, like a loaf fresh from the oven.

"Happy to share some of my ... opportunities." Darch swirled the wine in his glass, admiring the ruby red color.

"Think that wine came from one of your opportunities." Calvin smirked at his friend, but kept one eye on his brother, gauging his reaction.

"Do you mean—free trade?" Daron sounded flustered. Anne was accustomed to seeing her brother be his cocky self, charming the table, competing with other men, especially strangers, to establish his dominance. He seemed almost intimidated by this Darch, which didn't make sense.

Hewitt addressed himself to his mutton. "You sound surprised, Sutton. When Wales is almost all coastline, why wouldn't there be a brisk business running brandy and the like?"

"I wish the talk at my table would not be of illegal activities," Lady Vaughn said, calmly spooning up her crawfish soup.

Oh. Smuggling. Darch's business must be smuggling.

"Were there to be a new regiment of militia training hereabouts, I imagine the free traders would find their work more difficult," Hewitt remarked.

"The Monmouthshire? Duke of Beaufort has them lounging around the pubs of Monmouth, or pretending to drill in Brecon." Calvin snorted. "Wouldn't put them where they could be useful."

"I wonder that you've never thought of joining up with the militia," Hew remarked.

"Me? One son posing as a military man's enough for this family. 'Sides, Mum needs someone devoted at home, looking after her welfare. Can't count on the other to be here doing his duty. He'll be off sailing into the arms of some Caribbean light-skirt, or getting himself blown up in the arid East, trying to be a hero."

Anne put down her fork. Calvin's vitriol toward his brother made her stomach boil with acid. Or perhaps it had clenched around the idea of Hewitt embracing a woman. Pursuing her the way Calvin had pursued Mathry.

She focused on her host. Was that why he moved so awkwardly at times? Had he been injured somehow? His eyelids tightened—indication that he was annoyed—but his voice was calm when he answered his brother.

"Some of us protect from home, and some of us go to defeat the enemy abroad so he can't threaten British shores or British interests."

"What about our interests? What about this family?" Calvin snorted. "Haven't done a fine job looking after those, brother mine."

"I've done my best. I'm not to blame that Father died and left things as he did."

"You're to blame that you dismantled his most profitable investments before the earth had settled on his coffin," Calvin shot back. "What was it for, then? You liked your miserable Army conditions and thought we should be living in a tent as well?"

Hewitt's hand curled into another fist. Anne's insides did their jumping act, trying several different directions at once. "The Commons has been passing bills for years to end the slave trade. It is inevitable that the House of Lords will eventually choose the humane path. I had the sense to look ahead and invest in more viable ventures."

"The House of Lords will never end slavery and you know it," Calvin snapped. "Too many of them profit from it same as we did. All you did was take your bets off the winning horse. How is Mum to hold her head up to the Morgans with you making us paupers?"

Anne's muddled thoughts scrambled to follow. Hewitt did not support the slave trade. Did not profit from it. She'd heard wrong.

But she wasn't misreading the rage that rippled off him. He contained his temper, showing the strain only in his curled fist, in the tight set of his jaw as he forced his voice to remain even. "I am doing everything I can to see to Mother's comfort. Through just means." His gaze slid over his brother, dismissing him. "You should know. You've spent more than your share of the household allowance of late."

"Need to hold my head up too!" Calvin barked. "See what you reduced me to? Grubbing for a wife with money. Don't blame me I made a poor bet and chose one whose father squandered it all before I could."

He jabbed a finger at Anne, and she stiffened out of reflex, noting too late how straightening her spine brought her bosom into arresting profile. Darch noticed, and so did Calvin, and so did Hewitt. That bite of mutton tasted bloody on her tongue, though it was perfectly cooked. An agony of a blush swept up the sides of her neck, and she knew it must be visible in her cheeks.

She'd known it all along, hadn't she? It wasn't any attraction of her own person that invited suitors to ask for her hand. She'd never had men desperate to touch her, as Daron had been desperate for Gwen. She'd never been swept away by declarations of undying passion. She'd merely had men negotiating with her father to establish the price of her dowry, and she was only here because, dowry gone, Daron and Calvin Vaughn believed Anne might have an inheritance by other means.

Her heart squeezed in humiliation, but there was rage in there, too, as though she were borrowing Hewitt's heat. She had half a mind to march herself to Llandrindod Wells and tell Aunt Gertrude to save her money. Give it all to the workhouse to support widows and orphans.

"She's sitting right in front of you, man," Hewitt growled. "And if you've been pursuing her for a dowry, you're a bigger sand worm than I believed."

Anne shoved a bite of greens into her mouth before she did something that would prove her a ninny.

She hated sand worms, the legless lizard that looked like a snake. They were pale and corpulent, like Calvin, and when attacked they shed their tails, which would continue to wriggle in the most repulsive fashion. Like Calvin.

Did Hewitt mean that *he* would have been pursuing Anne for more than her dowry?

He was supposed to be putting a wrench in her marriage. Not instructing Calvin how to treat her once they wed.

Calvin narrowed his eyes, which had gone almost colorless with anger. "So you *do* want m' gel. *My* bride."

A tense silence stretched across the table, end to end. The growl of thunder pulled nearer. The heat grew so thick it was going to collapse the air and suffocate them all. Anne plucked at the puffed sleeve of her gown, peeling the fine muslin away from her shoulder.

Calvin continued to glare his brother. But Hewitt watched Anne's movement, his gaze riveted to her shoulder and the exposed slice of skin.

That odd heat gathered and sank low, past her belly, slithering between her legs. Good God, she wasn't about to start her courses, was she? They were unpredictable, but to start bleeding *here*, in this sheer muslin gown—she'd rather be stabbed with a fork and perish at the table than endure one more disgrace. She felt hot all over her skin, even after Hewitt looked away, back at his plate, as though he'd been found out doing something illicit and were trying to discipline himself.

A distant flash of lightning leapt from the glowering sky to light upon a far hill, and Anne felt the coming break. Finally. She welcomed the storm. Perhaps it would blow through her head as well, chase away these tangled emotions, and leave her thoughts clear.

Because she knew one thing. She could not, *would* not, marry Calvin Vaughn. She had to find a way to free herself from his clutches, a way that would leave her in charge of her own destiny and able to use whatever money was to come to her as she wished.

She didn't want to leave her family in penury. She wanted to help Daron.

But she wanted to make her own choice, finally. And here lay the opportunity before her.

I don't need to honor my father's commitments, he'd said. Some business at Acre had followed him home, something that, according to the Earl of St. Vincent, had put Hewitt Vaughn in chains. He'd returned to Wales to hide, the way smugglers concealed their boats and goods along the rocky shorelines.

When Gwen had tossed away her virtue, she'd been turned out and left to wander. So had Mathry.

The lightning flashed again, a dare, a promise, and Anne's nerves welcomed the bolt, the flare of determination. If Hewitt Vaughn would not do it, she must free herself.

She saw a chance. She meant to seize it.

And never let herself be trapped again.

CHAPTER EIGHT

The candle on the table beside his bed guttered in its holder, and Hew trimmed the wick. Sleep meant to taunt him from afar tonight, like fairy lights over the marsh, so he might as well read over his scribbled list of contacts.

He'd call upon each, make inquiries as to whether they saw the need for enlarging the militia, and whether they'd help stand the cost. Collect names of dependable men he could enlist. They need not all be able-bodied, but he wanted experience. Men who were motivated to protect their homes. Men who had reason to distrust Napoleon and the French.

Only the most generous would call Hew himself able-bodied. He shifted against the bolster of pillows, tilting the sheet of parchment toward the light.

He knew, logically, that the hand-woven silk brocade of his pillow was as soft as the shore of the River Ebbw those happy hours he'd spent wading as a boy, hunting for shrimps and eel or casting for brown trout. Yet he couldn't feel the delicate sensation of silk against his skin, only knew the temporary cessation of pain, now that he could strip off his shirt. He never thought he'd be grateful for the weeks of starvation, but they'd shrunk him enough that he could get his coats on and off himself, and the pressure of fine fabric against his skin didn't feel like being trapped in an iron maiden.

Eventually the marks would heal. They must. In the meantime, he had a glass of brandy on the table next to the candle. He'd declined the offer from Mrs. Harries, the housekeeper, to send up laudanum. He'd resort to it when the pain became blinding, if it kept him from becoming a beast, but he'd seen, often and up close, the results when a man dosed too freely with opiates. Hew needed to stay in control. In all things.

A gust of rain lashed through the open windows, tossing up the draperies like a harlot's skirts. The darkness outside was complete, the moon swallowed by clouds, and the boiling shadows resembled no earthly forms. The sleepy area he'd grown up in was changing before his eyes. The new canal he'd helped finance ferried out the bowels of the mountains, exposing to light the ores and coal that had been laid there in the first days of creation. Coal fired the forges that turned the ore into iron and smelted the silver from the lead to make fine and useful things, like the ammunition Hew shot at English enemies.

New men trudged through Newport every day heading to the mines for work, men who'd left hungry families or bleak futures in Scotland or the Welsh valleys or the isle across the Irish Sea. Hew had only had scraps of information from Daron about the recent attempt by some Irish rogue to kidnap the previous and new Viscountesses Penrydd, a dangerous debacle in which Anne had been involved somehow.

Anne, frightened, helpless, nearly hurt by a ruthless man— his thoughts sheared away. He had to help make the area safe. The forces of peace, a lock-up behind the pub and a magistrate who doubled as MP, weren't enough to stand against men like this Black Hound who had infiltrated the area. The Hound was gone, thanks to Penrydd—so Beddoe said—but the men he'd employed were turned loose, all of them accustomed to criminal trades.

And there was that squat and greedy French general, humiliated at Acre, who had returned to Egypt, but for how long? England and the Second Coalition were massing their armies to defend the German territories on the Continent and clip the expansion efforts of the French Directory. Napoleon wouldn't miss the chance to grow his country's power. The British Army might decide to deploy the Monmouthshire Militia to the southeast coast, where fortifications were underway to prevent an invasion from across the Channel. And who would be left to defend Newport and its vulnerable and increasingly lucrative trade?

French generals had turned their eyes before to the coastline of Wales, rocky and picturesque, where the smugglers already knew how easy it was to land ships unobserved. Hew would be making the same survey in their position, despite the defeat at Fishguard two years before.

That knowledge had driven him here, back to Rogerstone, back to Greenfield. He wasn't discharged, but he couldn't remain on active duty while his major laid his accusations before their superiors. So Hew had a new task, to survey defenses around Newport and manufacture a plan.

While his mother tried to enfold him once more within the confines of the narrow life he had fought to escape. The prodigal son returned to stand witness as the fingers of industry curled into his pastoral childhood home. And to see what had become of his family with his father dead, his mother increasingly bitter and haughty, his brother leading a life of dissipation.

And his brother's intended bride, a woman like none other Hew had beheld, being treated as if she were an unwanted piece of furniture instead of a goddess alighted on earth.

A boom of thunder rattled the windowpanes, and Hew pulled the coverlet over his knees. He couldn't make heads nor tails of Anne Sutton. She looked like a fragile nymph, with her narrow shoulders and slender limbs and the bosom of a classical goddess. He'd found her tearing apart flowers in the St. Sefin's church as though she were a vengeful Fury. When his mother fainted in his arms, she'd been one of the few to keep her wits about her, sensibly going for the smelling salts.

During the ride home in the carriage, he'd been subjected to the scent of her: wild rose and orange blossoms. She'd sprung up in the garden like the resident nymph as he explored his once-familiar home, trying to get his bearings.

And at dinner, she'd borne the insults and derision of his worthless brother with a magnificent, regal rage. Oh, she'd contained it—every line of her body showed her breeding and restraint. But there was no veil over her eyes, and those bright blue orbs betrayed everything.

Hew shifted position, trying to shake off the sensations that rose at the memory. Thou must not covet thy brother's wife. *Must not.*

The knock at the door penetrated, finally, his fogging thoughts. Not the hesitant scratch of a servant—and where were all the maids that ought to be about a house this size, anyhow? It was a thump both hesitant and determined, if such were possible.

Hew reached for his nightshirt and pulled it over his head, wincing as the fine fabric caught on the welts along his back. One would think the nerve endings there had been deadened. He wished it. But no sense terrifying his visitor, probably the housekeeper come to bring water for his washstand, or his mother to fret about the window he'd thrown open to the storm and the clash of sultry heat with cool rain.

"Enter."

The portal opened to reveal a figure in white standing on the threshold, like an angel come to conduct him to heaven.

Hew blinked to clear his head. He was sleeping. Or mad.

"You mustn't be here." His voice rasped, barely able to form words. Just like in dreams, especially the ones where he was tied again to the ladder, the fire falling on his back, the cleansing and consuming pain.

She stepped inside and closed the door behind her with a firm click. Her eyes flared, as if she were startled at the conventional sound. She raked that wide-eyed gaze around the room, looking anywhere but at him.

There wasn't much to look at. The dark paneling on the walls. The desk with his papers and the chair where Hew sat to pry off his boots. The empty fireplace with its painted screen, the tall double wardrobe, the nightstand where his candle danced as it caught a gust of air from the open window, where the draperies rustled and whispered like gossips at a ball. The hangings on the bed swayed, the medallions with their birds and foliage fluttering across the thick brocade, the canopy crowning the four-posted frame as if he were a king or an emperor.

Hew stared back, jolted by the blaze of blue in her eyes as her gaze lighted at last on him.

"You're alone," she whispered.

"Which is why you should not be here."

He ought to rise to face her, but his breeches were on the other side of the room, damn it. She was draped in a dressing gown, loose and ruffled, and still wore her hair in its arrangement of pinned-up curls. One or two had fallen loose to dangle over her shoulders. Silk slippers encased her tiny feet.

"Anne," he said hoarsely. "You must leave. You can't be found here. You'd be ruined."

She pressed the door behind her as if to ensure it shut tightly. "That is why I came."

Sense departed his head, simply lifted and swirled like a scattering flock of birds. She wore her shawl clutched about her shoulders, but the white fabric of her gown, thin and delicate, did nothing to conceal the shape of her, that lovely bosom and those long legs. She was built like a roe deer, all sleek limbs, huge eyes, and liquid grace. She stepped away from the door.

"You cannot—"

Words parted company with the rest of his sense as she pulled the shawl from her shoulders. She held up one slender arm and let the patterned silk fall onto his chair.

She stood in naught but the flimsy robe, and God above, it hid nothing.

"Don't remove your shoes," he said roughly as she did just that. "You'll take a draught."

"You might warm me," she said.

He stared, frozen, for a moment that stretched as if the clock had stopped on a still world. The wild moan of the wind keened past the windows. The candle capered, casting tempting shadows over her fair skin and the bone-white garment. Her breasts rose and fell with her fast breath, and she curled her toes into the patterned carpet. A shiver raked her frame, head to toe, and Hew rose from the bed without thinking.

"You'll catch your death," he growled. "Don't you know there's a storm out there?"

"I know. It's wonderful. The heat was driving me mad."

He caught up the shawl. God's toes, it smelled of her, powder and flower and soft woman. Thoughts struggled to form through the haze of sensation conjured by her nearness. Skin. Hair the gold of old coins. The rose-petal pink of her lips. He could not seem to look at anything but her lips.

Stiffly, he tried to settle her shawl about her shoulders. She slipped her arms around his back, clasping her hands, and looked up at him, her face as open and bare as a painter's canvas.

He couldn't breathe. She shivered again, but she wasn't cold. She was warm. So, so warm. Heat rose from her skin and curled toward him, carrying the scent of warm earth and clean rain.

Trying to haul words into his brain was like trying to push a wagon with a sixteen-pound cannon uphill. "You enjoy storms?"

"I adore them. This one makes me want to run about in it."

The thought caught his breath, of this girl in his arms running into the roil of weather outside, hands lifted as if she might catch the rain, her lovely face full of laughter. Ah, yes, she was in his arms. Hers still linked around his chest—he was afraid to move, lest she release him. And his hands had come to her shoulders, holding the shawl, but found some reason to slide over her arms and cup her shoulder blades. They fit in his hands like delicate wings, reminding him that he mustn't hurt her.

He mustn't kiss her, either. *Must not.* She wasn't his.

"Anne," he said, his voice scratching his throat. A small piece of logic pierced the fog in his brain, the haze whispering things he knew could not be true. "You can't wish to be ruined."

With her face tipped up, eyes locked with his, her mouth was within easy reach. He need only bend his head, the angle perfect, the most logical and inevitable of trajectories.

She moistened her lips, and his groin tightened. That was a trajectory he couldn't allow himself to consider. How he could pull her against him with his two hands and fit her body to his, as easy as sliding a cartridge into the bore of a cannon.

"I cannot marry Calvin," she said. "I *cannot.*"

Relief pounded him as if the fierce wind had thrust through the window to pummel his skin. Praise Venus. She didn't want his brother. Hew felt like raising his head and howling to the moon he couldn't see.

"Then don't marry him," he said. "Don't."

He shouldn't be crowding her closer, pressing his palms against her upper back. There must be space between their bodies. There must be space for words, for logic. She wasn't a spoil of war that he could carry back to his cot. She was Anne. Vixen. Venus. A nymph who tore apart boughs of myrtle with her hands.

Blood pulsed in his head. Not Calvin's. *Not Calvin's.* That meant she could be his. Hew's.

"I said no," she whispered. "They wouldn't listen."

Every line of her face was a study in softness. The flutter of her thick lashes, darker than her hair color, dewed with tears. The flare of her nostrils on that nose of hers, straight, strong, determined. The trembling of her lower lip. He wanted to kiss every plump groove of that lip. He wanted to suck it into his mouth and nibble.

He wanted his mouth on every part of her.

He struggled to keep the surge of his body at bay. "Then we make them listen," he said.

He wasn't certain what he meant. But he would do it. He would do whatever she wanted. He would do anything she asked.

"Kiss me," she whispered, lifting her chin. Her lips grazed his jaw, and his entire body jolted with the rush of blood.

Yes. God, yes. He wanted to roar his triumph over the hills, releasing it like a clap of thunder. She chose *him.*

He almost did it. He almost closed his arms and hauled her against him and let his mouth fall upon her, devouring. He would kiss her until they both forgot their names.

But say he did kiss her. Then what? What came after?

Hewitt Vaughn never did anything in the moment. He always, always had a plan.

Carefully he cupped her shoulders, holding her in place. She seemed delicate, but she wasn't. Firm muscle met his fingers. She might be slender, but she was strong.

"What?" he asked, searching her eyes with his gaze. "What are you asking me, Anne?"

"Kiss me," she said stubbornly, reaching her mouth toward his.

This wasn't right. She didn't want *him*. She wanted ... something else.

"And then what?"

Another growl of thunder shook the window casement. Hew swore it rattled the boards beneath their feet. Cold gusted into the room, and she shivered. Pink spots burned on her cheeks, pale as the linen of her shift.

"When they find me here," she said. "In your room. Then I am ruined, and he can't marry me. They can't make me."

The cold wrapped around Hew, digging through skin to bone. "Then what happens?"

His voice did not sound his own. His voice sounded to his ears as it had after the torture, when he'd stepped away from his body to watch, from a distance, what was happening to that heap of man-shaped flesh.

"I ruin you." He shaped the words through lips that didn't want to cooperate. "Then what?"

"Then I have to leave here," she said softly, her words a thread of sound against the swirling storm. "And I am free."

His hands felt numb and heavy, curled over her shoulders. She didn't know him. She didn't want him. She meant to use him to get something she wanted.

Wasn't that what people did? Wasn't that how the world

worked? It was only dolts like him, Hewitt Vaughn, who thought there should be more.

Who assumed he didn't deserve to have what he wanted anyway, so it didn't matter if he were denied.

"You suppose I will simply ... tumble you," he said. It wasn't the word he thought of first, but she was a lady, a gentleman's daughter. And she was not a seductress, whatever else she was about; her hands hadn't moved from their desperate clasp about his back. He felt the weight of her arms, a slender rope hauling him like a fish into her net.

His voice really was not his own; it was some beast coming from deep inside him. "And then you will go about your merry way."

She blinked. Her long lashes tangled, clinging together with their globes of tears. "Well, yes. Isn't that how it works?"

For his brother, maybe. And for hers. Not for him.

He told himself to straighten his arms. Told himself again. After a moment, his limbs obeyed him. He pushed her away.

She didn't let go, kept her hands stubbornly locked about his body.

"Anne," he said gruffly. "Go back to your room."

She shook her head. "No."

"If you don't want to marry my brother, then we will find a way to end it. I will help you."

Idiot! the beast inside him roared. *Take her! She's yours.*

She pushed herself close to him, breasts to his chest. Hew's mind blanked of thought. Pure sensation took over. Craven need, choking his mind like the dust storms that whirled up out of the desert.

Yours! The wind roared, ramming the glass panes of the window.

"This is how to end it," she said. "Kiss me."

He wanted to do more than kiss her. He wanted to consume

her. He wanted to raze her to the ground, and he wanted to lose his mind with her. Inside her.

To outrun, finally, the agony, and the humiliation, and the ghosts.

"What if you can't walk away?" He kept his eyes on her face, because her breasts were too close, and he felt the outline of her through the thin linen of his shirt. "What if this doesn't make you free?"

She hadn't thought this through. She didn't know what she was doing. She was an innocent; that much was obvious. She didn't know the first thing about what two bodies could do to one another. The pleasure. The entire cessation of pain, and of fears for the future.

She shook her head, and a gold ringlet swayed against her shoulder. Hew was trapped in the gleam of her hair in the candlelight, against the soft glow of her skin. He could *smell* how soft she was.

"I cannot simply walk away. They can find me and make me come back. I need you to do this for me. Hewitt." Her whispering his name untied something in him. The straight, clean lines of logic he usually thought in. "Help me. *Please*."

"Ruin you." The words were a dry crackle from his suddenly parched throat. He hadn't been this thirsty in the hottest days at Acre. "When you don't even know what it means."

"I know I want it to be *you*," she said, and pressed her mouth to his.

He was lost.

He saw it all. Even in a storm, even in the midst of mind-crushing agony, Hewitt Vaughn was strategic. He could see the end of things. He saw—or thought he saw—the end of this.

It would end with his being torn apart. Again.

Anne Sutton pressed her mouth to his, and he surrendered.

She tasted of flower petals and honey. Her lips were the sweetest delicacy, smooth as custard, firm as a bonbon. Her skin held the scent of myrtle. And she'd never kissed a man in her life. She simply mashed her lips to his and held them there, and Hew held back a chuckle of delight. She didn't know how to kiss. He was her first.

As if he'd ruin her. One didn't ruin a gorgeous mare with champion lines and a pedigree, didn't spoil her fine high step or dainty mouth with rough handling. One didn't manhandle one's hunting hound with the best nose and the finest instincts. And one didn't break the spirit of a proud, intelligent woman, nor despoil an innocent who'd never been awakened to pleasure.

Well, some men did. But Hew wasn't one of them.

He touched the side of her cheek, thumbing the corner of her mouth as he lifted his head. "Easy," he murmured. "Easy."

Her eyes flipped open, and her lips turned downward. "I'm doing it wrong."

He let his smile break free. Molten silver ran through his veins, like the ore buried in the Welsh hills. She was here in his arms. They had all night. And he could make her want him. Not whatever he represented, freedom, ruination, a thumb of the nose to his brother or hers. *Him.*

He hoped.

"There's nothing wrong, *sidan*, but what you don't like. So you must tell me what you *do.*"

He stroked the lines of her face as if he were a sculptor tracing a shape in his clay. Her broad brow and the elegant arch to her eyebrows. That bold nose. The round curve of her cheekbone, the delicate arrow of her chin. He traced the shape of her earlobe, and her eyes fluttered closed. Her breath whispered across her lips, and he touched those, too, her skin so soft beneath the coarse pads of his fingers. He'd been handling stone and iron for so long. He'd forgotten what it was like to touch a woman.

She opened her eyes. "You don't want to kiss me," she said, doubt swelling her tone.

"I do want to kiss you," he murmured, tugging at her full lower lip. "But do you down a whipped syllabub all in one go when the glass is placed before you? No. You savor it."

He pressed a kiss above each eyebrow, then to her temple, then cheekbone, each slide of his lips slow and deliberate. She tasted like a syllabub, rich cream with a heady wine within it. He progressed down the smooth line of her cheek, toward her mouth, and her breath came faster.

"I eat the syllabub all at once," she confessed. "I adore whipped cream."

He loosed the chuckle. Delight strained at his chest. What a pleasure for it to be delight breaking free, and not the raging beast he had lived with so long.

"Then," he murmured against the crease of her lips, "you must learn to savor."

She turned her head slightly, meeting his mouth, her lips parting beneath his, and the roar rose up in him. Arousal, yes, and triumph, yes. And the delight, such imaginable sweetness. Being allowed to touch Anne Sutton, kiss Anne Sutton, was the greatest gift he'd been given in his life.

This time, she relaxed and opened to him. This time, she tipped up her chin so he could slant his mouth across hers and capture her lips fully. The small sound she made in the back of her throat brought a surge of blood to his groin. He wanted her now, immediately, and he also wanted to kiss her for hours. Her mouth fit his perfectly, answering his question with a breathless *yes*.

The storm cartwheeled outside, the thunder like an attacking army, the lightning the crack of cannon fire, and he stood inside this room on the fringe of the dancing candlelight with a whole new universe in his arms, knowing he'd entered a perfect moment and wanting it never to end.

She broke the kiss and pulled her head back to look up at him. He could fall and drown in the deep wells of her eyes, such a deep blue, hazy with passion. For him. He'd done this to her.

He'd moved his hands from her shoulders to her back of her head, fingers clenched in her masses of hair. Her hands moved too, creeping up the back of his neck and stroking lightly, her fingers sending a lick of fire down his spine. He enjoyed the blaze of arousal, the full, heavy strain in his groin. It felt good to want, to know his body could still feel lust and crave release. Could still want to couple with a woman, after the sensations he'd been living with for the past weeks and months.

She swallowed, and he watched the flutter of skin at her throat. A pink blush rose across the top of her chest as his gaze dipped downward.

"Are you feeling this too?"

He brought his eyes back to meet hers. He smiled. "Yes, *cyw*."

"I want to savor," she whispered. Then she proceeded to outline his face with kisses as he'd done hers. Those lovely, soft lips skimming his forehead. His temple. His breath grew ragged. It wasn't just the brush of her lips, but all of her. The silken locks of hair that wisped against his face. The delicate tickle of her eyelashes against his ear. The elegant slope of her back as he dragged his hand down the long, sleek curve of her.

She didn't stop at his jaw but trailed kisses down his neck, the base of his throat. Darted out her tongue to lick his collarbone, as if she were tasting him, and his restraint snapped. With a growl he yanked her to him and captured her mouth again.

She chuckled, her lips pulling away in a smile. "You like that."

He liked *her*. Too much. She was delicious, and he couldn't get enough. He plunged his tongue into her mouth, too hungry for her to make a gentle probe first, to ask courteously. He licked into her mouth, tasting sugar and violets and clove. She gave a small whimper, clinging to his shoulders as her head tilted back before his onslaught, and he wanted to roar again at the satisfaction, but he also wanted to drink deep of her, to taste as much as he could. She was the most maddening bliss, a mind-blotting haze of need and pleasure. She was paradise in the shape of a woman.

He kissed her for minutes, perhaps hours, feeling no need to rush, while the storm blew and howled and banged around them, pounding like the blood in his head, in his groin. He wanted this for always, Anne Sutton warm and pliant in his arms. He could hold the rampant need at bay to keep her like this, soft, innocent, trusting.

But she was restless too, seeking the culmination of her desire, even if she didn't have a name for it. She leaned against his chest, conforming her body to his, but when she fit her belly against his groin, she went still.

His cockstand was unmistakable, stiff and proud, prodding into her waist above her hip.

Her eyes snapped open.

"That is what you do to me, Anne." The words came slurred and thick. He felt drugged with arousal, with her kisses. He brushed a knuckle along her throat as she swallowed hard. "That tells you what I am feeling for you."

"And that is ..." She licked her lips. "The instrument of my ruination."

His laugh disappeared into a groan at his body's response to the image that rose to mind. He dropped his forehead to hers, fighting the animal in him. The beast that wanted to lift her shift and take her now. One stroke, two, and he'd be spent. He was that hard for her.

"Yes," he said. Growled. "That is the *instrument* that I will put inside you. In your cunny. And then I will stroke you, hard and fast and deep, bringing you pleasure until you scream my name at your climax."

Her eyes flared wide, and her breath caught. "Oh," she said.

"But first." He fisted his hands in her shift, tugging lightly at the delicate material, pulling it taut over her breasts. Lord in heaven, her beautiful breasts. He loved the blush that spread over them when he described what he wanted to do to her.

"I want to kiss more of you. May I, Anne?"

"Oh." Her breath stuttered again. "You ... you may."

He pulled her toward him and swept an arm beneath her knees, lifting her. She was light as a blossom. She fastened her mouth to his, plunging her hands into his hair as he carried her to the high, four-poster bed. Her need, her surrender, heated his blood like a furnace used for smelting iron. She gave a little squeak when her bottom hit the mattress, the feathers giving way beneath her. Hew grabbed the hem of her shift, prepared to yank it over her head, but she shyly pressed her hands to the top of her thighs.

"I don't—I'm not—" A blush bloomed on her cheeks.

Such an innocent, so shy. He must be careful with her. "Shall I blow out the candle?"

She nodded quickly. "Yes, please."

The candle left a faint curl of smoke and the scent of sulphur as he whuffed it out. A shame, not to be able to see her luscious body. But he could examine her with his hands and mouth, map every inch of her that way. Hew stretched out on the bed, drawing her beside him, and captured her mouth again. He kissed her until her limbs turned liquid, until her hands left his neck and ventured down his shoulders, his arms. She stroked the muscle flexing beneath his shirt and, with a muffled sound from the back of her throat, wriggled closer.

She wanted him.

He let his hands roam, too. Stroking her lovely throat, the flare of her collarbones, the smooth span of skin beneath. He cupped a breast through the fabric of her shift, and she moaned in surprise as he flicked at the hardening nipple.

"Good?" he murmured.

She pressed her forehead to his shoulder, as if embarrassed to admit her body's own want, and nodded. So innocent. An odd tenderness warred with the triumphal beast. Hew hadn't forgotten his own initiation, long ago, at the hands of a Morgan relation, some buxom cousin come to lodge for the summer and with a mind to sample the local fare during her stay. He remembered how wondrous pleasure could feel, that first time with someone, and he wanted Anne to know that.

Whatever happened, he wanted her to have this: the knowledge of the bliss her own beautiful body could bring to her, and to another.

"My body tells you what I want, *sidan*," he murmured beneath her ear. "But you, my Anne, are more mysterious. You have to tell me what feels good."

"That." She gave a tiny moan and leaned into the hand stroking her breast.

"And what else might feel good?"

She scrunched up her brows; he could feel the feathering of the tiny hairs as she pressed her forehead against his chest. He wondered if she could hear how hard his heart was pounding.

"You said ... kissing."

Ye gods, yes. He pushed her onto her back and pounced. Her skin smelled of violets and tasted of cream as he kissed down her neck, along her collarbones, all the places his fingers had brushed. Her breath grew fast as he moved downward. He grappled a bit with the neckline of her shift—in the dark it took a moment to find the string—but then her breasts were free, both of them, and as delicious as he imagined. He bit back a moan as he bent his mouth to her, instead enjoying her sharp intake of breath.

"Hewitt," she squeaked.

He smiled. "Good?"

"Oh." She threaded her fingers into his hair, pressing into his scalp. "*Oh.*"

He was so hard and ready for her he felt himself leaking from his tip. Very likely he'd spend just from kissing her; it had been that long. All to the good, as he meant for this to be about her. Her ruination would be thorough and complete. He lapped, nibbled, nuzzled her breasts as her breath turned to short pants, and then he pulled a nipple into his mouth.

She cried out.

He let go. "I hurt you?"

"No." She shook her head, or he thought she did. The lightning was sporadic, giving him brief flashes of illumination, enough to see her hair spread over his pillow in golden waves, her eyes wide and dazed. Her breasts bare to his gaze, to his mouth. He was quite sure she arched her back, lifting them toward him.

"It feels good," he said smugly.

"Mmm." Her fingers plucked at his neck, his shoulders, slightly tugging.

He dragged his tongue through the valley between her breasts. "Tell me what you want, *sidan.*"

She moaned. "M-more."

"More what?" he teased, feeling wicked.

With a little mewl of determination she clamped her hands around his head and dragged his mouth back to her nipple. He laughed and dove in, tonguing the hard little nub, sucking on the peak, tugging it between his lips. Her hips lifted as she thrashed, moaning. So sensitive, his little Anne.

He brushed a hand down her thigh, and she clamped her legs together. But she kept her hands anchored to his head as he adored one breast, then the other. He brushed his palm up and down her thighs, then drifted his fingers above her apex, feeling the tuft of curls over her mound. She pushed her breasts into his mouth, her back arching off the bed, her breath short pants. He traced a finger along the crease between her thighs and she parted slightly, tentatively.

He was so hard and aching for her, but he wedged his cock between her hip and the bed, welcoming the friction. She wasn't ready for more. She loved him suckling her nipples, that was clear, and so he feasted. All the while he stroked her thighs, letting his fingers come closer, closer to her core. Then he slid his hand beneath her shift and stroked her bare skin. Smooth skin, soft as a bolt of silk. His cock bucked, demanding.

"Do you like this, *sidan?*" he whispered against her skin. Her nipple was puckered and hard as a pebble. "Do you want me to touch you here?" He touched the pad of his finger to her outside fold, the hair as smooth as her skin.

She bit her lip and nodded. "Y-yes."

He wanted to roar again. Blood pounded through him. "Yes, what, *cyw?*"

"Touch me," she nearly sobbed. "P-please."

He slid his finger against the tender skin, exploring, and she sucked in a breath, her fingers locking his head to her breast. He suckled with vigor, loving how she responded. Her entrance was slick and wet, and he gritted his teeth against the need to plunge inside her. Instead, he found her hood and the tiny nub of flesh beneath.

She clamped her thighs around his hand, but this time not in resistance. To hold him there.

There was a feisty, greedy girl inside that porcelain doll. Hew grinned to himself and set to his task in earnest, tonguing her nipple while he swirled his finger against that tender place. Soon her breath turned to short moans and her thighs tensed, quivering. So responsive, his Anne, like plucking the strings of a harp and producing beautiful music. She rose toward him and a soft mewl escaped her as her pleasure broke. Her head fell back on the pillow and he felt the throb beneath his fingers as her climax pulsed through her. She dug her hands into the feather tick, riding out the storm, and Hew wanted to howl again at the sight of the woman he'd satisfied. Instead he pressed a kiss to her shoulder, to her neck, as she swam the current, then eventually drifted back to shore.

She opened her eyes, turning toward his face in the darkness.

"So *that's* why," she whispered.

He laughed. He'd never laughed in bed before with a woman.

"Am I ruined now?" she asked.

"I hope so," he said. Because with any luck, after tasting real pleasure, she would want it again. With him.

She touched a finger to his chest, trailing it downward, over his shirt. "But you didn't—" The lightning flashed again, still raking the sky with an occasional glare, though the thunder had drawn off and the rain turned to a gentle patter. Her gaze landed on his cock, straining from beneath his shirt, engorged and more than ready.

"What shall I do?" she whispered.

Ah, that thread of boldness. He liked that about her, too. She reached toward him, hesitant, and he caught her hand. If she touched him, he would lose control, and he couldn't have that. Not now. Not here.

"Touch yourself," he said gruffly.

"Wh-what?"

"Put your hand where mine was. Feel where I touched you."

Eyes wide, she did, sliding her hand down her shift and between her legs. Her lips parted. He sat back, taking himself in hand.

"You can do that," he said, his voice scratching, "whenever you want. For yourself."

"I can?"

"Of course, you are welcome to come ask *me* to do it. Any time."

She let her eyes flutter closed again, concentrating as she explored herself, and Hew stroked himself, hard and fast, watching her. This wouldn't take long. Merely the sight of her was enough to send him over, but he wanted more of her.

"Put your finger in my mouth."

"My—what?"

"I want to taste you," he said with gritted teeth.

Still hesitant, eyes wide, she lifted her hand and slipped her finger into his mouth. He tasted the faintest trace of her essence, violets and clove, and that was all he needed. A groan ripped from his throat as he spilled into the cloth from his washstand, what felt like geysers spewing from him, molten silver. He shuddered as his release went on and on, trying not to bite her finger.

She drew her hand back, watching as he mopped himself quickly, then threw the cloth onto the washstand. Then she frowned.

"What's wrong?"

"You said you were going to—" She swallowed hard, but raised her gaze to his. In the flash from the window, she looked puzzled. And vulnerable.

She pushed out the words. "You said you were going to ... be inside me."

His cock bobbed at the thought, spent but not finished. He chuckled and lay down on the bed, pulling her against him. "And some day, I will. But I think we've done enough for your first time."

She sat up stiffly, scrambling her legs to the side as she tugged at the coverlet. "I need to be ruined."

He drew the covers over both of them, bending his arm beneath his head. "Stay here, and you will be."

"I—here?" She pulled the soft quilt up to her chin. She was so warm, nestled against him, and he loved that scent of hers, sweet as cake. "Doing what?"

"Sleeping," he murmured. "'S'been weeks of hard travel, and I'm home now, and this bed is very soft."

"I can't marry Calvin," she whispered into the dark.

He tucked his arm around her firmly, fighting a flash of jealous rage. "You won't."

She couldn't. She was Hew's. She'd come to him willingly, and while it wasn't what he'd planned—and God knew what he would do with her—he meant to keep her. Whatever hellfire rained down because of it.

~

HEW WOKE WITH THE DAWN, as was his custom. Outside his window, the sky was washed clean by the storm, a pearl-gray expanse skimming the unfurling green of the hills. The sweet, piping trill of the thrush spilled from a nearby tree, with the countering chirp of a long-tailed tit in response. Birds at his window. Green hills. The scent of the lime trees flowering in the garden. How strange, after the months and years of foreign lands, including a year in the desert. And how familiar, calling up a life he'd thought lost to him.

Anne Sutton lay tucked up beside him, her face turned

toward him on her pillow, one hand slipped beneath her cheek. Her soft, even breath was sweeter than any birdsong. She was proof that last night had been real. Touching her. Kissing her. Feeling her arch beneath his hand in the pinnacle of pleasure.

No, she would not be marrying Calvin.

A slight clang and rustle brought his gaze to the door. A young girl entered, a child, really, struggling with a heavy pitcher of water. She averted her eyes as she hurried to the washstand and poured her burden into the bowl. Hew hoped she wouldn't take up the cloth he'd tossed there; he didn't want a child handling the crumpled linen he'd used to catch his seed. The most potent release he could remember having in years, if ever. Because he had this woman within reach. Hew leaned back on his pillow and curved an arm around Anne.

The little maid turned, her eyes landing on the bed, and gave a frightened squeak. She looked at Anne, at Hew, who put a finger to his lips.

She ran out of the room as fast as she could go.

Hew had time to slide from the bed and don his breeches, then slide back in beside Anne's warmth before the silence of the house broke. He would not be having this discussion with bare knees. Anne stirred with a sleepy murmur, hammering the last nail on his certainty.

His gun was loaded, primed, and sighted. He was ready.

Footsteps first, pounding along the floorboards. That couldn't be his mother, who had trained herself to glide like a lady. But that was his mother's voice, raised in a querulous scold. She yanked open Hew's door, barreled inside, saw the figures on the bed, and stopped as if yanked by a harness.

The look on her face was—well, Hew had seen expressions of horror before. Not often directed at him, but it had happened.

"She's *here*," his mother shrieked.

Anne bolted upright, clutching the bedcovers to her chest and looking about wildly. She looked exactly like Snow White woken from her magic sleep, save a bit panicked.

"What—where—Hewitt," she said faintly. "And, er, Lady Vaughn."

"You didn't." His mother's nostrils flared. Actually flared. She stared him down. "Hewitt. You *couldn't.*"

"I did," Hew confirmed. He tensed his arm around Anne, but he knew not to show any other sign of weakness.

Anne's mouth moved, but speech escaped her. Her face was as pale as the linens on his bed. A huge rush of tenderness, of protectiveness, overtook him. She'd wanted to be ruined, but she hadn't thought it through, not fully. She hadn't imagined this part of it.

"Mother," Hew said, "before this discussion goes any further, let me make one thing clear. Anne isn't marrying Calvin." He waited until his mother's gaze swung to him, so he could be certain she comprehended.

"Anne is marrying me."

CHAPTER NINE

They were back in the parlor where they had dined the night before, this time with the sideboard set for breakfast. Anne's stomach rumbled, but she didn't believe she was hungry. She didn't believe she would be able to put food in her mouth ever again.

Her emotions had her in a roil, from head to toe, as if she were a teased-up skein of yarn, tangled past bearing. And she couldn't even sort out what she was feeling. The tangle of sensations writhed about her, and within her, like Medusa's snakes.

The paper on the wall was hand-painted with some bushy-looking pattern of blooms in a combination of sand brown and pea green. Anne focused on that. She studied the thick cornices that lined the ceiling. The elaborate marble mantelpiece and the carved panels that rose above it, classical figures surrounding a mirror. The tall sconces hanging from the walls. The bay window with its drapery. The pattern of the carpet—some exotic birds entrapped in vines and foliage.

Greenfield was opulent, but faded. Nicks and marks marred the surface of the long mahogany table at which she sat, Hew beside her, prisoners facing the tribunal of justice. Arranged on the other side of the table were her accusers: Lady Vaughn, who looked peeved. Calvin Vaughn, outraged. And her brother, green around the gills as if he were sick with drink.

"Explain this," Lady Vaughn rapped out. "This—this abomination."

Hew snorted and rose, turning to the sideboard and its silver covers holding back steam. "Abomination? I'm hardly the first man to steal his brother's bride, Mother."

"It's an outrage!" his mother squawked. Her light brown eyes bore a red rim, as if she'd been weeping. She pinned her anxious stare on Anne. "Did he—did my son—*force* you?"

Anne tried to push out words. Her voice had failed her somewhere between pulling on her round gown from the night before and furling a shawl about her shoulders as she hurried toward her inquisition.

"He didn't ..." Her voice was so small. She sounded like a fainting maiden. But she wasn't a maiden anymore, was she? That was the entire point.

"He did not force me," she said, and glory, she almost sounded calm. Like a woman in charge of herself and her emotions. Not a woman about to deposit last night's accounts on this polished if somewhat scarred table.

Hew continued pouring out the pitcher he held. "Anne came to my room—"

"She came to you?" Calvin broke in, adding his glare to his mother's. Anne shrank in her chair, wishing she could disappear into her shawl. She'd known there would be a raking-down, of course, if she were to go about ruining her reputation. But she hadn't imagined the specifics, and they were so much worse than what she could have conjured.

Daron continued to look sick.

"Anne came to my room to discuss her future with me." Hew returned to the table and set a cup in its dish before Anne.

Chocolate. As if she could abide anything in her belly at this moment.

"We concluded that she and Calvin did not suit." Hew leaned back in his chair, as casual as if he were entertaining morning callers. "But she and I do."

Calvin curled his hand into a fist and pounded it on the table. "You just want the money, you greedy cur!"

Hew folded one booted leg over his knee. He'd dressed as if he meant to go riding, and his casual polish offset his brother's fussy fashion. Hew glanced in Anne's direction. She felt his gaze on her face like a caress.

Like the way he'd touched her last night. Oh, heavens, she couldn't think of such things *here*. She'd go up in flames in her chair. What she'd done with him—what she'd felt—

She was ruined, indeed. One did not go back to genteel maidenhood after *that*.

But marriage? She gulped. Marriage was what she had hoped to escape.

"If you believe I was thinking about her dowry last night," Hew drawled, "then your upper story is unfurnished."

He meant he'd been overtaken by lust. For her. Finally, she'd driven a man to want something more from her than her inheritance.

You're not supposed to feel flattered by that, simkin.

Right. Angry. She should be enraged. She'd made plans to free herself from a man who wanted her for Aunt Gertrude's tiny portion and wound up with a man who wanted her for—what?

There was the rage. She curled her hands into fists on her thighs. They were shaking too much to bring the cup of chocolate to her lips.

"She is clearly a cunning baggage out to hook her claws into you. And you were so foolish, Hew?" his mother fretted.

"She was going to marry into the family anyway," Hew said. He adopted a casual pose, but something in him seemed coiled tight. Ready to spring. "So why not marry me?"

"Because you are the heir, and now you have fallen into her trap," Lady Vaughn snapped. "I wanted better for you, Hewitt."

Anne reached for the chocolate. If she were to be marched to the gallows, she wanted chocolate in her belly, rather than this seethe. One last dram of pleasure.

Though she'd had pleasure enough last night, hadn't she? Because of him.

Anne took a larger swallow of chocolate than she'd intended. It burned down her gullet, searing and bittersweet.

"I don't see how I could possibly find better than Anne," Hew remarked.

He was being so gallant. He was being so *frustrating*. What did he mean, she was to marry *him*?

"Because of the money!" Calvin roared again. "You just want it for your investments, instead of—"

Anne rapped her dish onto the table, startling them all. Even Calvin went silent, blinking at her.

"I am so relieved," she said to him, acid in her voice, "that I have not, in my faithlessness, dealt any blow to your pride, or to your heart. Clearly, your only concern is my supposed dowry, and who shall have the disposal of it."

Calvin moved his mouth like a fish pulled from the water. "No ... 'course I don't ... that is ..."

Daron shifted and regarded Anne blearily. "He won't 'elp us," he slurred.

"I beg your pardon," Anne said. "I presume you, also, are concerned about my supposed inheritance? Since that is the only reason to concern yourself with me at all?"

Daron blinked. "No reason t'elp our family," he said.

"Mum'll not have her fripperies. Father won' hold up his head. Turn us out into the street, this 'un'll."

"If you are to be connected to this family, then there is no way we will allow you, or anyone connected to you, to suffer penury," Hew said coolly. "Anne and I will see that your parents are taken care of."

The two of them. Together. As if they were matching salt and pepper boxes. Not Hew controlling her fortune or dictating her life, but they two making decisions together.

Anne rewarded herself with another sip of chocolate, since she hadn't cast back up the first.

Marriage. To Hewitt. She'd simply sprung from one trap to another.

As a wife, she would be his property. Her income would be his, her person would be his. He would want children. She would have to risk what Gwen had gone through, perhaps several times, all to carry on the Vaughn name, not even her own heritage. She would live here, or wherever he told her. She would have to plead for pin money and to borrow the carriage and have new gowns made up. She would walk into dinner on his arm and have calling cards embossed with Mrs. Hewitt Vaughn.

She'd been facing the prospect of marriage for years and yet she'd never seen its outlines so clearly. Married, she would be subject to her husband's whims, his peeves, his decisions about what she could or could not do with her time, who she could or could not see. He would have complete control over her person.

He would have unrestricted access to her bed. And she to his.

Anne clamped her legs together. Her capricious mind, rather than focusing on the issue at hand, kept drifting back to the pleasure of the night before. The astounding sensations she'd felt in his arms. The echoes she still felt in her body, between her legs. A memory.

And a desire to feel that again.

Lady Vaughn tried a new tactic, pleading. "Hewitt, you have not even been back a day. You haven't met any of the girls about. You do not even know Anne. You cannot imagine that a step such as *marriage*—"

"Mother." Hew set down his own coffee cup—black, no sugar or cream, Anne noted. He fixed his mother with a cool stare. "She was found in my bed. You can't imagine that I would do any but the honorable thing."

Anne's arms went cold to her fingertips, as if her shawl had slipped from her shoulders, leaving her exposed to the air.

He'd known this would happen. He'd *known*.

He'd *arranged* it.

She'd come to him bleating about being ruined, thinking she could be found in his bed, cast into the street with her things tossed out the door behind her, and walk away with her reputation in tatters, her head held high, freedom in both hands.

He'd planned all along for this result: that they would be required to marry.

Because Hewitt needed money to shore up the Vaughn family fortunes, and he also thought Anne had it. If she married Calvin, then he would be pleading with Calvin to invest in his canals or ships or whatever the solicitor had spoken about.

But if he married Anne himself—

She stood up, knocking a knee against the table in her haste, but it was as if her limbs were acting without her conscious direction. So was her mouth.

"I beg your pardon," she said. "This has been—a trying morning. I am overcome."

She whirled and headed for the door. A footman in livery,

approaching with a covered platter, dodged out of the way while another footman leapt before her to open the parlor door.

Daron scrambled after her. In the hall, she tried to remember which way lay her bedchamber, so she could march there in a righteous fury. He caught her wrist.

"Nan," he bleated. "The money—"

"If you say one thing more about Aunt Gertrude I shall scream!" Anne shrieked. "No, more than that, I—I will *bite* you."

She glared at him, astonished at her own feral snarl. She wasn't angry at Daron, was she? She'd done this to herself. She'd gone to Hewitt Vaughn's chamber of her own free will. And stayed there.

She'd thought she was springing herself from Calvin's trap, and she'd walked straight into Hew's.

"Nanny." Daron dropped her hand and ran a hand through his hair. Her usually debonair brother looked untidy, cravat hastily tied, his coat unbrushed. "I am in need of funds," he said with a groan.

"I have none to give you," Anne snapped. "Perhaps you might negotiate with my husband. I imagine there will be marriage settlements, and you will need to arrange them." Since, as a woman, Anne had no say over her own contracts. Over her own income or properties or person. Over the commitments that would trap her *for life* with a man she barely knew.

Other than in the carnal sense. Oh, Lord have mercy, she *must* stop thinking about being in his bed.

"Anne."

Hewitt caught up with her as she crossed the gallery that connected the side of the house with the reception rooms to the side of the house with the personal chambers. The sky outside, opening above the garden, above the river, above the grass-green hills, was as blue as the depths of his eyes.

Blast and damn him for a conniving liar.

"I was supposed to be ruined." She balled her hands into fists so she didn't do something appalling and unforgiveable, like strike him. "I should have been tossed out on my ear. Right this minute, I should be finding a coach to take me to Aunt Gertrude, and *freedom*—"

She caught the words on a sob. Tears? Now? She must not show weakness. But she hadn't known until precisely this moment that her escape plan had entailed fleeing to her lovely, silly old Aunt Gertrude in Llandrindod Wells, and now she was denied that.

Denied everything.

His jaw tightened. "You don't understand what it means to be ruined. It wouldn't mean freedom. You'd be cut everywhere. Your old life—"

"I don't want my old life!" Anne wailed. "I want a new life."

She pushed her fists against her mouth, appalled she'd said that. Ladies did not shriek. Ladies did not voice their desires in other but pleasant, modulated tones, and then they phrased them as requests, no harm done if they were ignored. Ladies did not insist on their own way.

Ladies also did not go to the rooms of unmarried gentlemen and asked to be ruined. So Anne had parted ways with lady-hood some time ago.

"Anne." Hew put his hand over hers. He was warm and solid. She remembered the feel of that hand, the blaze on her skin as he swept his palm over her, the boiling pleasure when he put his finger—

She focused on his mouth, on what he was saying. Now she recalled his mouth at her breast. The way she'd *pushed* herself against him, begging him to kiss her breasts. She burned with humiliation.

It must be humiliation. She could not stand here desiring

him, longing for him to touch her again, when he'd ruined every-thing else.

"I see no other way," he said quietly.

She grasped for the threads of thoughts in her mind. A way to *what?* She wanted to drop her head onto his shoulder. She wanted, outrageously, unfathomably, for him to put his arms around her and promise her everything was going to be all right.

She wanted him to comfort her, and she wanted to believe his promises.

"I know," he said, watching her with insistent eyes. Plead-ing. "I saw in the church. You do not want to be married."

"This cannot be what you want, either," she said, and a dangerous dampness welled at her eyes. "To be forced into marriage. To wed a scandal."

"What was the alternative?" he said softly. "And marriage ends the scandal. That is the point."

"I thought the point was the money," she said dully.

He brushed a thumb over her knuckles. "What money?"

She almost, almost believed him. Almost fell into that lucent blue gaze and let reason and sense be lost. Almost leaned into his touch, moving closer, seeking his warmth, inhaling the scent of him, outdoors and tobacco and the faintest hint of lime—

"The money *you* get now." To her astonishment and horror, her fist swung in his direction, landed on his chest. "The money your brother wants, and *my* brother wants, and *everyone* wants, except *me*—and you *tricked* me—and lied to me—"

"I did not lie to you," he said roughly, his voice edged with a flare of anger, though he didn't stop her as she swatted again and again at his chest. As if she could hurt him anyway, hard as the man was. His coat must be padded, for him to not even flinch. And his heart harder still.

"You came to my room," he reminded her, "and I warned you would be ruined."

"You tricked me," she cried. "You meant all along to marry me instead, but you didn't—tell—*me*—that." She emphasized each word with a blow.

Heavens above, she was going mad. She was actually striking a man, this man, the man she was supposed to wed. He caught her fists and held them, but gently, not with enough pressure to hurt.

"I didn't see another way, Anne. You can't expect I would leave you in shame, that I wouldn't offer for a woman found in my bed. For God's sake, who do you think I am?"

"I don't know." To her further humiliation, she sniffled. "I don't know you at all."

It was true. He was a complete and utter stranger. She'd known him for the span of a day, and she was going to wed him.

"But marriage," she said, fighting back another sniff. She would *not* give into tears. "There's no way out of it."

"We could have it annulled, if that is your wish," he said quietly.

"You can't annul a marriage. It isn't that simple." It was rage causing her tears, yes, righteous wrath. Not the sense of smashed hopes, or the wish that something, anything could be different, that she could have a real husband, in truth—

"If we prove I am impotent, or some such," he said.

She blinked at him. What man would make such a claim? What kind of man would submit to the examination that would be required? What man, if it would free a wife who didn't want to be wed to him, would claim impotence and go through the public humiliation of having it proven so, just to grant her liberty.

She'd seen his manhood last night. She'd watched, in the shadowy dark, as he found his own release by watching her touch herself. Dear God, that memory made her burn worse than anything else had. Sucking on her finger while he climaxed with a groan, as if all he needed was contact with her body.

She shivered. He would not be found impotent. No doubt he'd respond as readily to any woman set before him. He'd fail that test at the first.

"I would have to be caught in adultery," she said. "Then you bring a suit for criminal conversation, and a bill of divorce to Parliament." Which was expensive, and even more humiliating, and would lead to worse ruin than being found in Hewitt's bed. Divorce would destroy them both.

"You will *not*." He curled his hands around her wrists, as if he meant to physically restrain her from going to another man's bed.

Jealous, was he? Well, most men were about their possessions. Just look at how Daron and Calvin were behaving over an inheritance that hadn't even come to her yet, but which they already considered theirs.

And now it would be Hewitt Vaughn's. It had taken him less than a day to clear the board of his competitors. Fearsomely capable, this man. Could she blame him for seducing her?

But he hadn't. All he'd done was show up in his broad-shouldered coats with his clear, steady gaze and his strong hands and his competence in a crisis. Offered her a leaf of mint in a sunny garden while the sun teased out silver strands in his hair. Reproved his brother for insulting her at dinner.

Told her to leave when she knocked on his door in her dressing gown and slippers.

She'd thrown herself at his head. Come to his room begging for him to ruin her. No doubt many another woman had done the same, and that was why he was so accomplished at the ruining.

"We can live apart. Or file a bill of separation. You will have options, Anne."

"Those aren't options." Those would simply leave her alone. And he was a man of action, a man full of sensuality. Surely he wanted more than a wife in name only.

Women didn't have *options*, plural. A woman had one choice: find the most promising man she could to marry, one who would hopefully keep her economically secure and free from humiliation and public censure, and pray he did not die or turn into a sot or grow ill with disease.

Who could blame her for wanting her freedom?

"Then," he said, his voice heavy, "you jilt me."

Refuse to marry. She flicked her gaze up to his, her breath catching. "Now?"

"Not now." He curled his hands around her fingers. His were warm and strong. She remembered the calluses on his palm skimming her skin, the way she'd—

"Then when?"

"We pretend to move forward. We delay having the banns read at St. Woolos, draw out a long engagement. Say we are getting to know one another. And then—" His face tightened against a memory, that dent in his lip flattening, the scar deepening between his brows. "We find you a reason to cry off."

It had worked before in Llanfyllin. Anne went about her life with her betrothed in the background, marriage a distant dream. She had the safety of an agreement, and none of the duties.

That would hardly work if she remained *here*. With this man ever before her.

And he could line up all the possibilities as if assembling weapons against a siege, but there was no surety he would keep to his promise. No guarantee he would not change his mind.

They stood in the gallery, staring at one another, he holding her hands while the sun bloomed in the summer sky as if it shone every day in Wales.

She'd come to him because she thought he would set aside

honor. Surely that was scorn blazing in the eyes of the Earl of St. Vincent at the Penrydd wedding. *You*, he'd said to Hewitt, every part of his manner an accusation.

Me, Hewitt had agreed, as if he were guilty.

Yet if he were not a man of honor, why would he insist on offering for her? Why would he extend her the protection of marriage? None of this made sense.

He hadn't even done the deed properly. All he'd done was fondle and kiss, when he'd promised to—

She was *not* entertaining that thought. Anne brought her fists back to her own chest as if she could press her pounding heart into submission.

His eyes were so blue. He hadn't shaved yet, and dark stubble clung to his lean cheeks, his bold jaw. His facial bones stood out like that because the man had no extra flesh on him, nothing more than muscle and bone. The silver hair above his temples said he'd been through something that had aged him before his time.

She knew virtually nothing of this man, of his history, his temperament, or his character. And, if she did not find a way to free herself from this new snare, she would belong to him for life.

"Do not tell Daron I intend to jilt you," Anne said finally. "I will write my family and tell them I am betrothed. We can carry on the pretense, as you say."

She would not examine why that thought made her feel hollow. Wasn't he offering exactly what she wanted?

He unbent his fingers from around hers. "Of course. What-ever you need."

She answered him with a humorless laugh. As if any of this were about what she needed.

"By the way." Anne straightened her shoulders as she looked him in the eye. She might be trapped, she might be a *twymfat,* like Mathry said—*idiot,* she believed the Welsh word meant—but she refused to be a weepy, helpless mess.

"Congratulations on your forthcoming marriage, Captain Vaughn. You've won."

She wasn't used to delivering witticisms, or sallies, or even having the final word, really. But she was proud of herself for delivering this *coup de grâce* before she turned on her heel and waltzed away.

She only wished she didn't feel *quite* so pleased at the sense that Hew's eyes lingered on her the entire length of the hall.

CHAPTER TEN

She'd already done one thing she'd never dreamed of. Two things, really. She'd struck a man, when Anne had never in her life struck another person, not even inadvertently. And not just anyone; she'd struck the man she was supposed to marry.

After she'd been found in his bed wearing nothing but her shift, and that after allowing the man to pleasure her in ways she'd never known possible. That was the second unheard-of thing.

Now she did something else entirely out of character: Anne called for a horse.

A horse! My kingdom for a horse! They'd read several plays of Shakespeare's, she and Gwen, at the behest of their tutor. Gwen liked the wild poetry. Daron liked the insults and sexual puns and battles, and he would occasionally agree to act scenes with them. Anne grasped little of the language, but she was fascinated by Shakespeare's women. The weeping heroines who killed themselves for love or shame. The conniving queens. The girls who dressed as boys and got away with it, as if it were not another unheard-of thing for a woman to pursue her own goals single-mindedly.

"What kind of horse, miss?" asked the footman, wide-eyed, when Anne made her request. Greenfield, for all it lacked maids, did have footmen. She imagined Lady Vaughn had found some means, here on the edges of Wales, to avoid paying the taxes on manservants and windows, since Greenfield had both in abundance.

"Any horse," Anne said, trying to sound firm. In truth, she didn't ride often. She and Gwen were more like to ramble on foot, or take the pony cart and one of the workhorses when they and their nurse went out gathering herbs. She hoped the groom would not bring some enormous gelding it would terrify Anne to mount.

A few minutes later, as she stepped off the porch to the gravel front drive, she saw the coachman driving the carriage around from the stableyard. A pair of dappled grays with dainty matching socks pulled the traces, and a groom clung to the perch in the back.

"They'll take you anywhere you wish to go." Hew appeared beside her, sneaking up in that silent way of his.

Anne stifled the leap of her heart. He was tracking her. Trying to find out where she was going, but in a subtle fashion. That—resentment, surely—accounted for the blaze that ran through her body at his nearness.

"I only wanted a horse." She sounded surly. Well, she'd been trapped into marriage—again—and that could blight a girl's mood. Let him insist on marrying surly Anne. Headstrong Anne. An Anne who suddenly, without having shown any previous inclination for doing so, decided to speak her mind.

What was *happening* to her?

"You are not familiar with the area, and there are some rough elements in Newport these days," he said.

"You don't have to tell *me* that," Anne muttered. She'd been in the area longer than he had, a few weeks at least, while her brother and Daron laid their schemes. *She'd* been the one kidnapped by the Black Hound. Hew had shown up only a day ago.

And upended her world. Damn his mouth and the way she couldn't stop watching his face.

He turned to stare down at her. "I won't have you hurt."

"At least not until *after* the marriage agreement is signed, I'm sure, and you have some claim to my supposed dowry."

He held her elbow as she climbed into the carriage, ignoring her petulant tone. "Where are you going?"

As if he had any right to ask, Anne almost snapped, until she recollected that, as her presumed husband and the man who would control her life, he did.

"Away," she said curtly.

He closed the door and reached up to hold his hand on the window, where the leather shade was rolled up. "For how long?"

"As long as I wish."

"Return by dinner," he said firmly.

"We shall see."

"Have her home by dinner," he called to the coachman, and Anne heard the man's rumbled assent. She threw herself back into the upholstered seat, incensed. She couldn't even manage to run away in high dudgeon. She was in his carriage, leaving his house, in the hands of his servants, and he had every right now to dictate her actions. She'd settled the noose around her neck when she knocked on the door to his room and handed over the loose end when she stripped off her shawl.

She simply hadn't known it.

"To St. Sefin's," Anne called.

"Aye, mum."

This time, Anne paid attention to the sights and sounds around her. This place they called Rogerstone, after the ruined castle, was made of two towns, Tydu and Tregwillym, growing together like children growing out of short gowns. And this odd place, in transition, would be her home for a while longer. That hadn't felt real to her when it was Calvin insisting they marry. And now she was bound to Hewitt Vaughn. Who promised she could jilt him, whenever she was prepared to pull the full weight of scandal down upon her and her family's heads. But he was, by his own admission, not a man who felt bound by promises. So she might find herself well and truly trapped here.

She looked about with fresh eyes, and wondered if this were a place where she could be happy.

The scenery wasn't as dramatic as that surrounding Llanfyllin, but then, Llanfyllin was isolated within its valleys and hills. One had to choose to be there. The hills here were smaller as the land lowered into the sea, and the sky stretched further. Everything seemed more reachable.

She would swear the air carried the scent of salt and fish. Every tree seemed to be bearing fruit, and the wheat in the fields ripened toward harvest. Cattle grazed the hills in fat brown clumps, and the spring lambs were fattening themselves for the table while the ewes fattened themselves for another season of mating.

Every other created thing had its season and purpose—had its destiny—save for Anne. What was hers?

She knew it was a slender hope that Gwen would be at St. Sefin's. She was a new-made bride and would be in her husband's arms, likely already off on her wedding trip. Anne had spent last night in a man's arms, too, and for some reason she wanted to tell Gwen about it, as if their friendship had not been profoundly broken, as if Daron's betrayal and Anne's ignorance had not scored a deep rift.

The church of St. Woolos stood quiet among its overgrown graves, some tilting back into the earth, and across the hill the crumbling priory, once a shelter of impressive stone, lay as silent and dreaming. She heard birds and the low drone of insects, bees busy about their task, but the only creature she saw was the enormous goat cropping grass around the headstones in the cemetery, raising its head to stare with its odd, flat eyes as Anne rolled past.

Then the carriage turned into the yard at the back of St. Sefin's, and finally, there were people. The two black-clad widows were laundering clothes, one poking at the copper boiler with the washing bat, the other scrubbing a garment along the washboard. The two boys had the task of spreading wrung linens over every available surface, wooden frames, fenceposts, bushes.

The boys made her nervous. The blind one felt his way about with a shepherd's crook, not at all stumbling as Anne would expect from one who couldn't see, and the other one, the idiot boy with the round face and narrow eyes, chuckled all the time, as if the least thing delighted him.

"I don't suppose—the viscountess?" Anne called as she descended the coach. "Gwen?"

"She's off to the castle with his lordship to set up house, is our lady," said Widow Jones with a merry smile. "Ah, her lady-ship! What a fine thing to call our Gwen, aye, Mother Morris? Did you ever think we'd see such a thing?"

The crone turned and glared at Anne with beady eyes, muttering something in Welsh that ended with *Saes*, what the Welsh called the English. Which Anne was.

"Now, Mother, Miss Sutton was raised in Llanfyllin, she was, so a Welsh woman true as the rest of us," the widow chided gently. "Ifor, Tomos, here's Miss Sutton come to visit us! D' ye want to give the fine horses an apple, Tomos?"

"*Pert*," the older boy said, edging closer to Anne with a grin.

Anne edged away. "Er—Mathry?"

"Off with Mr. Ross to see to the castle as well, and there's a ring on her finger at last, to be sure," the widow said with glee. "Suppose we'll travel to Penrydd for their wedding, Mother, and stay in a fine, rich castle, shall we?"

The crone muttered as she turned back to poking the wash, but her mien seemed lighter, and she stopped glaring in Anne's direction. So Mathry had won a declaration from Penrydd's Scottish secretary. He'd seemed an acceptable sort of man, not anyone Anne would set her cap for, and not as commanding or capable as her Hew, who—

Anne threw a halter on those thoughts and brought them up short. He wasn't *her* Hew, was he? He was her pretended husband-to-be, but she had no claim to his affection.

She could hold him to the marriage, she supposed. Secure herself a roof over her head and some measure of economic security. Perhaps even pleasure, now and again, until they wearied of one another. And then she would be a wife like so many she knew, a polite acquaintance with the man whose name she bore, while they went about their separate lives and met over the dining table now and again to discuss the futures of their children.

Her belly rolled and bit like a feral dog, reminding her she'd put nothing in it but chocolate. She did not like that prospect for her life. She did not want that any longer.

She could take the carriage and go on to Llandrindod Wells. That was what she should do. Find Aunt Gertrude. Demand an accounting for this supposed money Daron was staking his future on. Get Aunt Gertrude's advice about her current dilemma and how to help her family. Or, hide behind her aunt's skirts until the tempest of her ruination blew over and everyone forgot Anne Sutton existed.

Have her home by dinner, Hewitt had said, as if she were already his to command.

It would take at least a day to reach Llandrindod Wells by coach, if she could find a coach to take her.

But would he let her go?

"Cerys is inside and can fix you tea," said the widow pleasantly, turning back to her task. "Mind there's a bit of a bother indoors, as we've someone in the mother's ward. But you're welcome nevertheless, Miss Sutton."

That was the thing Anne had learned about St. Sefin's: they never turned any seeker away. She tugged off her gloves and untied the strings of her bonnet as she headed through the door leading to the kitchen, where she'd sat with Gwen several times for tea. St. Sefin's didn't have a formal parlor, or they did, but the inhabitants rarely used it; everyone gathered in the broad, warm kitchen.

Cerys, Dovey's daughter, was there, singing to herself as she ground herbs in a mortar, one eye on the kettle on the hob grate. She was almost supernaturally lovely, with her green eyes and dark, springing hair, her skin the color of sandalwood. Unless one knew she were of mixed race, Anne thought, one might never see it.

Anne had never met a mixed person before. She had never seen a person from Africa until she came to St. Sefin's and met Dovey. Mrs. Evans. But then Dovey—Mrs. Evans—had not been born in Africa either, but in the West Indies, and Anne didn't know precisely how the woman had ended up here, only that Cerys's father had been Dutch, and properly married to Dovey.

Hew believed the trade in slaves must end, that Britain should no longer allow people to be kidnapped from African shores and carried across the sea in chains. He was opposed to it. If Anne gave it any thought—she never had, prior to this— she supposed she wanted such an awful practice to end, too. Those were human lives. Dovey—Mrs. Evans—and Cerys were as tender and brilliant as anyone else of Anne's acquaintance.

It unsettled her, how very provincial and sheltered her life in Llanfyllin had been, and how it had taken coming to Newport to open her eyes to what the world was like. How much of it she didn't understand.

"Black or green?" Cerys demanded, fixing her light-green eyes on Anne.

"I-I beg your pardon?" Cerys, who could not be ten years of age, had more confidence and authority in her manner than Anne did at four-and-twenty.

"Tea," Cerys said. "I've the fine black what we save for fancy guests, but I'd just as soon serve you nettle, as that's easy to come by and don't have a tax."

Good heavens, the child knew more about housekeeping than Anne did. "Er, green," Anne said, realizing that she had always in her life expected to be served the fine black tea, and now felt she would never again be truly deserving of it. "Is your mother about?" Perhaps Dovey would know about reaching Gwen.

"She's—"

The reply disappeared as another woman, a stranger, swept into the kitchen. A few years older than Anne, she wore her ash-brown hair coiled about her head and a simple round gown with one of those plaid Welsh shawls wrapped around her waist like the peasants wore them. Her hairline looked damp and her face, a set of bold and striking features dominated by large blue-gray eyes, gleamed with sweat. She rubbed a hand across her fore-head like a fighter energized after a battle.

"Bring the water, Cerys, and the caudle. 'Tis time."

The younger girl's eyes flared wide and she caught up a cloth to pull the kettle off the stove. "The babe is coming?"

"Any moment." The stranger swept a swift gaze over Anne.

"Ah, *iawn*, I could use another set of hands." She opened a cupboard and shoved a pile of rags at Anne as she stood awkwardly, about to protest, then nodded at Cerys as she poured the steaming water into a basin. "Come along."

"I don't—I am not here to—" Anne stumbled after her, doing the other's bidding despite herself. The woman had quite an air of command. She set off down a narrow hall off the kitchen, one Anne knew led to sets of rooms that had housed guests in the former priory and now served as a sort of infirmary.

It also served as a birthing ward. Gwen had mentioned that St. Sefin's frequently housed women who, for whatever reason, could not birth at home, or had no home to give birth in. The smell of a coal fire and lavender filled the broad stone room, which held about six cots and several small tables. Windows along the ceiling, too high to reach and cover as was the custom, let in light and birdsong. In the center of the room stood a birthing chair, unoccupied.

Dovey paced the room with a hugely pregnant woman leaning on her arm. The mother was disheveled, her gown stained, her dark hair plastered to her head with sweat, her cheeks hollow with pain. She moaned quietly with each step, cradling her swollen belly.

"A bit more." Dovey crooned soothing phrases in Welsh intermixed with the English. "There's a dear. We'll just walk a bit more then, and the *pwt* will be here."

The mother muttered something in another language, one more foreign than Welsh. Dovey kept up her soothing cadence.

"Na, all will be well, and the babe will be healthy. A fine, strong, dear one, and all the family will be proud."

Cerys, as if she knew what she was doing, placed her basin on one of the tables. Anne placed her stack of rags alongside. "You would not call an accoucheur?" Anne whispered, for that was the extent of her knowledge about childbirth.

Dovey lifted her head. "*Bore da,* Miss Sutton." She greeted Anne with civility, but Anne was quite sure Dovey didn't like her. "I sent for our usual midwife, but she's abroad, and Mrs. Lambe here is as good as one. You're a godsend, you are, Eilian," Dovey said to the woman now organizing the table, pouring hot water into another bowl and then swirling her hands through it.

"Mrs. Bernstein won't want a lying-in hospital anyway, even were there one near about, would you, Leah? They'd just insist the babe be baptized. And I've yet to meet a man-midwife not eager to use his tools, whether or not they are called for," Eilian said.

Anne stared at the mother, scandalized. What parent wouldn't baptize her child in the one true faith? She stared next at the new woman taking such command in St. Sefin's, and her thoughts snagged. "I've seen you about," she said. "The new pie shop, in High Street. That is you."

The woman inclined her head. "You make pies," Anne said, "and deliver babies?"

Eilian raised a brow in return. "A woman cannot be two things?"

Anne wasn't even *one* thing. She ought to leave; she didn't belong here. But there was something compelling about the primal scene of women gathering for that most sacred of observances, the birth of a new life into the world.

"You came back?" Anne echoed. "You are from here?"

The mother gave a sharp cry then, her hands gripping her belly. Eilian beckoned her forward and wiped her hands on a cloth before dipping them below the woman's skirts. Anne stared in fascination and terror.

"It is time," Eilian said. "Come to the chair. Cerys, hold her other arm. Leah, when the pains come, bear down."

"All must be well," the mother fretted. "This child must live."

"She's put her head down and is pushing out like the good strong girl she is." Eilian pulled up a small stool and settled herself as Leah lowered into the birthing chair. Anne marveled at Eilian's confidence, tucking her hands beneath another woman's skirts and touching her parts. Touching a *baby*.

"It must be a boy," Leah whimpered, screwing up her face as a pain struck her. "It *must*."

"Then it shall be," Eilian soothed. "Now push, *mam fach!*"

The straining and shrieking began. Anne's feet rooted to the floor. This was what Gwen had gone through, because of Daron. And her friend had given birth alone, in coldest winter, with no one to help her or save the babe in distress.

This was what she would go through to have a child, Anne realized as the hours wore on. The pain, the sweat, the shrieking. Birthing was a tedious process, sharp moments of action pierced by lulls where they simply stood and murmured encouragement while the straining woman panted and gathered her strength. And it clearly *hurt*.

Anne could not marry and face this torture. She would go to Aunt Gertrude, she would hide from her parents, and from Daron and his relentless need of funds. She ... she would work in a dress shop. Or a pie shop. She'd work in a butcher's if she must. Anything to—

"A set of cloths, Miss Sutton," Eilian, the pie shop lady, called. "Not the ones I've used. Clean ones."

"I don't—" Anne bit back the protest of her ignorance. She fetched a stack of soft rags from the table and stepped forward.

"A moment more," Eilian encouraged the mother. Anne watched in wonder and terror as the woman's face screwed taut in lines of pain. Dovey and Cerys stroked her arms and back from each side, murmuring encouraging words, more tender than anything Anne had ever witnessed.

"Once again—bear down, push him out—push, push!"

Eilian cried. Suddenly she sat back, something filling her hands. *"Baban!"*

Anne stared as the child emerged, its head enormous, its body long and stretched and covered with blood. Eilian whisked a cloth from Anne's hands and wiped its face, eyes, and nose, swiping a finger through its mouth. The infant opened its eyes with a mewling cry. Then Eilian set the thing and its cloth in Anne's hands.

"Hold a moment, me lovely, while I tie the cord." A long tube extended from the babe's belly, and Eilian quickly tied it with a piece of string.

Anne froze. She held a newborn child. A living creature, perfectly formed, unbelievably tiny.

"There we go." Eilian transferred the bundle back to her own lap, then beckoned Anne close. "Let's clean him, shall we? You do the feet."

Anne feared to touch it. How could something so small not break? But Eilian moved firmly, if gently, scrubbing the cloth over the wee head and shoulders, wiping off layers of stickiness and blood. Anne cautiously touched a foot. Five tiny toes, curled like a pillbug. The babe pulled its knees close to its belly, fists tucked beneath its chin, the way it had been formed in the womb.

"A boy?" the mother cried. "'Tis a boy?"

"Aye, a boy," Anne assented, for she could see that much.

"Baruch Hashem," Leah said, her voice breaking with relief. "A boy."

"A fine, strapping boy," Eilian assented. She looked on the thing with a soft, marveling gaze. Anne had to admit that, with the goo polished off, it did increasingly resemble a human child.

"Oh, here's the rest," the mother said with a gasp.

"Another child?" Anne cried.

"That will be the afterbirth, and we want it out, we do,"

Eilian said. "Hold this roaring boy for me, dear." She plopped the baby once more into Anne's hands. "When it's out, I'll cut the cord, and then we can swaddle your *bachan*."

Anne was clearly expected to hold it. The infant scrunched up his face and mewled, little fists striking the air. His eyelashes were tiny threads on his cheeks, his mouth a Cupid's bow, and thick dark hair thatched his head. Anne held the babe close to her body so she would not drop him as the tiny thing squirmed. The puckered face reminded her of a newborn kitten and how she'd spent hours with the stable cats and their litters, watching the pink sausages grow fur, open their eyes, and gain their feet. This was how the miracle of life began, right here with this bloody magic.

No, Anne thought, the miracle began with a man and woman doing what Hew had done to her last night—only he had not done the full deed, had he, likely to avoid this result. But would he want children of his wife? No doubt he'd be as concerned for heirs as this woman. He wouldn't be marrying Anne for affection, not after what she did, but only for convenience. To sop up a scandal. Have a wife without the trouble of wooing. Have a woman nearby to provide heirs as needed, and—

"That's that, then," Eilian said with satisfaction. She tipped the bundle in her hands, tissue veined purple with blood, into one of the basins, then snipped through the cord and peered at the child in Anne's arms. "Is our *bachgen* swaddled, me lovely?"

"No, I didn't ... I don't know how," Anne said humbly.

"Aye, then, here's the way of it," the other woman said breezily, and Anne's shame lessened. Eilian laid the child on the table and examined it briefly while the thing stirred and gave its soft, mewling cries. Then she wrapped it like a handpie in a fresh, soft shawl and took the babe to the mother, whom Dovey had cleaned up and transferred to one of the beds, propping pillows behind her back.

Leah held out her arms eagerly, her face soft with weary wonder, and brought the infant to her breast. Eilian watched, made a small adjustment, and the babe fell to sucking greedily. Eilian nodded with satisfaction and stepped back.

"We can leave you to rest now," she said with a fond smile. "I don't suppose you've a monthly nurse, Leah, not as things are."

"I will see to her." Mother Morris, the older of the crones, hobbled forward pulling the wooden stool. She'd settled herself onto it and brought out her darning before Anne even knew what to say.

"Splendid, Mother," Eilian said. "You'll call us if Leah or the babe have need."

Mother Morris responded with something in Welsh that must have been assent, for the others turned toward the door of the room, gathering up the detritus from the table. Cerys took the last of the rags, leaving Anne to take the basin of bloodied water and trail after them back to the kitchens.

She didn't know her place in any of this, but she didn't want to leave. She'd been part of something wonderful, a grave and important undertaking in which she'd been needed, and that had never happened to her before.

"Why doesn't she want her child baptized?" Anne whispered.

"They are Jews," Eilian said. "They live up in—Merthyr Tydfil, is it, Mrs. Evans?"

Dovey nodded and went to the scullery, where her voice floated back into the main kitchen. "She's the widow of a businessman, Daniel, who was murdered these weeks past by the Black Hound. Leah came looking for him to find out what had happened, whether any justice might be done. They have only daughters, and she feared her husband's family might turn her out unless this next child was their heir."

"And now he is?" Anne asked, placing her basin on the table. "The heir, I mean."

"So it seems. She ought to be able to keep her home, once she returns with the child. She says she cannot stay for the usual lying-in, there is a ceremony their rabbi must perform for the boy after a certain number of days. I hope she will be well enough to travel."

"We will make certain she is." Eilian moved into another smaller room Anne knew to be the stillroom. Gwen kept her herbs and her remedies there. "Red raspberry leaf?" she called out.

"There's some drying before the window. We've been making buckets of tea for Mathry," Dovey called back.

"I'll want some of the blessed thistle I saw in your garden," Eilian answered. "Have you goat's rue? Ah, here."

These strange words meant nothing to Anne, whose hands began shaking with the aftereffects of a trial. She realized she was sticky and she went into the scullery to wash.

Dovey finished wiping out a basin, then turned to face her. She was Anne's height, and hauntingly beautiful, with a slender neck, large eyes, and high cheekbones. Her mouth was full and curved into a smile Anne had never seen from her.

"Thank you, Miss Sutton. For your assistance."

"I did nothing," Anne said, not humble but honest.

"You came for a visit, I don't doubt, and we put you to work." Dovey's smile widened as she returned to the kitchen.

Widow Jones was there, stirring a pot of broth that had been simmering on the hob all this time, sniffing and then adding handfuls of herbs now and again. "Mother will want bone broth," the widow said, "and I say to add anise seed. Helps bring down the milk."

"And fennel," called Eilian from the stillroom.

Anne felt an odd squeeze about the heart, being here with

these women who were bent on the care of one of their own. So different from the kind of mornings calls she was acquainted with, or the customary amusements of her female friends.

Dovey started taking down bowls and dishes from the shelves above one of the worktables. "Gwen left last night so they might spend their first night at Penrydd, and I don't expect her back for a time," she said to Anne. "The viscountesses set sail this morning for Bristol, and we'll not see hide nor hair of them again, I wager. So I'm afraid it's just us if you've come for company."

Anne drew in a long breath. "I came to tell you. You'll hear I'm to be married."

Dovey's eyes were flat and hard, her lips tight, but her nod was polite. "To Calvin Vaughn."

"To Hewitt," Anne said.

The change in Dovey's face was almost comical. A clang sounded as Cerys dropped a utensil on the worktable.

"Captain Vaughn?" Cerys demanded. Eilian came out of the stillroom and stared at Anne, a stoppered jar in hand.

Anne's blush rose from her neck to her hairline. She must be as red as a raspberry herself.

"We—Captain Vaughn, Hewitt, and I—decided we would suit better than Mr. Vaughn—Calvin—and I would." And, oh, glory, wasn't that a fabrication.

Dovey looked cautious. "Well, you did find the pin, didn't you now? I suppose we're to felicitate you on the happy turn of events."

"The elder Vaughn?" Eilian sounded eager, yet somehow brittle, lacking the assured confidence she'd shown before. "Him as arrived yesterday. Hewitt. You're to marry."

"Er. So it seems," Anne stammered.

Eilian curled her fingers around the jar. "I thought you had broken with the Vaughns. This seems awfully fast."

Was the woman jealous? Had she looked upon Hew and wanted him for her own? Mrs. Lambe had made no mention of a husband, and Hewitt Vaughn was very fine to look upon. Not only that, he was master of Greenfield now, and in charge of its incomes.

And Anne could have him. All she had to do was go back.

"I-I wanted to tell you first. There will be gossip."

Dovey shrugged. "Shall you be married at St. Sefin's, too?"

She intended no such thing. This priory was the scene of her humiliation, watching her brother and Calvin make pitches for Gwen, then watching her old friend marry a viscount. But it was also the place she met Hewitt.

A Vaughn would want somewhere grander, perhaps St. Basil's in Basseleg, which the Morgans of Tredegar had made fine. But if she was the bride, and she were not to marry from her own home, then she could at least choose the church, could she not? And if she were to be married, she would want the ceremony to be here, in this one place where she had come bereft to Newport and found an odd sort of community. In this place designed to give shelter to the lost.

"Vicar Stanley could do it," Dovey thought aloud. "You'll need three weeks for the posting of banns."

"And a gown," Anne said, feeling more and more that she'd parted from her senses. Where was she to produce the funds for a new gown for a wedding, when she had nothing to call her own?

"That means they'll all be coming here," Eilian said. "The Vaughns. To Newport." Her voice still held that strange, brittle quality.

"Er—I believe they travel to Newport rather frequently," Anne said.

Eilian turned and abruptly vanished into the stillroom.

Dovey looked at Widow Jones. Cerys looked at Anne. Then

the girl approached, shyly, and smoothed her apron over her skirts.

"I'm an excellent flower girl, I am," Cerys said confidingly. "And I've done it before, you know."

Anne laughed. She didn't recognize the sound her own throat made.

Why was she behaving as if she were a happy bride in truth? She did not intend to marry Hewitt Vaughn. Not like this, with a snare drawn tight around the both of them. She was simply going through the motions, that was all, until she found a way to escape to where she was meant to be. The life she was meant to have, one of her own design and making, for once. Whatever that might look like.

And if she were to marry, as she'd been always told she must, then she wanted a man who chose *her*. Not her dowry. Not her name. Not the last straw he could clutch as he went over a cliff.

None of this was real, and yet, as the women closed around her, busy in their preparations for the babe and new mother, for dinner, and chatting of Anne's wedding the whole time—as if she belonged, as if this were her circle of friends in truth—Anne ached for all the things she had never known to want, and now well and truly would never have.

CHAPTER ELEVEN

There were a dozen things at Greenfield that needed his attention, and Hew couldn't focus on a one of them.

Anne had bolted, and he didn't know where she might go. Newport was too rough for a woman alone. He had to find her and escort her home. To Greenfield.

Unless she had left town altogether, to escape him and the trap she'd accused him of setting her.

His mother wanted Hew to sit with her in her favorite papered parlor and receive those acquaintances not invited to the Penrydd wedding, who would want to hear every detail. Her ladyship would hold forth as if she associated every day with members of the peerage and their wives, though Hew could almost wish a reminder about the guests, the flower arrangements, the food, the bride's gown. All he recalled was glimpsing Anne Sutton in the sanctuary. A sylph-like creature with a pile of golden hair, destroying a bough of myrtle as if by doing so she could vanquish her enemies.

Anne's big eyes meeting his over his prostrate mother as she waved smelling salts beneath her nose.

Anne's expression over the dinner table, hurt and angry, when his brother spoke of her as a movable good.

Anne's eyes when she stepped into his bedchamber and took off her shawl.

Anne's eyes this morning when Hew said that of course he would wed her. When she had accused him of tricking her into marriage because he wanted the money.

As if he were the type of idiot to want a woman like that for a dowry.

Hew looped the ribbons of his horse over one of the headstones resting at a gentle, abandoned angle in the cemetery encircling St. Woolos church. A goat grazing on the lush grass raised its head to regard him with narrow eyes.

"*Shwmae, gafr,*" Hew said. The goat went back to his browsing, satisfied by this greeting that Hew was not a threat.

"Captain Vaughn! I wouldn't expect you to speak Welsh."

Hew turned with a guilty start as the vicar walked around the yew tree casting its shade over the quiet yard.

"I know only a word or two here or there." The English worked hard to discourage the use of Welsh traditions and language, but Hew felt that only a great fool tried to make his home in a place where he couldn't communicate with the locals. Particularly if he relied upon those locals to produce his income.

The vicar gave him a friendly smile and a courteous nod. "Stanley," he introduced himself. "Took the living here shortly after you left for the wars, I think." His eyes twinkled. "But I've heard a great deal about you, as you might imagine."

A hot, tight prickle ran along the back of Hew's neck. It would have run down his back as well, had he any sensation there. "What have you heard?"

Had news of his infamy preceded him? *You,* St. Vincent had said with such a cold, haughty air.

"Heroics in the West Indies," the vicar mused. He carried a

basket full of plants and stopped near one tilting grave. With-drawing a trowel from his basket, he knelt and prodded at the roots of a tall weed with yellow flowers.

"Then heroics in Acre, we heard," the vicar said as he worked. "Single-handedly turned back the French assault and sent their general Napoleon packing back to—Egypt, I believe the papers said?" He rose holding the plant, stem, roots, flowers, and all, and placed it in his basket.

"Not single-handed." Hew's heart gave a sharp beat. "I had a company. There was a whole force of us, working together with the Ottomans."

He'd had a partner. Partners.

"Heard something about you helping to build a wall." The vicar resumed strolling, searching out more weeds. "Yet I thought you were a gunner, not a sapper."

In the Artillery, he meant, not the Corps of Engineers. And there lay the crux of Hew's trouble.

"So I am," he said.

The vicar nodded, then knelt for another excavation. "Don't suppose they're much for crossing lines of duty, the Royal Army, even in the heat of battle. Chain of command, and all that. Earn a man a court-martial under other circumstances."

"That it might," Hew said. Sweat rolled beneath his neck-cloth and down the back of his shirt. The vicar knew. He knew a great deal. He must have been talking to someone.

"Was this all in the papers?" Hew asked.

"No." The vicar straightened with another long plant in his hand. Ragwort. He shook dirt off the roots, careful to avoid soiling his pantaloons. "Had a nice chat with Lord St. Vincent. He filled me in on much the papers leave out."

Hew's sweat turned cold. If St. Vincent mentioned a court-martial, it must have been decided already. The summons would reach him any day. There would be no settling into

Greenfield as the welcome new owner. There would be no plans for marriage. There would only be disgrace.

"Where is the earl now?" Hew asked, his lips as numb as if he'd eaten of the ragwort. Noxious to horses and cattle, he knew. He'd learned some things about landowning and animal husbandry, despite what his father claimed.

"Left for Bristol last night." The vicar studied the ground. "Had lodgings there. The bride and groom left after you did, though the feasting went long into the night for us common folk."

A vicar, identifying himself as one of the common folk. Stanley was unlike the rest of his breed. Most vicars would be gentlemen's sons, if not the extra sons of peers, and considered themselves a cut above the people they served. This one went about with gardening tasks as if he were the sexton and not the one with holy orders.

"Why are you collecting ragwort?" Hew asked.

"So Gafr won't eat it." The vicar nodded toward the goat. "But Miss Gwen likes it for the poison garden, says it attracts bees, and Mrs. Evans says it's good for dyes. So I'll carry these over and let the ladies glean the wheat from the chaff."

He called to a young boy lounging beneath the yew tree, whom Hew hadn't noticed till now. The boy sat with a straw hat pulled low over his face, chewing on a blade of grass.

"Ifor," the vicar said, "I'm off to St. Sefin's to deliver my basket. Will you go with?"

The boy stretched and considered. He was a scrawny creature, in that stage where a boy grew inches overnight. "I'll bring Gafr back when Tomos is finished with the polishing," he decided. "S'pose he'll be another hour or so."

"He does love the polishing, and Miss Meredith has the patience of St. Melangell with him," the vicar said with his placid smile.

Meredith. Hew didn't recall a Meredith family in the area. She must be one of the ubiquitous spinsters upon whom the daily life of a church and its parish depended for their helping hands and free labor. The name registered somewhere deep in his memory, but Hew didn't have time to follow the thread as the vicar turned his way.

"Where you to, Captain, Vaughn?"

"I'll with you. I've a request to make." Hew unwound the horse's ribbons and led the animal as the vicar hiked over a brushy swale toward St. Sefin's, which rose in its stone glory on the opposite side of Stow Hill, the dirt road running between. "I have made a young lady an offer of marriage, and I wonder if you would solemnize our vows when the time comes."

If the time came. He was mad to behave as if Anne would consent to marry him. As if he might come within striking distance of such a lovely creature, and he a man mantled in shame.

The vicar's brows rose. Hew guessed he was somewhere around a score and ten years, only slightly older than Hew. Stanley was an Englishman, through and through, yet didn't have the English contempt for the Welsh.

Hew didn't, either. Sir Lambert had purchased Greenfield to bring home his new bride shortly after gaining his knighthood, and Hew had known no other home. While his parents had retained their sense of English superiority, especially living close to the border of civilization, Hew, being mostly raised by servants, had rather liked feeling he could move between two worlds. Though whether he belonged in either was a point of debate.

"I presume congratulations are in order," the vicar said. "And who is the lucky bride?"

Heat flashed over Hew's neck and ears, as if lit by the lightning of the night before. There was no other way but to brazen out the consequences of what he'd done. "Miss Sutton."

The vicar's brows winged upward. "Miss Sutton, as was to marry your brother?"

The heat intensified, a band of shame across his cheeks and brow. "The same."

No, not shame, Hew thought. He'd do it again in a moment, steal Anne away. She didn't belong to his brother. Calvin would only mistreat her. His brother had a roving eye, always had, and he wouldn't keep his breeches buttoned if he thought he could dip his wick somewhere new. He'd never honor and worship Anne as she deserved. Calvin would neglect her or, worse, be cruel, and in time that cruelty and negligence would break her fine spirit. Hew had seen it happen with his mother. He couldn't bear that to happen to Anne.

Hew would worship her, given the chance. He would cherish her. He'd never shame her, never scorn her. He'd make her fall in love with him, if he could.

Stanley tilted his head to the side. "This is an arrangement that suits both you and Miss Sutton?" he asked carefully.

As if a woman like Anne could ever love a man like Hew. Even the vicar saw it.

The man he'd been before, maybe; that Hewitt Vaughn would have had a chance with a girl like Anne Sutton. *Had* a chance with a girl like Anne Sutton. Had instead tossed it away to enter the Royal Artillery, and there, he'd become someone else.

Hew forced his head into a motion of assent, tasting the lie. "We have agreed."

"And your brother's feelings about the arrangement," Stanley probed.

Hew cleared his throat. "He will come to see the benefits to all involved."

In fact, Calvin had cornered him in the stables and chased away the servants, leaving Hew to saddle his own horse, glad the nervous mare stood between him and his enraged sibling. Calvin had been very specific about what injuries he would like to commit upon Hew's person in response to this vile betrayal.

It didn't help Hew to point out that Anne knew Calvin had only wanted her dowry. Calvin had demanded a groom hitch one of the workhorses to the pony cart, then headed out to Newport on some enraged venture of his own, leaving Hew to ride in his wake. Taking the last horse, since apparently Daron Sutton had asked for the other, and no one, including Calvin, knew what business their guest was about.

Hew had returned and lobbed a cannonball in the center of the quiet, orderly lives that had been going on at Greenfield. In less than a day, he'd come in and reduced this quiet country retreat to rubble.

Just as he'd been trained to do.

"The parties consenting, and being of age, I suppose we can read the banns here and marry you in St. Woolos," the vicar said with a wink. "You're certain I won't be stepping on the toes of Mr. Leyson of St. Basil's? I believe your mother attends services there."

The reason Hew had come to St. Woolos. Mr. Leyson, a chum of Calvin's and a man all too aware of what Lady Vaughn contributed to St. Basil's coffers, and to Mr. Leyson's living, would be casting Hew disapproving glances over the prayer book as he read the ceremony. Vicar Stanley didn't have a cock in this fight.

The vicar knocked at the back door of St. Sefin's, and a woman Hew had seen at the ceremony yesterday, the new viscountess's friend, answered.

"Mrs. Evans," Stanley greeted her, holding up the basket. "We come bearing gifts."

"Your lady is at the pie shop with Mrs. Lambe," Mrs. Evans said to Hew. "That's she as owns the shop, up in High Street near the old West Gate."

"Er, I thank you," Hew replied, recollecting his manners. What had brought Anne here to St. Sefin's? He had gathered yesterday that she scorned the place.

"She assisted at a childbirth earlier," the woman added. "Thought she might swoon once or twice, but she came through bravely, and we needed her hands. You might tell her so."

Anne? Hew stared. *Anne* had assisted at a childbirth? Shy, virginal Anne, who had been a woman untouched until last night, he would stake his life on it.

"Mrs. Bernstein is delivered?" the vicar asked.

Mrs. Evans nodded. "A boy, just as she wished. She'll keep her home and her place, from the sound of things, and have an heir. Named him Daniel."

"Then some good has come of the sorry business," the vicar said. "God does indeed provide."

Mrs. Evans took the basket and offered them refreshment, but the vicar declined on the grounds that a new mother ought to rest.

"And your brother took the carriage Miss Sutton came in," Mrs. Evans informed Hew. "Said you would arrange her way home."

"My brother?" Hew's nerves tightened. Calvin had come here also?

"Said he needed it for his business, he did, and I was to tell you he left the pony cart at the King's Head."

"Did he take Anne?" Hew asked, apprehension a grappling hook in his chest. His hands felt heavy, as if he were again manacled to the stone wall of the prison, or tied and waiting for the lash. The waiting had in some ways been the worst of it.

Mrs. Evans shrugged, her dark eyes reading Hew's features as if she could see the dark thoughts within. "That I can't say."

Anne had been found in Hew's bed, but that didn't mean she was safe. Calvin could take her back. He could drag her to Scotland and marry her over the anvil at Gretna Green, and the marriage would be legal, and Calvin would have his money. And Anne.

"I must find Miss Sutton," Hew said. His sweat stank of iron, foul with fear for her.

The vicar chattered as they walked down Church Street, past the rows of houses and shops. River silt and smoke from the lime kiln lay rank in the air. The sky had lost its summer glow and lay burled with clouds, a fuzzy gray like the catkins on a willow. It suited Hew's mood.

Anne intended to jilt him, in due time. The break would leave her embroiled in shame, just as Hew was. She'd be prey to fortune hunters and desperate men, like his brother. Jilting Hew wouldn't be safe. It wouldn't be wise. Somehow, he had to protect her.

"That Mrs. Bernstein as was at St. Sefin's," the vicar was saying. "Her husband, Daniel, was killed by the Black Hound's men. Some dispute over money the Hound said he was owed. Mr. Bernstein came to Newport to invest in the new bridge."

Stanley gestured toward the river, where the Usk coiled like a smooth snake, dappled gray and lazy in the heat. "You can see there, they've begun building to replace the old wooden one. Five arches, it's supposed to have. Died while I sat by him, the poor man, but the family brought his body back to Merthyr Tydfil to be buried in their own plot." Stanley shook his head. "Sorry business. And he'll never meet his son."

"The Hound," Hew said. "That's the man Daron Sutton tried to bargain with to strike at Penrydd. He let all the ladies Penrydd be captured, along with Anne, and himself."

He felt a rising rage against Anne's brother. Even that morning at table, when his sister's honor was under discussion, Daron hadn't issued a challenge to Hew for besmirching her. He'd moaned about whether his sister's marriage to Hew would benefit him.

Did *anyone* in her family stand up for Anne? Was she nothing but a pawn to them?

"And Penrydd doled out justice, after a fashion. Haven't seen the Hound here since, and don't expect to." The vicar looked around them. "But that's not to say his men have all slunk back to their burrows and dens."

"I had the same thought," Hew said.

Down the street he spotted two familiar figures, one wearing the coat he'd sat down to dinner in at Greenfield the night before. Daron Sutton in the company of Rafael Darch, both of them passing into the small stone building that was once the house of the murenger, the man whose task it was to see to the upkeep of the town walls, back in the medieval days when Newport had them. Now West Gate was dismantled, the old prison was gone, and the central gate stood over the market as more decoration than defense.

Newport had no defenses. Enemies could come by land or sea, pouring down from the rough hills, pulling their boats up on the sand of the tidal river. There was nothing to stop the coming, and there was nothing to stop the taking.

A third man, much shorter than lanky Darch, looked up and down the street, then made his way into the shadows after the other two. The lookout, announcing the all-clear.

What was Sutton doing in the company of Darch?

Hew didn't follow the thought, because they reached the pie shop, and he peered through the multi-paned window fronting the street into the broad room inside. One woman, a bit older than Anne, stood behind a wooden counter, offering Anne a packet of oiled paper.

Anne, ten times lovelier than she'd been that morning, peeled back the paper and sniffed its contents. Her expression of pleasure, the fluttering of her eyes, small upturn of her mouth, and the lift of her pert chin, clenched Hew's gut like a fist. Then she nibbled at the contents, parting her dainty lips, and her head fell back on her neck as her expression melted into rapture.

The fist in his gut pulled heavy and tight. Hew had brought that look to her face last night. He wanted to be the reason it was there again.

He stepped inside the shop. The scent hit him first, heated spice and sweet preserves, thick as a veil. Through a rear door lay the back room with the ovens, the kneading trough, the boxes of dough and bags of flour, and leaning against the wall, the long-handled spades that the baker used to place and remove items from the oven.

The front room held shelves beneath the window laden with pastries and loaves, and the shelves behind the counter stood stacked with bags and baskets and tins of all kinds. The air shimmered with heat from the oven which ran most of the day, as housewives and maidservants in and around Newport bought the family's dinner and their farthings and ha'pennies to trade for the luxury of serving their family a hot meal.

Hew saw only Anne as she turned to him with the paper in her hand and that glow on her face. She looked different than she had this morning when she'd glared ferociously at him, a vixen spitting as she realized she'd been trapped. Now, she glowed with calmness and warmth, like a goddess of the earth, a woman who dispensed her bounty and wisdom with graceful largesse.

The sight of her, the scent in the air, the heat, all of it

contrived to make Hew feel like his skin had lifted and something might slide through that space next to his flesh, into his marrow.

He entered a room holding Anne, and he came alive.

"What caused that smile?" His voice grated from his throat.

The woman behind the counter went still, staring at Hew. The vicar entered the room behind him, boots tapping the wooden floor. Anne held out her paper, and he moved toward her like the moon pulled by the sun.

"Artichoke pie," she said. "You won't believe how divine it is."

He took a bite of the pie, his mouth next to where her mouth had been a moment ago. Like she had, he held the morsels in his mouth a moment, letting the complex tastes sweep over his palate. He swallowed and mirrored her smile.

"Nutmeg?"

"Mace. Isn't she clever?" She turned toward the other woman. "Mrs. Lambe. This is Hewitt Vaughn of Greenfield—Captain Hewitt Vaughn of the Royal Artillery, I mean. Captain Vaughn, Mrs. Lambe, lately returned to Newport, proprietor of this shop."

Her dreamy look slipped as she made the introductions and the world intruded. Then her face shifted again, and he saw the moment she remembered she was angry with him. Her lips tightened, and two lines divided her brow as she scowled.

He wanted dreamy, sensual Anne back.

"Mrs. Lambe." Hew gave a perfunctory bow, then stiffened. A prickle passed beneath his lifted skin. The warning he got before an attack.

The woman seemed near him in age, a score and a handful of years. He'd never seen her before, yet a needle poked at his consciousness, the tug of the long-forgotten but once familiar. "You are from Newport?" he asked warily.

"From Rogerstone, rather," she said. "But I went away when I was an infant and have not been back these many years."

"Welcome to Newport." Had he done something to anger her? Had he intruded on a moment with Anne and thus stirred the resentment crackling from her?

"We ought to welcome you. Captain," she added, stiff as the paddles she used in her oven.

He let his attention drift back to Anne, where it wanted to be. "Is there more pie? We could take one home to Mother."

"Of course. Because I am to return by dinner."

At least she hadn't eloped with Calvin. The relief was so great it shook him. He felt like he'd been set down on land after weeks at sea. "Have you seen my brother? Or yours?"

"Neither," she said frostily. "I have been at St. Sefin's all day."

"Assisting at childbirth, I hear."

The other woman abruptly departed for the back room. She had not even greeted the vicar. Hew studied Anne's face, saw the flicker of uncertainty, a brief wash of wonder, then determination as it settled in. She tightened her lips and lifted her chin.

"I did. Yes."

"Mrs. Evans says you are to be commended."

Those lovely lips of her quirked up at the corners. "She did?"

A compliment from Mrs. Evans meant something, then. Would she be as pleased at praises from him?

"I did not know you had skills as a midwife."

All the softness fled from her face. She looked like a guilty girl caught trying on her mother's wig and diamonds, being scolded for her presumption. "I haven't."

Blast. He had lost every skill he'd ever had at flattering a woman. If he'd ever had any, which was in doubt. "May I drive you home?"

"You did not trust me to find my own way?" She tilted her head to the side.

Hew's heart rapped in his chest, a prisoner banging on the thick door of his cell. She'd come to him in desperation, trying to escape his brother's snare. It didn't mean she wanted Hew.

"I hear Calvin took the carriage, leaving you without transportation. I'm told he left the pony cart for us."

He could not simply say that he wanted her company? Had he ever known how to woo a woman?

No, because he never wooed. He simply accepted what fell into his arms or his bed. The Morgan girl, that first summer, and other times she contrived reasons to visit her kin. Willing girls of Woolwich and London. Caribbean beauties in the West Indies sharing their time and charms while the battalions plotted their next moves against the French.

He'd never had to pursue or entice or cast out lures. He'd never poached on another man's woman, either, despite what was said about him.

Until now, of course. When he'd stolen his brother's bride.

He watched Anne as she wrapped the handpie and tucked it in her reticule. She'd come to his room to use him, and seemed shocked at the consequences when they'd been discovered. But how could she be, really? She was innocent but not stupid. She must know what happened when genteel girls were discovered in a soldier's bed.

They must wed the soldier, with all his train of baggage, with all his scars.

He didn't want to be a sentence of doom for her.

Mrs. Lambe returned with a small basket she handed to the vicar. "For you, Mr. Stanley, your almond loaves." Stanley's face lit with a bashful grin. "Miss Sutton. A tort for the servants of Greenfield." She held out a second basket. "Only for the servants, mind. With my compliments to Mrs. Harries."

Anne took the basket. "I shall see it delivered."

Mrs. Lambe smiled, finally, but only for Anne.

"Do call again, Miss Sutton. Here, if you like, or at St. Sefin's. I am as often there, these days, but Mrs. Reece can see to anything here. She is my partner and my right hand."

"And you are mine," sang a woman's voice from the back room, with an accompaniment of giggles that suggested she was not alone there.

"I shall." Anne smiled back. This woman, this midwife and baker and maker of pies, had, in the span of an afternoon, won Anne's trust and regard.

Hew could admit he was jealous. *He* wanted Anne's regard.

And he'd done nothing to deserve it. He never would. He wasn't that man any longer.

CHAPTER TWELVE

The vicar struck off in his own direction, and Hew had Anne to himself. He sensed she was not in the mood for wooing as they walked down High Street to the King's Head. She thought he'd come to collect her for dinner, and the regal lift to her head, along with her pointed silence, said she did not welcome his pursuit.

That *look* she'd tossed him when he'd issued his instruction, desperate for reassurance that she was not fleeing him, that she would return. Hew feared anything more he could say would only harden her to him. She had come to his arms, but he had broken her trust in him when he snapped the shackle of marriage around her ankle.

Because he could not let her be turned out of Greenfield, shamed and ruined. And he could not let her go now.

She took care to keep her skirts from sweeping the dirt and seemed oblivious to the attention she drew. Men stopped their business on the street. Tradeswomen came to the doors of their shops to look at the well-dressed lady. With the modish pelisse over her round gown and the smart cap with its bows and feathers, she was a fashion plate come to life, all leg and bosom.

Newport could have seen nothing of the like in years, the way passersby stared, drinking in her beauty. Hew wanted to drink of her, too.

Was it haughtiness, that she did not acknowledge the stares? Or was she simply unaware of how mesmerizing she was?

She'd known she need only step into his room last night and remove her shawl, and he would drop to his knees at her feet like the clodpole he was. Starved for a gentle touch, nearly unable to bear the sweetness of her body, the softness of her skin. Memories taunted him, thick in his blood.

Hew sobered when he found the Greenfield pony cart and the draught horse stabled at the inn, and the information that Calvin Vaughn had inquired about stagecoaches north.

"Did he leave on one?" Hew demanded.

"Nay, he'd his own cart and cattle. Set out on the road to Chepstow shortly after noon," said the proprietor, a Mr. Trett.

Anne said nothing, but her gaze flickered to Hew's set jaw, the leap of muscle as he clenched his teeth.

The taut silence held as Hew helped her into the cart, then drove back up Church Street to St. Sefin's. She didn't step inside as he collected his horse from the pen holding a nanny goat and kid. She merely waved to a strapping young man who was at the well, drawing water, who gave her a broad grin and an awkward flap of his arm.

Hew joined her in gazing from the heights of Stow Hill to the marshland that embedded the River Usk as it wended its way to the Bristol Sea. Spits of sand clogged the channel, and the bank of the river changed with the tide, the mudflats growing and shrinking again each day. Towers of purple loosestrife clustered empty land dotted with marsh orchids and meadowsweet, flinging its fragrance onto the breeze.

The view would look brown and dull to many, but to Hew, it was balm of Gilead spread over the wounds of Acre. He'd thirsted, all those long, dry days in the desert, mouth burning with the taste of dust and brine, for exactly this.

"I spoke to Vicar Stanley about our marriage ceremony," Hew said. "I thought it best that word spread of our betrothal ahead of the rumor that you were found in my bed."

"I mentioned as much at St. Sefin's, and for the same reasons." She drew her bottom lip between her teeth. "Where do you suppose your brother went?"

She wasn't coming to him a glad bride, smiling at her chosen one; she was escaping a worse fate. Best he remember that.

"I'd say he took off in a pelter, sulking that he did not get his way." Hew looped the reins of his horse around the back panel of the cart so the animal could follow them home. "But if it were me, I would be off to the bishop at Gloucester Cathedral to obtain a common license. Then he could marry you without banns."

She lifted her chin, a tiny gesture of defiance. "But not without my consent. I was kidnapped once and didn't like it."

Anyone who thought about harming Anne, or attempting to harm her, would find themselves in range of Hew's cannons. But he sensed she might mount her own resistance. There lay a streak of adamant in her that it seemed she was just now discovering for herself.

"Is that the canal you spoke of? At dinner." Pink touched her cheeks, as if she were guilty of something. The color brightened her wildflower eyes. He could make a life's study of the shades and colors that moved across Anne Sutton's face, and never weary of the task.

"This is the Monmouthshire Canal." Hew pointed north toward the wooded hill of Malpas and, beyond it, the land hefting itself into mountains full of iron and ore. "That is the main arm and runs up to Pontymoile Basin. Over twelve miles long, with forty-two locks." He knew the names and numbers would mean little to her. His family didn't care for the venture either.

"That," he pointed to the west, though the hills obscured the view, "is the arm that comes down from Crumlin, the one I am most invested in. Eleven miles and thirty-two locks. The Cefn Flight, which alone is fourteen locks, is there." He shifted his arm, and she dutifully peered in that direction. "That, my dear, is a marvel of engineering. Raises the water level one hundred sixty feet over a span of eight hundred yards."

He moved his arm a click west. "I hold that parcel of land, there where the tramway runs, so I am allowed to charge a toll on my stretch. The Morgans of Tredegar are doing the same. We stand to make a great deal of money once traffic increases. But the problem is not enough water is filling the flight, and we need more volume of water to ship more volume of goods."

Anne turned toward the east, holding her hat to her head as the wind kicked up, thick with the scent of mud and salt. She smelled of wildflowers, too. "And they are loaded onto ships there?" A horse plodded south along a towpath that followed a curve in the Usk, towing a boat laden with limestone.

"There, on that stretch we call the Town Pill." Hew pointed to the small inlet where the canal ended south of Newport Castle and the Green. From this distance, the wooden cranes used to lift and lower walkways looked tiny, like matchsticks, flimsy evidence of mighty human endeavor.

"The larger ships simply pull up on the sand. You see there is only one wharf. There needs must be more. At first the canal stopped at the castle, but there is a current near the bridge, so they built a bit farther." He led her eye south, where an elbow in the Usk created a natural wharf. "What we should do is extend the canal all the way to Pillgwenlly, then build up more wharves around. Then the ships need not come up as far, and there will be less congestion in the river."

He gestured toward the bridge where the wooden scaffolds were going into place to hold the workers as they ferried and sank stone. "I contributed funds to the bridge as well, over and above what was levied. Newport is growing. Greenfield's fortunes can grow with it."

There was so much to think about, so much to decide. Bleddoe had laid out all the opportunities, and all the problems, in one great line that rose before Hew as steep as the Fourteen Locks, and as slow to navigate.

"Is that what you mean to do, now you are home?" Anne faced him, her face guarded but curious despite herself, as if she didn't wish him to see her interest but couldn't stop herself asking. "That is, are you done with the Royal Artillery?"

His back prickled, that ever-present weaving of dull pain punctuated by a sharp startling fire, as if he still felt the lash. Nothing of what he'd done, or was doing now, was a secret; surely he could tell his erstwhile bride.

He took the ribbons and clicked his tongue at the horse to walk on along the dirt road toward Bassaleg, leaving Stow Hill. "I do not know yet if the Royal Artillery is done with me."

It hung before him like an axe on the wall, the threat over his future. Anne couldn't marry a man who'd been court-martialed. It would give her the perfect reason to cry off, of course, but the scandal around her would worsen. An extra cloak of shame to follow her, all because of him.

"For the moment, I've been charged to look at ways to reinforce the Monmouthshire Militia. Design defenses if we must for this area, to protect the shipping and prevent invasion from the French. They've done it before and may try it again. The Monmouthshire could be enfolded into the regular Royal Army if there is a threat from the French, and their going would leave Newport undefended."

"Like Fishguard." Anne nodded. "When La Légion Noire

invaded Britain. But there the Welsh women lined up with their black hats and red shawls so they looked like soldiers, and they frightened the French into submission."

The truth of Fishguard, Hew had heard, was that the invading force, mostly recruited prisoners and pardoned criminals, had turned their attention to looting the local homes and public houses. When the locals massed, armed with farm implements and fury, the threat of the coming militia on their heels, the drunken soldiers quickly surrendered.

Fishguard may have been a debacle for the French, and the Irish who backed them, but the short-lived invasion also served up a lesson on Irish weather and British defense to any canny generals paying attention.

"If you admire those women, then you are not like other *Saes*, who view all things Welsh beneath them." He couldn't resist the opportunity to tease her and was rewarded by the heightened blush and flash of color in her pure blue eyes.

"I know all about Jemima Fawr with her pitchfork." Anne tossed her head, reminding him of his mare that morning, kicking up her heels as the wind frisked with her mane. "And if you're Welsh, Hewitt Vaughn, I am a Frenchwoman."

"*Bonjour, mademoiselle,*" Hew teased further. "*Je suis enchanté de faire votre connaissance.*" He was delighted to make her acquaintance.

"*Monsieur Vaughn,*" she returned with a flawless accent. "*Le plaisir de la rencontre est à vous.*"

The pleasure of the encounter was all his. Hew tilted his head back and laughed.

She swayed on the bench seat beside him, as if startled by the sound he made. Hew was startled, too. He hadn't laughed since ... since the West Indies.

Oh, there had been the ribald jokes aboard ship as the Navy sailed them to the Mediterranean and Acre. There had been the usual jests about the hardtack, the rum rations, the lack of women. There had been crows of delight when Smith's men captured French boats and confiscated their artillery. There were bitter, satisfied chuckles when the French army with all their bluster and rage had failed in their assaults on the city, and took sick with plague besides.

But a laugh, a true, honest laugh, born of pleasure—that was a gift he'd been lacking for a long time.

Hew turned toward her, ready to extend the jest, and pleasure flickered and died at the tight frown on her face.

"Do you wish for children?" she asked in a rush.

She had him off his guard, and he answered without his usual reserve. "I always hoped I would have them, someday." It was the kind of distant dream a soldier allowed himself in his bunk at night: the promise of dry land somewhere with good and plentiful food, entertainments instead of duty, a woman's curves tucked beside him at night, and children to raise to their name and place in the world.

She turned to stare at the shadowy mass of Twym Barlwm, ever-present on the horizon. As a boy Hew believed the legends that a giant was buried there, the mound the swell of his enormous belly, the hump at the top his belly button.

Six years ago, he could have been bound to this woman. He could have been the one who came forth as her protector against the hard winds of the world. The husband who indulged his genteel lady with compliments and pin money, who gave her a fine home and gowns and children, and who let her oversee the household accounts to her liking and suffered house parties and dinners with her friends.

Instead, he'd run off to the West Indies to fight and drink and man artillery for no-flint Grey and naval commander Sir John Jervis, recently made the Earl of St. Vincent. And Anne knew he hadn't wanted her.

The thought of those six lost years sat like a brick on Hew's throat. What if he had said yes? What if he had traveled to Llanfyllin and said their vows in her parish church before all the friends who had known her from birth, with meadowsweet strewn over the church floor and champagne flowing at their wedding breakfast. What if Anne had been lodged at Greenfield all this time, drowsing in the walled garden like a pollen-drunk bee, sitting down to table with his mother and father, safe under their roof and untouched while her father's fortune vanished and her brother lost himself in gambling and bad bets.

Hew wouldn't have been home any more frequently. He would have left her there at Greenfield, his bride, alone with Calvin. And his brother would have respected Anne's marriage vows to Hewitt as little as Hew had respected the bond binding Calvin and Anne.

"Do you wish for children?" he ventured to ask. He knew so little of this woman.

"I have names picked out for nine of them. Four boys and five girls." She twined the string of her reticule around her fingers, the string digging into the kid of her gloves. "But today I saw what that entails, and I—" Her voice was high and thin. "What I saw is pain and blood and terror. Gwen's child died. Leah's still could. I do not know how women bear it."

"If I do not have children, then Calvin will inherit Greenfield," Hew said slowly, keeping his eyes on the road. He did not understand what she was telling him.

She straightened her shoulders in that way she had of steeling herself. "I am only saying, that could be a reason. That you refuse me."

"You were found in my bed, Anne. I am not going to *refuse* you."

"I suppose you are right. I must be the one to cry off." The string pulled so tight about her slender hands that her fingertips must be going numb.

The brick moved down his gullet to Hew's chest, lodging there. His heart pulsed against it, painfully. He would rather be standing with his back bare, wrists tied to the ladder, dozens of silent men watching him bleed as the only sound in his ears was the hiss of the cat-o'-nine-tails through the air and the dull smack as it sank into flesh. He would rather be flogged again than hear Anne Sutton say she did not want him. That she did not want him to touch her again.

"Wait," he said dully.

"I-I beg your pardon?"

"Wait. A few days more." They passed the high mound of the ancient hillfort and rounded Pye Corner into the intersection of Bassaleg, where the old roads spouted a new tramway. Another venture Hew supported, had invested in. He felt he might fall and be buried under the weight of all he must do, but the most important was to keep Anne from bolting just yet.

"It has only been a day," he reminded her, surprised to realize that was true. He felt he were living lifetimes in the span of hours, so deep was the upheaval she had brought to his life. "You might let some time elapse. Decide where you can go. Wait for the carriage to return, so I might take you there. Come up with a reason to end things that ..."

He trailed off. She wanted to end things. And he did not want her to leave.

But neither could he give her what she wanted. Certainly not what she deserved, a whole man who could come to her with honor in his clean hands and a soul free of scars.

"Very well." Her words were a whisper, snatched away by the breeze. They might be in for another storm. She untangled her reticule from her hands, head bent, gaze focused on her task as if it might save her.

They were nearly to the old heap that was Rogerstone Castle when her voice came again, a gentle hum on the breeze. "I hope, after all this is over ... we might remain friends?"

"No, Anne."

That much was clear to him. This woman, in the blink of an eye, had uprooted everything he believed about himself. She'd torn the dull, unformed thoughts he'd had for his future into shreds. He was alone on a storm-tossed sea. Standing in the middle of a walled garden while the army beyond battered at his walls. Left again to die in an Ottoman prison, of plague or infection or rat bite, whatever took him first.

He didn't have the goodness, the nobility in him to wish her well upon leaving him. To watch her go gladly into the future she wanted, without him. He turned his face away, hardening his expression, hardening his heart.

"No," he said again. "I wish you well. I will do whatever you ask of me. But you and I can never be *friends*."

CHAPTER THIRTEEN

Anne couldn't say precisely what brought her back to St. Sefin's the next day. What drove her away from Greenfield was a combination of many things. The prospect of sitting with Lady Vaughn, who was again at home to callers, of whom she seemed to entertain a great number. Everyone of her acquaintance wanted to hear about the marriage of the viscount to the Welsh woman who had gone on trial, it was said, for running a brothel from an ancient priory, and then had got herself and two viscountesses kidnapped by an Irish criminal. At some point in the discussion, the scandal of what Anne had done must out. She did not wish to be peered at and hear the whispers that she was a hussy.

Hew left early in the morning on business. Over breakfast he said he was going to inspect the Fourteen Locks and see for himself how they functioned.

"Why would they need you?" his mother inquired. "You're an artilleryman, not an engineer."

"A gunner, not a sapper, you mean?"

The harsh note in his voice made Anne look up from her salted fish. She could read him now, and tension lined his mouth and eyes. He clenched his hand around the butter knife in a way she had come to recognize.

"They are quite separate occupations, I thought." His mother seemed genuinely perplexed. "You wouldn't have been trained in building batteries or whatever."

"You would be surprised what accommodations must be made in the heat of battle, madame," Hew replied.

Lady Vaughn fretted with her soft-boiled egg. "But that is why you are in trouble with the Army now, I was told. Isn't the Duke of York himself reviewing your case, as commander in chief?"

"And how would you know that?" Hew asked.

Anne was glad Calvin was not here to see this. He would leap upon his brother's weakness with glee, a carrion eater at feast. The whereabouts of Calvin Vaughn were yet unknown, as he had not appeared for breakfast nor sent word to the house, but Anne for one was glad of the reprieve.

Daron was not at breakfast, either, though he had been at dinner the night before with tales of visiting some place called Goldcliff. Anne, admittedly, had been watching Hew more than her brother, and she saw Hew's eyes narrow at this divulgence. It seemed Daron had spent the previous day in the company of this man called Darch, and planned to do so again.

Anne was glad her brother had found a friend to divert him. Perhaps he would forget to be outraged with her over shaming the family name, etc. etc.

"I—em. Jane Morgan, or rather Jane Homfrey now, she may have mentioned something. Did you know she is expecting again?" Lady Vaughn said, her tone bright as gold paint. "This is her fourth already, I believe. Only think, Hewitt, you could have married her when she was widowed by that naval captain, and then you would be one of the Morgans, too."

"Jane is twelve years older than I am, Mother, and she was

in love with Captain Ball since she was a child." Hew calmly buttered a slice of toasted bread. "She never saw me as more than an amusing nuisance, and neither did her sister Elizabeth."

"Elizabeth is ten years older than that man she married," Lady Vaughn said testily. "It could have been you marrying a Morgan at St. George in Hanover Square at the height of the season, but no. Elizabeth fixes on a bastard, the son of a general and a prostitute. The fits Lady Morgan must have had with such a pedigree in the family."

"Are you relieved that my scandal is so much the less, then? I am hardly the first man to have robbed his brother of a wife. The Bible is full of examples. It's practically part of Scripture."

"Please *do* spare me such irreverence," Lady Vaughn sniffed. "It has been strain enough on my nerves to have you return under a cloud. I thought you such a hero, and so I told all my friends. I don't know how I shall support myself if you end up in prison, much less support a supposed wife. And your brother—"

"Had his chance with Anne, and did not marry her though the betrothal was proposed years ago." Hew rose and held out his hand to Anne. "Shall we have Mr. Stanley post the banns this Sunday, my darling? Three weeks is already too long to wait."

Anne hadn't finished her chocolate, but she stood also, setting her fork to the side. At least she had enjoyed her coddled eggs, which swam in her stomach as Lady Vaughn glared.

"I—so soon?" Just yesterday he had proposed they lengthen their engagement. Give her time to look about her and come up with a plan.

He swept a thumb across her ungloved hand. A bolt of sensation rushed up her arm, swift as wildfire, setting the fine hairs on end.

What was he doing?

"I regret that business calls me away today," he murmured, looking down at her. Though low, his voice carried across the fine papered parlor, and his mother no doubt heard everything. "I would rather be wooing you."

"I ... I have things I must attend to as well." Good heavens, her wits had scattered. He smelled of open woods and the sea breeze, and she fell under his spell with a word. His eyes were incantations, his heat on her hand an alchemy that turned her thoughts into mist. Where he touched her, she became something else. Base lead turning to gold.

She didn't have a single notion what she meant to do with her day, other than compose a letter informing her parents she meant to marry Hew and not Calvin. Why couldn't she *think* with this man near her? He drew close and she stood riveted like a post that had been sunk into the river, a support for the new bridge.

Not a reed in the breeze, as she always had been, but a sturdy support. Meant to bear a great weight.

"I shall see you at dinner?"

His voice took her back to his shadowed bed, to her body trembling from the peak of pleasure, her hand touching herself at his gruff command. By the saints, she couldn't turn to a puddle here in the dining parlor in front of his mother. She couldn't press herself against him and beg him to touch her again.

If they were not to be married—because she planned to jilt him, because he did not want to be *friends*—why then this play-acting? She clung to his hand and stared up at him, mute, miserable with confusion and longing.

"I want my mother to see that I chose you," he murmured in her ear as he guided her from the room. His hand curled around her elbow was a warm shackle. The ring one put in the nose of a bull to draw him. "I want her to tell all her friends that I lost my head and seduced you. I stole you from Calvin because I wanted you for myself."

She leaned toward him, wanting these words, wanting to believe them. That he had longed for her. Chose her. Longed for her still. A pool of heat gathered between her legs in that awakened place. She was turning to gold there, too.

"Take a groom with you if you go anywhere." Hew lifted his other hand and brushed a finger over her cheek, freeing a curl she hadn't realized had plastered itself to her skin. To his mother, it would appear they stood together in the hall, murmuring sweet nothings to one another. Him gazing at her with adoration, her staring back up at him, caught in his snare.

Unwilling to free herself, even if she could. "I shall."

"I will think of you all day."

He must be saying this for his mother. Keeping up the pretense that they were besotted. That they had both gone mad and broken the chains of convention and courtesy, the contract between their families, because a passion like that the poets spoke of drew them together.

Then, at least, she would not be the whore alone, tempting him past restraint and begging him to ravish her, throwing away her honor for calculated intent. If they loved, they could be understood. Perhaps, in time, forgiven.

This show of tenderness was to protect her. She melted before it.

And felt something bold and wild light within her. She wanted him not to be acting.

His mother was watching. The tiny maid who lit the fires and brought her hot water that morning was coming down the hall from the wing with Anne's room, likely having just tidied her chamber. A footman in livery stood near the sideboard in the dining parlor, able to see them from the door. And here was the housekeeper, coming through the baize door from the kitchens. They were on full display.

Anne planted her hands on either side of his face. Her palms were cold and his skin warm, his jaw shaven and smooth. His eyes flared.

"Think of *this*," she said, and pushed up on her toes to kiss him.

He might have stood still before her assault, but he didn't. He lowered his head to meet her, slanting his lips across hers, and his arms snaked around her, palms cradling her back. She felt the heat through the muslin of her gown, the linen of her shift, the cotton twill of her stays. He kissed her as if he had been waiting—*craving*—for her to step into his arms. He kissed her as if she were chocolate spiced with vanilla and cinnamon and he meant to drink her down.

Hunger roared between them, like a great cat that would snap her up whole. The world spun before her closed eyes. His arms were iron bands around her, as if she'd been caught up in a vise. But his mouth—his mouth was a feast for all her senses, taste and touch and scent. He was every delicious thing she'd tasted in her life, and when he made a sound, a low, raw grumble deep in his throat, she wanted to melt against him like treacle in utter surrender.

Just in time, Anne caught the last thread of her wits, the vanishing reminder of her intent. She broke free from his devouring mouth and stepped backwards. Her balance was not steady, but he held her, kept her from tipping over.

His eyes had darkened to a storm over the sea. He looked at her as if he meant to swoop her into his arms, carry her back to his bed, and do all the things he had sworn he would do and hadn't.

"Good day, sir," Anne said, giving him a prim smile. Then she turned and left him, doing her level best to glide like a swan, like the carefree hussy who had just kissed her chosen lover and would do so again as soon as she pleased.

She wouldn't be anyone's pawn any longer. And she could act a part, too.

SHE TOOK NOT a groom but Daron, and she drove the pony cart, not he. To her surprise, he did not protest but sat beside her, lost in gloom. Anne wondered if he remembered that years ago he had taught her how to drive a horse, taught her how to be gentle on the ribbons and look for the smooth part of the road and think of the space her vehicle would need to make a turn. She drove now to assert her own independence, to show that she could do a thing all by herself, though the cob was unfamiliar to her. But Daron seemed uninclined to applaud her moves toward self-reliance.

"Calvin did not tell you where he went?" she asked curiously. "I had thought you two as thick as thieves."

Daron glowered at the passing countryside as Anne guided the cart down the steep and narrow paths. The clouds held a blue-violet cast to the gray, reminding her of Hewitt's eyes. Everything called to mind Hewitt Vaughn. The man had planted himself in her psyche.

"Peeled off without a word," Daron muttered. "When the plan was for us both. I'm the one as found out about Gertrude."

"What do you mean, found out?"

A man emerged from the Tredegar Arms, the coaching inn that stood where the road branched at Bassaleg. He was dressed the gray flannel of the Welsh working man and tipped his black felt hat to Anne as she drove past. She raised the tip of her riding whip in acknowledgement, accustomed to male regard. But when Daron slouched on the bench seat and quickly looked away, she wondered if the stranger's small, mocking smile had been aimed at her brother instead.

"Read their post," Daron muttered. "Had to know how bad it was, didn't I? The pater was too busy rating me for trying to hold my head up as a gentleman to give me the finer point of the matter, and you know Mumsy can't keep a figure in her head for a minute, much less add two to make a sum. Knew she was fretting to Aunt Gertrude about how to dispose of you, so took a peek at the matter."

"And?" Anne's lungs compressed. She was far too desperate for answers to affect modesty and chide him for being indiscreet.

"Dear old Gertrude told Mum not to worry her head, you'd be provided for." Daron crossed his arms over the bright bronze buttons on his waistcoat and slumped further.

"Daron, you fool."

Anne had never in her life talked back to her brother, never dreamed of scolding him. Not when he wheedled her for pin money, which she gave him, only to find out later he had lost it at play or spent it on drink for his friends. She had not chided him when he squandered the small payment from the breach of promise lawsuit when the baronet's daughter he was meant to marry jilted him for her Italian music master.

She had kept her mouth shut when Gwenllian, her friend and companion, was sent away because she had tried to tempt Daron into marriage. Anne held her peace as her dowry disappeared and her marriage prospects dwindled to one Calvin Vaughn, who would agree to take her dowry-free on the basis of his father's long friendship with hers.

She had not shrieked down curses upon Daron's head when he brought Anne to Newport to try to win Gwen back, once they learned she was an heiress; she had helped him. And she had not screamed at him when she ended up trapped on a criminal's boat with dung bombs going off all around them. She had stayed calm like a lady, proving her birth, and had never spoken against the brother she had loved from youth.

Because that boy was engraved on her heart. And when she looked at Daron, she saw still the boy who laughed and held out his arms when young Anne toddled to him, flowers clenched in a chubby fist. He'd swoop her under his arm so she could fly like a goose. He had called her Nanny, a treasured name she allowed no one outside the family to call her. She still saw that boy who had walked alongside her pony as Anne clutched its mane, terrified of falling, and who had as a young man looked over all the other young men coming to call on his sister to ensure they were upright and well-mannered and would never insult her.

She had gone so long thinking of Daron as her protector that she still could not quite believe he would use her with such calculation. She had been willing to give her all to make him laugh, make him happy, keep him from disgrace. But she saw now that boy who had always accepted her worship as his due had become a man who believed the world ought always fall in line with his wishes, and whatever resources he could find were his, no matter whom else he injured.

"Fool?" His head snapped up. Above all, Daron could not stand an insult to his pride.

"A-a *nincompoop*," she said, hurt overtaking her. Had he ever thought of *her* in all his calculations? No. "Aunt Gertrude might not have meant she would leave me money. I doubt she has any to give me. Likely she meant that if I didn't marry, I could come live with her and be a companion, and not be a charge on Mama and Papa."

He straightened his shoulders, offended. "There must be money. Look at the way she lives."

"And you think it must all go to you, instead of disposed as she would wish?"

Daron gaped at her. "I am the heir!"

And that was the heart of it. He was the golden boy, the shining hope of their house, the proof that a collier's son had leapt into the ranks of the gentry. Anne was their ornament, but Daron was their legacy. Daron was born to command all, and Anne was born to bend with grace as she gave it to him. As women had been shaped to do from the first moment in the Garden of Eden, or so they were told.

Anne recalled the tiny, wicked hope that had reared its head at dinner when Calvin Vaughn leered at her about being a dried-up spinster who would be eager for his touch. She had thought about taking Aunt Gertrude's money herself, if it came to her. Ruining herself at the hands of Hewitt Vaughn—she veered away from the specifics of *that* memory—and walking away with money to establish herself on her own.

Where? How? And in defiance of everything her family requested of her? Everything she owed to them?

"Besides, Nanny," Daron said, and his tone was pure, scandalized hurt. "I am the one who is acting in the interests of this family. *You* would leave us with nothing, the way you're going on. Thinking only of yourself these days."

"I refuse to marry Calvin Vaughn. Daron, you see the way he is. Surely you've heard the whispers, what the servants say. I cannot marry a dirty dish."

"He's the one as would share the money with us," Daron grouched. "Can't say your Hewitt would. Or is any better than Calvin, come to that. Don't you know why he was sent home from Acre in disgrace? Did he tell you that, or is he too busy weaving pretty lies to lure you into his bed?"

Anne's neck grew hot. Hew hadn't needed cajoling to lure her into his bed. She'd leapt in feet first.

What money? he'd asked, as if he didn't know. As if it weren't part of the consideration—the sole consideration—why he would want to marry a woman no one else wanted, a woman whose suitors and admirers and friends had peeled away one by one, going off to begin their lives as gentlewomen and viscountesses. While Anne was left all alone with her beauty and her virginity and all the dainty charming skills she'd been taught, and which had gained her nothing.

"Why was Hew sent home? Mister—Captain Vaughn. I thought he was supposed to be a hero." She caught the slip, but she'd betrayed herself.

"Ask him, as you're bedfellows now. Cutting your true groom and your brother out of everything. Seizing the kitty all for yourself, aren't you? Bet you won't have a penny for your brother when it's all done."

"Hew said he would ensure our parents are not in penury. They won't lose Vine Court." Anne gritted out the words. Once again, his focus was all on Daron. Not a thought for her future happiness. Not a single question whether any of this was what she wanted.

"And what if I want more than a tiny house and plot of farm in the Welsh hills, in the hind end of nowhere? What if I want some stature in the world? Your Hewitt can't give that to me."

"Neither can Calvin Vaughn," Anne argued. She pulled up the horse as a clump of sheep wandered across their path, their sheepdog nipping to move them along. One of the animal's black ears flopped down endearingly, and it looked up at Anne with a grin. "I don't think he can be trusted, Daron. I wouldn't rely on him."

"Much you know, Nanny. But that's why I'm meeting Darch. He's a man as can set me up in the world. Could have as much influence as the Black Hound did, if he wanted."

"I hope you are not getting caught up with Mr. Darch. He does not seem an honest businessman."

Anne steered the cart along the narrow track passing the

ancient hillfort. The ridge commanded a view of two rivers, the Ebbw and the Usk, and Hew said the fort was likely used by the Saxons, and perhaps the Romans, and perhaps the British who ruled the isle before them, the descendants of Brut. Lords of the land, those who held the hill encampments, and come what may to the people who lived in the valleys. The ones born to be pawns for the greater, and at their mercy.

She was no more than a woman in the world, and that was the way of the world, was it not?

"Stay out of my business, Nanny. If you're only out for yourself, then I have to see to my own affairs. I'm meeting Darch at the Fleur de Lys, so don't look for me later, and don't go meddling. No telling tales to your bedfellow, neither. I'll find my own way back. I'll find my own way anyhow, now you've left me in the lurch."

"Daron!" That cut deep. She'd always been loyal, obedient. She'd come south with him to help lure Gwen back into his good graces. She'd run to pull Gwen into the trap he'd laid the moment she learned the Black Hound had turned on him and held Daron in his grip.

But he saw none of this, gave her credit for none of the ways she'd upheld him. *Saved* him. Instead he leapt down as she stopped the pony cart in the back yard of St. Sefin's and slouched off down Church Street, muttering. Abandoning her.

Anne pressed a hand to the shard in her chest as she watched him walk away, once her handsome and godlike brother, now a young man with a blurring jawline and a well-fed belly pushing out his waistcoat. He was walking away from her, as had Gwen, as had all her other friends. She wasn't his favorite anymore.

She wasn't anyone's favorite.

Dismounting, Anne pressed her face into the side of the horse's neck, seeking comfort from the animal if she could find it nowhere else. The great beast stirred and stamped, huffing a breath, but she didn't fear it as she had before. It felt good to touch something large and warm and strong. As if she could gain courage.

As if she could gain any insight as to what in blazes she was supposed to do next.

All her life, Anne's future had been laid out before her as clear as a painted landscape. She knew what to do. Listen to her nurse and her governess and her mother and the teachings of the Church, and she would grow into a gently bred girl who deserved the praise and admiration of those around her. Her mother would teach her the manners she would need and her father would bless her marriage to a gentleman of some lands, perhaps the son of a titled man or better yet one in line for a title himself.

Her husband would give her standing in the neighborhood, a generous table to preside over as lady, gowns to wear and a carriage to go about in, children whose little minds and natures it would be her charge to shape. She would live to be a credit to her husband and her family and her parish, and she would be buried with all honors in her husband's family tomb and her name spoken of with a blessing, for the few years she was remembered.

Anne had often, as a game with Gwen, tried to imagine the face of her future husband. He had, in her mind's eye, looked much like Daron. Like Calvin Vaughn, blond and blue-eyed and full of lazy charm. But now she faced a reality so much different: a sharp-jawed, somber soldier with silver in his hair and a hardness that came into his eyes at times. A man with a warning against his name and a stiffness to the set of his shoulders that she was certain, now, came from injury.

A man who said aloud that he need not be honorable, but who treated everyone in his life with strict courtesy, even if they did not deserve it. A man who did not spend his coin at the card table or racecourse or pub with his friends, but who spoke of investing, of building things, of securing an income for his family and the people who depended upon him.

A man who knew the secret ways of pleasure, and taught them to her.

A cheerful whistle startled Anne out of her reverie. "*Haia* and well-met! That's Greenfield's cob, innit? I recognize the step of you, Cadfael, I do."

The blind goat boy came forward and lifted his hand, and the horse in the traces pushed his nose into his palm in greeting. The boy scratched his muzzle with practiced ease. Gwen said the boy's mother had gotten the pox, which often caused blindness in their infants, and so he'd been left on the church steps at St. Woolos. The sight of the boy's scarred blue-white eyes no longer made Anne quite so nervous.

"Hello, Ifor, it's Miss Sutton come for a visit again," she said.

His grin broadened. "I knew that. You smell of meadow clary, y'do."

The older boy, the simpleton, edged close to the cart. In his arms he cradled a hen. "*Pert,*" he greeted Anne with a grin, reaching out to stroke her skirt.

"Mind your toes, Tomos, Cadfael won't care that you've new boots," Ifor remarked. "Miss Sutton, Tomos says you're pretty."

"Thank you, Tomos," Anne said, looping the ribbons around the cob's neck. "I hope I may leave the cart here for my visit?"

"Aye, that you can," Ifor said agreeably. "Tomos can help me unhitch Cadfael and we'll set him loose to graze with Gafr. He's turned out of the churchyard while the vestry meets."

"*Cyw,*" Tomos said, holding out his arms to indicate the chicken.

"Er. Yes. A fine chicken. Very fine," Anne said, and Tomos beamed.

"*Helô*, Miss Sutton!" Cerys called from across the yard. She stood beside a hedge of brambles spotted with blackberries, a basket over one arm and a bonnet dangling down her back, purple juice staining her fingers. She looked like a nymph of summer, smiling and carefree, and Anne waved back, charmed by the girl's irresistible sunniness.

"We'll have blackberry wine," Ifor said gleefully. "And elderberry, too. Mother Morris knows a spot. And Tomos and I are after hazelnuts. Mrs. Evans makes them into butter."

"*Cyw*," Tomos said solemnly, presenting the chicken once again. He'd lost his customary grin.

"Oh. Hmm." Anne stroked the dark red feathers, silk beneath her fingers. The chicken jerked its head, comb flapping, and trained one beady eye on her. Then, with a satisfied cluck, it settled further into its nest in the boy's arms. Tomos lifted the beast to rub his cheek against its fat back.

"*Cyw pert?*" He directed a hopeful look at her, and Anne's heart softened.

"The loveliest of chickens," she agreed, and only as she spoke realized she'd understood the Welsh words.

"Oh, Miss Sutton! Wonderful that you're here." Eilian stood in the kitchen along with the ever-present pot on the hob, an assortment of plants spread out over the oaken worktable, and the baby on the table beside her, swaddled in flannel. "You can help me bathe wee Daniel."

She said this as if Anne could absolutely be trusted to dandle a day-old infant. She greeted Anne as if she were already a boon companion. And Anne realized why she had come here, of all places: it was the one place she felt welcomed, and useful. In the drawing room of Greenfield, the talk over tea was always of family health and the doings of the neighborhood and occasionally the broader gossip of the kingdom. The women of St. Sefin's *worked*.

Anne stripped off her gloves and laid them and her bonnet on a chair, smiling at the newborn with his tucked-in face, lips shaped in a pout.

"Is it safe to bathe them so early?"

"Mother Morris says no," Dovey sang from the stillroom, whence came sounds of chopping and some rustling about. "Don't let her catch you at it."

"Just a bit of a wipe down," Eilian said briskly, unwrapping the babe with efficient hands. She dipped a cloth in the basin of warm water and handed it to Anne, giving her a sideways look. "So. The gentleman as collected you yesterday."

"Hewitt? Mister—Captain Vaughn." Anne's neck heated. She concentrated on tugging her cloth along the baby's toes, round as the tiniest mushroom caps.

"He's the eldest, aye? And his mother's pride and joy, I hear."

Anne shrugged, affecting diffidence. "There seems much to admire. He was very well-liked as a young man, always beautifully behaved from what I have heard of Lady Vaughn's acquaintance. None but the usual boyish mischief and tricks, and he was always protective of his brother. Mrs. Harries says it was a picture to see the two of them together, so devoted."

And what a change now between the brothers, the distance, the disdain. Which Anne had only deepened by her actions. She concentrated on baby toes.

"There were never any other children?" Eilian asked casually. She cleaned the babe's belly, dabbing carefully around the stub of the umbilical cord. "No sisters?"

"None that I've heard of, only the two boys." Anne cupped the baby's foot and he kicked slightly, flexing his tiny knees. The way the horse had pressed back against her, a fellow creature seeking touch.

"I heard that Mathry's child was Calvin's," Eilian said.

Dovey materialized from the stillroom, a jar capped with cloth in her hand. "We wouldn't be gossiping, would we, Mrs. Lambe?"

"Mathry as much as told me herself," Anne confessed. "It seems Calvin pursued her, then turned her off when she submitted and paid the price."

"So he's done to many a one hereabouts," Dovey said shortly. She poured several flakes from her jar into a stone mortar and began grinding with the pestle. "They most of them came here to St. Sefin's for aid, and good fortune for us, the vicar looked the other way."

"Why would he disapprove?" Anne asked in surprise.

Dovey raised her brows. "He don't, but the town fathers look down on a woman alone, heavy with child. A decent household isn't to take her in. She's shunned and pushed along when it's known. Nipped out of town like an ewe with a dog at her heels."

"There's a law on the books at Newport," Eilian said. "I know them all now as they were read to me when I arrived, weren't they? We foreigners are given an education on the way things are done here." She screwed up her face, letting Anne know what she thought of certain of these rules. Or being called a foreigner, because she hadn't been raised in the borough.

"An unmarried woman carrying a child can't stay in a home above three days. Then there's a fine thereafter. Three shillings each day, if I recall rightly."

"She is fined for being pregnant and unmarried?" Anne was shocked.

Dovey nodded. "If she stays in Newport, aye, and I imagine it's the same all over. Only the workhouse might get a stay from the fine. The vicar argued for us before the aldermen that St. Sefin's were a hospital and the girls came for care, so it was left to us to charge them as we wished."

"Fined for being a woman alone," Anne repeated. She stroked the baby's knees, marveling that the shape of him could be so perfect, all the parts in place that would, with nurture and God's grace, grow into a healthy boy and then a man.

"I had to prove I would support myself before I could pay my fee to become a freewoman here." Eilian pushed a lock of hair off her forehead. It was warm in the kitchen, with the stove always going. "Pay to not be a foreigner any longer, but a true citizen of the town. But as a woman with no husband, I must convince the council I had land or money or work to support myself. They don't want women coming in and setting up as bawds."

"You had to pay to set up your own household? How much?"

"Twenty shillings. Would have been forty, were I a man." Eilian dabbed around the baby's tiny fingers, and he reflexively clenched the cloth. Anne's heart clenched at the tiny being, so driven by instinct, so determined to survive.

"So you no longer have a husband, Mrs. Lambe?" Anne asked delicately.

Eilian grinned. "Never did. There is no Mr. Lambe, least-aways that I know of. But an unmarried woman falls under more suspicion than a widow. So it's the widow of a baker I am."

"A baker and a cunning woman," Dovey observed.

"My father was a baker, and me mum a baker's wife, wasn't she," Eilian said with playful indignation. "But aye, it's apprentice to a midwife I was, back in Abergavenny. A fine cunning woman she was, and the best midwife in the Bannau Brycheiniog. That's the Brecon Beacons to you *Saes*," she told Anne.

"And who is the other woman running the bakery with you? She was there yesterday," Anne observed.

"That'd be Mrs. Reece, a widow true, and another as knows the baking trade. When I learned she was coming here, where she was born, I thought it easiest to come with her. I'd have too many eyes rolled my way with suspicion did I come a woman alone."

"I thought it was acceptable for a widow to live on her own," Anne said, thinking of Prunella.

"If she's money enough, she can go anywhere," Dovey said, then paused. "So long as she looks like the rest of them."

Anne floundered, unsure how to address a prejudice she had never experienced, never would experience.

"Gwen told me your husband died," she said to Dovey. "That you were left to raise young Cerys alone." She stroked the baby's thighs, lean from the struggle of birth and carrying the folds of skin he'd grow into. "Like Leah will be raising Daniel here alone."

Dovey nodded, working her pestle. "We lived in Bristol and were married proper, lines of the register in St. Thomas the Martyr for anyone who cares to look. But I got a fair number of looks after his ship went down, a woman and child and no man. Landladies raising the rent. Shopkeepers telling me so kindly they hadn't work for me when they hired the next girl who came in the door. So I came across the Channel looking for better, came to the priory looking for a place to stay, and Gwen found me."

"And then you found me." Evans limped into the room, a crutch tucked under his arm. The empty sleeve on the other side was pinned to his coat so it didn't dangle free. Dovey smiled up at her husband, her face shining with tenderness, and he dropped a kiss on her brow.

Anne looked away, uncomfortable at the sight of the man's

mauled body, and perhaps too by the glow on Dovey's face. The glow of a woman who had found her love.

"And now I'm respectable again, I am," Dovey called after him as he moved on to one of the storerooms. "As much as I can be, I suppose, married to a rogue such as you."

"'Tis why I kept all the better men away," Evans called back. "Left me your only option, dint I? Gibraltar took my arm but not my wits."

Dovey chuckled and added more herbs to her pestle, a contented smile on her lips. She wouldn't trade her husband for anyone else, not even a whole man, that Anne could see.

"Marriage," Anne said slowly. "'Tis the answer to every-thing, isn't it? For a woman."

Eilian nodded. "So they want us to think. And so they try to make it, men like the aldermen as write up the rules. They want the woman yoked into marriage, and if it's a bad lot she's drawn, a sot or a fool or a man who raises his hand to her, it's a pity. Only death can set her free." She patted Daniel dry after his washing and then laid out the swaddling cloth, showing Anne how to cross and fold and tuck until he was wrapped like a twist of spiced nuts.

"Like Mrs. Gossett," Dovey said soberly. She set the pestle on the table and held out her arms, and Eilian put the babe into them. Dovey cuddled the infant, cooing at him, while Eilian took over grinding the herbs.

"Who is Mrs. Gossett?" Anne asked, taking the basin and cloths into the scullery.

"I can take you with me when I visit," Eilian said. "Her husband was a bare-knuckle fighter and prone to use his fists on her. He's stopped of late, praise be, p'raps because she's breeding again, or perhaps because Lord Penrydd had words with him. Who knows if he's changed his ways. And she's three other babes in that house of theirs, and nowhere to go if she wanted to leave him. Nowhere to go but here, to St. Sefin's," she added when Dovey opened her mouth to protest.

"But the aldermen could come and make her return to her husband, couldn't they," Anne guessed. "Even if he beats her."

"And they'd have some scripture at the ready to back the law." Eilian nodded. "The wife and the man are one flesh, or some such. St. Peter's a busy one, that he is, keeping all those bad marriages together."

Anne poured the dirty water into the deep trough of the scullery and hung up the cloths to dry on the line that held other baby clouts, also drying.

"I thought I could break my betrothal to Calvin Vaughn if I were ruined," she said. It was easier to confess when she was in this low side room, dim with green light through the foliage against the small window. "So I arranged to be found in Hewitt's bed."

The two other women stared at her as she emerged from the scullery. "And?" Dovey asked, rocking the babe in her arms.

"I didn't think it through," Anne confessed. "Now Hew thinks he must marry me."

Eilian's eyes were round. "D'ye want to?"

"I thought I could simply leave if I were ruined." Anne flushed with shame now to think of her own stupidity. Or rather, naivete, for how was she to know the ways of the world when no one had taught her? "I thought I could simply walk away. But now I see it is not so easy."

"You might have caught," Eilian said at once.

Anne shook her head. "We didn't—that way." She gulped. "But as you know a bit about midwifery, perhaps ..." She swallowed her shame and forged ahead. "Perhaps you know how I might ... keep from conceiving. Until I am ready to go through what Leah did." The thought filled her with cold fear. She could die. A baby could die. What woman could ever bear for a man to touch her, knowing what could result?

The pleasure, Anne supposed, a hot flush chasing away the cold in an instant, as if she had the ague. There was a great deal to be said for the pleasure.

Dovey nuzzled the head of the infant, who squirmed in her arms. "It's pain, yes, Miss Sutton," she said gently. "There's no way around that, if you want the result. But a babe is a fine and precious thing, if it's with a man you love, who loves you." She smiled as her daughter came into the kitchen, bringing her basket and the scent of warm, ripe fruit. "And then you get a Cerys, to bring sun to your days, and white hairs to your head. *Pfft*, child, how am I to scrub those stains from your apron?"

"We'll soak it," Cerys said breezily. "Mother Morris will show me how to make a paste." She held out her arms to take the babe, as confident as any seasoned mother.

Anne watched them, the infant and child. That was the done way to have both such things, the pain and travail of childbirth. Childbirth within marriage, if she wanted safety for herself and a babe. Of course, she could stay at St. Sefin's and wait for a child to turn up on the doorstep, like Ifor had at St. Woolos, if she indeed wanted a babe. But to care for it, a woman alone, was made twice as difficult by law and custom.

She was terrified of the pain, yes, but she had that list of names after all. And Hew needed heirs for Greenfield. Anne suspected he would be the kind of father who lofted his son on his shoulders and allowed his daughters to lure him from the ledgers to play with kittens in the stables.

"I can find you the herbs to keep from catching, though it's never a sure thing, mind." Eilian tied a hat over her cap and reached for another basket, hanging from a peg beside the door. "Come with me now to take some cuttings, and you can go with me to Mrs. Gossett later, if you wish."

"I don't wish to be a burden," Anne said humbly. It felt wonderful and strange to be included in this women's business, in the real and vital work that women did to support their lives. The most she'd ever done was approve menus and give servants orders in her mother's stead. She knew so little of housekeeping, and even less of the real ways women lived beyond the houses like Vine Court and the papered drawing rooms enclosing gentlemen's daughters.

"But I want to learn," Anne said, lifting her chin. "I want to learn everything."

Dovey smiled. Eilian grinned and held out another basket. "Aye, then. Let's begin."

CHAPTER FOURTEEN

Anne was pleasantly weary as she drove the pony cart into the stable yard at Greenfield. Her mind buzzed like sleepy bees making honey of all she had learned that day, and her muscles, too. She hadn't done this much walking since those long days outdoors with Gwen. She looked forward to a quiet dinner and hearing how Hew had spent his hours.

Greenfield blushed rose in the mellow late afternoon light, the windows casting back silver gleams, the ivy on one wall green with life. It was a house that had made peace with the land that held it, a lovely house, serene in symmetry and splendor. Anne allowed herself, for the briefest moment, to imagine this was her home. She was returning after a day spent—doing what, she couldn't yet imagine. Calling on the ill of Newport and nursing them with her remedies. Delivering babies. Doing some good in the world.

And coming home at the end of it to a husband who would smile to see her. Sit next to her in the parlor the way he'd sat beside her on the pony cart yesterday, his masculine body a thrill and a comfort at the same time. They would spend the evening tending to their home and one another, and then retire to bed—

She shook herself free of the fancies falling about her like the soft light of dusk. Her marriage to Hew was a charade. She didn't want a marriage forced by custom or circumstance or threat of ruination. She wanted ... something more.

He strode toward her across the packed earth of the yard as if he were a compass needle and she his true north. As if he had been waiting for her. Lean and strong in his dark blue coat, legs flexing in his pantaloons, a hint of the military in his tall black boots and straight shoulders. He was a man who commanded, a man with authority over himself and others.

The bolt of bald desire shocked her. Ladies were not to feel this kind of raw longing, or, if they felt, were not to heed but to deny.

She didn't know how she was supposed to do that. A groom took the reins of the horse, and Hew came to her, his face a mask of courtesy, with a smolder beneath. He held up his hands, and Anne hesitated only a moment before tipping into them.

A wall of sensation sprang up around her, prickling heat and firm, warm flesh and the scent of the summer lake she had loved as a child. She fought the reckless urge to press her face against the lapels of his coat, run her nose through the folds of his cravat and kiss the heated skin beneath. He called up some strange craving within her, and like a sprout pushing its way out of the seed that encased it, everything in her reached toward him.

"You've time to change," he said as he set her feet on the ground. "But not much more than that, I'm afraid."

He didn't release his hold on her waist, and she didn't step away. She ought to.

"What has happened?"

"Mother is hosting a dinner party," he said grimly.

"I know how to behave at dinner, Hew." Did he suppose she didn't? Of course, he'd seen little evidence of her behaving. That kiss this morning, in plain sight of his mother and half the servants—His gaze fell to her mouth, and his fingers clenched about her waist. Heat radiated from his fingers.

A delicate lady would not heat all over when a man touched her. A delicate lady did not *crave*.

Of course, a delicate lady wouldn't have done most of the things Anne had been doing lately. That elegant shell her mother had tried so hard to cover over Anne was falling away, and the woman emerging beneath, raw and vital, bore almost no resemblance.

"She said she wishes to announce your engagement." He seemed struggling to connect his thoughts. Because of her? Did she distract him, the way he turned her mind into seeds that scattered on the merest breeze? She smiled at that thought.

"That means," he added, "everyone will want to know the wedding date."

"Oh." The smile fell away. She had thought to have time to decide, to plan. To tease out of the great burl of tangled emotion in her chest a clear apprehension of the future she wanted, and the way towards it.

"What shall we say to them?" She drifted her fingertips down his arms to his wrists, relishing the strength, the heft, the heat of him.

"That kiss," he growled, his gaze hunting over every feature of her face. "I can think of nothing else."

Anne chuckled and was amazed at the sound, husky, seductive. Was she the type to allure a man, now? Did the new Anne have this power?

He lowered his head and she tipped hers up to meet him. Apparently the new Anne was a harlot without shame. A wanton who wished to spend her days and all of her nights kissing Hewitt Vaughn.

"You wouldn't be mauling m'sister in plain view, would you, Vaughn?" came Daron's drawling voice from the direction of the house. "Had the decency to save it for the bedchamber, before."

Hew lifted his head, his jaw tightening. "She is my affianced," he said to Daron.

"Yet I would've sworn she was promised to y'r brother."

Anne sighed. Her brother was a fool, to insult his host. Where did he think he could go if Hewitt turned him out? The Suttons had been staying at Greenfield at the invitation of Calvin Vaughn, but Calvin was gone and Hewitt was here. And Hew had said outright he was not a man to honor commitments merely on principle.

Daron looked a bit bosky already, his blue eyes glassy and his cheeks flushed. Whatever his doings with Darch, they had involved drink. Anne's stomach clenched.

"So the trap is closing," she said to Hew, her voice low. The trap *she'd* made and caught them both in. He'd come home for a reprieve from war, from fighting, and she'd merely built him another kind of prison, the very one she'd been trying to escape.

He unclasped his fingers, and cold curled around her waist as his hands fell away. Her lips tingled where his had briefly touched them.

"I don't know how my mother intends to tell the story," Hew said, "but it will be lions eating Christians in the Coliseum, once the gossips get hold of the news."

Refuse to marry. His eyes had captured the twilight, that liminal space where magic happened. Anne studied the scar between his brow, that groove above his lip where she wanted to drag her finger across his mouth to the cleft in his chin.

"You might refuse me," she said quietly. "This is all my fault. You shouldn't have to bear the blame." He was the prodigal son, the hero of Acre returning in all his glory, and she had robbed him of his triumph. Worse, she'd added to his disgrace.

He stared down at her as if she wasn't some penniless, conniving girl who had tossed over his brother for him. He stared at her as if he could see all her fear and uncertainty and years of fruitless hopes, and he meant to offer her solid ground at last.

"I am not going to refuse you, Anne." He stepped back. "Now change your frock. Hop to it."

Anne paused before Daron, who lounged against a fence post of the stable yard. The groom and all the stableboys pretended to be about their business, putting the cart away and walking the horse, but Anne knew they were being observed.

"I hope you will do nothing to shame the name of our family," she said, rather surprised at herself for finding the temerity to lecture her brother.

Daron returned a feral grin; he saw through her, as always. "Nanny's going to scold me about better behavior? The wanton found in the bachelor's bed? Rather too late for me to go about it, I'd say. You've torn the pride of this family in two."

Head high, Anne went inside.

She'd face a hard road as a woman alone, she'd learned that today. But a harder path lay ahead of the woman in a marriage for the wrong reasons. Raising children alone while her husband spent their income the way Daron had tossed her dowry into the wind. Being trapped, like Mrs. Gossett had been, with a man who spoke with his fists.

Better to find a trade and work her fingers to the bone at it, the way Dovey and the widows of St. Sefin's toiled. Better to pay her twenty shillings to the aldermen, as Mrs. Lambe had done, and find a means of employment. The council of a town might tell her where she might live and where she could sell her goods and how often she must go to church, but a husband would have so much more power.

Of course, a woman in love happily handed over that power, as Gwen had, as Dovey had. But they had found men they trusted, and they knew their husbands well before they made that vow. Anne had known Hewitt Vaughn for mere days.

And he had offered his hand and his future to her, though he knew as little about her. The act of either a desperate man, or a very honorable one.

Or a man who did not believe having a wife would change much of anything, and he would simply go on as he always had.

Or perhaps a man in immediate need of funds to repair his family fortunes, who believed an heiress stood before him.

In her room, the young maid was pouring hot water into the basin of the washstand and laying out drying cloths.

"Can you fetch my cambric gown from the clothes press?" Anne wet a cloth and began scrubbing her face clean of the grime of the day. "The one with the scarlet panels in the bodice and the gold sunbursts along the hem. There's a sheer tunic to go along with, and a matching veil for my hair."

It was the most luxurious ensemble she had, her one gown made in the height of fashion, or what had been the height this spring when she and her mother went shopping in Shrewsbury. Their strained budget had provided one new gown to prepare Anne for her journey south, the journey to secure Anne's marriage to Calvin and Daron's marriage to Gwen so that that the Sutton coffers might begin taking in money rather than bleeding it out.

How very surprised her parents would be at the turn events had taken. They would not at all be pleased by the part Anne had played, so outside everything she'd been taught.

The girl carefully opened the top doors of the mahogany

clothes press and stared into it. "Aye, what's the cambric, *bonesig*—Miss?"

Anne patted her face dry and went to the tall piece of furniture. "How old are you, child?"

"Ten, Miss." The child bobbed a quick curtsy.

"Young to be a maid, aren't you?"

"Aye, but Mrs. Harries said I'll do. Too young to catch the eye of the gent, s'what she said."

Anne's fingers went numb as she reached for the gown she sought. "Does she mean Calvin? She's hoping you'll avoid Mr. Calvin Vaughn?"

The girl's eyes flared with horror and she took a step back. "Oh—Miss—I didn't—I'd never—that's to be your husband, is that one, and I—"

"I'm not to marry Calvin," Anne said quickly. Seeing the maid's startlement, she kept her voice gentle. "Calvin meddles with the maids here, doesn't he?"

The girl's cheeks turned the color of an orange poppy. "Oh, Miss, I mun say ... I ought've said nothing, I don't know a thing, I—"

"Child," Anne said again, and she thought this must be the new Anne speaking, the Anne who had held and washed a newborn baby while speaking with Eilian and Dovey of the rules hedging in single women and the fines that fell on a woman who caught a babe outside marriage, while there was no consequence for the man who had put the babe in her.

"You needn't try to protect me. It is my duty to protect you. You are wise to stay out of Mr. Vaughn's way—that is Calvin, I mean," she added, feeling her own cheeks grow tight with heat. "Do not get within his arm's reach if you can help it. And if he says ought to you, flirts or tries to cozen you, run to me or Mrs. Harries immediately."

"Yes, Miss," the girl said, eyes round as hazelnuts.

"I mean this," Anne said, fearing the child was only saying what she thought Anne wanted to hear. "If you do not feel safe. If it does not feel right. Come to Mrs. Harries or me."

The girl paused, then nodded gingerly. "*Gwnaf*, I will."

"Good." Anne realized she had taken the girl's arm, as if she could put her own will into the child, and let go immediately. When had this new boldness in her come about? But the thought of Calvin Vaughn harming this girl—or Mathry, or Gwen, or anyone—made her blood boil. And if she did not have the power to stop Calvin, Anne saw, finally, that she had the power to protect this girl, or try. "What is your name, dear?"

"They calls me Mair, Miss. After Miss Meredith, she as raised me."

"And who is Miss Meredith?" Anne took the cambric gown and inspected the creases. She hadn't the time to press the light fabric, given Hew's urgency. She'd simply have to come to the table rumpled and hope the tunic, lightly embroidered with matching rosettes, would mask the worst of it.

"She's a lady as lives in High Cross, a right fine lady she is, and takes in girls like me, with no mum to look after us." The girl drew the matching tunic from a drawer and ran an admiring hand over the delicate fabric. "She's a friend of that place as you've been going, St. Sefin's. Many an orphan as came there's gone to the charity school with Miss Meredith."

"How did you—never mind. I should like to meet this Miss Meredith," Anne said, and meant it. She had a new interest in these women with charitable impulses. Like Dovey. Like Eilian. Like Gwen. They, too, were the pillars of a little community like this, but in a far different manner than a woman like Lady Vaughn.

Anne had been raised to become a Lady Vaughn. She had no pattern for becoming anything else.

"Will she be at dinner tonight, your Miss Meredith?"

"Oh, no, it's all Lady Vaughn's high friends tonight, as many ladies as she could scratch together," Mair said innocently, hanging the tunic from a peg and searching the drawers for the matching hair accessory. "And a few men too, she said, so as to entertain you."

"Men to entertain me?" Anne echoed. "Though I am to marry her son?"

Mair looked up quickly, her face paling and flushing poppy-orange again—she really did have the most revealing skin. Anne hoped she wasn't as transparent as this child.

"Never mind," Anne said. "Lady Vaughn is hoping to divert my attention, I don't doubt. She thinks I am an adventuress and, if she dangles better bait before me, I might snap at it, and so leave both her sons free.

"And," she guessed further, stripping off her day gown and tossing it on the bed, "I don't doubt the young women are to tempt Mr. Vaughn away from me, and save him from the clutches of a girl with little standing and no dowry, who has turned out to be a bad bet."

Mair took up the discarded gown and shook it out, then draped it over a chair as deftly as any trained lady's maid. "I dun s'pose the captain could do better than you, Miss," she said. "You is kind, and you's pretty. That's a fair way to his favor, I should think."

"You are ten, and too young to be thinking of courting." Anne's voice came out muffled as she pulled the gown over her head. She'd wear the same long-boned stays she'd had on all day rather than taking the time to change them for her shorter set. "In fact you are too young to be working. You ought to be at school learning your letters."

"I's been a scullery maid since I was six," the child said, regarding Anne with surprise. "Orphans as I needs to earn they way. T'won't get handed to them on a salver."

Anne heard the echo of a familiar proverb in her declaration, perhaps wisdom handed down from the revered Miss Meredith. "At least you've a skill to earn your keep," she remarked. "I'm for deciding whom I might marry to give me a place in the world and hold me there. I suppose that does make me an adventuress."

"Thas the way of the world, that is," Mair said with a shrug as she set to buttoning the back of Anne's gown. "But the captain seems a fine one, that he does."

"Fine indeed," Anne acknowledged, her chest tightening as she arranged the bodice of the gown so the ribbon lay beneath her breasts. Hewitt was too fine for the likes of Anne. Too handsome, and, she was beginning to suspect, honorable after all. The way he'd played at affection that morning so his mother might think he was wooing Anne in truth.

Hewitt Vaughn was too good to be ruined by the girl Anne had become, a girl without prospects, and lately without shame. She would have been a proper match six years ago, young and pretty and empty in her head. Lady Vaughn was right to want better for him.

The sound of traffic in the house increased, the front door opening and the patter of evening shoes and heeled slippers clicking on the marble tile of the hall. Anne decided to keep her hair in the coils she'd worn all day rather than take the time to brush it out and repin. She donned the tunic, which tied at her shoulders like a Roman toga and wafted about her upper body, and tucked the comb into a roll of golden hair. The small veil fluttered behind, hiding the simplicity of the arrangement.

At least the curls around her face still held. Her cheeks were pink with a hint of the sun that had come out from the clouds while Eilian walked her through St. Sefin's herb gardens, Cerys frolicking at their heels as lively as the young goat that followed them about. Anne would use that memory to give her strength to face what lay ahead. She dabbed a bit of color onto her lip and picked up her fan.

"What's the secret to making Lady Vaughn like me, d'you think?" she asked, as if Mair were her reliable, beloved Pym of Vine Court and not a ten-year-old scullery maid. As if the new Anne had some affinity with children now, especially half-feral, too-wise ones like this girl, or Cerys. A girl that would never have come into the orbit of the old Anne, yet here they were.

Mair sighed. "Wish I knew."

Anne followed the voices to the formal parlor, Lady Vaughn's favorite, papered in saffron and gold. The chairs and chaise had been pushed back against the walls to allow guests to circulate. The enormous chandelier dripped with candles, and all the windows were pulled shut, making the chamber close and warm.

Hew stood to one side of the room with two young ladies hovering about him like butterflies. Over their heads his gaze landed on Anne, and held. She stared back at him, ensnared by the currents in his dark blue eyes. His bold stare was making a claim on her, and she, gaping back like a ninny, acknowledged it.

She shook herself lightly and went to Hew's mother, dropping a gracious curtsy. "Your ladyship."

"I mislike that I cannot find another harpist," Lady Vaughn fretted. "None here are as skilled as Miss Ewyas." She turned to the matron beside her, done up in glittering jewels and a Norwich silk shawl. "Did you know the new Viscountess Penrydd used to harp for me?"

"So you've said, Winifred. Once or twice." The older woman smiled indulgently. "And this is your Miss Sutton?"

"Anne, this is Mrs. Hawkins," Lady Vaughn said crisply. "Of Gaer House."

"That lovely ivy-covered manor on the road to Cardiff,"

Anne said. "The one that overlooks the old Roman hillfort? How do you do."

Anne made a delicate curtsy, wondering how she'd been described to her ladyship's friends. Not with the highest praise, she gathered from the curious, evaluating way Mrs. Hawkins studied her. But then, gentlewomen always did that, trying to place another in birth, station, wealth, accomplishments, and comparative influence. Hoping that the one being evaluated would come out a little less in the equation, leaving the other an advantage.

Anne had youth, beauty, all the customary feminine graces, and a good family to count in her favor. But her lack of money wiped her attractions off the board. A lack of secure dowry meant she had no value as a marriage prospect. And Lady Vaughn knew this.

"So you are the girl who has enchanted Calvin? A good match, I'm sure. All the more since I do not think Winifred will let her eldest go to any mortal woman. She speaks as if Hewitt walked on water over there in the Holy Land." Mrs. Hawkins smiled, though Anne wondered if a veiled taunt lay in her words.

Her ladyship tightened her lips in a frown. "Calvin and Miss Sutton have been promised for years. I am sure Anne would not like how it would reflect on her were she to jilt him now, after all this time."

Anne gaped at her ladyship. "Calvin," she repeated, as if she were a bird learning speech.

Lady Vaughn turned to her friend with a thin smile. "Young people these days are so headstrong. Not like you and I, Florence, who went where our parents bid us."

A cold draft crept up beneath Anne's tunic, clutching her arms. Lady Vaughn could not think, after all this, Anne could still be pressured into marriage with *Calvin*.

No, it must be she was taking care to keep a cap on any gossip. Hew and Anne could be cut throughout the neighborhood if their indiscretion made the rounds. Anne had been trained to learn the family associations of an area and she'd gleaned the knowledge she needed over those many teas when Lydia and Prunella, the dowager viscountesses, called at Greenfield.

Florence Hawkins was a Seys, a family who had been high officials under the reign of the great Elizabeth, and her father had been High Sheriff of Monmouthshire. Her husband's family were burgesses of Newport and touted their connection to a French duke who had somehow escaped the scythe of the guillotine. Florence Hawkins would be one of those Anne must impress and not offend.

"I was fortunate that my parents gave me to a man I found I could love," Mrs. Hawkins said mildly. "I wish you the same good fortune, Miss Sutton."

Anne nodded and gulped back the sudden clot of rage in her throat. She could not love Calvin Vaughn. She had tried to escape him. She knew all the more surely, after Mair's divulgence, that Calvin Vaughn was not a man she could tolerate. What more must she do to be free of him?

"My dear Eleanor." Lady Vaughn greeted another lady who joined them, an older matron with a majestic turban and a modish silk gown, a saffron open robe over a petticoat of butter yellow. On her head sat some combination of a silk cap, gauze ribbon, and feathers, all mixed together.

"Mrs. Kemeys, this is Anne Sutton." Lady Vaughn made the requisite introductions with a wave of her gloved hand. "Anne, Mrs. Kemeys, wife of George Kemeys of Malpas. Her brother-in-law, William, owns Newport Castle."

Anne dipped another curtsy. The Kemeys were one of the oldest families in the area, hailing back to the Norman kings and their barons. This evening wasn't an introduction; it was a gauntlet.

"Calvin's intended, are you?" Mrs. Kemeys smiled. Apparently all of Lady Vaughn's friends labored under the same misconception. "I admit he's a fine-looking boy, but this Hewitt of yours is rather splendid, Winifred. I do so adore a man with that military physique."

All four women turned to regard Hew, who had managed to draw another gentleman into his circle. Hew had swapped his tall boots for white silk stockings and black pumps. His long-tailed coat of dark checked olive green cut away to show a golden waistcoat with a light but intricate embroidery along the hem. A white cravat billowed at his neck, and his jaw was freshly shaven around the slightly rakish slant of his sideburns.

Anne did her level best not to stare at the cut of his coat, the fit of his breeches, but she knew the power and heat that lay beneath the correct appearance, and the secret was a lava pit opening up within her.

"Eleanor, since Anne knows so few people here, you might introduce her to your nephew, Robert," Lady Vaughn prompted.

Mrs. Kemeys nodded. "Robert is studying to be a surgeon in Bristol. Isn't your Anthony studying medicine also, Mrs. Hawkins?"

"Such accomplished young men," Lady Vaughn simpered. "They will turn Miss Sutton's head from my Calvin, I fear."

Anne's chest ached, as if she'd been given a sharp rap on the ribs. It appeared her ladyship wished *both* her sons could be free of Anne. She wouldn't be trying to protect Anne from Calvin, as Mrs. Harries tried to protect her maids. Lady Vaughn was one of those species of women who agreed that men were meant to do as they wished and women were meant to hold the world together as best they might, bearing the consequences to home and family when a man went astray.

Lady Vaughn would never choose Anne for Hew.

But Hew hadn't exactly chosen Anne, either.

"Anthony has just received his medical diploma after rigorous study in London," Mrs. Hawkins said with the complaisance of a doting mama whose son was a source of pride. "I am so pleased he has agreed to establish his practice here in Monmouthshire. He intends to become an accoucheur."

Anne's ears pricked. A man midwife. She wondered what Mrs. Lambe would think of having a medical man for a rival, and if she would account this doctor's practices any better than others she had known.

"I would adore meeting them both," Anne said absently, wondering how soon she could make her way to Hew and pull him aside. Their scandal wasn't yet known; to this crowd, Anne was still betrothed to Calvin. She must ask Hew what to do.

Robert Allard, would-be surgeon and the Kemeys heir, was shy and perfectly unobjectionable. He regaled Anne with accounts of recent surgeries he had attended, and she wondered at her own strong stomach as she smiled and nodded along. A week ago, she would have fainted at the account of a man having his leg taken off. Now, compared to childbirth, amputation of a limb seemed a less painful ordeal, and far quicker.

Anthony Hawkins was a fine-looking young man who carried himself well and was devoted to his studies. He spoke of his mentors until Anne knew all their names, Dr. Baillie and Dr. Fordyce and the anatomist, Dr. John Hunter, and knew every anecdote from his time studying at the University of Douai in France. He was earnest, an advocate for reform, and Anne thought he would have a soothing manner for a physician. No doubt he would have a long and profitable career. She couldn't summon the least bit of interest in him.

William Griffith was barely eighteen years of age, and showed it in his puppyish manner. Henry Powell, apprenticed to an attorney, was very grave. John Jones had an extremely high opinion of his own cleverness for having been born to Mr. Jones, Esq., of Llanarth Court, a stately manor house to the north of Newport and a fixture on tours of picturesque Monmouthshire. Uninterested in Mrs. Jones's discussion about how much he had won in a recent cockfight in Bristol, Anne finally drifted over to Hew's group, hoping to insert herself at his side.

The two young women, introduced as Margaret Griffith and May Powell, greeted Anne with hostile civility. Like Mrs. Kemeys, both young ladies wore yellow, one a cotton round gown with a spotted print and the other a delicate muslin with a gathered bodice and small train. Apparently yellow was the color of the season, and Anne hadn't known. The other women dotted the room like daffodils in bloom, and here she was with scarlet touches on her white, like the whore of Babylon, or a blood-spattered sacrificial lamb. The golden sunbursts that had called to her in Shrewsbury now put her behind the current mode.

What was she doing here? In these rooms, in this house? Once, presiding over a party was the sum and pinnacle of Anne's identity. She lived for the compliments of admiring gentlemen, the envious gazes from other girls, the covetous glances of matrons who wished their daughters as graceful and cultivated as Anne.

Now it struck her as simply an elaborate show. The inane conversation, the efforts of the gentlemen to display their wit and stature, the efforts of her fellow young ladies to depress or outmatch her. The heavy scent of perfumes and cologne and expensive wax candles. The display they made of themselves in expensive fabrics and jewels, bought by the toil of others.

At St. Sefin's, Anne had fallen easily into the rhythm of

small but necessary tasks and the gentle flow of conversation about the matters of the world. They had, through no virtue of her own, given her a place in their community. Ifor knew her scent. Tomos had let her pet his chicken, which she'd later learned was the highest honor he could extend.

Here, she was an insect trapped to a board, flung open to everyone's inspection without the thin barrier of glass to defend her. Lady Vaughn watched her like that sheepdog from earlier, as if she were guarding her flock. As if Anne were a scarlet temptress set loose in Greenfield's decorated rooms, or a donkey who had wandered into a paddock of well-bred racehorses.

Mrs. Kemeys had tried to bait Anne with Mrs. Hawkins's son as if she were a kestrel on the hunt. And May Powell, far from envying Anne's looks or gown or family name, was delivering a glare that said she wished the floor would open and the devil take Miss Sutton to the fiery furnace of hell.

"Anne. This is Mr. David Edwards, the engineer working on the new bridge." Hew tucked his hand beneath Anne's elbow and drew her to his side. Her gloves were three-quarter, a barrier between his hand and her skin, and yet his heat sank through. The breath left her body, exactly like the time she and Gwen had been playing lawn tennis and Anne took a ball straight in the belly.

"Mr. Edwards. We've been watching the work progress. It seems quite an ambitious project." Anne managed a correct response, even though her head whirled at Hew's touch, the citrus notes of his cologne.

"I told him what I think of the Fourteen Locks," Hew said. "Dadford's construction is brilliant, no one's denying that, but if some of the locks were widened, more water could support heavier boats."

He smiled down at her, his features animated with the delight of having a mechanical problem to solve. He was more unguarded than she'd ever seen him, and the absent stroke of his thumb over her forearm shot every thought from Anne's mind like a hound flushing a covey of pheasants.

"I take it you had some engineering training, Captain," Edwards remarked. "Yet I thought you were a gunner in the Artillery, not a sapper with the Engineers?"

"Our training at Woolwich was thorough, and necessity can call upon a man to play many roles, especially in a place like Acre." Hew's manner was easy, but he rolled his shoulders back as if consciously loosening tension. "The question is, how to determine how much more volume is needed, and how to test a new design? Is Dadford even available to oversee renovations? He left for another project when the Crumlin Arm was declared finished. And there will be no little expense to the new work, so we must ask if the original investors are willing to buy more shares."

He'd been one of those investors. "You said the Cefn Flight is one of the highest rises in the country, and one of the most complicated," Anne remembered. "Shall you have to fix all of it, or merely certain parts?"

"That," Hew said, "is an excellent question." He beamed at her, and she found herself leaning toward him, soaking up his approval like butter on toast.

"Mr. Vaughn, I thought you were a military man, not a builder. You were telling us how you meant to organize a new company of militia to protect us from invasion from France." May Powell, with a playful pout, tapped her fan on the back of Hew's shoulder, teasing the sticks along a slope of muscle.

Hew didn't acknowledge the bold touch, though he shrugged his shoulders again, a flicker of unease crossing his brow. "That is my charge from my superiors, and I ought not neglect it," he replied. "Which is why I cannot resist hearing what Mr. Edwards has to say about his bridge and the traffic it might support when finished. Heavy enough to handle a train of sixteen-pounders, along with shot? What about twenty-four pounders, in the event Newport must man defenses against a siege?"

Anne settled her arm against the crook of Hew's, surrendering to his possessive touch. Let May Powell try to peel him from her, the little cat.

"How are you to take an artillery train through these roads, Captain?" she teased Hew. "The road to Cardiff is but a narrow track, and I can't image the road to Christchurch is much better."

Hew's grin widened. "And you've come to know this area, have you, Miss Sutton?"

She only knew Cardiff and Christchurch thanks to Eilian and Dovey as they chattered their way through the garden, identifying plants with their properties and whom in the area they'd helped. Hew's approval made her unfurl like a dove preening her feathers.

"You'd be bringing this artillery up the river, I assume?" Edwards asked. "You could fit Royal Navy ships in our channel, I'd warrant, and make use of their carronades."

Hew turned to him. "Where's a ship of the line to dock in the Usk? We have one wharf at the Town Pill, and that's stone. We need more wharves, wooden ones, with cranes and moveable walkways."

"You said they need to extend the canal down to Pillgwenlly and build wharves there, too," Anne reminded him.

"That I did." Hew spared her another approving glance, and Anne tucked in a smile of satisfaction as May Powell glared. "Have you an interest in building more than bridges, Edwards?"

"These Welsh names are such a mouthful, Mr. Vaughn." Margaret Griffith gave a trill of laughter and tapped her fan on Hew's other arm. "I wonder that Miss Sutton can pronounce them. I own I cannot manage such barbaric syllables."

"Captain Vaughn," Mr. Edwards said, with a quizzical smile at the girl. "You know, I hope, that this man is a hero of Acre?"

May Powell, not to be outdone, turned wide brown eyes on Hew, her voice breathy. "Do tell us about your heroics, Captain."

Hew's arm went hard as steel beneath Anne's fingers. She smelled his own scent, the way she had in his bedchamber, that rich blend of cloves and pine and summer earth. He was sweating.

"There is little to discuss. The forces of the British Navy turned back the French, and Napoleon slunk back in defeat to Egypt. If he abandons his hopes of conquering the Middle East entirely, he is like to return to France and take an interest in the Directory's wars on the Continent. Or," Hew turned back to Edwards, "take an interest in our prosperous isles. Have you heard of the new fortifications going up at Dover? I'm wondering if we should do something similar here with the sea wall at Goldcliff."

"If you're going to build us wharves, build a racecourse! You'll get in the way of the free traders do you shift things about at Goldcliff," John Jones said, sliding into the conversation with the arrogance of a young man who expected to be welcomed anywhere. "I hope your forts won't go driving up the cost of brandy and tobacco, Vaughn."

"Captain Vaughn," Mr. Edwards said with a trace of annoyance, "and I would think you would take his advice on fortifications. When Commodore Smith seized half a dozen French ships trying to reach Acre, this man took their own artillery and deployed it against them. The little general spent a month drilling through Acre's walls, and what did he find?

Captain Vaughn had built *another* wall and mounted their cannon upon it. The French were beaten back by their own guns."

"And the plague," Hew said. "The second wall was really Farhi's idea—he was advisor to the Pasha Jezzar. And Antoine de Phélippeaux designed the wall. I aided only in the heavy lifting."

"The papers gave you more credit than you give yourself, Captain," Edwards noted.

May Powell widened her eyes. "Captain Vaughn. How cunning you are."

"And how brave." Margaret Griffith batted her eyelashes.

"How did you manage to mount cannon upon the wall?" Anne asked, curious. "I'd imagine they're rather heavy."

"Ramps, ropes, and pulleys," Hew said, turning to Anne. "The French have designed a lighter carriage which can fire heavier shot than ours. We put the four-pound cannons and six-pound howitzers on the walls, with some of the heavier guns behind. I can explain Gribeauval's system of artillery to you, if you wish."

A light kindled in his eyes that she hadn't seen directed at the other girls. Anne gave him a provocative smile. "Shall I have use for that knowledge at any time?"

"Not with me around to defend you." He held her arm against his side, the pressure light and somehow shattering. A gust moved through her body, lifting her like a flower petal in the breeze.

"A Frenchman helping you against the French? A traitor to his people," Jones drawled.

"Antoine escaped to Britain early on in the Revolution," Hew said. "A monarchist in his sympathies, and an antagonist of Napoleon's from their days at school. He and Smith were great friends after Antoine broke the commodore out of prison in

Paris. He was the engineer among us. I merely did as he instructed."

He rolled his shoulder again, throwing off some harsh memory. Anne's arm moved with his.

She slid her fingers beneath his palm, where he held her arm tucked against his side. "You must not discount what it meant to keep Acre. The Pasha Jezzar still holds his territory, and Napoleon will not be Emperor of the Orient, thanks to you."

He squeezed her fingers, briefly, as if her touch anchored him. She felt again the emotion that swept her when Eilian placed a minute-old newborn infant in Anne's arms. As if she'd been born for this precise place, this exact moment.

As if up until now she'd been a laurel tree, and his touch turned her into a woman.

"I thought Lord St. Vincent said Vaughn was a traitor." Daron butted into their circle. His eyes glittered, his cheeks held a hectic flush, and even from this distance, Anne smelled drink on his breath. "Weren't you thrown in prison, *Captain?*"

Hew's easy manner turned to an iron as hard as his guns. "At the order of my major, yes, I was imprisoned for a time." He spoke evenly, but his expression showed every defense dropping into place: the straight shoulders, tensed eyelids, grim mouth. Anne wished she could reach out and hold that coldness at bay, bring the easy, smiling Hew back to her.

"And the charge?" Daron taunted.

Hew snapped out the word. "Insubordination."

May Powell took a slight step backward and opened the leaf of her fan. Margaret Griffith rearranged her skirts so they no longer brushed against Hew's boot.

"And that's why you're up for a court-martial now." Daron sneered.

"For building a wall?" Edwards' brows rose in confusion.

"For crossing lines of command," Hew said. "I'm a gunner, not a sapper, as you said."

"Thas why they buried you here with some meaningless task." Daron shook his head. "As if the French would dare invade British soil. The Frogs are off preying on the weak, trying to build their little empire. And you're here, Captain Vaughn, about to have all those honors stripped away." Daron glanced at the other young women, inviting them to share his disdain. "Shame."

"The matter will be decided by the proper authorities," Hew gritted out. "And if I did wrong, I'll take my punishment for it."

Anne wished she could smack her brother across the mouth and stop his cruel taunts. That Daron, who had never bestirred himself to a useful task in his life, should sneer at a military hero who had taken blows in a battle for a just cause. And who now, returned home, actively searched for ways to shore up his family's fortunes and invest in the town he found growing exponentially.

"You forget the French tried to invade Wales just two years ago," Anne said tartly. Without thinking she laced her fingers through Hew's, exactly as if she were promised to him and had the liberty of a public touch. "I don't imagine many of us would know the first thing about defending ourselves, but Captain Vaughn is trained to do exactly that. He's only been home a few days and already has found ways to improve the area. *Some* men interest themselves in more than how to line their own pockets."

Daron stared at her, then narrowed his eyes at Hew. The back of Anne's neck prickled. She'd declared her allegiance, and it was not to her brother. Not anymore.

John Jones, noting that Lady Vaughn was starting to dispose the party toward going into dinner, took Margaret Griffith's arm.

This effectively cut out Mr. Edwards, who was standing right beside the girl.

"Miss Sutton," Jones drawled, "you show your loyalty to Greenfield already. What an addition you'll make to the Vaughn family."

"Perhaps it's not Calvin she's after," Daron said. "P'raps she wants a bigger prize."

That was all it took. Daron held out his arm to May Powell, who leaned close with a curious whisper. The gossip that Anne was faithless and Hew a seducer of his brother's intended would blaze through the room before everyone was seated at table.

Anne realized then that her fingers were solidly entwined with Hew's, his arm anchoring hers to his side. He was firm and strong and the heat from his body warmed her in ways that were not appropriate for a genteel drawing room. She couldn't tell if her stomach were turning flips because the gossip was out—despite Lady Vaughn's best efforts—or because Hew watched her with consideration, curiosity, a hint of shadow in his eyes. Guarded, still, and not entirely convinced she was his ally.

She was, though. They were in this together, sink or swim.

Good thing Anne knew how to swim.

"We've been betrayed," she murmured.

"Betrayed how?" He moved his thumb over the back of her hand. The motion soothed and excited her interest at the same time, a response that did not at all feel as contradictory as it should have. Everything in her was rushing headlong toward him, without the slightest regard for her safety, and everything in her was convinced he would catch her and break her fall.

"Your mother was trying to contain the scandal. She was telling her friends I was yet promised to Calvin."

Hew could still be taken away from her. That was the thing. She'd tricked him into seducing her, snared him with his own sense of honor. She couldn't force him into a ruinous, loveless match with her when he deserved so much more.

Where did that leave them, then, trapped in their own separate vises?

"Which of us do you want to stand by you, Anne?"

She stared at him. "You don't know?"

"You are not easy to read."

That seemed manifestly untrue. Surely her emotions were written plain upon her face. Her emotions of this immediate moment, at least.

But she had no business letting sentiment or whim dictate her movements. The world held infinite dangers for a woman alone. She must be wise.

She turned toward the dining parlor, following the other guests as they trailed in, paired or singly. "My mother taught me a lady cannot afford to be transparent. She should not let her inclinations be known until she has secured the gentleman's interest."

"Believe me, I have no desire to compel you against your will," Hew said in a low voice. "But if your brother spreads tales, I can do no less than stand by my offer to you."

Marriage. Lifelong, irrevocable, unbreakable in the eyes of God. Anne shied away, keeping her gaze trained on the table as it came into view, a broad mahogany expanse draped in gleaming white linen and laden with cut glass bowls and crystal goblets. All of Lady Vaughn's wealth and taste on lavish display. Outside the windows, the green forested hills rolled out into an opulent vista, further sign of Greenfield's splendor.

This was the world she'd been born and bred to, and she'd moved through it all her life like a puppet on a stage, following the script set out for her.

That script had failed her, brought her to ruin and nothing. She'd seen a path forward today, in the kitchen at St. Sefin's, when she realized she could learn what Dovey and Eilian and Cerys knew, the ways of plants and women's pathways and healing. When she'd understood she could step out into the unknown and trust her own wits to catch her.

Marriage to Hew was just another version of the old path that had failed her. Even if his arm were strong beneath her hand, his heat a solid and steady wall. Marriage was a pen that would curtail the futures of both of them, yoking her to a path she no longer wanted to tread.

Besides, she'd sacrificed her right to be ranked among the May Powells and Margaret Griffiths of the world when she threw modesty and chastity and decorum to the wind and tucked herself into Hewitt Vaughn's bed. But this was his world, the world he'd gone abroad and fought to protect, the world he'd come home to for peace and shelter and ease. He deserved a lovely, gentle, pure woman who would adore him, would thrive in this potted life, the flowering lady at his side. Not some fierce creature eager, nay, desperate to stretch her new wings.

His arm beneath her hand was only there because she had forced it. And their alliance was not one of fascination, or even affection, but because she had left him no other choice.

She couldn't hold him—either of them—to that.

CHAPTER FIFTEEN

She'd asked him to refuse her. She'd as much as advised him to repudiate her here, before all his mother's guests.

Was that what she wanted?

Hew was a man of discipline, a soldier. He was accustomed to enduring discomfort. He was used to forcing his will against his feelings like an iron plow breaking dry sod. He was practiced at rigor and denial.

Yet he couldn't keep away from Anne Sutton. And he didn't want to.

No man alive could ignore the soft allure of her beauty. The way the candlelight cast a honeyed glow over her fair skin and struck glints of guinea-gold from her hair. The delicate arc of her fingers as she held her cutlery. The demure, quietly amused curve of her mouth as she spoke with her dinner partners, Robert Allard, the surgeon, on one side and David Edwards, the engineer, on the other.

Both men looked as fascinated as Hew felt, unable to glance away when she lifted her cornflower-blue eyes to theirs. Anne Sutton, with her quiet radiance and subtle grace, was a woman a man would pursue to the edges of the earth. She was a woman whose face would linger in the chest of the man who'd left her, creating a hollow ache that couldn't be filled until he returned to hold her in his arms.

Hew desperately wanted to hold her in his arms again.

"Mister—Captain Vaughn." May Powell, seated to his left, looked pensive. "Do you really suppose the French might try to invade us?"

She'd dropped the provocative smirk and the flirtatious flutter of her lashes. He guessed her slight lisp was not affected.

"It's happened before," he reminded her. "The Duc de Choiseul thought to cross the Channel in 1759 and raise the Jacobites in Scotland. The next year, the Royal Navy captured François Thurot in the Irish channel after the French sent him to stage an invasion. And you would be too young to remember the Armada of 1779, but the French fleet came within sight of English shores, causing widespread panic. I sailed with men who'd been under Admiral Hardy's command when he chased off the French and Spanish that summer."

Hew passed her the bowl of stewed cucumbers near his plate. "The English Channel is one hundred fifty miles at its widest, scarcely more than twenty at the Strait of Dover. The French thought as recently as last summer to bring their Army of England upon us. The plan was to draw off the Royal Navy by sailing the fleet to the West Indies, then turn back to England and attack. Napoleon was only lured away by the promise of taking Egypt."

She tasted a cucumber, and her lips puckered. "So we ought to fear?"

"Suppose they might assay an attack again," Hew said gently, "but not fear they might land."

She hesitated, then laid down her fork and nodded slightly. "Thank you."

He slid his gaze toward Anne. She was watching him, her

quick eyes moving from him to his companion, now dipping a spoon into her soup. Her eyes didn't narrow with jealousy or displeasure, nor her luscious lower lip curve into a pout, as another woman might do. Instead, she smiled, as if she understood that the girl was afraid, and Hew had tried to soothe her.

A strange heat prickled his shoulders, not quite the ache of his wounds, but something else. He was accustomed to women pouting and flirting and fighting around and over him; women habituated to military men didn't stay demure for long. But he'd never had a woman's approval for his manner, his actions. He'd never wanted such.

Until Anne.

Margaret Griffith, on Hew's right, was not through with her provocations. "Captain Vaughn." She leaned forward, affording him a view of her breasts nestled into the shelf of her low neckline. She was a generously shaped young woman, moreso than Anne, who was comparatively slender. But Miss Griffith's bosom, even on admirable display, didn't tempt his eye the way the sheer tunic Anne wore made him hunger to lift the veil and peek at the treasures beneath.

He tried to focus on Miss Griffith's words.

"—prison," she was saying, licking her lips with curiosity. "But how long were you held captive?"

His back ached, but from a memory, not from sensation. He doubted he'd ever have sensation there again. "Not above a handful of weeks. A month, at most." It had felt like a lifetime. An eternity spent in a circle of hell.

"But what had you done?"

A band of fury tightened across his forehead. "I went against my major's orders. He said I obeyed a foreign authority over his. Which is treason." The subtle taste of his white soup was gone, erased by the taste of bile.

He wouldn't tell Margaret Griffith the true argument had

been over a woman; the story made Hew look a fool. A courtesan coming to offer herself, reeking of neroli oil and her lover's tobacco, a rich silk gown gone too long without cleaning. He'd supposed it nothing at the time; women were ever trading themselves to soldiers for a bit of reward, coin or favors. Hew was selective. A woman who'd been claimed by another, particularly a superior, didn't tempt him. He'd service himself before he'd be embroiled in a jealous love triangle. He'd assumed his commander would know this of him.

But the major didn't care whether Hew'd had his whore. The major only cared that she'd wanted Hew. And when Hew ignored the man's orders and worked with Farhi, carrying out his and Antoine's plans, their fortifications had defeated Napoleon. Hew emerged the hero of Acre, one of those whose quick minds and ready hands had saved the city, and the major came off looking a narrow-minded fool who couldn't satisfy his own woman.

A sentence of a hundred lashes wasn't the greatest punishment he could have ordered. He didn't want to kill Hew with his own hands, only humiliate and permanently scar him. Let the courts set the noose.

"But what will happen to you?" Miss Powell asked, eyes wide.

"The matter is being discussed higher up the command," Hew said. "They'll decide whether to discipline me or hold a court-martial."

"Death is the sentence for traitors," Miss Griffith said, and she was not wrong.

The fire spread down his back, the claw of memory. Anne hadn't seen his scars, hadn't touched them. She didn't know yet what he was accused of, what he'd done. He had no right dragging a delicate beauty into his beastly embrace. Soiling her with the muck of his nightmares, the rubble he'd made of his career, his life.

But he couldn't stop looking at her anyway. The price of damnation. She was the pure, good, beautiful thing he once could have had and now would never be worthy of.

"I think you are a hero, Captain Vaughn," May Powell said softly. Her brown eyes shone with admiration. But it didn't move him like Anne's glowing at him did.

Hew cast his eyes down the table, looking for a gentleman—not Sutton—to drink with him. He couldn't hold Anne to her promise, not with the sentence hanging over him. They would have to end things as agreed.

He wouldn't be able to let her go. He was as bad as a shepherd boy ambushing his favored dairymaid behind a hayrick. He was more fevered for her than he'd ever been for the Morgan cousin. She would need to sever them.

And the longer he made her wait to do so, the deeper the blow would land.

She must see how ill he fit in this glittering world, Hew thought as the party rose from table and adjourned to the drawing room for music and cards. He wasn't one of these men in their tailored fashions and curled hair and polished boots whose talk was of corn prices and the winners of the latest race. Hew didn't know how to speak to these women as lovely as a flock of wood pigeons, fluffy and collared and cooing, their eyes bright and inquisitive. When other men had been learning to dance and pay compliments, Hew had been learning to build fortifications and take apart a gun.

Yet this was Anne's world, the decorated rooms and lovely gowns, the parties with their chatter and music, the table laden with dishes and gossip. And Hew wasn't a man who lived by his wit; he was trained to build things.

Or blow them up.

"Fearsome smart lady," Robert Allard said, coming to stand by Hew before the tall French windows that let out on the paved terrace running behind the house. "Knew Cicero when I quoted him."

"Miss Sutton?" Hew didn't need to ask. The focus of Robert's interested stare was the same as Hew's.

Anne stood talking with Mrs. Griffith and the tall, severe spinster who served as the Powell aunt and chaperone, an older woman Hew had not yet seen wear anything other than a look of grim concentration. Anne, on the other hand, wore a small, steady smile, a permanent curve of pleasure, as if everything were a delight to her. It softened her face and balanced her bold features, giving her a look of animation and intelligence that Hew knew was not feigned.

"She's had an excellent tutor," Hew allowed.

"I think her Latin is better than mine." Anthony Hawkins joined them, seeming to know already the topic of their discussion. "And possibly her Greek. She mentioned the works of Hippocrates."

"But not a bluestocking," Allard said. "Likes lawn bowls and archery. Don't think she hunts, though."

"But she sails," Hawkins added. "Mentioned boating around Lake Tegid. Told me the legend of the monster who dwells below. The *afanc*, think she called it."

Anne had won these two young men over completely. And why shouldn't she? She'd been bred to be a gentleman's match. He saw it in the smooth grace of her manner, the conscious economy of her movements, the straight bearing in her shoulders and the modulation of her voice. Women who followed men who followed the drum were loud and bald about the expression of their feelings and desires; women who serviced sailors on leave didn't mince their ways either. Anne was cast of a different mold.

"Promised to your brother, I heard?" Allard asked, so casually that at first Hew almost missed his remark. He lifted his hands when Hew swung on him with surprise. "Thought your mother told mine."

An unseen hand clamped around Hew's windpipe. "Did she say? Tonight?"

This was Calvin's world. Calvin knew how to hunt like a gentleman, shoot like a gentleman, dance and flatter a lady as a gentleman did. Hew was rough-edged and scarred in mind and body, accustomed to employment, activity, danger. These gentlemen standing with him were the matches Anne Sutton was meant for. Not Hew.

Hew's hands sweated in his gloves, aching for action. He could not give her up to one of these men. Not now that he had tasted her.

"Heard different from her brother. Said the lady don't consider herself bound to Calvin." John Jones strolled up to them with his pampered, arrogant air. His blue evening coat sported a high velvet collar, his neckcloth was an artful rumple of chalk-white linen, and his hair piled thickly across his brow.

His dark eyes, and his lips, held a smirk. "Sutton said his sister's been making sheep's eyes at you instead, Vaughn."

"Sutton said that?" Hew's voice came out hoarse, strained by the sudden lack of air. A red-black haze darkened the edge of his vision. That this jackanapes should even say Anne's name.

Jones wouldn't have a single scar on his body beyond the badge of a childhood prank. His easy, elegant grace said he didn't. His back wasn't a mass of scars he wore like a hair shirt beneath his fashionably cut coat. He was the one who wielded the cat-o'-nine-tails; he didn't bear the marks.

Allard and Hawkins wore the look of men who'd been forced out of duties to stand in line and watch one of their fellows stripped for the whipping, a lesson and a warning to all of them. Green around the gills at the thought of carnage, but unable to look away.

"As much as hinted you were playing a game of beggar-my-neighbor. Or you're the sort of brothers who share and share alike?" Jones wore a thin, malicious smile. "Interesting chap, that Sutton. Full of ideas."

Daron was spreading tales about Anne. His own sister. What did he mean to accomplish, other than ruin and discredit her?

Lady Vaughn called for music and ordered the footmen to set out chairs before the spinet and the Welsh harp. With a nod of her pointed chin, she tried to direct Hew to take one of the front seats. Put him front row to the charms of the other woman, as if he weren't bound to Anne.

Hew shook his head. Anne wanted to be free of him. But he didn't want to let her go. That night, when she'd come to him as pure and clean as a moonflower touched with dew, he'd looked ahead and saw a dream of a future where she came to him willingly, smiles on her lips and a flush on her cheeks and her hands reaching for him. A future where she chose him. Wanted him.

But then he'd sprung his trap. She would never trust him now.

Daron Sutton didn't take a seat, either. He leaned against a chaise that had been pushed to the side of the room. He took out his watch and studied the face as if he had better things to do with his time and was only here, a guest of the Vaughns, lodging and dining at Greenfield, on sufferance.

What did it gain Daron Sutton to poison opinions about Anne?

Unless he wanted to make it impossible that Hew could claim her. Unless he wanted to leave her nothing but Calvin, in line with whatever devil's bargain her brother had made with

Hew's. The very bargain Anne had sought to escape by turning to Hew.

A man who stole his brother's bride was the worst sort of rascal. Little wonder his mother didn't want to allow the idea, much less condone a change in Anne's affections.

But a man who let a beautiful, vulnerable woman fall into the clutches of a rake who wouldn't value her—what was the name for a man who allowed that?

Margaret Griffith seated herself at the spinet and began the musical entertainments with a sepulchral rendition of "Tom Bowling," the lament for a sailor lost at sea. The prickle rose beneath his Hew's collar.

The sentiment of this song made him furious. Of course death was a glorious rest when one's life was rope burns and splinters, sea spray crusting the skin, rum and hardtack rotting the innards. He doubted any tar who'd been impressed into service for poor pay and bad rations, flogged for the slightest infraction, then discharged with no pension when sick or wounded would be remembered for singing mirthful tunes. Miss Griffith wrung every note of pathos she could, and Mrs. Griffith dabbed her handkerchief at one eye as the last notes hung in the room.

Anne listened with still attention, head slightly bent, hands folded in her lap. The veil of her hairpiece floated on a draft of air each time someone near her shifted, revealing the white nape of her neck, delicate and tender. Hew knew the soft skin would smell of meadow flowers. He longed to press a kiss there.

May Powell, not to be outdone, followed with "A Soldier's Adieu," a Dibdin tune Hew recognized and had no doubt was meant for him. Miss Powell had a pretty voice and sang with a slightly melancholy air, accompanying herself creditably on the spinet. When she finished, her eyes sought Hew's, and she blushed a dog-rose pink. Hew suddenly regretted that he'd never had a sister, a friendly and confiding sort of sister, an ally who could offer insight into the inscrutable world of women.

Silence fell as Miss Powell returned to her seat, and Lady Vaughn pointedly did not look at Anne. But Anne rose anyway, her tunic fluttering lightly. She moved toward the spinet, head held high as if she were gliding over water, and settled herself on the bench.

She poised her fingers over the ivory keys, and Hew held his breath. Then a bright, fast, merry tune spilled from her finger-tips, and she broke into the raucous, rousing "The Pedlar," another Dibdin tune. She sang with a broad, rough accent, as if she were a traveling man indeed, and instead of singing "Christmas comes but once a year," she put in "sweethearts come but once a year," like any merry damsel who was accustomed to men bidding for her hand.

Hew worked to hold in laughter. It was a near thing, given the appalled expression on his mother's face, and the shades of amusement, puzzlement, and horror ranging over the faces of the matrons as Anne sang of nymphs and shepherds wooing their loves, love-powders that could make any woman a Venus, and taking pleasure's key to open scenes delicious. She ended with a resounding flourish, and the reedy tones of the spinet echoed through the drawing room as she drew back her hands.

"La," said Lady Vaughn, "that was certainly lively. Miss Griffith, would you play for us again?"

Margaret Griffith came forward with an expression that said she had no notion how to follow Anne's display. She dithered over sheet music, then resolved on "Robin Adair," a popular Irish tune that could not fail to please, being so familiar. She wouldn't try to outdo Anne; she would, instead, make her feel out of place.

Hew observed the faces of the company. The other young men regarded Miss Griffith with polite interest. John Jones watched Anne, his gaze boring into the back of her head as if he were studying each coil of her styled hair, or attempting to see into the thoughts behind her calm, inscrutable façade.

Daron Sutton circled the room, a silver flask in his hand. The swagger of his gait told Hew the man had been drinking steadily since dinner, if not before, and was more than top-heavy. He stood next to Jones and they whispered back and forth for a time.

Then Jones shifted his gaze from Anne, to Hew, back to Anne. And sneered.

The back of Hew's neck prickled in warning. These two were up to mischief. He'd place money on it, and he was not a gambling man.

Succeeding in her turn to the burden of impressing the company with her musical accomplishments and ladylike grace, May Powell placed herself again at the spinet. This time she furnished another popular, familiar Irish air, "Eileen Aroon." She gave the song a wistful quality at odds with the admiring sentiments of the lyrics. Her chaperone's face took on a faraway look, but Lady Vaughn nodded with each measure, smiling with approval. She would wish a wife like May Powell for Hew, he didn't doubt.

When May abandoned the spinet, Anne rose again, though their hostess had expressed no invitation. Hew held his breath in anticipation.

She went to the tall Welsh harp standing beside the spinet and seated herself, pulling the instrument against her left shoulder. The melody she began was simple but rippling with melancholy. And then she began to sing.

Hew supposed it was an Italian aria from some opera he didn't know. He didn't care. His chest broke open, his heart beating painfully open to the air. She was a gorgeous mezzosoprano, her voice rich and velvety, and her voice filled the room, swelling and falling with perfect modulation and control, emotion spilling from every note.

Hew felt once more as if he'd been tied to the mast, skin bare to the elements, but this time the lashes that fell didn't draw blood. These blows landed deeper. He was truly, excruciatingly aware that this woman, with her divine voice and her air of utter self-possession, was a being permanently above his grasp. A celestial entity that he had sullied with his touch, and would sully further if he tried pulling her down to his level.

The last echo of her song lingered in the room, and May Powell stared with awe. "What was that?" she whispered, as if hesitant to break the spell.

Anne shifted the harp back into place. "The song is '*Che faro senza Euridice*,' from the opera *Orfeo ed Euridice* by Gluck. That is the song Orfeo sings when he breaks the taboo to look upon Euridice when he is leading her from the shadows of hell, and so, she dies in his arms."

"A dark subject for a drawing room," Lady Vaughn snapped.

"It is the most beautiful, most haunting expression of love I have ever heard." The Powell aunt spoke up. Her voice was firm, almost masculine in its confidence and authority. "He loves her so desperately he cannot live without her, he defies death itself to reclaim her, and then by his own eagerness and desperation loses her again. What tragedy could be more magnificent, more painful?"

Margaret Griffith gritted her teeth and gripped her fan in her fingers.

"So who is the Orfeo this Euridice wants to come carry her off?" John Jones wondered, his voice dripping with disdain. "The brother she's contracted to, or the other?"

Hew saw the blow land in Anne's slight sway, the white hand that tightened around the frame of the harp. The sudden, bleak tightening of her mouth as she caught back the words she wanted to say, because she had no defense, and Jones was the type of man who would only press his attack if she made a protest.

Hew turned on him. "Why would you say that?" His voice was the low growl of approaching thunder, the boil of a coming storm. "Why would you say such a thing?"

Jones widened his eyes, his mouth in that perpetual arrogant smirk. "Honest question. Can't see why brothers would fight over a little nothing," he said.

A nothing. That was what Anne would be reduced to if news of the scandal got out, that she'd broken her betrothal with the nearest man at hand. Those of her own class would judge her harshly. She'd never be welcomed again in these circles she was born to—she'd never be allowed.

She could not have thought this through when she came to his room that night. Hew could free her from Calvin, but there was only one way he could free her from disgrace. And he could not bear for this beautiful creature, who had made one headstrong, independent decision in her life, to spend the rest of her life paying for that choice with the derision of her peers.

Hew stepped forward. The same way he had stepped forward whenever his instructors asked a volunteer from class. The way he had stepped forward when Antoine needed help and hands erecting his new defenses. The way he had stepped forward when his sentence was read before all his men and the next step was to bare his back for the lash.

"I had thought to save our announcement for another time," he said, catching Anne's gaze.

Her eyes widened, and the purse of her lips made her nose stand out, that one bold note in her sweet face, the sign of a character that could not be broken.

But her heart could be, if he didn't do something. "Ought we tell them, my love?" he asked her.

She turned her head slightly like a dove would watch a fox approach from the corner of its eye, pretending innocence. "Now?"

She hadn't quite grasped his intent yet—he could tell from her puzzled expression—but was playing along. His clever girl.

"I think so." He reached her, grasped her hand. Her fingertips were rough and slightly reddened from the imprint of the harp strings, and her palm was warm and dry. Such slender strength in her, he could see that now. She would bear up under rejection, humiliation, being an outcast from the world she knew. But she deserved so much better.

Much better than him. But he was the only line of defense available at the moment. He was the only gun in her arsenal.

"Mother, if you will permit me? You have already given your blessing, I know."

His mother glared at him, striving with every scrap of her will to force him to silence. But she knew what he was doing, and knew the result if she spoke against him here, in her own drawing room, among the most important people of her acquaintance. Winifred Vaughn had not become a knight's lady because she was a fool.

"It is my very great honor to inform you all," Hew said, surveying the various expressions turned upon him—shock and surprise and, in a few cases, furious jealousy— "that Anne Sutton has agreed to become my wife."

A murmur ran through the room. Mrs. Kemeys leaned close to Mrs. Hawkins. Mrs. Griffith turned a betrayed, accusing stare on Lady Vaughn. The Powell chaperone, the aunt or some such, looked at Anne with steady curiosity, but her gaze bore no malice.

"I thought she was to marry your brother," Margaret Griffith burst out. Clearly, she and her mother had harbored hopes of Hew, no doubt encouraged by her ladyship.

"Our family has been in negotiations with the Suttons for quite some time to make an alliance," Hew replied. He curled his fingers around Anne's and tugged her gently so she left the harp and stepped to his side. Her hand fit so naturally in his, fingers intertwined like honeysuckle climbing a fence. She fit at his side, too, as if her curves had been shaped for his body. He could turn his head and brush his mouth across the top of her cheekbone, just beside her ear.

His pulse pounded in his ears. "Calvin was the proposed choice for a while, since I was away," Hew explained to Margaret Griffith, to all the doubters who would debate his worthiness of Anne, his deserving to have her. "But when I returned, we discovered an affection we cannot deny."

May Powell gave a little sigh, as if she found this admission very romantic. Anne clung to Hew's fingers as if she might find anchor in him if a storm of disapproval began, if the strong wind meant to blow her away.

He tightened his grip. He would not let them bend her. He would hold her to him as long as he could.

His mother's guests watched them like spectators at a play they couldn't bring themselves to like. Hew's temples throbbed. Was he making the wrong move after all? Was he binding Anne to a world that would no longer accept her, no matter how much she belonged in it?

"To affection." The voice of David Edwards, the young engineer, cut through the murmurs in the room. "A toast."

"Indeed. A toast." Lady Vaughn summoned a footman and before long, liveried servants were circulating among the guests with glasses of champagne. He doubted his mother had meant to break into her stores that night; champagne was dear, given the import tax, unless his mother was a patron of the free traders like Darch and his ilk. Hew would ask her about it later. For now he focused on Anne, handing her a glass as one of the hired footmen approached them, trying to hold her eyes, seeking her approval for his bold action.

He'd announced, in public, that she was bound to him. He'd slid the bolt home on a betrothal as surely as if he were her jailer in prison. He could bind her to him, but he couldn't make her *choose* him. He couldn't force that.

The tilt to her chin, the elegant and forced serenity with which she accepted congratulations, and the way she avoided looking at Hew told him prison was precisely how she felt about the matter. She looked like a proud rebel who'd felt the iron shackle close about her ankle but meant to go to the gallows with head held high, come what may.

CHAPTER SIXTEEN

The scent of the river at night rose to meet Hew's nose as he walked the landscaped grounds behind Greenfield. Sir Lambert had liked to sit in this park that tamed wild nature into a pleasing vista of sweeping lawns, cultivated shrubbery, and well-spaced trees.

In daylight, the prospect offered the soothing promise of a refuge, a pleasure garden shaped for human enjoyment, no trace of the rugged wilds or barren stretches, rocks and mires, fens and caves that could elsewhere swallow a man. In the light of a near-full moon, with the gravel paths and dewy lawns silver ripples dappled with the deeper shadow of trees, it was a place of magic.

A place where one would expect to see the *ceffyl dŵr* rising from the mist-limned water of the river, the magical horse that sometimes took the shape of a fair young maiden. Or a *nelferch*, one of the beautiful water spirits who would emerge from the water to marry a mortal man, bringing him cattle and gold, until he displeased her and she disappeared back beneath the waters to leave him grieving and lost.

"So you're set on m'sister."

Hew paused at the sound of the slurred voice, then turned with slow deliberation. He'd heard the gravel crunching behind him and expected it was Daron.

Her ladyship's other guests had gone for the night, summoning their carriages and making their way across the countryside by the light of the July moon, the thunder moon as the old farmers called it. Hew couldn't turn off her brother without insulting Anne, and he didn't want to drive Anne away, wanted the exact opposite in fact. But Sutton's lurking slouch, his bleary, sneering gaze, and his hunted, hungry look were grating on Hew's nerves.

He'd seen enough men wearing that look to know what came next. Sutton was a man in trouble, and determined to climb out of his pit over the bodies of others he dragged down with him.

"I've offered to marry her," Hew pointed out.

"Because ye tupped 'er first and was caught at it."

Daron swallowed a belch. Hew wondered where the man had procured the spirits he reeked of; Lady Vaughn no longer kept such liquors in her house. They reminded her too keenly of how liberally Sir Lambert had indulged in drink, and what consequences followed for his family when he did.

"Because I esteem her," Hew replied.

It was the answer he had given to John Jones and Margaret Griffith and all the others who had made sly inquiries that evening, demanding the motivations for his surprise announcement. Anne Sutton had enchanted him. One need only look at her to see the appeal.

Anne wore a mantle of rose on her cheeks as he said this over and over, and she accepted the congratulations, forced or sincere, with a calm, courteous smile and a graceful murmur of thanks. She was the consummate gentlewoman. It was proof he'd done right, acting to salvage her reputation for as long as he could, for as long as the pretense would hold.

Her grace was also the mark of every reason she was too good for Hewitt Vaughn.

Daron shook his head. "Just out to spike yer brother's wheels."

"I do not see how," Hew bit out. "Calvin is not here to insist on a claim. He took off at the first sign she preferred me."

There was still no news of Calvin, no note to their mother, no report from someone who had seen him turn up at a coaching inn or ale house. Where had Calvin gone, and what was he plotting?

"Then ye orter be talking wit me 'bout a marriage." Daron's speech tripped over itself despite his look of concentration, visible even in the half-light.

Hew continued walking. "To ask your permission in the stead of your parents?"

"To talk settlements," Daron said sharply. "What're you offerin 'er?"

Hew whirled back to face the sullen man. "I'm the owner of Greenfield. This land, this house, is mine. Just what did Calvin offer, that I wouldn't be an improvement?"

Daron thought this through. Hew could practically hear the machinery of his mind grinding; drink had not oiled the mechanism. "Calvin said 'ee 'ad all that."

"Well, he doesn't, and he wouldn't, unless he was counting on me turning up dead after Acre."

"Said you hant been heard of fer months," Daron grouched. "Said it was good as 'is."

Hew's blood turned cold, as if he'd been poured full of silver moonlight, icy light instead of blood in his veins. Anne had warned him Calvin had been speculating on gaining Greenfield. Had counted on it.

Counted on Hew's death.

"Sorry to disappoint," Hew said coldly, "but I'm still here."

"And now you wants Anne's money."

"I don't know what you're talking about."

Daron blinked over this. "Then why'd ye offer at all?"

Hew gritted his teeth. *Because she was found in my bed, you slow-top*, he wanted to shout. But he had the sense that, for all his current lack of sobriety, he oughtn't alienate Daron Sutton. The man seemed a fool, but a fool could be cunning when it came to his own preservation.

"Because," Hew added, "I told you. I esteem her."

Daron waved this off, and another rush surged through Hew's veins. Cold rage. Her own brother wasn't looking out for Anne's welfare, negotiating her future happiness. Sutton kept coming back to the money.

"M' parents don've the blunt," Daron clarified. "'S all gone. But Gertrude. Aunt Gertie. Fine lady. She's the gelt. But she's only given it t' Anne."

Hew had already told Daron he wouldn't leave their family in penury; apparently that wasn't enough. "What did Calvin promise that I haven't?" Hew asked.

"I cud stay 'ere. Live here." Daron blinked slowly. "An ee'd set me up fine as a gennelman."

"Calvin invited you to take up residence at Greenfield," Hew clarified. It wouldn't be unheard of for a husband and new wife to offer a home to her unmarried brother. But it would be a decision for the master of the house to approve.

Daron nodded. "Says there's opratunities hereabout. Business opra—business. Make me a rich man. Oper—opportunities," Daron slurred, "as you doan find inland places like Llanfyllin." He squinted his eyes at Hew. "But you doan know the firs thing about 'em. You can't semme up fine."

Another tide of cold surged through Hew. "My brother offered you business opportunities? What kind?"

"Darch." Daron slitted his eyes. "What Darch does. That Jones was talkin' bout it tonight."

"Free trading."

Daron shifted his eyes right, then left. He swayed, as if the movement unbalanced him. "Sssh."

"You are correct," Hew said. "I can't connect you to such opportunities. I cannot condone them. I took an oath to uphold English law. Besides, I see the purpose in taxes. We need a trained military to fight English wars. The Prussians pay their soldiers. The French pay their soldiers."

Britain couldn't defend itself from an invasion with just militia. It needed a navy to protect its ships on the high seas, and it needed an army to keep Britain's enemies from doing things like taking over the Orient and cutting off their access to India and the East.

And it needed to pay those men, both to put themselves in danger, then support their widows when they got themselves maimed or killed in the service of God and country.

Hew had a feeling, if he explained this to Sutton, it wouldn't have an effect, now or at any time when the man was sober. He seemed the type able to cling to a belief in the face of all logic and evidence. And cling, moreover, to a sense of righteous self-preservation above all, no matter who else was hurt in the process of enriching himself.

"So you won'elp me." Daron slitted his eyes.

"I won't condone smuggling, nor any activity that goes against the law. I will help your family through honest means."

"So, live like you." Daron swept a scornful glance up and down Hew's outdated attire. "No fashion. No address. No bit of fun for the side. All business, all march, all law and right and toeing the line. Live pinch penny on the coppers you give me, like a wife."

"Or give you leads on honest businesses to invest in," Hew said. "My solicitor—"

"Damn your eyes." Daron's snarl was sudden, like a feral beast that found itself cornered. "Damn your righteousness. Where's it come from, anyway, a man up for court-martial?"

A band of cold clamped around Hew's throat. "I've been charged with nothing yet."

"Yet." Daron snarled. "But you'll marry m' sister, all on your righteous horse, and take her money. To bribe yourself out of a sentence? Thas why you wan'er? Make m' sister yer whore just to—"

Hew stepped forward. He was taller than Daron, and while the man had a stone or more of flesh on him, Hew was all lean muscle.

"Say that again," Hew said with low, deadly calm. "Call your sister a whore to my face, one more time."

"Thas what you—"

Hew's hand shot out for the other man's throat. Just in time, he clenched his fist on air. He held his knuckles before the man's nose, a warning.

"I have offered your sister my hand. I will defend her honor with my life. And if you keep spreading tales, smearing her reputation, making it so she cannot hold up her head among these people who will be her neighbors, I will call you out. I don't care which you choose, swords or bullets. My money is on me for the field of honor, Sutton."

Daron's sense of self-preservation finally kicked in. His eyes widened. "Yer a madman. No gennelman."

"No," Hew said, pulling his fist back to his side. "There is nothing gentle about me at all."

Daron narrowed his eyes again, his expression of cunning

and hatred visible even in the shadows. Hew tensed his shoulders and let the man walk away. Let Daron think he'd made his point, had the upper hand. Better than starting a brawl with Anne's brother. The lady already had enough reason to accuse him.

Anne. She stood on the set of shallow stairs that led to the verandah of flagged stone that ran along the back of the house, where the French doors let into the gallery and the windows looked into his study. She wore a shawl draped around her gown, and in the silver glow of the moon she was a statue of Greek antiquity, a column of poured light, a lady of the lake dripping magic.

A goddess of old coming to visit her wrath on mortal men.

"What were you speaking of?" she asked Daron, her voice low. Hew heard the music in it and wondered why he hadn't noticed before what a rich, powerful voice she had. He remembered her song, the haunting lament for the lost beloved, the cry for where redemption could be found.

Hew moved toward her. He had been moving toward Anne Sutton his whole life and only just now realized that.

"Tied yer garter but good, haven't you?" Daron said, his voice a grim crack in the shadows. "Chose the close-fisted one to cast yer lot with. The milksop. He'll not raise you nor any of us. All his counters are for Greenfield."

"This is his home. That is his right. It was you and Calvin who planned otherwise."

Her voice was equally cool, but Hew sensed a painful rigidness in the line of her shoulders and spine. She, too, saw where Daron's thoughts went, and he hadn't a care for her.

Daron looked her up and down. "After everything Mum and the pater have done for you. What I've done for you. This is how you repay us."

His words were careful, sharp points that fell clearly, not

slurred in the least. Daron pushed past her, climbing the steps, and Anne's shoulders slumped.

Hew didn't have the right to draw her into his arms. He'd tossed a net over her head like a hunted reedling on the river bank, but that didn't mean she would come to his hand.

"What are you doing out of doors?" Hew asked.

She moved down the gravel path toward him. Moonglow bathed her neck and the artful coils of her hair. She looked made of spun sugar, impossibly sweet, and when she stopped before him and tilted back her head, her eyes were silver pools of light.

"What am I doing? The same thing you are, I suppose."

He traced a finger over the gloved knuckles clutched at her bosom, holding her shawl together. She smelled of night flowers, of fancies that rode to earth on showers of stars.

"I've been wandering the paths in the moonlight, waiting for a magical woman to rise from the mist over the Ebbw and come to me." Hew glanced at the stars wheeling above their heads. "Or descend on a spill of starlight, though one hears less about those."

The corners of her mouth perked up. Her smile wavered when a thump behind her said Daron had slammed his way into the house, but she held his gaze.

"Don't be absurd," she said. But she allowed him to slip his fingers beneath her palm and lift her hand.

"I am Orfeo, searching for my Euridice," he said.

He wasn't customarily fanciful; the moonlight must have touched his head. Or the sight of her, every pure and astonishing thing that he would never, with his bloody, soiled hands, be allowed to touch, to hold.

"Now you make fun."

He tugged lightly, coaxing her to walk beside him. "I would never mock such beauty. I had no notion you could sing like that. You made my mother speechless for five entire minutes. She adores fine music."

"I hardly think I will win her over by singing."

"I think you could win anyone by your singing," Hew said. "Like the sirens that lured Odysseus. You have certainly captured me."

The enchanting corners of her mouth pressed into a solid line. "You made it sound as if you'd won a prize."

He tucked her hand beneath his arm, the way he had pulled her to his side in the drawing room. It felt right to have her close. Necessary.

He'd sprung a trap on her again, this time before all his mother's friends—the people that, should she live at Greenfield, would become her friends, her community, her neighborhood.

"Your brother forced my hand," Hew said quietly. "He was spreading tales that you were found in my bed. My mother had tried to keep it a secret, so you could be free of me, I suppose. But John Jones heard, and what he discovers, he will make sure everyone knows about in the span of an hour."

"You could have refused me," she said. "Let me twist on the wind. Hang myself with my own rope."

"I told you I would not refuse you. You must be the one to jilt me." He tried to keep the growl out of his tone.

"Now?"

"Take what time you need. To decide what you want." He was doing it, keeping his voice level, the register of logic and reason, not howling need. "Only, where will you go? And who will support you?"

"I suppose it is ridiculous to think I might support myself."

"How?" He musn't let his voice go sharp, reveal his hurt at the thought of her leaving. Weakness was despicable in any man, but more so in a man of the military, a man who was supposed to be made of iron and powder, not bone and blood.

She stopped in the pathway. The look she turned to him was so full of dismay, of appeal, that again he felt the overwhelming urge to pull her to him, wrap her in his arms as if he could be her shelter, her defense.

"I don't know," she said. "And I hate that I am so helpless. I hate that I know nothing. Of how to take care of myself, of how to—" She stopped, bit her lip, and a shadow moved over her face, a blush touched by moonlight. "I know nothing of how to be alone, and nothing of how to be married. I know *nothing*. Except how to sing."

"That is no small thing."

This despair came from the thought of being married to him. Hew tried to force back the haze that laced his vision, that primal need to grab her, hold her, keep her. The beast in him wanted to weigh her down, chain her at wrist and ankle so she couldn't escape.

"Will it earn me my supper? Will it earn me anything?"

"I suppose this is the sign that you are well cared for," Hew said slowly. "That you are loved. Your family has protected you. Sheltered you."

"Bartered me," she said bitterly. "And much good it has done them, for how far my value has fallen."

Hew felt that phantom shiver down his back, the memory of the cat-o'-nine-tails sinking its hooked barbs into his back, tearing flesh. If he held her, kept her, she would be disgraced by the marriage. Chained to a man who'd been court-martialed, if he wasn't shot for treason first.

She would hate him for it.

"Your brother would rather Calvin for you. He thinks I am the worse bet."

She pulled her lip between her teeth. "My brother is showing himself a fool. He has already squandered my dowry. I fear he will make a worse mess for himself, trying to find ways to support himself. Dishonest means."

Heartbreak laced her voice, bare as a vein of ore in the mountain. Hew squeezed her hand. She was slender and warm.

"I will try to advise him. He should not be involved with Darch."

"I fear he will not take advice. He is—" She caught herself. Such admirable self-control the woman had. Such unruffled calm, a will of iron, for all that she looked soft as silk. "He is not the brother who raised me," she said, something forlorn in her voice. "Not the brother I loved. That brother would never try to sell me. He would have given me the moon."

Hew wanted to sink his fist into Daron Sutton's sulky face. He ought to have given his sister the moon. She deserved it.

Hew would give it her, if he could.

"My brother has changed as well," Hew said, walking along the path beside her. She moved like a whisper at his side, as if she were indeed made of mist and moonlight. "Calvin was always a selfish little bastard, even when we were small. He'd cheat when you weren't looking. He'd cheat if you were. He always wanted to be the favorite. He was, with our mother, and often with our father, too. But I never thought he could become —" He hesitated. "I'd hoped reaching manhood would teach him better."

"You ought to have been your father's favorite." Anne glanced his way. "You are the eldest. The heir."

"One would think that the way of things, wouldn't one? But I was a disappointment."

"A military man? A hero, a disappointment?"

"When I was supposed to stay and take up the reins at Greenfield, yes. My father wanted a John Jones Junior." There was the bitterness in his own voice, bare as a blade. "A rousing Corinthian who could ride to the hunt, take any fence, lose his money on a horse or a cock or the card table with a jaunty grin. I liked to save my money to buy things I wanted. I liked to build things, not squander or play. I was too serious, too somber. He preferred Calvin's company to mine, and so did our mother, to please him."

Anne turned toward him, a whisper of her alluring scent rising from her skirts, weaving into his brain. He feared she could peer through his wooden face to the memories that were surfacing, the boy scorned by his father, the young man who again and again watched Sir Lambert walk from the room, shaking his head and muttering that he should be cursed with a tradesman's son and not a gentleman. His father's back turned toward him, always.

That was reason enough to stay away for the funeral and after, doing estate business with the solicitor by mail at Southampton. Too cowardly to return to Greenfield one more time, knowing he would never redeem himself, never be good enough to earn his father's approval, no matter what he built, no matter what cities or islands or ships he saved, no matter how many decorations he received. He wasn't the son his father wanted. He was a gunner, a builder, a soldier, a captain of men, but he wasn't a gentleman of culture and leisure, not now, not ever.

Anne lifted a hand and traced the hair at Hew's temple, where the brown had turned silver during his illness in prison. Her fingertip was a bolt of lightning touching earth. His heart tripped in its beat.

"I wish I had known." Her voice was a whisper, yet it filled his senses, weaving into his mind like a spell. "All those years ago, when my parents first chose you." He almost didn't hear the next words; they might have been conjured in his mind, a sigh made of starlight. "I wish I might have known you then."

"Anne." The need overpowered him; he was helpless before

it, like a tide that slammed ships toward the rocks, throwing them to their doom. He could no more hold back from kissing her than he could turn away the lightning her touch roused in him.

She placed a hand on his chest, stopping him as he lowered his head. "I know you did this for me," she said quietly, and her voice trembled, but not with the controlled emotion she had shown while singing. The words tumbled out of her, as if she same tide were tossing her. "I trapped *you*. I never meant it—I didn't think—"

She clenched her teeth on her lip, drew in a short breath, and struggled on. "Of course you would offer for me, because that is your nature. I had thought you lacked honor, and I was wrong. Honor was what drove you at Acre, was it not? You did what was right, what was necessary ... and it caused you nothing but trouble."

Trapped. The word echoed in his mind, an accusation. He was confining her. She'd offered him an opportunity he'd never dreamed—

"I do not want to be trouble for you," she said, her voice breaking on the last words, and the tide surged, blotting out every thought.

"Anne." There was only need for her, the desperate desire to touch her, the wish to show her what he felt. The need to tell her she was beautiful, she was perfect, she was his dream of a woman made flesh, and if he were to be skewered through the heart for kissing what he could not have, he would kiss her anyway.

Her lips were cool and soft and fit against his perfectly. She lifted to his mouth like a nightflower coaxed by the moonlight to unfurl its petals. He meant to seduce, to entice her to him, but she offered no barrier, no reserve, merely slipped open her lips, and the small, pleading sound from the back of her throat as his mouth came down on hers shot through him like an elf bolt. He plunged his tongue inside her mouth as if he were taking a fence and she met him, bold and sure, her fingers digging into his forearms as if she were using him to hold herself upright. She tasted of lemon and vanilla and smelled like cardamom, like all the exotic spices of the world, and every conscious thought shot out of his mind like a covey of pheasants taking flight.

There was only the gravel beneath their feet and the night air dancing along his fevered skin, along his hands where he'd clamped them to the side of her face to hold her and kiss her, and the heat from her body made him want to sink and dissolve and disappear, lose himself in her forever. As if in union with her, he could be purified. As if she were the last rock in a drowning world and if he stretched himself out upon her, he could be saved.

"*Anne.*" Her name was a summons, an incantation, a plea. She swayed toward him, melting in surrender, and he lowered one arm to clamp around her, to catch her back and haul her against him, against the hard, aching length of his body. He couldn't stop the growl when she came in full contact with him, when her sweet yielding softness melded against him and hot need roared to life.

He froze, sure she'd pull away. An innocent woman, a graceful roe in the field, and he was rutting against her like a buck in heat. He'd deserve if she broke the spell. He'd deserve if she pulled away and left him hard and aching for her, without release.

She moaned again. Slipped her arms around his back, gripping his coat. Then she shifted ever so slightly, bending her knee and lifting it toward his hip so that the rutting part of him slid not into her belly but into the sweet arch between her legs, and he knew by the cant of her hips that she had placed herself precisely where she wanted to be, that she felt the same hot need and he could answer it. With another feral growl he pulled her hard against him, plunging against her, the hard shaft in his breeches sliding the soft muslin of her gown between her legs, and her soft cry told him he'd struck true.

He didn't know how he held her, how he kept them both from falling, but as they stood on the gravel path beneath the moonlit trees, with her beautiful body wrapped around his, he pressed between her legs and knew he was pleasing her with his body by the way she trembled and whimpered, by the way her hands dug into the thick scars of his back, by the way her breath fluttered against his mouth as he kept kissing her, kissing his Anne, telling her in the only way he knew how that she was beautiful, so soft and brilliant and beautiful, she made him mad with desire. He had never seen or felt anything more perfect and if he died of pleasure bringing her to her peak, then he would count the sacrifice well worth his life.

She gave a soft cry, her fingers closing convulsively, and he froze, terrified he had hurt her.

"Stop?" he asked raggedly, lifting his mouth from her.

"Hew." She buried her face in his neck, her lips touching his throat above his cravat.

"I'm not—I oughtn't—we ..."

"Don't stop," he said, his voice grating like the gravel beneath his boots. "Touch me. Take your pleasure, Anne."

If he could only have her, hold her. If there were some way other than words he could bind her to him. If he could make her *want* him, even only for this.

She sagged against him, and he shifted his grip, one arm around her lower back to hold her against him, then slipped his hand beneath her knee, hitching her closer. He almost buckled and fell as she moved, pressing her sweet, soft self against his cock, the movement timid at first, then wanton, urgent. She rode him to her pleasure, and he felt by her trembling and the softs pants of her breath when the tension built in her, when it came to the breaking point, and when she broke, spasming against him, holding on to him for dear life while the great wave lifted and shook her.

It was the most beautiful thing he'd beheld in his life.

He couldn't have stopped himself if he wanted to—the feel of Anne, his beautiful Anne, finding pleasure in his arms was too much for a mortal man. Hew let himself spill in his breeches and panted at the hard, sharp relief of it, the temporary reprieve from madness.

"Oh," Anne breathed against his neck. She pulled back her leg and he released her knee, setting her carefully back to earth. Slowly, the world stopped spinning, righted itself, and stillness descended. "Oh," she said again.

He rested his forehead on the top of her head as she pressed her face against his neck. "Oh," he agreed, relishing the way she melted against him. As if he were all she wanted.

As if he could bind her to him with this, against her will and better judgment if he must.

The purr of a nightjar broke the silence, punctuated by a few pleased chirps. Hew smiled. It was exactly how he felt. Anne, in his arms, soft and tousled and pleasured. Pleased by him. With him.

"Hew, I ..." She burrowed against him, her shoulders tensing. He couldn't bear for her to explain or apologize. Couldn't bear for her to feel ashamed of her wantonness, her greedy demand, when it meant so much to him that she should lose herself in his arms.

"Ssh," he whispered into the silk of her hair. "It is just pleasure. Let it be. It is good."

"Oh. Just pleasure." She stepped away, releasing him. "Yes. I-I must go."

"You needn't." His voice cracked. He'd forgotten how to

form words. "Jilt me yet," he managed. "There is time." He wanted to hold her as long as he could.

But she drew back, and he focused all his will on releasing his fingers, lifting his hands. A nearly impossible task, when everything in him wanted to haul her back against him, carry her inside to his bed, and claim her fully. She was his. *His.*

She hurried away, the delicate embroidery on the hem of her white muslin gown sweeping along the path as if her feet didn't touch earth. He watched the sway of her hips and the straight, proud line of her back. That lithe, lissome body was imprinted on his own, a hot outline against the cold air rushing in around him. Off she went, the water sprite returning to her element, the fairy creature leaving the mortal she'd seduced and captured and ruined.

A few steps from the terrace, she turned to face him. She stood under a linden tree, her expression in shadow as if she were dissolving already, a dream he was never meant to have.

"I cannot do it, Hew," she said in a low, trembling voice. "I do not want to live a lie."

Then she turned and swept up the steps, crossing the verandah, slipping into the house as silent as a wraith, as if he had not held and kissed her and revealed himself to her. As if she had not just torn his heart from his chest and borne it off to keep it always, a hollow and worthless prize.

CHAPTER SEVENTEEN

Evidently, the new Anne was a complete, wanton hussy.

She chose her gowns with the intent to allure. She'd guessed the scarlet-tinged gown with its sheer tunic would set her apart with its vaguely Grecian outlines, and it had.

Instead of asking polite questions meant to draw her companions into conversation, the new Anne tested the impact of an interested smile or a gently teasing question. Not on the young men beside her, who were eager to flatter, but on the straight-backed, somber master of the house, who glowered down the table from his high seat and looked impossible to please.

Which made a smile, a softening, an amused glance from him more precious than gold.

When a good girl would be in her chamber, reading sermons and saying her prayers, the new Anne sought out men in shadowed gardens. The new Anne kissed that somber, brooding master in the moonlight. The new Anne threw herself into his arms and twined her limbs around his body, rubbing against him like a cat that had chosen its mate.

She was glad there were no other drivers on the road to perceive the blush that burned her cheeks as she turned through Bassaleg toward Newport. She'd abandoned all sense of decorum and modesty. She'd fallen into the planetary pull that was Hewitt Vaughn, seduced by his blue eyes, his straight-lipped mouth, the way his features animated when he spoke about locks and bridges and wharves. The way he looked at her as if she were the centerpiece of a feast he'd give his soul to be invited to.

The way he kissed her as if the world would end when he stopped.

He had told her to decide what she wanted. She was afraid what she wanted might be *him*.

And if everything else she'd longed for had turned to dust in her mouth, why would this be any different?

There was no one in the stable yard of St. Sefin's. Anne unhitched the pony cart and let the horse into the grassy paddock holding the goat, remembering to check that the trough held water, and somewhat surprised to accomplish all these things herself. Not that the water mattered; the iron sky that had been lowering all morning finally opened and released its first windy spatters of rain as she heaved the bar of the paddock back in place, again, all by herself. One hand on her hat and the other holding her pelisse to her neck, Anne ducked into the kitchens, which were customarily warm, quiet, and welcoming.

The kitchens were a damp, steaming, rowdy mess.

Quarreling voices drifted from the scullery, the widows in a brangle about something, their words floating out on the acrid odor of lye. The kettle screamed on the hob, and something in the oven was burning. Dovey wasn't in evidence, nor Cerys, but Tomos was, sitting on a stool in a corner, holding his hand to his chest and sobbing.

Anne went to him first and laid a hand on his shoulder. "Tomos, what is it?"

"Cyw," the boy blubbered and held out his pudgy hand. A red triangular mark stood out on the flesh between finger and thumb.

"Oh, dear one, did your chick take a fit and bite you? Poor, poor boy."

She looked around for a way to distract and soothe him. What had Pym always done when Anne was in a fret? She spotted a jar of licorice sticks on a high shelf and pulled it down. "Here, have a licorice." Soothed the stomach and any upset, Anne had found for herself, and the same was true for Tomos. He popped an end of the stick into his mouth, and instantly the tears cleared.

"Hiya, I wants one of those." Ifor stamped in from a storeroom, a small cask beneath his arm that he plunked on the wooden table. "Licorice, is it, Miss Anne?"

Anne laid a stick in his outstretched palm. "Hello, Ifor. Do you know where I can find bandages? Tomos has a little nip on his hand."

Ifor nodded and squatted next to Tomos, patting the other boy's arm. "Cyw is loose in the church," he reported. "Lodged under a pew and won't come out. Cerys is trying to lure her with grain. Told me to go out and dig up a worm, which I might at that. Don't cry, Tomos, Cyw just took a fright when Cerys was playing her trick on the vicar. She'll come out when she's done with her sulk, Cyw and Cerys both."

He nodded toward Anne. "Bandages in the still room, Miss Anne, second shelf above the table, basket to your left."

"Thank you." Anne swept up a handful of the rags for handling hot things and pulled the kettle off the hob, silencing the scream. "Whose tea?"

"Something for the lady in the infirmary, or the babe,

mayhap? Miss Dovey is seeing to her now, but she don't know the herbs. There's something gone wrong, I dunno what, and the widows can't settle what to do." Ifor tilted his head toward the voices in the scullery, not raised in anger, but sharp with concern.

Anne pulled the bread pan from the oven and regarded the dark crust. "Either it's burned or this is bara brith," she said.

Ifor sniffed, then chuckled. "Bara brith. Missus Evans don't make it quite like Miss Gwen did, but none of us is to tell her that. Are we, Tomos?" He turned with a small frown to the boy beside him.

"Cyw." Tomos shook his head mournfully, cradling his bitten hand against his chest.

"Yes, you're next, Tomos." Anne set the bread out to cool, then went into what she hoped was the stillroom, a place she'd seen Gwen duck in and out of on her visits. The bandages were right where Ifor predicted, beside a jar of sweet-smelling salve. Anne brought out both, pulled up a chair, and set to the business of wrapping Tomos's hand. She'd never tended an injury in her life, but she hoped the application of a bandage would resolve whatever hurt to his hand, and his pride, the boy had sustained from his pet.

She was right. With a smile of relief, Tomos admired his bandage. "*Hapus*," he pronounced.

"Hapus?" Anne looked to Ifor.

"Happy." Ifor gave Tomos's arm one last pat. "Your world is white now, all right? Hold, I hear Evans about. He'll want a hand with that calf."

"Calf?" Anne asked just as Dovey's husband came into the room.

"Trett at the King's Head bred his milker, but now he wants her weaned so he can have his milk back." Evans leaned on his crutch, taking in the room at a glance. "I told him we could graze the calf here for a time, Ifor, but he's to share the milk with us as he might. Would you like cow's milk with your tea, Tomos, instead of goat?"

"*Buwch?*" Tomos blinked away the last of his tears, a grin forming.

"I know that one!" Anne exclaimed. "It means cow."

Evans smiled. "We'll make a Welshwoman of you yet, Miss Sutton. And you might slice up that bara brith if you wish."

"I—" she started to demur. She hadn't cooked it, didn't know its purpose, what if she did something wrong? She was only a guest.

She bit back the protest. The new Anne wasn't an ornament. She wasn't useless. She *acted*.

"I shall, at that." Anne ruffled through drawers until she found the knife for slicing bread. The loaf fell open, releasing a warm yeasty smell, showing the dark spots of currants that had been soaked overnight in tea. She added a scoop of salted butter that Widow Jones made herself and pushed the plate across the table to Evans.

He picked it up with his one hand, nodded, and took a bite. He had strong teeth, all intact, and muscles flexed in his forearm, showing where his sleeve had been rolled back. He wore a simple waistcoat and a cravat looped around his neck, which would be undress in any other scenario, but for some reason his workman's attire, and his missing arm, didn't upset Anne as they had before. Now that she looked, Evans was an attractive man. The brown hair falling slightly into his eyes held traces of silver, much like Hew's, and the lines carved around his eyes and mouth suggested a man of strong spirit who had endured much.

Like Hew.

"Did you know Hewitt before he left?" Anne asked, slicing bread for the boys. "Since you both—well, I suppose you might not have." Hew was in the Royal Artillery, and Evans had lost his arm in service with the Royal Navy, she'd heard.

"The captain? He'd already commissioned as an officer when I arrived, shipped out soon after," Evan answered. "Came back once or twice to see his mother, but didn't have business at St. Sefin's. I think Gwen harped for them on his visit. Her ladyship had a festival day. Hewitt was always her favorite, she made no bones about it. But the lad didn't return for his own father's funeral, and we thought that odd, we did."

Ifor stretched out his legs, balancing his plate on his belly as he savored his treat. Tomos, watching him, did the same, injured hand forgotten.

"No one as much mourned Sir Lambert, did they," Ifor remarked.

Evans nodded. "That Calvin is cast in the same mold, one as—" He caught himself, seeming to recollect that Anne was promised to Calvin and what he said next wouldn't be wise. "Well. You'd know him better than I, perhaps."

Anne shook his head. "Calvin wants to marry me for a dowry that doesn't exist, and Hew—Captain Vaughn—has offered to save me from scandal." Her cheeks heated at her own admission—why was she confiding in this man, this utter stranger? "But I know so little about what kind of man he is," she concluded.

Other than that he was good, and strong, and cast of honor to his core. Fiercely intelligent, fiercely kind, a lover of fine music as much as his mother, and a man who could not stand to watch a gentlewoman be shamed in his home. And so he had acted as if they were in love, as if he were the besotted bridegroom in truth, and she had gone mad with a fever and threw herself into his arms like the shameless hussy New Anne had become. Begging for him to hold her, choose her, *want* her. Love her.

The imprint of his body, the burn of his lips, the grip of his arms about her, holding her up, she could erase none of that from her senses now. He was pressed upon her like a seal. He had said it was just pleasure. Not something more.

The gossip that Hewitt had stood up before all his mother's guests and claimed Anne would make the rounds of the country houses today as fast as morning calls could be paid. All it meant was that Anne had an even less clear idea what she must do.

"The vicar'll know more of Captain Vaughn, should you ask him," Evans said. "Stanley knows the great families hereabouts and reads the English papers besides. But I don't think the Captain's a bit like his brother. Saw him tend his mother at the wedding breakfast. Read how he beat the French back from Acre, then got himself thrown in prison for it. Dovey, that's my missus, she told me Hewitt made the captains of the ships he owns stop trading in slaves. He'll carry only honest cargo."

This was confirmation of what Anne already gleaned for herself. The man she'd trapped into offering for her was a moral man, one with strong beliefs about fair treatment and just works. Not a dirty dish, like his brother or hers, and not a man who would exploit others, like his brother. And hers.

Anne pinched off a bit of bara brith for herself and nibbled on it. The bread was surprisingly tasty.

She desired Hewitt, and he desired her. They could marry and pretend they loved, save face with the world with that lie.

But she didn't want to live a lie. That was what she'd wanted to tell him, but with him standing there, as splendid as a god striding over the land he commanded, his hair rumpled from her hands running through it—she hadn't found it possible to speak.

Because he might say no. The answer might be *pas de tout*, as everything had been of late, for her. And what would she do with herself then?

"Here now, my love." Evans straightened as Dovey charged into the room, her arms full of bed linens. "That's a full load ye have."

He stretched out a hand to take part of her burden, leaning on his crutch. The white linens bore the dark crimson and rust of bloodstains, old and new. Dovey curled into the crook of his arm.

"I can't stop the bleeding," she said, her voice muffled against his shoulder. Her body trembled with distress. Anne had never seen Dovey other than sleek and perfectly put together, as if she were dresser to a duchess and not making do in a falling-down priory on the edge of the civilized world. "I don't know what to do."

"Shh, my love, my little bird. You've done all that you can and more. You're an angel, that you are. Did you call for Mrs. Lambe?"

"Aye, Ifor went to ask after her this morning. She said she'd come, didn't she, Ifor?" Dovey raised her head, blinking tears from her large, lovely brown eyes, and her gaze fell on Anne. Then Ifor with his plate, and Tomos beside him licking his fingers, then the largely demolished loaf of bara brith.

"Aye, said she was for looking in on Mrs. Gossett, then'd come here straight away." Ifor popped the last bite of bread into his mouth. "Miss Sutton saw to Tomos's hand."

"Did she. And the bread. Did I hear the kettle?"

"I stopped it but didn't know what you wished," Anne said, gesturing toward the hob. "Shall I start tea?"

Dovey let her husband take the soiled linens from her and rubbed her eyes. "I don't know. I'm so tired I can't hook two thoughts together. Do I give her yarrow to stop bleeding, or will that bring it on? Was it blackberry tea or raspberry?" She glanced toward a door leading deeper into the priory. "Where is Cerys?"

"Rounding up a chicken in the church, I believe," Anne said, since Ifor had his mouth full.

One corner of Dovey's full mouth hitched up in a crooked smile. "Did I ever imagine I'd be here," she said, looking around her as if momentarily bewildered. "Walking over the shades of dead sisters. With fowl loose in the sacristy and two hens quarreling in the scullery." She shook her head. "They'll just have scrubbed the stains out of the last batch of linens."

She leaned into Evans and the nest of his arms, and his hand stole around to press her shoulder toward him. He turned his head and printed a kiss on her forehead. Dovey's shoulders slumped in a quiet exhale as she drew strength from her husband. There was something so tender in his gesture, so protective, and at the same time, the flex of muscle in his lean cheek as Evans kissed his wife made Anne's stomach jump with impossible yearning.

Desire wasn't enough. What she wanted was *this*. A man whose arms would hold and bear her up when she was sinking. A man who would stir in her the devotion that shone in Dovey's eyes as she lifted her head to look at her husband.

He pressed another kiss to her temple, then the side of her mouth. "You need rest, my love," he murmured. "You were up all night."

Dovey sighed and straightened, pulling herself from his embrace with clear reluctance. "I'll rest when she's better." She ran her hands over her hair. "Miss Sutton, might I have some of your bara brith?"

"I am quite sure 'tis *your* bara brith, Mrs. Evans," Anne said self-consciously, picking up the knife. But the gentle request made her stomach flip again in that odd fashion.

They all had folded her in with them like spiced currants in the bread, giving her a place in their community. This community that, to Anne's mother and Lady Vaughn and perhaps all the other well-bred women at Greenfield last night, would be considered one step above stable muck in quality. And Anne was honored—*thrilled*—to be accepted here.

One of the merry outcasts of St. Sefin's. At last, she had found a world where she belonged.

The door to the yard flew open and heavy footsteps tramped down the short hall. Eilian stepped into the kitchen, pulling off her cap and shaking raindrops from her hair.

"Throwing rain out there, it is," she said. "A *glaw bras*, I call it. Big fat plops of it."

"The *glaw gochel*, my knees say. The heavy rain." The older widow, the crone they called Mother Morris, hobbled out of the stillroom and, with an impatient yank, took the soiled pile of linens from Evans. "The little mother's a-bleeding still and we can't seem as to stop it," she announced with no other greeting, though she gave a curt nod upon spotting Anne.

"The blackberry tea?" Eilian asked. "Cerys was gathering leaves for me."

"I started the water." Dovey looked to the hob, where the kettle sat quietly steaming.

Anne picked up the green stems laid along the worktable. "These?"

Widow Jones emerged from the scullery, wiping her hands on the plaid shawl she wore tied at her waist. "Not enough," she said. "We need horsetail."

"Best as a powder." Eilian laid her hat on a small side table. "Have you any?"

Dovey worked her fingers at her temple, attempting to relieve a headache. Evans rubbed circles on her back, and again, his touch seemed to give his wife strength and ease. "I can't recall," Dovey said.

"I'll need fresh nettle, lots of it," Eilian said, then glanced around. "Where's my *pwt*?"

"In the church with the vicar," Ifor reported. "Tomos and I can fetch your nettles, Miss Lambe. Miss Sutton fixed Tomos's hand right good."

Tomos held up his bandaged hand. "Cyw," he explained.

Eilian gave Anne a curious smile, welcoming, but adulterated with something else, a restraint Anne didn't expect. "Survived the do at Greenfield, did you?"

Anne fumbled with the brambles. "You heard?"

"The boy as delivered our morning bread came back with some stories. A rival for Rosemond Mountain at Greenfield last night, and fair Rosemond's the best singer on the English stage, they say."

Anne felt her cheeks burn. "I am not nearly a Rosemond Mountain."

"And you spurred Hew—Captain Vaughn into making a declaration, then and there." Eilian moved to the worktable beside Anne and began stripping leaves from brambles, far more efficiently than Anne. "The most romantic thing in Newport in a decade, according to Mrs. Jones, who stayed home with the headache. One Mr. John Jones called on his mother for breakfast, and she and his sister heard all." Eilian slanted a sidewise glance at Anne. "You'll say yes, then?"

Anne pricked her finger on a bramble and puffed out a quiet curse. Being around this company, their ease and banter, their lack of affectation, made her lose the strict decorum she'd been trained to uphold. "I'm not certain." She let her hands rest on the table, trying to still their trembling.

She wished she could confess all: how much she wanted Hew. How much she wanted, at all the wrong times, for this something between them to be *real*.

Eilian observed Anne's discomfiture and changed tack. "Mrs. Evans, are you for nettles, too? We'll need a great many. The juice must be fresh, not dried."

Anne pulled her gloves out of her pocket, craving a reprieve from Eilian's inquisition. If the news were making the rounds indeed, then she was signed over to Hew already. This wasn't a family agreement, as she'd had with Calvin, but a public pronouncement as good as reading the banns.

Jilting him, after this, would be so much harder.

"I'll help."

"Bring a hat." Dovey held out a straw hat with a wide, deep brim. "That sweet cap is like to melt in a *glaw gochel*."

The hard, splattering raindrops had pulled back to a mizzle as the two women stepped outside. Dovey led Anne with confidence to the edge of the pasture, beyond the paddock with the animals, where stands of nettles grew in profusion, their deep green leaves gleaming with fat drops of rain. Along down the row, Tomos and Ifor set to work, Ifor running his hands along the plants and Tomos occasionally tipping the basket at a dangerous angle as he reached for a likely-looking leaf.

"I've heard from Gwen," Dovey said without preamble as they began to gather nettle leaves. "She asked about you."

"Asked what?" Anne's conscience pricked her. She could have written to Gwen, in care of the Castle Penrydd, but she hadn't thought of her friend in days.

"How you were going on. How we were treating you. If you'd managed to get free of Calvin Vaughn."

"I've managed." Anne wondered what her old friend would say of the methods Anne had chosen, throwing herself into the arms of the better catch—though hadn't Gwen done the same, when a viscount came her way?

But this was different. Gwen had fallen in love. She knew the man she married, knew who he was without the lordship and the properties and the robes of state.

Anne knew so little of the man whose neck she'd settled her noose around. Oh, she knew his character; he was deep and clear as a well of pure water, that she and anyone could see. He was strong and stubborn and he wore a quiet confidence that came from his own accomplishments, not his birth.

And he kissed like a fallen angel.

"What will you tell Gwen?" Anne asked.

"What ought I tell her?" Dovey replied. She glanced up, then away, and Anne felt that quick gaze like a pinprick on her skin. This Dovey had become Gwen's closest friend, taking Anne's place. Taking more than Anne's place, for the Gwen Anne knew had been a kept girl, practicing her harp and her Greek letters with the tutor, buying ribbons in the Llanfyllin shop, perching on the pew beside Anne each Sunday sharing a prayer book. Blushing and sparkling each time Daron Sutton teased her.

The Gwen Anne found at St. Sefin's had become a woman, honed by fate and fire. She knew passion and pain and despair and abandonment, and she'd forged friendships deeper and stronger than she'd ever felt with Anne. Gwen had saved lives and healed spirits. She and Dovey took in Ifor and Tomos, gave the widows a place to stay, took in a grieving widow about to give birth and braved whatever the councilmen might say about harboring a pregnant woman who had no man.

Gwen had lived and grown and learned in the years they'd been parted, and Anne had merely trod the same shadowed rooms, having the same conversations with the same friends, watching suitors fall away one by one as her dowry diminished. She'd been waiting for marriage, for her deep and true life to begin, to make that sacred passage into womanhood.

And now here she was, with nothing to call her own, not even the scraps of her reputation. No *life*.

"Did Gwen ever speak of me?" Anne pulled handfuls of nettle leaves from the stalks, stuffing her basket. The green left streaks on her dainty gloves that would likely never scrub out.

She'd need thicker gloves for this gardening work. "Did she speak of her time in Llanfyllin at all?"

Dovey shook her head, the bow beneath her neck fluttering where she'd tied a hat over her coils of hair. "She never said a word. I had no notion where she'd come from, her people— nothing of that. I hadn't known she had a babe until we took in Mathry."

Anne swallowed hard. Daron never spoke of the child he'd fathered, the child who had not lived. Anne, to her shame, had thought it at first a relief when she'd learned the babe had not survived birth. She'd thought Daron and Gwen could start fresh. Their love could reknit them like a grafted plant, and the fruit they bore would be strong this time for the sanctioned union.

Fool that she was. Marriage couldn't sanctify a union foul at the root. Daron had never given a thought to that child, or Gwen, until he saw the letter saying Gwen's father had died rich and left her his lands and mines.

Anne's father would die destitute and leave Daron a burdened estate and Anne nothing. It would look as if she had trapped Hewitt Vaughn to secure her own position, to make herself safe with a gentleman who had a home and pin money to offer her.

And such would be the foundation of their marriage: her desperation, and his honor. Thin soil for love to grow in, to be sure.

"I thought she would be happy with my brother," Anne blurted as she tore another handful of nettle leaves free.

Dovey lifted her brows. She was an intelligent woman, quick of mind. She knew precisely what Anne meant.

"Did you now?"

"I didn't know his character," Anne said. "I hadn't seen ... or perhaps I refused to see?" She shook her head. A small, cold drop of rain rolled down the back of her neck. Setting foot in Newport had changed her, started breaking apart her belief in the world and showing her something new.

"I had thought he would come to save her. Not cause her more distress."

Dovey simply shrugged. "Water under the bridge now, that is. She's Lady Penrydd, and she'll have her coronation robes with her bars of ermine and her three-and-a-quarter-foot train." Dovey snorted, showing what she thought of the regalia. "Your brother cannot touch her."

No, but he could still touch Anne. Could still hurt her.

As if she caught the thought, Dovey looked full in Anne's face. "But you were kidnapped by the Black Hound too. The viscountesses thought they would never recover. How did you?"

Anne offered a rueful smile, recalling how Prunella had treated her nerves with bracing glasses of Canary wine, insisting Anne join her. Those fond confidences with the young dowager viscountess had gone a fair way toward helping Anne ignore her brother's betrayal.

She wondered where Prunella, the Dowager Viscountess Penrydd was now. If she were holding to her breezy statement that she might never marry again. As Penrydd was likely to provide the jointure she was due, no doubt Prunella could live comfortably as an independent woman, keeping her own home, her own company.

Anne couldn't conceive of such freedom.

"I still dream of it sometimes," she confessed. "Of that horrible, huge man who told me he had my brother, and I must bring Gwen to the ship or Daron would die." She shuddered. "And the small man with him who told me what the Black Hound had done—who else he had killed. I still think of my fear. And how Gwen poisoned his drink so we might escape." She tried to laugh, shrugging off the claws of memory that wanted to dig in and shred her. "Sometimes I think I still smell Penrydd's dung bombs in my hair. And your Evans helped make them, did he not?"

Dovey smiled, and was there a touch of smugness to that smile? She was a woman secure in the knowledge that she was loved, and loved by a good and faithful man. A rare enough thing in this world, from what Anne had seen.

"He's a hand, my Evans."

"And you are newly married as well," Anne observed, feeling shy to probe another woman's affections. Yet she knew so little about the world, even less of men, and nothing of how to frame what she felt. "I thought Mr. Evans had worked here at St. Sefin's for some time?"

She might earn herself a reproof, for she hadn't really spoken with Dovey before. She'd thought the woman aloof, regarding herself too good for the likes of Anne, who was no more than the daughter of an obscure English gentleman buried on a Welsh estate, when Dovey had traveled oceans and borne a daughter and already buried one husband—more life than Anne had ever lived.

But she saw better now. Dovey was simply reserved by nature, not a woman to wear her heart on her sleeve, too wary of how that heart could be thrown down and trampled by a world where she was marked as different by the color of her skin. Anne tried to comprehend what that must feel like, and couldn't. To always visibly stand out. To be distrusted. To have every action studied and questioned, to always be given the lesser portion.

As a woman of her class, Anne knew what it was to be watched and judged, but it was not the same. It could not be. And yet in the teeth of prejudice and fear and the guilt of people like Anne, Dovey lived life on her own terms, helping others, loving her daughter, daring to give her heart to someone new.

Dovey's was the smile of a woman wholly in love. "Evans was with us almost from the beginning. He's a Pembrokeshire man, you can hear in his speech. I thought him handsome from the first, that rugged look of a man who's been dragged to hell and back."

Anne nodded. Hew gave her that same impression, with the lines around his mouth, the silver at his temples in a man not yet reached thirty years. The way he held himself sometimes as if his back were one giant plank or a shield of steel and wouldn't bend like other men's did.

"But I knew going soft would be throwing a stone after him," Dovey added, grabbing fistfuls of nettle. "He'd been through so much. Safer to brangle with him rather than follow after like a mooncalf. But when his lordship came and left, and Gwen was different ..." Dovey examined a handful of greenery, plucked out a stem. "We talked about what to do, how to keep St. Sefin's going if Gwen went off with the lord. And after he told me right full how he felt ... well." Dovey's face glowed. "I knew I had nothing to fear, not any longer."

Anne's heart twisted on itself, envy biting like a stoat with its little poison fangs. This was love, pure and true. And it wasn't the mannered love of the courtly songs of old or the maddening desire of the ballads, which were ever driving a fair maid to self-harm. This was a love like in that poem by William Blake that had so struck her, the one where the lovers were twining trees with streams flowing at their feet and turtledoves nesting in their branches. A root-deep sweetness that bore flowers, then fruit, and endured steady days and nights together. A love that would survive storms and accusations and a hostile world, because the lovers leaned on one another.

Anne couldn't imagine Calvin Vaughn being a nest for anyone or anything.

But Hewitt Vaughn ... there was a man with deep roots. There was a man who could offer shelter.

"Did you know him?" The words tumbled out before she could stop them, and the rain, caught on a gust beneath her hat, stung teasingly on Anne's cheeks. "Hewitt—Captain Vaughn." She tried to gulp down the urge to confide, but it wouldn't abate. She wanted so much to be *seen*.

"I wanted to break from Calvin," Anne said, "and Hew stepped forward to declare for me. I'm sure he doesn't mean anything but honor by it. Now I've got us both in a tangle and I don't know how to get free."

"The question is, I suppose, if you want to marry him." Dovey pulled a tall bush toward her and stripped off several leaves.

"Yes," Anne said, taking a fistful from her own branch and stuffing it into her heaping basket. "That is the question."

They took their full baskets inside and set to soaking, then crushing nettle leaves. Evans returned with a clutch of tall stems waving long green spikes, which the Widow Jones said was horsetail, and hung it to dry in the stillroom at once. Cerys, with her nymph-like grace, strode into the kitchen with the fat hen in her arms, her hair tousled, a scratch on her cheek, and an expression of serene triumph on her face. Tomos welcomed his beloved pet without an ounce of acrimony for its earlier bad temper. He sat crooning to the hen, smoothing her feathers while Cyw clucked and accepted the homage she was due.

Anne paused to look about her. Were she home at Vine Court, she'd be in the drawing room with her mother, practicing on the spinet or embroidering a dainty design. Ready to chat with callers about the weather and the coming harvest and who had worn what to church the week before.

Here, among the residents of St. Sefin's, she felt again that unfamiliar tug of purpose. Of belonging. As if she stood poised on the precipice of something made just for her. And her work mattered, for before long, Eilian had a wooden cup full of green, strong-smelling juice which she handed to Anne.

"This will do for Leah," she said, "and you can hold the baby while I see to her. We'll likely need another set of sheets."

Without protest, Anne followed the other woman down the hall to the wide room they called the mothers' ward, once a dormitory for women travelers seeking hospitality at the priory. Eilian was scarcely older than she was, Anne thought, about Hew's age, and yet the woman already had a store of useful knowledge about herbs and midwifery and doctoring. She was calm and capable and could be called upon in a pinch.

Anne wanted to be such a woman. She knew that now.

Leah looked poorly, her olive skin sallow, her hair hanging in damp strands. The high windows let in the gray clouds, casting a quiet shadow over the broad room. Leah gave Anne a tired smile as she handed over baby Daniel.

"Miss Sutton. Mrs. Lambe. I'm afraid I've become such a trial to you."

Anne read her face; her fear was greater than that. Leah had other children at home in Merthr Tydfil, and she needed to return with the son and heir of the house so her husband's parents would provide for them.

"I came here expressly to hold little Daniel. I see no trial in that." Anne took the baby to the table and laid out the fresh clouts she'd brought. She also laid out a fresh swaddling cloth, scented with rosemary and chamomile. She feared she'd fumble, with the mother watching, but she did a rather creditable job of cleaning the child, folding his bottom into a clean clout, then swaddling him as Eilian had shown her.

She was rewarded by Daniel opening his eyes and peering at her, his eyes as dark and bright with interest as a baby bird's.

Eilian performed a brief examination of her patient, then gave Leah the cup of nettle juice. "Your bleeding is heavier than most, Leah, but not the worst I've seen. We'll give you fresh nettle juice twice a day and keep on with the blackberry tea."

Leah gripped her hand. "Am I dying? Please. If I am, I must prepare."

"*Nac wyt*, little mother, you aren't in danger," Eilian said lightly. "Your body is shedding all that it made to nourish wee Daniel here. 'Twill take some time to move it all out, a month or more."

Leah rolled to one side as Eilian stripped away the soiled linens. The new mother smiled at the sight of Daniel intently studying Anne's face.

"He's taken a liking to you, Miss Sutton."

Eilian nodded. "Knows you're one of those saw him into the world. Almost like a godmother."

Anne froze. "Do you—have godparents in your—?" She fumbled the question, feeling again the weight of her ignorance.

Leah gave a small chuckle. "No, not like you gentiles do. But at his *bris* he will have the *sandek* to hold him during the circumcision, so perhaps that is something like a godfather."

"Every babe needs a hut full of aunties to help raise him, and Daniel will always have us," Eilian said, and again Anne felt humbled at how easily she was drawn in to this circle. Exactly as if she had a part to play, something to contribute. Eilian gave Leah a sponge bath, and Anne watched and learned about postpartum care while performing her role, holding the baby and crooning softly to him.

"I feel so much better," Leah said after she was dressed in a fresh shift and new bedding laid, her hair brushed and braided, and a bit of bone broth to follow the nettle juice. She looked better, refortified. The care from others at this tender time would help her be strong for her baby, and Eilian had known just the cure to help her.

Those things could be taught. Anne could learn them.

"You've a lovely voice, Miss Sutton."

Anne looked up to find both women staring at her. She'd chosen a silly little ballad, something about a fairy child and a forest, she scarce knew half the words she crooned to the baby. It was a tune Pym sang to her, and Anne had always liked it.

"Thank you," Anne said. She was often complimented on her voice. Could this be her purpose, what she was made to do? Run away to the English stage and try to make her fortune, singing for strangers, turning herself out in her finery to be judged and dismissed by cold foreign eyes? The thought made her blood run like the rain out of doors.

Perhaps there was no place for her paltry skills, no place at all, and she must simply go into the future she was led to, like a fish caught on a hook.

"And you've a lovely boy," Anne added, peering back at wee Daniel, who had tired of his examination of her face and was trying to focus beyond her head. Holding the child now felt— strange. She no longer feared she would break him. Rather the small, warm weight in her arms was an anchor. She could understand, suddenly, the fuss people made over these tiny beings.

She could see herself, for the first time, holding her own child in her arms.

"I don't know how you face it." The words tipped out of her, exactly like the other confessions she couldn't keep holding in. Somehow she had found herself again in a realm where she had friends, where people *listened* to her, and she could not stop drinking in the goodness of that.

"The bearing and the raising, I mean," she said, cradling

Daniel. "So much can go wrong. I never really thought how difficult it must be."

Leah gave a little laugh. "It becomes easier in time. Though one becomes more tired, perhaps."

"But women do it," Anne said. "Again and again."

"For look what comes of it." Leah's smile at her son held wonder and fondness and the fear only a mother could feel when she held a newborn babe up to the cold, hard world. "The raising is its own pleasure, as is the making of them," she teased. "And now, I have something of my husband for always."

Not always, Anne thought, thinking of Gwen's lost babe. Human life was so frail and so brittle, could be snuffed in an instant.

And yet the having. She saw again the look on Hewitt's face when he heard Anne sing. When he saw her standing on the terrace last night. When he raised his head after their embrace and looked into her eyes and she felt like the most important person in the world, like she had discovered something more beautiful than anyone in history had ever known, that what rose up between them was a delight and a mystery and a sacred power as old as human time.

More than just the urge to kiss. Much more, but what it was, she hadn't any way to frame or understand. She'd never seen anything close to what she felt for Hew, unless it was the sweet devotion she saw on the face of Evans as he smiled on his wife.

"The best things come at the highest cost," Eilian said simply, washing her hands in the basin she'd brought.

Leah nodded. "That they do."

Anne handed Daniel back to his mother, watching the way they turned toward one another instinctively. The strings of her very being thrummed with a knowledge much like what had come over her when she lay caught in Hewitt's arms last night, her body sated, her heart moving in ways she didn't expect. She wanted these things that could bring her pain. She wanted love, and children, and a home of her own to look after, and friends she might disappoint at any moment, and a pet that might bite her if it took a scare. She didn't want to tread the safe paths of decorum any longer.

But there was so much she didn't know, the first being how to go about addressing her feelings for Hewitt Vaughn. It was like stepping off a cliff with her arms full of rocks.

But if she didn't take the plunge, she'd never know if she could fly.

CHAPTER EIGHTEEN

What had she meant, she could not lie any longer? Had she meant she would not lie with him? They'd already shared pleasure—God, just the memory of holding her, touching her, made Hew's legs weak. His thoughts kept veering back to Anne in his arms like iron filings clinging to a magnetic stone.

Or was there something else she was deceiving him about?

The kitchen of St. Sefin's smelled of crushed greenery and damp poultry. Vicar Stanley sat at the heavy wooden table with one of the black-clad widows, drinking tea.

"Captain Vaughn," Stanley said with his friendly smile. "I'm to start reading those banns, I hear?"

How he wished. Three weeks, and then he could say the words that would bind Anne to him, and he could have one thing sure.

"You're a son of Sir Lambert's, you are," said the older woman, a dark, glaring eye fixed on Hew.

He cleared his throat. "Yes. The eldest, Mother." He spoke in Welsh, as she had, and she dipped her chin as if confirming something to herself.

"Where's the other gone to? Your brother."

Hew shook his head. "I wish I could say. Is Anne—Miss Sutton about? I saw the horse and cart in the yard." She'd driven alone, unhitched Cadfael alone, and taken care of the animal alone. The cob greeted Hew's mare amicably when he'd put his own mount in the paddock.

"She's making the rounds with Mrs. Lambe." Stanley leaned back in his chair, a man at his ease. "I called to speak with Mrs. Bernstein and was engaged in the pursuit of a chicken. Fortunately, it was recovered and peace has been restored. The children are outside with it now, gathering nettles or so they say, and your Miss Sutton and Mrs. Lambe are in the mothers' ward."

"This Mrs. Lambe." Hew waved away the offer of tea from the widow. "What do you know of her?" Anne had been spending an awful lot of time in her company, and the woman was an unknown entity. She could be coarse, unprincipled, manipulative, and Anne was too sweet to—

"Why not ask her yourself?"

Mrs. Lambe appeared in the doorway leading to an inner hall, holding a handful of dirty rags in her hands. Anne came up beside her, holding a basin and cup.

Anne looked as delicious as usual, her gown plain but tidy, a patterned Welsh shawl slung around her waist, her hair primly tucked beneath a dashing little cap. Her eyes widened when she spotted Hew, her delicate lips parting, and it took all his self-control not to cross the room and pull her against him like a besotted bridegroom.

"What are you doing here?" Mrs. Lambe spoke, directing her words at Stanley. Hew wondered why she sounded strained, her words harsh. The vicar scrambled to his feet, recalling he was in the presence of ladies.

"Taking tea with Mother Morris." He reached up to remove the hat he'd already laid on the side table, and the man's face fell as he realized how ridiculous he looked with his hands groping through the air above his head. Hew sympathized. He did the same thing with Anne—missed every chance to impress her, took every opportunity to act a clodpole and not the refined, gallant gentleman who deserved her hand.

She found pleasure with him—he was good enough at *that*, at least—but for the rest? He'd seen last evening her graceful ease with his mother's guests, the way she'd commanded the room with her performance. She was bred a lady in her bones and every inch of her manner. He was a broken soldier, a scarred man who had failed his family, his commander, his father, and the friend who had saved his life.

He didn't deserve her. Hew's skin prickled at the acknowledgement. But he was her best of a miserable set of options, and with that, he might lure her. Trick her. Trap her, just like she'd said. That was why he was here.

"And you." Mrs. Lambe's gaze moved to Hew. He'd thought she had blue eyes, but they'd turned a stormy gray-green. He could tell from this distance, so piercing was her stare. Hew's eyes did the same.

This woman, too, had Sir Lambert's eyes. How could that be?

"I am here for Anne," Hew said, looking to her for rescue from this strange, challenging woman.

"Is ought amiss?" Anne moved forward with her trained grace and set the basin and cup on the table. Then, as naturally as if she were the lady of the house and its hostess, she took the teapot and poured into the widow's cup, then the vicar's. The widow patted Anne's hand in approval.

"Not *Saes* after all," Mother said in her rough voice. "And neither's he, for all that he fought for them." She nodded toward Hew. "Hero of Acre, is it?"

Anne, who didn't understand the Welsh, gave her a perplexed smile. Hew answered in English, certain the woman spoke it. "A hero to some, until the court-martial comes through." Might as well say it, through the burn of shame along his back, the place where he was supposed to feel nothing. "Time will tell."

"Time always tells," the widow said in Welsh.

"Time always tells," the vicar said in English, not knowing he repeated the sentiment. "And Captain Vaughn's a hero."

"In your eyes." Mrs. Lambe still trapped him with her accusing stare. "Is that why he is free to judge us?"

"Not judge," Hew said. "Only ask. You are new to the area. I am lately returned. I am curious."

She held his challenging stare for a moment, then turned with a sharp move and stalked toward the scullery, head held high. "I run a pie shop," she said.

The vicar attempted a smile. "And rather more, I'd say, considering all your help to those in need." He waved a hand through the air again, a gesture encompassing their environs.

His reassurance meant little to Mrs. Lambe. She was already in the scullery. Mother Morris snorted and sipped her tea.

Anne watched her friend's retreat, then glanced at Hew, curiosity in her gaze, before she started tidying the countertop. She held her shoulders back, her chin lifted, but her movements were easy, natural. She was at home here in a way she wasn't at Greenfield, where she wore that guarded look, always.

Hew wanted her to feel at ease at Greenfield. He wanted her to feel at ease with him.

"Will you drive with me?"

"Where you to?" She raised her high, arched brows, then a smile broke across her face. "Listen to me—I *am* becoming a Welsh woman."

"All the better for it," Mother Morris cackled.

"*Ta,* Mother, thank you." Anne seemed to understand the Welsh this time; she was learning the language. She smoothed her hands along the plaid shawl she was wearing for an apron, then untied it from her waist. "I will go with you, Captain."

Finally. She was moving toward him, not away.

She stepped close to gather her pelisse from the peg, and her scent rippled through Hew's head. She smelled lush and flowery and rinsed clean. She was too good for him, too pure. He wanted to put her on a pedestal beyond his reach and fall on his knees in adoration. He wanted to draw her to him and caress her body in every way he knew how, until she was once again limp and sated in his arms, ready to surrender her soul.

But then she'd be marked with all the sweat and grief and pain of his muddy world, and once the vows were said, she could never be free of him.

Unless he could make her want him, despite all.

She helped him hitch up the pony cart, calling the gelding to her with a cluck of the tongue, and Cadfael came obedient to her hand, just as Hew would if she ever summoned him. Ready to submit his neck to the yoke in return for her strokes of approval. He helped her into the cart, noting the green juice staining her gloves.

She smiled as she caught his notice. "Nettle juice."

"Are you learning teas and tisanes? Cures and remedies? They say that Mrs. Lambe is a cunning woman."

"If by it they mean the women with knowledge of midwifery and plants that poison as well as heal, then yes, Eilian seems to know those things." Anne twitched her skirts so they fell about her half boots. "But very often that term seems used in aspersion, not approbation. I think the male physics and surgeons want everyone to believe their medicine is the better way, or the only way."

"Is that what you learned from Hawkins and Allard last night?"

He sounded jealous. He averted his face as he tied his mare to the back of the cart. *Fool.* He couldn't chide her for looking out for a better chance for herself. What if one of those men could offer her more than Hew could?

Then he'd find a way to spike the man's wheels and ensure *he* was her only choice, Hew decided. Proof through and through he wasn't a gentleman.

"I learned their approaches to surgery and to use of forceps in giving birth." She made a face. "Men seem terribly fond of their tools."

Hew bit back a snort of derision and hauled himself onto the seat beside her. At once, her scent reached out and coiled about him. "I can explain to you about grades of artillery, if you would rather."

Stupid—that would not win her. One needed to speak with a lady about subjects pleasant to her if he wished to woo. Hew knew that much about the business, at least.

She twisted slightly and observed the saddlebags he'd deposited in the back of the cart. "Where are you taking me?"

"Through Newport, first. Do you know what your brother is about these days?"

He should not have asked so bluntly. She drew back, her guard up, her face somber. "He has not confided in me. Do you know something?"

"He's been seen again in the company of Rafael Darch. Their association began well before I returned, I'm told. It seems Darch has been training your brother up to his business, or attempting to."

"Free trading." Her voice was quiet but not surprised. Everyone knew of the open defiance of customs law that took place along the shores of southern England and western Wales. And the reputation of smugglers of being ruthless to anyone who crossed their purposes.

She sighed. "I wish I could say I could not believe it of him. But he has been ... pressed for funds of late."

And not the type to take up an honest trade. They both knew that.

"Worse than that," Hew said, guiding the horse down the wide lane that led to Newport. "He's been asking about the Black Hound's business. Who is taking up what parts of his interests. And he's been seen in the company of known associates."

The little man Hew had seen in the street the other day, for example. A chat with Evans, out of Anne's sight, had confirmed him as Morys, one of the Black Hound's henchmen. He'd taken part in the kidnapping of Anne and the ladies, which was how Evans knew him.

Her brother was trying to insinuate himself with the associates of a criminal who had been feared throughout south Wales, but Sutton didn't have the stones or the steel to be a businessman in the vein of the Black Hound. He'd get himself jailed or killed.

And Anne would suffer for it.

Hew braced himself for the changes in the town, the missing West Gate, the torn-down Market House. That strange sense of disassociation, that he belonged here, was *of* this place, and yet no longer knew it. He'd often accompanied his father to town to bring his mother to market, to take a pint at the Bull Inn with the other burghers, to listen as Sir Lambert weighed in on local affairs, his name as a knight and gentleman holding just as much weight as a Kemeys or Jones or Herbert, almost as much as Morgan's.

Hew knew these landmarks like he knew his own face: the House of Refuge, an institution for the poor, built by the Earl of Pembroke centuries ago, with the Pembroke arms in stone above the door. The half-timbered house where Charles II had stayed prior to the Restoration. The old Cross House with its great granite cross in the front yard, the purpose of which was long forgotten and much speculated about.

It wasn't a lovely town, or a large and sophisticated one. But Hew heard its heartbeat, a song of possibilities. He could make a home here. A future. One holding a wife and a family and a place in town affairs as great as his father'd once held.

If he didn't end again in prison.

If Anne would consent to be that wife. He wanted none other.

He passed the Fleur de Lys, where he'd learned, with a few discreet inquiries, that most of the tax-free goods trading through Newport were stored, at the direction of one Rafael Darch.

"If you know something, Anne, please tell me." He tried to keep his voice gentle, confiding. Reassure her she could trust him. "I want to keep your brother out of trouble, if I can."

She pinched folds of fabric over her knees, a nervous gesture he found endearing. But the look she cast him was anxious and full of despair. "I would if I knew. But Daron no longer confides in me. He—"

Her voice hitched, and she stopped. A rush of heat flooded Hew, so many emotions he couldn't untangle them, but it felt like the same heat that goaded him into battle, to fight for what was right, to stop an attack. Anyone who hurt Anne was his enemy, and he would blow them to smithereens given the first opportunity.

Even her brother. That made him a beast, and one more reason he wasn't worthy of her.

Damn it, he had to *try*. He couldn't just stand back and hand her over to another man, even if that were what she wanted.

"I will protect you," he said, his voice rough as the road beneath their wheels. "I will do what it takes. Trust me, Anne."

She turned those large blue eyes on him with a considering gaze. She did not trust him, not yet.

But she didn't deny him, either.

"Daron wants me to marry your brother because he has some agreement with Calvin," she blurted. "He believes he cannot manipulate you."

"That much is true. But *you* do not want to marry Calvin."

"No." She turned to face ahead, watching the homes and shops as they passed. She craned her neck to look into the pie shop and waved at the woman in the window, an older woman dressed in black with streaks of silver in her hair.

What do you want, Anne?

He couldn't force out the words. Because he was a coward. Because he didn't want to hear that she might want something, or someone, other than him.

What would it take to win this woman?

He'd only needed to see her blossoming at St. Sefin's, see her command the party at Greenfield, see her walking through the garden of his home to know he wanted this woman by his side always, to learn from and discover for the rest of his natural life.

But he wasn't the future she had planned or wanted for herself. He wasn't the man she had dreamed of, he was certain.

So how could he, in good conscience, do his best to woo and win her when she deserved so much more than he could offer?

～

"THIS IS MARVELOUS," Anne said, and she meant it.

She stood and peered into the narrow channel lined with cement and half-full with water reflecting the slate-blue clouds, much the shade of Hew's eyes. He stepped next to her, slipping a hand around her waist, his fingers digging gently into her side as he urged her away from the edge.

"It is marvelous, until you fall in."

His worry coaxed a smile of delight to her lips. His hand on her waist sent a giddy rush of air through her body, lifting her like a leaf. She wanted to curl toward him and press every inch of her body against his.

Hello, New Anne.

Old Anne warned her it wasn't proper. Even if they were alone for the moment, standing on the grassy verge of the canal with the woods of the Welsh hills all around them. The Crumlin arm of the Monmouthshire Canal was a busy thoroughfare channeling iron from the mountains to the Newport docks. A boat would come through soon, and even if Hew were not recognized on the spot, a man of his description and a woman of hers would quickly be identified if gossip circulated about a couple caught in an embrace on the Cefn Flight.

But if he were her betrothed in truth ...

"Marvelous," she said again, turning to regard the locks carved into the hills, framed with timber and lined with stonework, a staircase for a giant. "The timber gates let the water drain out, lowering the boat to the next level, then the next."

"And the weirs and reservoirs hold water in reserve in case adjustments must be made."

He fell into step beside her as she climbed the sandy trail to peer into the higher lock. The fit of the stones, the mechanism of the gate, everything about the engineering fascinated her. He didn't clamber ahead and then wait impatiently for her to catch up, Anne observed. He paced at her side, inviting her to use his arm for balance.

She did. It was good reason to touch him, and she liked touching him.

"How does one know how to make it all fit together? I wouldn't know where to begin with designing such a project."

"Referencing similar projects, if possible. In this case I think Dadford had to make guesses. It's a matter of trial and error, building, testing, revising the plan if one must. It's remarkable, how it all works together, though there are ways it can be improved."

"And you can see them. You know what they are. What to do."

He looked into her face, and his gaze held, tracing every feature. His look was bold, and her heartbeat quickened.

"It's simple mechanics, at heart. Judging how much volume you need, knowing how water moves. And having good builders, which I think Dadford did. This masonry is sound and will last for centuries."

"You know engineering *and* artillery," Anne said. She liked that he didn't condescend to her. He didn't dismiss her interest because she was a female. He spoke to her as a companion, an equal.

She felt, when he looked in her face, that he *saw* her. Not the image of Anne she projected, and not the image he wanted to see. He was listening to what she told him, and he saw beneath her to the skin, to her confused and keening heart.

She turned toward the saddlebags he'd placed on a grassy patch of ground, marking the spot for their picnic. She was not certain she wanted to be studied so carefully. Was not certain she could bear for the proud and silly and longing parts of her to be seen.

"Why do you dislike when people call you the hero of Acre?" she asked once he had opened the saddlebags and she had laid out their picnic.

"Because I didn't act alone," he said at once. He opened a bottle of Canary wine with a quick, capable twist, and Anne's gaze snagged on the size and strength of those hands. Her skin lit with a glow where those hands had touched her.

"It wasn't even my idea, what we did." He fortunately did not notice her sudden distraction, how she had forgotten how to unpack a basket. "Commodore Smith and his crew captured the half dozen French boats bringing Napoleon his guns. Antoine de Phélippeaux designed the fortifications and taught me what to do. Farhi, the Jewish vizier to the Pasha Jezzar, he found us the materials and the men to help. I made sure the artillery was fit for use and helped to mount it. If I was a hero, we all were."

His lips tightened, and his eyes flared as if with a sudden blow of emotion. "Antoine more than any, and he died for his pains. The plague, after he survived everything else."

"And you were put in prison?" Anne asked softly. She handed him one of Mrs. Harries's pies, watching his every fleeting expression. She wanted to desperately to know this man. To *understand* him. "Did the French capture you?"

"No. My commander charged me with insubordination because I took my orders from Farhi and Antoine to go around him. He wanted a pitched battle, British might for British glory. He thought subterfuge was the coward's way. Even though we saved countless lives, especially among the residents of Acre.

When the French overran Jaffa, it was slaughter. It was ... women and children—"

He stumbled, then paused. Anne swallowed the bitter taste in her mouth and focused on unwrapping her pie.

"It shames me to say it, but you should know. My superior officer was angry with me because he thought I had taken his woman."

She froze, fingers curled over the oiled paper like talons. "What do you mean?"

"He'd found a local woman. A—courtesan. He was besotted." Hew frowned at the golden-brown crust of his pie. "He discovered she made an advance to me."

"Oh." Anne shoved her own pie in her mouth so she did not reveal the jealousy, the rage, that sheared through her at the thought of another woman in Hew's arms. Pleasing him. Pleasured by him. Someone more beautiful and seductive, who might be in the back of his mind even as he—

"I turned her down."

She glanced up and her gaze collided with his, blue and steady on her face. "I do not poach on other men's claims," he added.

"Oh," she said again, considering this. Hew did not *poach*. As if a woman were an acre of property or a hound or a gun, not to be borrowed without permission.

His eyes widened. "I phrased that badly."

Anne clapped a hand over her mouth. "Did I speak aloud?"

She adored that crooked smile of his, bashful and burning all at once. "I wish you would always speak your thoughts to me. Whatever they are."

"I could wish the same." She lowered her hand, resisting the urge to fret with the fabric of her skirt, a nervous habit. "I am not sure I will remain sanguine while I listen, though. Gwen was the only person who spoke frankly to me, whether I wished it or not, and we quarreled often."

Anne winced now at the memory of her younger, righteous self. The Anne so certain that what she wanted was just and proper and true. Then she had come south to Newport, into a world where she was no longer the hub and darling center, and the shreds of her old self were falling away like linens cut up for rags. She was still discovering who stood in the midst of it all, the Anne she was becoming.

But this man had played a part on her shattering, and he had a part to play in her recovery. She was certain of that.

She managed a smile. "As a woman who also did her part to entice you, I suppose I have no call to be outraged that other women have tried the same."

"Anne—may I call you Anne? Or is it yet Miss Sutton?" He unwrapped a paper full of chicken pieces, baked with spices and breadcrumbs, and laid one on her plate.

Warmth climbed her neck, circling her throat. "It is Anne to you," she whispered. "Given our other intimacies."

He didn't draw back. He was so close, his shoulder nearly brushing hers, that strong, firm shoulder she'd clutched when she gave herself to him. She smelled him, that combination of spice and earth that haunted her dreams, the musk of the man himself, muscle and iron. His lips drew close to her ear, and she shut her eyes as his breath drifted across her neck, calling up tiny currents of light that raced from her skin to her core.

"I have been thinking of those intimacies. All of last night, and all of today." His voice, a low murmur, was as heavy and warm as a hand on her cheek. She *wanted* his hand on her cheek. On her neck, her throat, her breasts, her—everywhere.

She squeezed her eyes shut. How was she to prevent herself from turning toward him, tossing aside everything in her hands so she could wrap herself around him again, press her body to his chest, claim his mouth? She wanted to claim everything about him. She wanted to plant herself in his arms and never leave. She wanted him bound to her by oath and fire, sealed to her in that most primal of promises. She shook with longing and the fierceness of her cravings, raw, unchained, unlike anything she'd known.

Anne opened her eyes. "You did poach me," she said suddenly.

He reared back his head, eyes flaring. Something about the gesture, about the sheer masculine grace of him, wore her restraint to the merest thread. He sat like a king of the forest, a primal force tucked beneath the veneer of a gentleman's coat, but beneath the tailored clothes beat a wild heart, a passionate nature, a vein of tenderness with iron beneath. Not forged iron, fired to the hardness of steel, but iron as it came from the earth, able to bend under blows, but not break. Not ever break.

"I was to be your brother's," she reminded him. "But I came to your bed, and you took me."

The words were out before she considered them, and the blush climbed to her brows. *Took* had such a carnal sound to it.

"You were to be mine first," he said softly. "Don't you remember?"

"You turned me down."

Say you regret that now. Say if you had only met me. Or, now that you have met me, say you would have chosen me.

It mattered that he might have chosen her, once.

"Would you have accepted me?" He turned the question back on her.

"It was not given me to accede or refuse. My parents had that power."

"Would you have chosen *me*, Anne?" he asked softly. "If you could?"

She tore off a piece of chicken, still warm, the crispy skin parting to reveal the tender meat beneath. "Can you see yourself being married?" she asked instead. "To me."

"Yes." He didn't hesitate, but he didn't hold her with that smoky gaze, rather turned to his own plate. "Can you see yourself with me?"

She nibbled at her chicken, looking across the meadow and into the brown trunks of the trees as if she could peer through to the rise of mountains beyond.

"All my life, I've been told I must marry. It was all I was meant for. Trained for. When Calvin went for Gwen, I was at sea. And when I saw Gwen taking everything I thought I should have had ..." She swallowed hard, the crumbs clinging to her throat. "But Prunella—that is Penrydd's sister-in-law—and the women of St. Sefin's, Dovey, Eilian, they have shown me there are different ways a woman can exist in the world. I might more choices than I thought." She closed her eyes, breathing deeply. The air smelled of water mint and harebell. "And when you said you must marry me because I'd ruined myself ..."

"Nothing about you is ruined, Anne."

He sounded so certain, his voice a low rumble, soothing as the lap of waves upon the shore.

"I think, now, there should be more to it," she said. "To marriage. Money should not be the reason. Or station or name. Nor to stave off a scandal. I think ... in the end there must be more. For a marriage to be strong and true."

Dovey and Evans had known each other for years, worked side by side in the keeping of St. Sefin's and its fragile residents. Gwen had kept Penrydd in her care for weeks, learning who the man was at his core, with naught else to define him. If Anne could bring Hewitt nothing else—not a dowry, not a family with wealth and connections or a title and a name reaching back to centuries of nobility—then she ought, at the least, bring him her heart, her loyalty and affection and the promise to put no other before him.

How could she bear to vow all this to him knowing in return that he wed her only for honor, a slender shield of respectability, and once yoked to him she was bound forever, no matter whom he might go on to be enticed by, no matter whom he might love?

She could not bear that. She was both too proud and too sensitive to be the abandoned wife. She would not be able to lead a separate life, knowing this man existed in the world. She would always long for him. She would always want to be with him. She would seek him in everything she did.

And if he did not want her the same way, she would slowly bleed to death from the thousand tiny cuts of humiliation. She would die of a broken heart.

"Good marriages have begun on less ground than what we have," Hew said softly.

But did that mean he *wanted* her, in the ways she was asking? She could not press the question past her lips. She'd had a lifetime of being taught to be quiet, docile, demure. A lady did not trouble or demand. She was graceful courage in every circumstance, soft pride when her heart was broken. She never offered more than she ought, and she never showed weakness or disappointment or despair.

"We know so little about one another," she whispered.

What she meant was, could he love her? A love that was honest and deep and true, a treasure they could mine their whole lives and find the delights never ceasing.

She had no right to ask for any of this, any of the things that a couple might share in love and devotion and mutual sacrifice, because she had not wooed him, she had not won his heart. She'd chosen him on a mad, selfish impulse before she even knew what a deeply honest and just and true man he was, and she'd trapped him in a scandal just as surely as she had herself.

Ask him anyway.

But New Anne had not yet vanquished the old Anne, at least not the old chains that bound her. That deep-driven belief that she would only be loved if she were quiet and pretty and *good*. Those foundations ran to her core, and they were made of stone.

He leaned forward. Close enough to kiss. Close enough that she could press her mouth to his mouth, pull his full lower lip beneath her teeth, slide her hands to his jaw where the beginnings of stubble would be the softest velvet against her palms. Perhaps he would slide his tongue into her mouth in that way that made her feel he wanted to devour her, that made her turn to liquid in her legs and between. She was turning to liquid now, and—

"Someone is approaching." Anne drew back her head.

A dog bounded into the clearing, crashing through the stand of ash trees and buckthorn bushes. The spaniel spotted them and charged, jaws parting, paws thudding into the thick grass. Anne froze in terror.

"Bran! *Sefyll*," a woman called in a voice of command.

The dog skidded to a halt and panted, tongue lolling. Bright eyes regarded Hew, and Anne, with great curiosity.

"*Lawr*," the woman said. The dog dropped into a prone position, paws tucked, and regarded the chicken on their cloth with a gaze of absolute longing.

Hew rose, rotating his back and wincing, as if he'd gone stiff. "I beg your pardon," he said automatically.

Ever the gentleman. Anne breathed again. The dog sat quietly, licking its lips, as intent on the chicken as a hound on its prey.

The woman was older, perhaps the age of Anne's mother, clad in a long black cloak with a small net veil fluttering from her hat. She wore the clothes of a gentlewoman and had the gait of one, her black half boots sinking quietly into the grass as she neared them.

"I beg your pardon for the intrusion," the woman said. She spoke like a gentlewoman, too. "Bran has the impolite habit of not waiting for an invitation. I am terribly sorry he disturbed your picnic."

"We hardly expected to be alone. In fact I think a boat is approaching now." Hew indicated the top of the staircase of locks, where the prow of a narrow boat had appeared. Men's voices sounded in conversation, and one of the workers cranked a great wheel to raise the wooden gate. With a splash, water began to fill the lock below.

The men on the boat above sat back at their leisure, waiting for the slow process to complete. One waved to their little group, and Anne waved back. Then she realized the older woman had waved, too.

"I am Hewitt Vaughn of Greenfield," Hew said, "and this is Miss Anne Sutton." Anne inclined her head, not certain if she should curtsy.

"Miss Sutton." The woman gave Anne the briefest of nods before turning her attention to Hew. "Captain Vaughn of the Royal Artillery. I heard you'd returned. In fact, I have been hoping to meet you."

"You might call at Greenfield," Hew said courteously, glancing at the dog. At a signal from the woman, the spaniel rose and trotted toward them, pushing his nose into Hew's hand. Hew scrubbed the animal's head and the great tongue lolled.

"I do not think I am welcome at Greenfield," the other woman said, a dry amusement in her tone. "I am Miss Meredith."

"The vicar's Miss Meredith? He spoke of you. And your charities."

"*The* Miss Meredith?" Anne rose, shaking out her skirts,

and stepped to Hew's side. "We have one of your young protegees at Greenfield. A girl named Mair."

Miss Meredith nodded. "I hope she is going on well for you, and minding her manners. She's a spirited girl, but a quick learner."

"I enjoy her company. But she made me curious to meet you." Anne held out her hand. The woman pushed the veil back from her face, and Anne's jaw dropped.

"Forgive me," Anne said, collecting herself. "You look very like someone I've met in Newport. Mrs. Lambe, who runs the pie shop."

Miss Meredith nodded, though her eyes flicked toward Hew as if waiting to see what he made of this conversation. "Eilian is my daughter," the other woman said. "She ... went away to live with friends when she was small. I am gratified to have her back."

Anne shook hands, the other woman's gloved fingers firm in their grip. Eilian had not mentioned family in town. Had she returned on account of this woman?

"You must be very proud of her," Anne said. "Such skills she has for healing. And the pies are delightful."

Miss Meredith laughed. Odd that she was Miss—would not a widow go by Mistress? "Mrs. Reece is to be credited for the pies," she answered. "But Eilian is indeed canny with her herbs and remedies. I was glad to see her become a healer. She has a gift for it."

"She is teaching me," Anne said.

Hew turned toward her with some surprise. Ah, she had not mentioned that.

"At least, I plan to ask her," Anne said. "To take me on as her apprentice, if I might."

"So you will be staying in the area for some time, I hope," Hew said softly.

She held his gaze, searching for meaning in it. His eyes were the iron-blue of the sky above them and just as vast and unknowable.

She turned to Miss Meredith. "Forgive me, but why would you not be welcome at Greenfield?"

The woman wasn't looking at Anne, her eyes still trained on Hew with a wistful expression. "That is for Captain Vaughn to say, is it not?"

Hew looked politely puzzled. "I am sure you may call whenever you like, and I hope my mother would be courteous."

"Ah." Miss Meredith drew backward, as if he'd swatted at her the way one might chastise a puppy. "So that is the way of it. I see." She turned and whistled for her animal. "*Dere, Bran.*"

The animal shot to her side obediently, though not without casting one last hopeful look at the cloth laden with food. "We must be on with our walk, or Bran will grow naughty. Good day, Miss Sutton. Captain Vaughn ..." She hesitated, her eyes resting on Hew with a sort of pained tenderness. "It is good to see you home," she said finally.

Hew bowed his head slightly. "Good day, madame. I should like, someday, to hear more about your work."

"You may call upon me in Pensarn Cottage, at High Cross," she answered. "I would be happy to speak with you. Someday." She moved away, her dog trotting at her side.

"That was an odd exchange," Anne remarked.

Hew shook his head. "There is something there I do not understand. Why should she think my mother would not receive her? She seems a gentlewoman. The vicar spoke highly of her charitable works."

"And Mair spoke of her as nearly a saint. Perhaps Eilian knows something."

Hew stood over their picnic, half-eaten. "Do you suppose

we should—?" He made a half-hearted gesture indicating the food.

Anne found her appetite had whisked away in the hope that Hew might kiss her. Besides, she had no wish to sit and eat with the men in the narrowboat, laden high with iron, mere yards away in the long process of descending the staircase.

"We might stay if you wish to see the locks in action," she said.

"I've seen them." Hew squatted and began gathering the scattered bits of food. "It only confirms what I suspected. There needs to be more water, for look how slow they are going, and there is another boat approaching above." He waved to the top of the staircase, where more voices drifted down from the top of the hill and the prow of another boat edged into view. "The locks must be widened, and then we will need more wharves on the Usk to ship all this ore. I know I am right. It is only a matter of finding someone to listen."

His mouth twisted, and Anne saw the grimace he'd given her when he spoke of being imprisoned for insubordination. She wanted to ask for the rest of the story. How he'd been freed. What happened next.

What he would say if she summoned the bravery to speak and tell him she might *want* to marry him.

But the moment had fled, and her courage with it. She helped roll up the cloth and tuck the bottles and dishes and cutlery back into the basket, where Mrs. Harries or the kitchen maid would have the unpacking of it and perhaps enjoy the food more than Anne had.

She held her silence until they neared his home and she saw the carriage standing in the forecourt of Greenfield, footmen unloading a significant pile of luggage at the back. "Who could that be?" Anne asked as Hew drew the pony cart up behind.

More visitors his mother had summoned to attempt to divert Hew's attention from Anne?

"That is our carriage," Hew said, a grim set to his mouth. "Calvin must have returned."

"And with him ..." Anne's stomach knotted, flailed, and then sank as she recognized the monogram on a leather trunk banded with iron. "My parents."

"How can you—?"

"So that is where he went. To Llanfyllin, and Vine Court." Anne wanted to curse, to scream, to clench her hands into fists and shake them at the sky. "He brought my parents to make me stand by my promise to marry him."

Her mouth tasted of ash and lye. She had missed her chance with Hew indeed, for now her choice would be taken away, and there was nothing she could do about it.

CHAPTER NINETEEN

"Of course you must marry Calvin. We made all the agreements with Calvin. He could very likely bring a breach of promise suit against us for this, and how on earth would we pay? Whatever were you thinking, Anne?" Her mother, huddled in the deep leather seat of the Vaughn family coach, pulled her Norwich shawl around her neck and sent Anne a reproachful look.

"Daron won two thousand pounds when his gel ran off with her Italian music master." Her father, seated beside Anne on the facing seat, grabbed for a leather strap as the coach jounced over the now-familiar road to Bassaleg. "Where do you suppose we would find those kinds of funds, child?"

"It was good of you to travel all this way to ensure that I marry a man who will be kind to me," Anne said. "I am so overcome by your concern for my welfare, I know not what to say."

She clung to the strap on her own side of the vehicle. The coach, despite being a newer, London-made model with the latest springs, was a far less comfortable ride than the pony cart, and her teeth clattered in her head. But Eliza Sutton would throw herself into the salt marsh before she would put herself atop a horse.

Her mother frowned. "Are you being pert? Richard, is she being pert? After I suffered how many thousands of miles of travel through the wildest country?"

Aunt Gertrude, snugged into the seat beside Eliza and taking up the greater portion of it with her enormous petticoats, guffawed with laughter. Aunt Gertrude was not standing anywhere close to the lingering specter of death, as Daron had led Anne to believe.

"'Twas scarcely above a hundred miles, Eliza, and the Brecons are the most beautiful country God ever made. 'Tis time you set foot out of your valley."

"England is the most beautiful country God ever made," Anne's mother answered with a haughty sniff. "Sometimes I wish I'd never left Telford."

"Calvin compelled you to travel all this way," Anne asked, "merely to insist I marry him, and not Hew?"

Her mother glared. "How free you are with the given names of both your intendeds. I never thought to raise a pert daughter."

"Nor a lightskirt." Her father's look was just as severe. "Vaughn had best be mistaken in his accounts of what you've been about with his brother."

Anne looked to her aunt. "And how did you get caught up in this, if I might ask? Of course, I am delighted to see you, Aunt Gertrude. It has been far too long."

"It has, indeed. I find there are one or two matters I must settle." Her aunt stretched her legs out, compelling Anne's father to bend his knees to the side, which he did with another glare. "Writing letters has become tedious, and this seemed the best way to speak with you."

"We have time now," Anne said. "Until we reach—where did Daron insist we meet him?"

"Some place called Pillgwenlly," her father grumbled. "Friend of his wants to take us for a pleasure cruise. Poor day for it, boding rain."

"It always bodes rain in south Wales," Anne replied. "Wait an hour, and you'll see what kind."

Her mother pressed her lips together. "How is there more than one kind of rain?"

"There are many. There's the *glaw trwm*, the *glaw bras*, and the *glaw gyrru*, all types of heavy rain, and then—"

"You're becoming a Welshwoman, then?" Aunt Gertrude said with a chuckle.

Anne smiled softly, remembering sitting with Mother Morris in the kitchen of St. Sefin's pressing nettles for their juice while Cerys pattered in and out with her baskets. "I've never lived anywhere else, and am not like to."

Hew would stay at Greenfield, she suspected. He was planning his future there, putting down roots. He was done with the Royal Artillery, or they were done with him.

Would he stay if Anne were forced to marry Calvin?

She would not agree, and they could not force her without her consent. They lived on the cusp of the nineteenth century, not the mediæval age. No vicar would pronounce them wed without hearing Anne's vows.

She wished Hew had come with them, though there was no room in the coach to seat him. He could have ridden alongside on Cadfael, like a knight of old on his destrier. She would feel safer if Hew were with them.

Calvin had made a great fuss about uniting the Suttons as a family, and Daron had made plans to host his newly arrived parents in some grand fashion. As Daron's plans of late had been little devoted to the welfare and pleasure of others, Anne admitted some degree of apprehension about the business.

"This is all about the money, I imagine." Anne spoke above

the creak of springs, the rustle of fabric, and the whining of the wooden planks of the carriage as it shifted over the uneven terrain. "Daron took it into his head, Aunt Gertrude, that you meant to make me a bequest of some sort, and he believed he ought to stand in line for an inheritance as well."

She could not bring herself to say outright that Daron wanted to take whatever came to Anne. She could not bring herself to say aloud that her playmate and guardian of old had abandoned her and the golden boy she had once worshipped had become a man she could not respect or even like.

"He never would be so—" her mother began, speaking over her father's "I never told him to—"

Her parents fell silent and looked at one another nervously.

Aunt Gertrude folded her hands in her lap, fingers encased in dainty lace mittens. "How interesting," she said. "Yet I could have sworn I addressed that letter to Anne, and sealed it."

"It is as though nothing we do or make is our own," Anne said to her aunt. "Not our property, neither our skills nor our earnings, not even our decisions over our own bodies."

Her aunt nodded. "It is why I counsel every young woman to become rich and independent. That was my plan for you, at any rate."

"I thank you for it. That seems wise advice."

Her mother chewed a lip, a gesture she herself held to be unladylike. "Daron would never to do anything to hurt us or this family."

"Indeed? That was not your sentiment when he filled Gwen with a babe," Anne said sharply. "I recall he was forbidden to contact her after she was turned out of our house."

"That was his own choice," her father grumbled. "I counseled him to take responsibility for her. Own his mistakes like a man, and pay the girl to go away."

"He did not," Anne said, her voice catching as she recalled

the conversation, sitting in the kitchen of St. Sefin's, when she learned the truth from Gwen. The frothy scent of yeast rising in the air, undercut by the acrid sting of soap. Her friend's taut face as she recalled her disgrace. "He had nothing to do with Gwen until the news came that David Carew had been knighted and died, leaving all his wealth to his daughter. Daron brought me south because he thought we could persuade Gwen to marry him. Did you know that?"

Her father directed his scowl out the window. "I said it was brazen of him."

Her mother picked at a thread on her shawl, frowning. "It would have solved our problems. Carew left Gwenllian his mines, Richard. All of them."

Aunt Gertrude looked back and forth between the couple, a wry smile twisting her lips. "How very, very interesting," she said. "This is all because that ship sank, Richard? But I thought the insurance paid handsomely."

Her father's expression darkened. "Insurance paid for that," he said. "But not the debts my son has accrued since then."

Anne's mother twisted a fringe of her shawl around one gloved finger. "We raised him as a gentleman, Richard. He is accustomed to that life. You cannot expect a young man—"

"I was given my wealth, too," her husband interrupted. "I do not deny it. But I stewarded my inheritance. I thought of my wife and children. I could have spent it on stables and hounds and the quarterly races, taken you shopping in Shrewsbury twice a year. But did I?"

"No." Eliza gave her husband a sour look. "There were no shopping trips."

"I suppose it is time to turn him out," Anne's father said grimly. "See if he lands on his own two feet, like the other did."

"Gwen married a viscount," Anne remarked. "So it all turned out rather well for her."

Her mother stifled a small cry. "A peer of the realm. The Penrydd title and estates, we heard. Anne, could you not even—"

"Oh, I made a bid for him," Anne retorted. "I'm not a complete ninny. But he was well caught by then, set on Gwen and none other. He foiled Calvin's plan to ruin Gwen and thus force her into marriage, and then he saved all of our necks, including Daron's, after Daron went to the Black Hound to try to trade Gwen for the viscount's debts. So you see, Mother, Calvin threw me over first. I turned to Hew so I too might—how did you put it, Father? Land on my feet."

Aunt Gertrude's eyes flared wide. "So you *were* kidnapped, gel? I thought you were embroidering the story."

Anne breathed through her nose, remembering the terror. "Daron proposed me as a bride for the Black Hound. He knew Penrydd would pay a ransom for Gwen and the viscountesses, his stepmother and sister-in-law who were captured with us. There was no one to pay ransom for me. So he had arranged a bride-price if the criminal wanted me."

"He would never," her mother cried. "Anne, such vile accusations—"

"He *did*," Anne said fiercely. "And he has been consorting with blockade runners and free traders and other criminal elements since then. So beware whatever invitation my brother has extended, I beg you. I fear it will not be to our best interests."

Her father set his expression in stony lines. "I won't be tricked by my own son. Take him over my knee if I have to."

"It'd be too late for that, Papa." Anne curled her hand around the leather strap. "Why have we stopped?"

Aunt Gertrude peered out the glass window at the sight of a tall, two-masted brig tied up at the wharf. "I take it we've arrived for our cruise? How lovely. I haven't been boating in an age."

Anne's half boots sank into the thick sand as they disembarked, a heavy pull at her ankles. A small, sleek two-masted brig sat nosed in beside the stone wharf, sails rigged but deck empty. A wooden crane on the wharf lifted heavy casks from a second, larger brig pulled up along the sand, swinging the cargo into a waiting wagon. Anne anchored a hand on her hat to hold it against an uprush of wind. Hew would have something to say about this, some design already sprouting in his clever brain about how to improve the loading mechanism. She wished again he had come with them.

But he was not hers to keep. She had not won him fairly in the first place. Whatever happened with her family—and she would not marry Calvin under any circumstance she could imagine—Anne could not let them force a marriage to Hew. She could not let him sacrifice his future. Not when he had already escaped prison once.

He was the very man she would have drawn for herself if given a sketchbook, down to the gleam of mischief in his eye and the cowlick at the back of his head that showed he was not a man to be subdued. And she *would not* have him take her out of pity.

A man approached them, a little man with tousled brown hair and a leather jerkin. "You!" Anne recognized him. "Minikin."

"Morys," he said, tugging the brim of his cap. "Ladies, guvna, won't you come this way?"

Anne turned to her father. "This roustabout worked for the Black Hound. He helped kidnap me."

"Helped save your hide, I did," Morys cried, nimbly bracing Aunt Gertrude as her shoe turned on the sand. "And the Hound got as he deserved."

Anne surveyed the shapely curve of the ship before them, rolling on the Usk's gentle tide. The rain was coming; she smelled the wet underside of the clouds rolling up the channel. She'd come to know not only the rains of south Wales but the clouds that presaged them. A quick fist of longing squeezed her chest. When she broke with Hew, where would she go? Where would she find a home?

"I do not like this," Anne's mother announced as a crew member directed them to sit in the small rowboat hung by ropes along the side of the ship. The yawl swayed as men cranked the winch to raise them, the shore dropping away like Anne's stomach.

"Daron!" Elizabeth called when her son's golden head appeared at the rail above them. "Why must we take a ship, my darling? I'd do very well to have my feet on solid ground after the past days."

"I've a surprise for you, Mother," Daron called back. His face looked eager and tense, his eyes resting on Anne. "You'll like it."

"Salmon cakes for tea?" Aunt Gertrude asked. "I do adore salmon."

"Something better," Daron promised, then directed a scowl to the sailors operating the winch. "Hurry."

"But why would you not invite Lady Vaughn or the others, dear?" their mother asked as her face came level with her son's. "If she is to be our hostess, it seems polite."

"Her ladyship mislikes boats. She'll be waiting for us at Greenfield when we return." Daron, disregarding his mother's outstretched hand, reached for Anne.

She ignored him, climbing over the rail herself, hauling her muslin skirts after. Calvin, waiting at Greenfield when she and Hew had arrived, had barely let Anne meet her disheveled parents and accept a kiss on the cheek from Aunt Gertrude before insisting they change and meet Daron at the dock for the welcome he'd planned. Mair had laid out the gown Anne wore to Gwen and Penrydd's wedding, and Anne, too upset over what the appearance of her parents portended, had not quarreled.

"Is Hew here?" Anne asked, looking about. The deck of the ship was empty save for a few crewmembers about their tasks, securing sails, pushing casks toward the crane. "I do not understand what all this is about."

"Come, then." Daron towed Anne at his side like a child pulling a wheeled toy. The smooth planking of the deck rolled and shifted, the cool breeze nipping around the collar of her pelisse with a playful bite. Daron's fingers were cold through his gloves. The sails belled and snapped in the wind, and the masts creaked in ominous chorus. Daron pulled her down a short set of wooden stairs leading belowdecks, and Anne blinked as the dim engulfed her.

Her heels echoed on the polished planks of the captain's quarters. Light filtered through tall, narrow windows set like a row of smiling teeth in the stern of the ship. The dark wood of cabinets and heavy furniture curved around them, but the middle of the room was bare. In it stood Rafael Darch and beside him Calvin Vaughn, wearing a dark suit and a smug smile.

Anne's throat closed on sudden dread. She swallowed hard, reaching for bravery. "What is he doing here?"

Calvin crooked his fingers toward a shadowed alcove. "Come forward, vicar. We've the witnesses and her parents. No time like the present."

"Calvin, what does this mean?"

Behind her, Daron filled the stairwell as if standing guard. He tugged a finger beneath his cravat, his gaze shearing away from her narrowed glare.

"Delighted to have you here at our happy event. Sudden, but needs must. Can't wait a moment longer to become the happiest of men." Calvin chortled, baring his teeth in the shape of a smile. "Haven't you sussed it out yet, pet? They're here for our wedding."

~

"TELL ME I MISHEARD YOU, MADAME." Hew fixed a stare on his mother. "Anne isn't to marry Calvin. She's to marry *me*."

The back of his neck prickled as panic rose in his chest. He hadn't persuaded her of this yet, of course. He'd been so close to asking her today in the grassy verge beside the Fourteen Locks. Had wanted to bend a knee, take her hand, and, in the sight of God and the crew of the narrowboat with its cargo of iron from the Welsh hills, ask this most elusive and maddening of women to marry him.

When he had nothing to offer her. Except his heart. But that was better than what she would gain from his brother.

Lady Vaughn huddled into the plush chaise as Hew approached. The drawing room felt shadowed and close, the lamps failing to penetrate the dull afternoon light. A storm brewed in St. George's Channel, and it would sweep up the Bristol Channel soon; the rising pressure rang in his ears.

"Hew, she's turned your head. I do not blame you. The girl is more wily than any of us thought. But Calvin secured her long ago."

And what Calvin wanted, went the unspoken logic, Calvin got. It had always been that way. Hew was the eldest, but Calvin was the favored child. Hew had always been too loud, too coarse, too thoughtful, too idealistic, too ambitious, too gentle, or too stubborn, depending on his father's mood. Calvin was made in his father's image and could do no wrong in his father's eyes. Hew must be denied, disciplined, bent to his father's will to shape him as the heir and successor to Greenfield and the family name. Calvin might do what he liked, and every treat he pointed to was placed in his hand.

Hew curled his hands into fists. Not Anne. Calvin could not have Anne for the asking. She belonged to Hew. She had given herself to him, and he'd accepted this most precious gift. No more needed to be said.

"Where have they taken her?"

"I don't think—"

"Madam." Hew gritted his teeth. "I know my wishes are not your primary concern in this instance. I know you do not like her. But her brother has been dealing with dangerous men, and if he has caught Anne up in it, the consequences could be grave."

"Hewitt!" her ladyship cried. "You are my son—my only son. I think of nothing but you."

Hew reared back his head. "You have two sons, madame, and the second is determined to bring us both grief, I fear."

His mother spread her hands over her face, a gesture he had never seen from her. He had never known her to despair, to crumple, to weep. She was never anything but the brittle statue of a lady, ruling her kingdom but little pleased by it.

"Calvin is not mine," she said from behind her hands. "I took him in at your father's command. He sent away the daughter, but insisted I take the son."

Hew stared, afraid to move toward her, feeling the floor might crumble. An enormous piece of his life had just fallen away. "Calvin has a different mother?"

"A maid. I sent her away at once, as I had all the others, but a son, your father would not forfeit."

"Did you say I have a sister?" Hew put a hand out in the air, looking for something to lean on. There was nothing nearby.

"By my lady's maid. My trusted Rowena." Her ladyship

lowered her hands and stared at them bitterly. "My husband took both of us at my marriage, but when I found he had used her, I-I turned her out. I thought that would be the end of it."

She curled her hands into fists. "After Calvin, I at last knew the man he was. I swore to him then I would take in no more bastards, nor would he have any honest children from me unless he could be faithful." Her voice broke. "He was not."

"This explains it," Hew realized. "Why he was so hard with me. To punish *you*."

His mother shook her head and raised her face, full of pleading. "I was not his choice," she said. "I was never his choice. He considered it too high a price for an heir. I would not see you make the same mistake and bind yourself a woman you cannot love."

Hew crossed the rug and dropped to one knee beside the chaise. His mother's expression tore at his heart, even as his mind warned he was losing time.

"I chose Anne for myself, Mother. I love her already. Out of every woman in the world, I would choose her, again and again. She *cannot* marry Calvin. What I will do if he takes her from me—let me simply say, the consequences will shame us all."

His mother managed a watery smile. "No worse than being found in your bed again."

So that was the reason she turned so hard against Anne. Her betraying his brother was a treachery skating too near her own humiliations, her own old heartbreak. And for him to choose one who might be unconstant ... Hew took his mother's hands, stopping her nervous plucking of the ribbons and her waist.

"She is good," was all he could manage to say. When there was so *much* Anne was, and so much she meant to him. She brought the sun with her when she stepped into a room. She made him feel strong and capable. She looked at him and saw not the soldier or the son or the brother or the Greenfield heir, but the man he was aside from all these things.

And when he held her in his arms, felt the heat of her desire, tasted her surrender, he felt a whole man again, reformed, not the bloody, scarred mess left after the siege of Acre and the slice of the cat-o'-nine tails. He was *himself* again, thanks to Anne, and if he lost her—

If he lost her, he would never again be the man he saw in her eyes. And losing *her*, her own beautiful self, was the worst harm he could ever be dealt.

"When I bring her home," he said softly, "I hope you will take the chance to know her. But you must tell me where they have taken her first."

CHAPTER TWENTY

"Of course I will not marry you."

Anne was astonished at the calm in her voice as she delivered the words. Old Anne would be quaking in her half boots. Old Anne would be weeping with nerves. New Anne glanced out the window, saw the clouds rolling in, and drew a rush of power from the gathering storm. If only she could shoot lightning from her palms, she would clear all this away in a moment.

She whirled to face her brother. "If it's a matter of the money, beg it of Aunt Gertrude yourself. You don't need me." She stabbed a finger in her aunt's direction before turning with a shame-faced smile. "My apologies, Aunt."

"Oh, I would do the same." Aunt Gertrude shrugged. She affected calm, leaning on her ebony walking stick with its elaborately carved ivory head as the ship rolled lightly. But the tightness in her face, around her ears and jaw, betrayed her discomfort. Aunt Gertrude was going to be seasick.

"But I don't have the money, boy. And if I did, I'm not sure I would help your father anyway. I most certainly would not hand it over to you to spend on whatever you will."

"You said you would give Anne an inheritance." Daron's face too, was taut, but with a different kind of sickness. When had her brother gone from greedy to obsessed? "Where's mine?"

"You insolent child," Aunt Gertrude said softly. "Your father did not take you over his knee near enough, did he?"

"Now, Gertrude." Anne's mother stiffened. "We did not desire your instruction when our children were young, and we do not require it now."

Aunt Gertrude stamped her cane on the floor, where it echoed against the planks, sticky with whatever resin was used for polish. "You spoiled him, Eliza. You and Richard gave him everything he wanted, and when he disobeyed you, did you correct him? No. You laughed and let him go his way. Let you reap what you have sown, a spoiled, willful—"

"That is the outside of enough." Anne's father frowned.

"You might save the recriminations and family spats for later," Calvin struck in. "We've a wedding. Vicar—"

"Wait." Darch held up a hand. Calvin and Daron instantly fell silent, and Anne saw that he somehow had both men in his thrall. Vicar Stanley swallowed hard, his Adam's apple bobbing beneath his white clerical collar.

"You said there was money, Sutton. And you said her marriage to Vaughn was the way to secure it. Now it seems that is not the case."

"He supposed I've a fortune, and I don't," Aunt Gertrude barked. "The nerve of you all! Let me off the ship this instant."

She turned to leave, but Daron blocked her way. The room was not warm, but he was sweating. His sweat smelled sour, like old drink, not the lovely warm spice of Hew.

Hew. How Anne wished he were here. He would know what to do.

"Let me past. I'll die on this boat before I'll be held for ransom by a spoiled boy." Aunt Getrude raised her chin.

"Best hope it doesn't come to that, you old harridan," Darch said sharply. "You're here, all of you, because Sutton claimed you were worth geld. Enough to pay the debt he owes me and more."

"What debt?" her mother yelped at the same time her father barked, "How much?"

Aunt Gertrude overruled them all, thumping the floor once again with her cane as she whirled on Darch.

"I don't owe you a scrap, you insolent pup, much less an explanation. But I will say this. What money I have is tied up in a trust for Anne, and Anne only. No one else can touch it, not her brother, not her father, not her husband, not God himself. It is hers to dispose of, hers alone, precisely because I do not wish her hand to be forced. For *any* reason."

"Here now, calm yourself, Aunt Gertrude," Calvin said with a mocking smile. He reached for Anne's hand. "Gel agreed to marry me. Love, and all that. Can't help if she wants to give me all that she has and more, can I? Luckiest of men, etcetera."

Anne pulled away from his grasping hand, cold and moist as an eel reeled from the river. "I said I won't marry you. I'm going to marry your brother."

Calvin scowled. "Trollop! Threw yourself into his bed to get Greenfield. Think I don't know that?" He pushed his face close. "You'll marry me if you know what's best for you."

Anne shied backward, her stomach flailing. "I'll throw myself over the side of this ship first."

"Then you'll drown when the tide comes in, or I'll leave you stranded on the sands." Calvin sneered. "Save us all the fuss, there's a good Nanny, and let the good vicar say his words. Took a bit of convincing to get him here, but he's a man as loves a pretty love story."

"I do believe," the vicar said in a mild tone, though his eyes were wide, "that Miss Sutton is contracted to Captain Vaughn. The captain spoke of it to me mere days ago—"

"Promised to me first!" Calvin roared. "*Me*." He clamped a hand around Anne's wrist. "Now quit being a hussy and say the words."

Darch watched with fascination as Calvin attempted to wrestle Anne before the vicar, Anne resisting every step. Daron threw himself in front of Aunt Gertrude when she raised her cane. Her parents fell back in confusion, clutching each other in alarm.

"Vaughn, you said the gel was willing," Darch put in.

"And you said you'd witness my wedding in return for my help against the excise men," Calvin snapped. "Said I'd be your partner, and I will. Put in my share to cover expenses, get my share of the revenue. But have to ... get the capital ... first!" He hauled on Anne's wrists and she yelped.

"I won't marry you! I promised to marry Hew."

"Then I'll kill him and take his widow!" Calvin's face transformed in fury.

"And I'll kill all of you if I don't get my money." Daron's voice was a hoarse croak, yet somehow the more terrible. So was the pistol in his hand. Anne recognized it as one of a set of dueling pistols that had been on display in Hew's study at Greenfield.

A man had a chance of walking away from a pistol shot at dueling range. But Daron stood far closer than that.

"Whoa. Easy, easy." While everyone else stood frozen, staring at the weapon in Daron's palm, Darch raised his hands above his shoulders, his voice as calm as if soothing a horse. "I'm not here for a murder. That's what'll get you hanged."

Daron wiped the sweat off his face. "You can keep to your smuggling runs and hiding your casks of brandy, Darch. I've a bigger operation to run. I'm the new Black Hound."

"What in the world," Aunt Gertrude barked. "Is the boy run mad? Richard! Since when is there madness in our blood? This must be your doing, Eliza."

"You cannot be Y Gwyllgi," Anne choked out. That was the monster who had kidnapped her and Gwen and the viscountesses. His men had beaten Leah's husband to death over money and he had meant to kill Penrydd, too. "Penrydd defeated him. The Black Hound disappeared. He was swept away by the Severn bore after Pen and Evans blew up his ship and rescued us. You cannot think to be what he was, Daron!"

"Not be rich? Not be powerful? Not be feared?" Daron curled his fingers around the trigger guard. "You all think I am nothing, all of you. You'll learn better."

"Daron, my son—" Their father bit off his words when the pistol bore swung in his direction.

"What, Father? You taught me to shoot. You know I'm fair with a close target."

"Threatening us won't gain you what you want," their father said through gritted teeth. "And you're frightening your mother."

Daron's face softened as he regarded his mother, who clutched her husband's arm, whimpering.

"I'm doing this *for* you, Mother. So you won't be in want. So you needn't worry about who will keep you. I will."

"Sutton," Darch drawled, his hands still raised, "if you shoot at this close range, you'll put a hole in the side of my brig. I'd rather you didn't."

Daron swung the gun on Anne. "Marry him, Anne. Say the words. I promised Calvin I would share your inheritance with him. I'll pay my debts and have more money than Midas. Calvin will ensure the Newport officials don't come close. We'll have an empire, and you'll be taken care of so long as you do what you're told."

Anne set her jaw on the words that wanted to spill forth. Daron, the beloved boy of her youth, had never denied a thing she'd begged of him. But begging would not avail her now.

Daron swerved the pistol toward the vicar. "Now say the words."

"Ahem. Who brings this woman to be wed to this man?" Vicar Stanley managed. "You know I must see a special license—"

"We're at sea!" Daron shouted. "It's done when you say it is. We'll sign the license later."

"After I have the money to pay for it." Calvin cackled. He looked desperate, Anne thought, watching Daron with apprehension. But when Calvin looked at Darch, she saw real fear. Darch was the dangerous one—but why?

Her father cleared his throat and puffed out his chest, pushing his wife behind him. "I cannot consent to this marriage. I won't give my daughter to you, Vaughn. Not like this."

Anne closed her eyes briefly and choked back a cry of relief. Her father, in the test, would stand by her. "Never mind that *I* already objected," she managed to say.

"Richard." Their mother moaned and clutched her husband's coat sleeve. "Richard, I believe I might faint. Why does Daron have a gun? Just let him marry Anne. Gertrude, this is all your fault!"

"*My* fault? Did I drive them to this madness?" Gertrude banged her cane on the floor, her plump body swaying with the increased rocking of the ship. "I already told him they can't touch the money. It is Anne's."

"And she'll sign it to me as soon as we're married," Calvin snarled. "Now hold your peace or I'll have your nephew plug you, you old beldame!"

"Hew," Anne whispered, saying his name like a prayer. "Hew is going to stop this. Stop all of you."

"Stop us how?" Darch asked curiously.

"I don't know. He'll think of something. He's a gunner *and* a sapper."

Daron advanced on the vicar. "You. Say the words. I've two pistols on me, and Darch has more."

Stanley swallowed again, his shoulders moving back. "If y-you shoot me, you know, there will be no sanction at all upon this marriage. I can't say it will hold in any case, given—"

"Do it!" Daron screamed. Then he tipped to one side—they all did—as the boat lurched beneath their feet. Behind her own cry and the shouts of men above deck, Anne heard a bellowing *boom* and the splinter of wood, smelled hot tar and sulfur.

Darch pushed Daron aside and charged toward the stairwell. "Someone's firing on my ship!"

~

"GOD'S TEETH, Vaughn, you were right." The Duke of Beaufort grinned as he peered at the splintered hole in the hull of the brig racing in the tide before them. "Landed the shot right where you said you would, and didn't need to turn broadside at all."

"That's why they call them bow chasers." Hew patted the bore of the cannon beside him, still hot from the charge and the explosion. "Handy for firing on ships ahead of you. Put one on the stern and you can fire on a ship chasing you, too. Broadside presents too much field for damage if they return fire. Keep a narrow profile and you're harder to hit."

The master's mate raised his spyglass as men poured onto the deck of the other ship, turning out to inspect the damage. "They're past the seawall but not yet to the Point," he reported. "Like to turn in at the Goldcliff Pill, I'd say."

"And Darch will know the area. That bloody Monk's Ditch

is lined with smuggler loot," the duke said grimly. "How far could they make it if they sailed on?"

"Tide's in their favor, but Cap'n put a nice square hole in their hull, port stern," the mate answered. "They'll be taking on water afore they hit the Severn."

Anne was on that ship. So were her parents, her aunt, her brother, his brother—half brother. Hew hadn't time to think about the consequences of his mother's revelation.

He'd pushed the cob as hard as he might to Pillgwenlly, poor Cadfael getting his first good gallop in years. And there, tied up at the wharf, was a beautiful brig, the *Fierce*, dispensed for the use of the Monmouthshire Militia, which Beaufort commanded.

A worker had straightened from leaning on a stack of crates and approached Hew at once. He recognized the little man he'd seen at the smuggler's hideout with Darch.

"You," Hew said.

"Morys." The other jerked a thumb over his shoulder, indicating the square-rigged brig curving its way down the Usk toward the Bristol Channel. "Yer lady's aboard, and all her folk with her. They've the vicar and the Vaughn dandy with, and he as thinks to be the new Hound." Morys spat into the sand.

"You'll swing for helping them."

"I'll get a pardon from His Grace for turning informant," the small man said, scrambling after Hew as a sailor on the *Fierce* lowered the yawl in response to Hew's hail. "Vouch for me, won't ye?"

"Hero of Acre." The Duke of Beaufort grinned and advanced, arm extended, as Hew stepped on deck. "Shake my hand."

Hew did, reflecting that his mother would faint with joy to know her son had touched a ducal glove. "I need your ship to foil a kidnapping."

"And a smuggler. Suspected Darch for years, but never been

able to catch him at it. Carried off your lady, did he? Well, the King won't stand for that, and neither will I."

The duke's expression beamed excitement. Henry Somerset, fifth Duke of Beaufort, peer of the realm and nearly three-score in age, was a man of action. His crew ran up the sails and cast off faster than Hew had ever seen.

Hew stepped back as the gunner's mate swabbed the cannon, cleaning and readying it for the next round. "How many gunners are they mounting?" he asked.

The master's mate swept his spyglass back and forth. "Looks like four guns on each side. Not sure what size—"

Hew plucked the spyglass from him and knew in an instant. "Ten pounders. Light, but then they're made for blockade running, evading ships and not attacking. Your eighteen-pound cannonades can take them, Your Grace."

"Beaufort to you," the duke said genially, "and we're not going to sink her with women aboard, I'd wager."

"No," Hew said grimly, "we are not."

The mate blinked as Hew handed the spyglass back. "Ye mean to run 'em onto the Welsh Grounds, Cap'n, sir?"

"Those spits turn to quicksand with the coming tide," Morys, who had attached himself to the rescue effort, spoke up. "Darch knows that."

"I don't intend to wreck them," Hew said. "Only bring them about so we can board."

"Those smugglers've been running goods through Goldcliff for a while now," the master's mate said. "But the deeper channel's to starboard, on the Avonmouth side. He'll run into the gravel bank here, or the Bedwyn rocks just ahead. Unless he's light enough in the ballast that he thinks to float straight through."

"We're not light enough to follow," Hew said. "I have to stop them."

"I say." The duke pointed. "Who's the gel?"

Morys chortled with delight. "His mort, and no mistake. Knew she wouldn't let the rotters hold 'er."

Hew blinked as a head of golden-blonde hair, gleaming like a fresh-struck guinea, emerged on deck. Anne ran to the railing, her pelisse soaring behind her like a sparrow's wing. Across the yards that separated them he saw her white face, and the fear in her bright blue eyes stabbed his heart. She stood dangerously above the hole he'd put in the smuggler's ship, and Hew prayed the deck would not give away beneath her.

"Hew!" She waved her arms wildly, joy and relief chasing one another across her exquisite face. She was hale and they had not hurt her.

"Tell the captain to come around!" Hew cupped his hands to shout back. The wind was against him, blowing the words back in his face.

"What?" Anne shouted, placing her hands to her ears.

"Tell Darch to heave to! Turn into the wind!"

The smuggler ran to the wheel to confer with the helmsman, while sailors converged on the capstan to pull ropes. If they loosed the sheets to full sail and weren't high enough in the water, they'd run aground on the sands. The *Fierce* couldn't clear the sandbanks known as the Welsh Grounds until the higher tide flooded the estuary. The militia ship had a heavier draught than the smuggler's, carrying more guns and a full crew.

He had to get to Anne.

"Daron," she began, then whipped around at a shout behind her.

Her brother charged onto the deck, waving a pistol. Calvin pounded up the stairs behind, then Vicar Stanley stumbled onto deck, looking as if he'd been keel-hauled. Sutton ran straight to his sister.

Hew heard part of their exchange as the *Fierce* drew nearer, but it was enough to see the gun and Anne's fear, her mouth open in protest. His blood turned to ice, a roar filling his ears. Anne was in danger, and Hew was a bloody boat length away. He curled his hands into fists around the railing of the ship until he thought his knuckles might burst their skin.

"Let her go, Sutton!"

"She's my sister," Sutton screamed back, closing a fist in Anne's hair. She swung at him, without success, back arched and arms windmilling.

"Call this off, Calvin, or by God I will shoot you out of the water," Hew bellowed.

"You'll do what, *Captain?*" Calvin's sneer cut across the distance, rife with disdain. "You're no hero. Not even a decent gunner. You'd never've ended up in prison if you were worth a groat to the army or anyone. We all know it."

Calvin didn't know the half of it; he didn't know what had come after prison, for Hew. He couldn't bear the questions on Anne's face.

"Reload," Hew ordered.

"Yes, sir." The gunner's mate scrambled to push the cartridge into the gun.

"Fuse three point five." Hew held out his palm. In a real fight he'd have another gunner and six soldiers to assist him. He'd have a trigger line, not a linstock for firing, but this was an older cannon, without a gunlock.

In Acre, in the last stage of the siege, he'd fought with confiscated cannon, one powder monkey, and a quarter gunner who'd taken grape shot to the hand, and he'd still won.

"This all I got, sir." The gunner, a boy with the accent of the Black Mountains, handed Hew the line from the supply bucket. Morys watched with interest, craning his neck to see.

Hew pricked the fuse into the touch hole, the action so familiar he could do this blindfolded, in his sleep. "Home."

"Stop him!" Daron demanded, shaking Anne so hard that she cried out.

"Won't shoot us!" Calvin taunted. "Can't be that mad."

"Loading shot." Hew picked up the wooden rammer and drove in the ball, an iron round shot, heavy, lethal. "Prime her, soldier."

The gunner's mate scrambled forward, ladling powder into the pan at the touchhole. "Primed and ready, sir."

Calvin gripped the rail, leaning forward to hurl his insults. "Parents'll never let her marry you, you know. Worthless. Reason our father hated you."

"Run out your guns!" Hew roared the command. It took all of them, the master's mate, gunner's mate, and Morys, along with the duke, straining the gun tackles to heave the cannon into place at the bow. The carriage dropped into place like a key in a lock.

"Hold your fire!" Darch bellowed from the helm of his ship.

Finally. "Then heave to, Darch, and put a stop to this." Hew pointed to the man behind him. "I've the Duke of Beaufort on board. His Grace says kidnapping's a hanging offense."

Daron swung the pistol on Darch, training the gun on the smuggler while holding Anne like a squirming cat. Darch swallowed his reply, raising his hands in the air. Even from this distance Hew could see the man's eyes were stony flints. He wasn't with them, but he couldn't help Anne.

A cold calm he knew well rolled through Hew, lifting his limbs. He moved to the rear of the cannon, levering the heavy mechanism that sighted his gun.

"Left two hundred," Hew called out, his training at work even though the duke didn't know the commands. "Elevation minus five minutes."

"You won't, er, fire *at* them, Vaughn," the duke said. "Right-o?"

"Course he wouldn't!" Morys scoffed, then caught his chuckle. "Would 'ee?

Sweat gathered across Hew's back, that familiar, ominous prickle. He braced his legs and found his sight line, feeling for the roll of the ship. He'd trained on land and at sea, in swells larger than this. But he'd never had a target that meant everything.

Anne was trapped at the rail, her brother's elbow around her neck while he held Darch at bay with his pistol. She fought and screamed, but Sutton had Calvin to help subdue her. The rest of her family huddled near the stairs, too far to help, too weak to intercede. Only Hew could stop this.

Calvin leaned over the rail, his face turning crimson. "You lost, Hew! Admit it. You've finally lost. I've won, the girl and the money, and you're nothing but a—"

"Five seconds!" Hew bellowed, lifting the linstock.

The long wooden pole held the burning match at its tip, lit and ready. Sulfur sizzled in the damp air, and Hew welcomed the burn in his nostrils, his throat. This was his element. This, he knew. His gun was his arm, an extension of his body. He could shoot in the rain, through the mud, through a hell of return fire. He would not fail. He waited for the next swell, counting.

Calvin faltered. "You wouldn't—"

"Do it!" Daron screamed. "Try to stop me."

"Three!" Hew shouted. "Two ... one ..."

The men behind him fell back, hands covering their ears. Anne paused to stare at him, mouth agape. Awe transformed her face as she watched, but not a hint of fear. His magnificent woman. Hew lifted the linstock, meeting her eyes, and she read his command as if she heard it. She dropped to the deck, throwing her arms over her head.

The ship rose on a swell, in time with the beat of his heart.

"*Fire.*" Hew dipped the burning match to the fuse. It hissed like an asp shooting from its burrow, and the touch hole ignited. The boom of the cannon echoed in his bones, a euphoric rush. The gun recoiled into the breech line, straining the tackles, a veil of smoke drifting from the bore.

The ball soared through the air, whistling like a shepherd boy at play, and rammed into the keel of Darch's ship, slamming the brig sideways. Hitting the wind, she lurched and stilled, her sails furiously fighting one another as they belled with air.

Daron staggered, the bore of the pistol cutting empty air. Anne rose with her teeth latched on her brother's hand. He howled and loosed her. She sent one flaming look at Hew, her face fearless.

"Come fetch me!" she called.

"Anne, don't!" Hew rushed forward, guessing her intent even as she hiked up her skirts, showing dainty stockings and her favorite boots. Nimble as a goat she hopped onto the rail of the ship, then swung her legs over the side as if she were a child on a picnic at her favorite lake. She'd told him of that lake, of her summers upon it, but—

"I can swim!" she shouted, her voice nearly cheerful. She sent one smug glare at Calvin, who lunged for her, and then, as the ship listed, she slipped out of his grasp and plunged into the cold, frothy water.

CHAPTER TWENTY-ONE

She couldn't swim, not in this. The Bristol Channel at rising tide was nothing like her quiet Lake Tegid. She had just killed herself, when what she wanted was to be with Hew.

Anne fought to the surface, kicking her legs wildly, pushing water with her arms. Brine filled her mouth, and she choked.

Her feet hit something, and she found her footing. Sand. Her choke turned to a laugh. She was on a long spit of sand. *Saved.* She need only wait till Hew arrived. She heard shouts from both ships and the creak of ropes, smelled scorched wood. She felt wild and free in a way she never had in her life.

A swell knocked her to her knees. This was *not* Lake Tegid. Here, where the Bristol Channel turned into the Severn Estuary, the land was a funnel for the water, turbulent and greedy, with an unpredictable bore that could arise any time and wash everything before it. Hew had spoken of it in his discussions about wharves and shipping and navigation with the men.

Hew. He was coming. She'd never seen anything so magnificent as Hew with his cannon, determined to blow Darch's ship out of the water to save her.

Sand closed around her hands, and she yanked them free.

Honestly, she need only stand here on this sandbar until he came, and—

Another wave pitched her into the water, sand sucking her legs up to her knees. Good Lord, it was like quicksand. She pushed aside her skirts, wet and tangled, and tugged at her feet. She had to get free. She had to keep her head above water, she had to wait, she had to be with Hew—

"Anne." An arm snaked around her middle, pulling her face from the water. She knew the chest she was hauled against and sputtered a half-laugh, half-cry of relief.

"*Hew*." She turned and threw her arms around his neck.

The tiny boat rocked. Morys held the oars, steadying them as Hew sat with Anne in his arms. She scrubbed her face into his neck.

"You saved me."

"You saved yourself. I've always wanted a woman who rose from the sea. My very own water sprite."

Anne laughed into the curve of his shoulder. He smelled of gunpowder and salt. She curved her hands on either side of his cheeks, lifted her head, and kissed him.

"They didn't make you marry him?" Hew murmured against her lips. "You didn't say the words."

"It wouldn't have mattered. Calvin didn't have a license." She drew back, fear clutching her heart in its wild leap. "He said he would kill you to have me. He said—"

"Shh. We'll sort everything. I promise."

"So." Morys cleared his throat. "Ready to board, Cap'n? 'Pears His Grace has his men rounded up and himself'll be wanting answers, I don't doubt."

"So do I," Hew said.

"His Grace?" Anne asked, looking up to see that Hew's ship had secured Darch's brig with grappling hooks while his men boarded.

"The Duke of Beaufort, commander of the Monmouthshire Militia, and my commander now, I think," Hew said. "Come, love, I know you don't like kidnapping, but will you away with me?"

Anne gripped the sides of the yawl as the sailors hoisted them. Oh, she hated this part, the swaying in midair with naught but tiny bits of wood to hold on to. "I'll away with *you*, but they can't hurt you, can they? The duke will stop them?"

"*I* will stop them," Hew said, "and they won't hurt you. I'll be sure they can never hurt you again."

"And a pardon for me, remember," Morys remarked, stowing the oars. "Helped save the lady, I did."

They were a bedraggled group, assembling on the deck of the *Fierce*. The duke held court as calmly as if he stood before his peers in the House of Lords or at ease in his own drawing room, his backdrop lowering clouds laced with crackles of lightning as the promised storm drew near.

"Darch." The duke regarded the smuggler, who stood at indifferent ease, shoulders back, though his hands were bound behind him. "You're responsible for the cargo on this brig, none of which has paid the King's tax?"

"Not I, Your Grace," Darch drawled. "The cargo belongs to Sutton here." He nodded at Daron.

Anne gaped from her safe place snugged at Hew's side, his arm firmly around her. "Daron? Smuggling?" Her dismay was real.

"And the contraband stowed at the Fleur de Lys, which Mr. Morys has described?" the duke inquired.

Darch nodded. "Sutton's also."

Daron huffed and turned on him. "Set me up! Sell me out! You—" He whirled on Calvin. "Tell 'im! Tell them all."

"Tell what?" Calvin backed away, palms raised, his pale

blue eyes wide. "You said you're the Black Hound. We all heard it."

The duke frowned. "The Black Hound is responsible for a great number of crimes around Newport and Cardiff. Has been for years."

"Not me!" Daron yelped, struggling as several of the duke's men stepped forward to bind his hands. "Someone else! Darch's trying to frame me, he is—"

"You demanded my ship," Darch said. "You commandeered my cargo. Morys will vouch for it. Then you kidnapped your own sister for the purpose of forcing her into marriage with this one—"

"No harm done!" Calvin bleated, waving his hands through the air. "Didn't marry her, did I? Gel said no. That was the end of it. Wasn't that the way of it, vicar?" He turned to glare at Stanley.

"Vicar," the duke said, "I want a full accounting of events from someone I can trust."

"Of course, Your Grace." Stanley swallowed hard. "Only, might we stand on solid ground for that?"

"Please, let's," Anne's mother said plaintively. "This has all been very distressing. I'm certain my nerves are shattered for life." She leaned against her husband as he offered a protective arm.

Neither of her parents had inquired after Anne's welfare. Instead, her mother fretted about Daron, worrying that the bonds were too tight around his wrists, promising his father would clear him of all these nonsensical accusations, and soon.

"Miss Sutton." The duke turned to her. "I'll want an account from you as well. In the event you wish to bring charges."

"Of-f c-c-course, Your G-grace," Anne said, teeth chattering from cold or fear, she wasn't certain which.

"Charges?" Calvin yelped. "Anne, you won't bring *charges—*"

"We'll discuss this when she's warm and dry," Hew said, pulling Anne close against him. He glanced at the master's mate. "You heard His Grace command our return to port. Tell the helmsman." He turned to the duke. "You can grapple the brig into the mouth of the Usk, I'm sure, but you might want to beach her near the Ebbw for repairs. She won't make it to Pillgwenlly."

"As you wish, Captain." Beaufort grinned. "She's your ship now to command."

Darch made a sound like a smothered moan, his shoulders dropping in defeat. "She'll need repairs after the holes he put in her," he muttered.

"Some of the best shooting I've seen. Demned fine gunner you are, Captain—pardon my language, ladies." The duke clapped Hew on the back, shaking his shoulder. Hew winced, and Anne clutched her arm around his waist.

"The brandy," Daron cried. "The tobacco. The tea. It goes to *him?*"

"That goes to the customs officer, but the ship's a spoil of war, ain't it?" the duke said heartily. "Or she's my prize to give away. One of those two things."

"Your Grace." Calvin pushed forward. "You should know this man is a disgrace. He left the Artillery under a cloud. Any day word will come of a court-martial—"

"Not when I speak to the King," the duke said genially. "Stopping a smuggler who's been plaguing this coast for years, *and* capturing the Black Hound? Good God, his work at Acre had him in sight for a knighthood even before this. We sent him home with a charge to plan British defenses so you all aren't speaking French a year from now. Your brother's in line for honors, son, and if you've any sense, you'll rise along with him."

"Beaufort. I shall be the first to congratulate my grand-nephew to be." Aunt Gertrude made her way to Anne's side, her cane echoing on the polished deck. "But we can do this back in Newport, I hope? Granted, they won't have a tearoom like what we're accustomed to in Llandrindod Wells, but we'll make do."

"Lady Poultenay." The duke graciously offered his arm. "How do you do? I profoundly regret what these men have put you through, such a delicate bloom as you are."

Aunt Gertrude cackled with delight. "It's Gertrude to you, Duke, as it always has been." She linked her arm through his as Beaufort led her off, matching his gait to hers. "How is your lovely duchess, and your very many beautiful children?"

Anne looked up at Hew as the others drew away, leaving them apart for a moment. She drew a deep sigh of relief, though she could imagine, with the need to confront her parents later, the ordeal was not over.

"Spoils of war." Hew pressed a kiss to her forehead. His lips were cool and firm. An electric charge hung in the air, the clouds over his shoulder bristling with energy. "Does that mean I get to keep you?"

"That means *I* get to keep *you*," Anne said, and kissed him back.

THEY HAD a riotous welcome at St. Sefin's, with everyone running everywhere at once to heat water, find dry clothing, and fetch fresh linens to make up beds. Aunt Gertrude and the duke went to sit in the chapter house, the best the priory could offer for a formal parlor. Anne's parents followed, offering pleas and explanations for Daron's behavior. Cerys set herself to the serious business of making the ducal tea. Dovey and the widows ransacked the kitchen for proper refreshments and sent Ifor and Tomos to the pie shop for baked goods, coins from Aunt Gertrude weighting their pockets.

Eilian came from the room where she'd been attending to Leah and pulled up short at the assemblage in St. Sefin's kitchen, wafting the smell of damp wool.

"Anne? Why are you wet? Captain Vaughn." She veered her glance away from Hew toward his brother. "Mr. Vaughn. Mr. Stanley? What is the meaning of this?"

"Mrs. Lambe." The vicar swept her a deep, awkward bow, reaching for his hat and finding he lacked one. "I regret the strange circumstances under which you find us, but I'm afraid we must beg your—"

"Oh, for heaven's sake, speak straight," Eilian snapped. "What has happened?"

"We, er, were caught up in a, em—"

Anne stared with fascination as the vicar, whom she had always known to be eloquent grace, stumbled over his words. "That is to say—"

"Vicar," Widow Jones called, coming from the chapter house, "His Grace wants you."

"Ah. I must go. The duke wants me." Stanley vanished down the hall.

Anne tried to catch Hew's eye, but he was staring at Eilian, who stared back. Anne noticed for the first time they shared the same straight nose and decided tilt to the jaw. The same changeable eyes, now green-tinged like the Irish Sea.

Dovey cocked her head as she loaded the tea tray. "Cerys, *pwt,* with me," she said. "Widow?" They whisked away to attend the duke, while footsteps sounded from a different hall.

"Eilian, my lamb—"

The woman pulled up short at the sight of them. "Miss Meredith?" Anne asked, confused.

The older woman's gaze riveted on Eilian's face, then Hew's. "Ah," she said. "You know."

"I just learned," Hew said softly.

"Learned what?" Calvin brushed at the shoulder of his coat. "By God, I could use a brandy."

Miss Meredith cleared her throat. "She is your sister."

Calvin recoiled. "Not *mine*."

"Half-sister." Hew turned on him. "And I am your half-brother."

Calvin blinked. "The devil you say."

"Eilian is my daughter. Your father sired her when Lady Vaughn brought me here as her lady's maid upon her marriage. She and Hew are three months apart in age. My lady and I might have gone through our time together."

Miss Meredith turned to Calvin, her lips tight. "I am not your mother, however. She was a chambermaid. Your father believed everything at Greenfield was his, including the help."

"And my mother turned you off for it." Hew's voice cracked with tension. Anne slipped her hand into his, wondering at these revelations. He'd never been sure of his place in this family to begin with, and now to learn it was nothing like he'd believed ... what might this mean for him?

For them?

"She wasn't—where's th' other, then? The one you say is m'mother." Calvin licked his lips, his eyes wide with confusion.

"Dead, now, may her soul be at peace," Miss Meredith said. "The good burghers of Newport wouldn't have her in the town, staunch Christians as they are, and there was no place like St. Sefin's to take her. I fear her lot was a hard one, and unhappy."

"I'm the favorite. Mother always favored me. Father, too." Calvin looked to be sweating, his gaze darting everywhere. The hatred when his gaze fell on Hew was palpable. Anne squeezed his hand all the harder.

Miss Meredith spoke for him. "Sir Lambert wished to punish my lady because she refused, after you, to take in any more of his bastards. She vowed he would sire no more children on her until he was faithful. He never was."

"You knew this?" Hew asked.

Both Eilian and Anne watched Miss Meredith's face, the wistful sorrow turning up the corner of her mouth. "I said I was not welcome at Greenfield. She is free to call at Pensarn Cottage whenever she likes."

"But she sent you away. You and your daughter." Hew's voice was low, the emotion kept at bay. Such control the man had, Anne thought.

"Mother, you needn't," Eilian began.

Miss Meredith held up a hand, her eyes filled with pain. "It is time for the truth, my darling. Yes, I had to send Eilian away. Everyone knew what had happened. Milady gave me the cottage at High Cross so I would not starve, but the councilmen —the rules—I could not keep her."

"I had a happy childhood." Eilian curled her fingers around her mother's hand. "I was loved. They spoke well of you, and I understood why you could not visit often."

"You're lying!" Calvin yelped. "Filthy lies. I won't stay to hear this." He turned and darted out of the kitchen. The outer door slammed.

"How will he get home, I wonder?" Eilian's eyes were wide.

Hew shrugged. "I'll deal with him later. For now, I owe you both an apology, but Anne ... she fell in the water. Is the bath ready?"

"Come, chick." Eilian held out her hand to Anne, but her gaze lingered on Hew. "I need no apology from you, Captain Vaughn. Only—I have wanted you to know me."

"I won't be my father," Hew said, a grim set to his mouth. "I won't put my honor above what is right. I would be proud to acknowledge you, in public if Miss Meredith wishes, and in private if she would have it so. You have been an inspiration to Anne." He turned to press a kiss to her forehead, and Anne melted into him.

"You need a wash as well. You smell like gunpowder still." She hesitated, clinging to his hand. "You'll stay? Here?"

Hew nodded. "We needs must settle some matters, you and I."

"Yes, we must," Anne said softly.

~

SHE MADE short work of her bath, cleaning herself in the hip tub that Eilian and Cerys filled for her. She dried quickly and drew on a wrapper, an old one of Gwen's, and went to find where they'd put Hew.

She found Leah first, dozing in the mothers' ward. She opened her eyes at Anne's soft footstep and smiled tenderly. "Come in, my dear. He's awake. I think he knows it's you, and he wants to say hello."

"He knows me?" Anne took the baby with delight. Daniel opened his eyes in that foggy way newborns peered toward voices they recognized. "Then I am indeed one of his people."

"May you be blessed for the help you have given us, and may you be blessed in your own children," Leah said, pressing Anne's hand.

"May it be so." Anne nodded, swallowing down the lump in her throat. A warm rock filled her belly, heavy, solid. She had done this, helped this woman and her child. And she could do this again and again.

Hew was in a smaller room that had once been bedroom to a long-ago nun. He sat on the narrow bed, coat and waistcoat discarded on the covers, trying to pull his shirt over his head.

"Let me help."

"No." He turned suddenly, clamping her wrist. "Don't—I don't want you to see."

"Hew." She swallowed that aching lump. She wanted so badly to touch him. "If you are to be my husband, darling, you must let me see you."

His eyes flared, turning that dark blue she knew now meant interest and desire. "No jilting?" he asked softly. He turned his hand to slide his palm against hers.

She caught her breath and shook her head. "Unless you want—"

"I want *you*." Before she could finish the thought he hauled her to him, his arms a hot vise across her back, her breasts pressed against his chest. He fell on her mouth as if he'd been starving for days, kissing her as she'd wanted to kiss him in the meadow. Land and sky tilted and fell away, leaving only his arms, and the world between them.

"You would marry me?" he growled. "You would say yes?"

"Yes."

His kiss stole her breath and gave it back again, as if he were drawing out the last of the old, broken Anne and giving her back to herself, new, whole. As if the flame lit within her found its answer and twin inside him.

She tugged at the hem of his shirt, wanting to touch him, wanting him as close to her as possible.

"Off."

He laid a hand over hers, his face sobering. "It will frighten you. Disgust you. I can't imagine what it looks like."

"Let me, my love." Gently she tugged, and he opened his hand. She pulled the shirt over his head and stifled her gasp as he turned to cast it aside.

She stretched out a hand but caught herself an inch above the angry wounds. "Does it hurt still?"

"Phantom pain. I cannot feel a thing from here—" he pointed a finger to the top of his shoulder— "to here." He moved the finger to his waist.

The stretch of skin between was a coil of red welts, healing to scars. Anne pressed her palm to the raised ridges of flesh. "How many lashes?" She held back a sob.

"My major ordered a hundred, which is a light punishment for the Navy. The colonel came in and stopped him at fifty. He said the major had no right to use official discipline for a personal grievance, and not on a man weak from prison fever."

Anne laid her cheek against his back and slipped her hands around his waist. He was warm and firm, so very solid. She drifted her palms over the light hair dusting his chest and felt beneath the muscle the strong, steady beat of his heart. His strong, valiant, courageous heart, bent on justice and right.

"I will take your scars if it means I can have you."

He turned to press a kiss to the top of her head. "Anne." His voice came out rough, like the gravel against her hands when she'd thought she would drown on that sandbar before he could reach her. "God knows I want you, but I cannot—I must not bind you. It would not be fair. I might yet be court-martialed, despite what the duke said. He is not the one who will decide my sentence. The judgment will come, and I could not bear for you to suffer because of me."

"I will rise with you, and I will fall with you, if you let me," she whispered. "I want to be with you, Hew."

She slipped her hand lower, across his belly, and smiled against his shoulder at his sharp intake of air. He wanted her, and being a man, bless him, he could not hide it. She peeked downward and smiled all the wider. There was the evidence, stretching out his buckskin breeches.

"Minx." He clasped a hand over hers. She loved the rough weight of his palm, the corded muscle in his forearms, the dizzying strength of him. He was so much *more* than her, a huge sturdy cliff she could curl beneath, and know she would be safe always.

"You want my body," he taunted. "But Anne, I am not the kind of man you are meant for. I'm not a man who is worthy of you. Your kindness, your goodness, your wit—that heart you hide beneath all this golden beauty." He pressed a kiss to her cheek, to each side of her lips. "I see it. I see you."

"I want *you*, Hewitt Vaughn. All of you. Why do you think I came to your room that night?"

"So you didn't have to marry my brother," he murmured against her lips.

"Because I wanted *you*." She rained kisses over his face, crawling over him as she pressed him back upon the bed. "I saw you minister to your mother. I saw you sit at the table at dinner, and I could see you were a man of honor, a man of strength. A man I could admire."

"A man of clay." But he didn't push her away. He reveled in her kisses, caressing her in return, sifting his hands through her loose hair, sliding his palms along her skin as if he were handling a treasure of gold. "I want you to be free, my darling. Not tricked. I want you to make your own choice."

"And I choose you, for you are the match for me, Hewitt Vaughn." She pressed a kiss to the tender place beneath his ear, feeling the muscle jump beneath her lips. "But I am the one who tricked you. Forced your hand. I will not have you compelled to take me for honor."

"Dear God, Anne, I want *you*. Honor is the least of it. Wherever you go, I will follow and beg you to take me. I will never cease wooing you, for without you—I could have said yes to you six years ago. Why didn't I?" His eyes burned blue as he stared into her eyes, and Anne felt the shock of rightness to the seat of her soul. This man, this place, this moment—everything in her life had led her here.

She climbed over his hips and hiked up her skirts, settling herself against his eager manhood. His eyes flared with passion, and she loved that look, too.

"I accept you now," she said. "You are mine. Now claim me back."

He anchored his hands to her hips, fingers digging into her flesh, his face transfigured with pleasure and longing and wonder. For her.

"I was yours the moment I stepped into this church," he said hoarsely. "I saw a goddess of the spring, tearing apart a bough of myrtle, and I was caught in her spell as sure as if I'd stumbled into a fairy ring."

She moaned softly, moving against him. "Liar," she breathed. "The way you glared at me—"

"Because I knew whatever I'd never thought to have in my life, it was there, standing before me. And if I could not have it—have *you*—better I had died at Acre, or in prison, or from the lash."

"You have me now," Anne panted, moving toward her climax, and his. "Say it. Believe it. I am yours."

He arched his back and caught his breath, clenching his teeth. He was holding back, she saw, drawing out the moment with her. Their moments together. She loved him for it.

"Anne—I don't wish to trap you. I want you to have what you want."

"You, my love." Anne leaned down to kiss him on the mouth. "I choose you. Now choose me back."

"God, yes," he breathed. He grabbed her hips and thrust up into her, driving her to the brink and over.

"Stay with me. Be with me," she sobbed as the pleasure keeled her over, rolling her like the waves that had dragged her down in the channel. But she would surface again in Hew's arms. He would always bring her back to the light.

"I will be with you always. I promise."

He slipped out of her and pulled her against him, squeezing her legs and thrusting once, twice between them to finish. Anne smiled, watching him reach his peak. She would always love watching this beautiful man come apart for her. With her.

"You were supposed to be with me," she chided gently.

"I am. I will be." His eyes were a hazy blue-gray with passion, his lips curling at the corners. "But I won't give you a babe if you do not wish it."

"I believe I might, one day. I am less afraid lately." For everything beautiful came with a price. She knew that now. Anne laid her head on his chest and surrendered to the sense of completeness, of safety, of belonging that she felt with Hewitt Vaughn in her arms.

"No one else," she said a while later, startling out of her doze at a sudden thought.

"Hmm?" He pulled a lazy hand through her hair. She lay atop him still, the sheet stretched over them both.

She lifted her chin to look him in the eye. "I won't share you with others. No lady's companions, no chambermaids, no sweet, fresh buttercup girls. I will be a jealous wife."

"Then prepare to meet all my needs, *wife*." He chuckled. "I won't tolerate other men looking at you, you know. No clever tradesmen or knowledgeable surgeons instructing you in their trade. I will be a jealous husband, too."

She kissed him again. "And I'm afraid I won't be one of those potted wives. The kind who only move from the kitchen to the parlor to the nursery. I want to do what Dovey and Eilian do. I want to learn a real skill, and I want to use it to help people."

"I want whatever makes you happy, *sidan*." He ran his

hands down her arms, like a potter sculpting clay, and Anne knew herself to be fully alive. She knew where she belonged, and it was here, with him.

"You do." She slid her hands over his jaw, coming out in stubble, and ran her finger along that delicious groove above his lip, feeling his smile as she claimed him for her own. "I'm for Captain Hewitt Vaughn, and none other," she murmured. "You are man enough for me."

EPILOGUE

"St. Teilo's toes, it's hot." The Viscountess Penrydd pulled off her bonnet and fanned herself. "Are you hot, Anne?"

"I think it perfectly pleasant," Anne remarked. The sun shone in a sky lazy with autumnal blue, and a warm breeze wafted through the garden behind Penrydd Castle. That towered edifice, built for pageantry and not for defense, lay snugged at the foot of the great forest of Wentworth, the gray bricks gleaming with the same air of contentment that mantled its mistress.

Anne pointed at Gwen's belly, outlined by the Welsh shawl knotted at her waist. "Perhaps the future viscount is the issue. You're growing quite fat, Gwen."

"Don't let Pen hear you speak that way," Gwen said lazily. "He's determined we'll have a daughter. And I'm not as fat as Mathry." She waved a hand at the third woman of their foursome, out gathering flowers to decorate the table for the evening's dinner.

"Mrs. Ross to you." Mathry giggled and tapped her cheeks with a handful of comfrey. "Finally brought my Scotsman up to scratch, I did. Had you lost all hope of me, Mrs. Evans?"

"I never doubted the man was tripping over his feet for you." Dovey smiled and heaped her basket with hydrangea. "Much like Sir Hewitt the first time he saw our Anne."

"Sir Hewitt," Gwen marveled, sending Anne a triumphant grin. "How was the knighting ceremony at St. James?"

"Terrifying," Anne said frankly. "I was certain I'd trip over my train and fall at the King's feet. Or forget to walk backward out of the Queen's chamber when she held her drawing room to honor us wives."

"But now he's a Knight Bachelor, and you are the new Lady Vaughn," Gwen said. "How is the other Lady Vaughn adjusting?"

"I have no say in the menus or the entertainments at Greenfield," Anne admitted. "But I am so busy learning from Eilian and Mrs. Evans here, I have little leisure at any rate. And she has put me in charge of the staff, so I might at least hire maids, now that Calvin has decided to take an extended tour of Italy." Anne laughed and shook her head. "And I am summoned to sing all the time for her friends. Her ladyship does adore music."

"Your parents must be very pleased by Hew's elevation," Gwen observed.

"They were more pleased to discover he has powerful friends. The Duke of York, the commander of the Royal Navy and Commander-in-Chief of the Army. Commodore Smith, who was with him at Acre. Viscount Howe, the Lieutenant-General of the Ordnance—he oversees the Artillery," she explained for the other women, "and the Master-General, the Marquess Cornwallis, one of the most senior military officials in the country—they all spoke in Hew's favor. Not to mention the Earl of St. Vincent, who once sailed with our mutual friend the Viscount Penrydd. And I suppose Pen wrote a letter for him as well?"

"He may have done, once or several times," Gwen admitted,

pulling a stem of hellebore through her fingers. "*I* have not yet been bidden to one of the Queen's drawing rooms."

"Yes, well, you'd only been a knight's daughter for a moment before you wed a viscount, and then he carried you away on a wedding trip to explore your mines and count your riches," Anne reminded her. "I don't doubt you'll have your chance to wear your ermine tails and your coronet with its sixteen pearls when Parliament opens its next session. And the Queen only had me, I think, because the Duke of Beaufort was in London as well. Hew is very much in his pocket planning improvements to Newport, now that General Napoleon is confirmed to be back in France."

"And what of your brother?" Mathry dared to ask.

Anne pursed her lips. "Still being held for the assizes. I think the evidence will show he could not be the Black Hound, or at least not responsible for all his crimes. But Mr. Darch has suddenly turned into an honest businessman, while Daron was only too eager to make everyone around Newport and its environs aware he meant to take over his operations. So I think Daron can only be pardoned if Hew speaks for him, and even then, there is like to be a hefty fine."

"Aye," Mathry said seriously, "but did you get to keep the brandy? Because a certain housekeeper of a certain castle has a brace of hard-drinking men to keep, and—"

"Peace," Gwen laughed. "I hope all our stores are got by honest means, Mrs. Ross. If we're to have a future magistrate and Member of Parliament in our family, which I think we will."

"Good heavens." Anne blinked. "Would I be spending the season in London too, in that case?"

"What fun we'll have when you are!" Gwen walked the gravel path to where Anne stood peering under the blowsy petals of the dog roses. "Ah, you've found the hips. Good for digestion and for passing water." She plucked one of the red-orange berries and rolled it between her fingers. "Mother Morris swears they are good for the eyes."

"And the skin," Dovey called.

Anne smiled, though her eyes smarted as she helped Gwen place rose hips in her basket. "There is so much to learn."

"But you have good teachers. I like this Mrs. Lambe."

Anne nodded. "That's not even her name. She's just pretending to be a widow. I don't think she's been any closer to a man than I was before I married."

"I wonder if she'd like to be close to the vicar?" Dovey snickered. "For certain he'd like to be close to her."

Anne dabbed the corner of her eye with a gloved finger. "Don't let Mr. Stanley hear you. He likes to pretend he treats her like any other member of his flock."

Gwen reached out and took Anne's hand. "Are you feeling low over Daron?"

"Yes." Anne sniffled. "And outraged that he turned on me, when why should I be? He turned on you. I suppose it is his just deserts for abandoning you."

"I only hope you will not let what happened to me—with my other child—frighten you away from something you want."

Anne blinked away the tears. "I won't. Hew has said he can wait until I am ready to have children. I think in time I may be. And until then, I have a wonderful cunning woman who knows the herbs to keep me from catching." She turned her hand and clasped Gwen's palm. "Besides, I have you, and Dovey, and Mrs. Ross to help me when the time comes."

"We are fortunate in our marriages, aren't we?" Gwen remarked. She glanced at Dovey, her face softening. "And in our friends."

"The wisest of women, we are," Dovey agreed, sauntering over and allowing Gwen to take her other hand.

"Amen to that," Mathry said, and blew them a kiss. "Ah, the moment's ruined. Here's one of the husbands come to fetch his bride—and it'd be the most newly wed among us, wouldn't it?"

"I won't be ashamed for wanting the company of my lovely wife over the coarse lot you call husbands," Hew said.

"Oh, high in the instep now he's got his knight's badge, is he?" Mathry laughed.

"I manage to tolerate him." Anne's whole being grew soft and warm, watching her husband walk toward her down the gravel path with a smile meant only for her.

The other men turned out into the garden, continuing some heated discussion. "Hewitt's right. End the trade first," the viscount was saying to Evans. "Then you cripple the economic engine, and the landowners have less grounds to object when the whole business is abolished. Of course it might take years to bring the Lords around—"

"We ought to be supporting the revolution in Haiti, like the American president is," Ross argued. "Milord, tell your military friend here—"

"We've lost him, he's a man in love," Penrydd said, going to the side of his own lady. "Can't say as I blame him."

Hew tucked Anne's hand over his arm and walked the paths with her. She smiled up at him, enjoying the calm blue of his eyes, the cornflower hue of the sky, and the firm, solid warmth of his arm beneath her palm. Here was where she felt most at home—beside him.

"All's well with the viscountess?" he said softly. "I know you were nervous about her invitation."

"We're friends again. It feels good to have things repaired."

"And does she approve of me?"

"As long as you are making me this happy, I think she approves." Anne gave him a twinkling smile. "And only look at me! Capturing a knight. Higher than my mother hoped. Sir Hewitt Vaughn, hero of Acre."

He brought a hand to her lips. "I only hope I might give you the life you deserve. You were meant for grand things."

Anne stepped close to him. "This is the life I want," she whispered. "With you."

After a moment he lifted his head and held her gaze as if he would seek out every corner of her being. "Do you finally trust me, then? To take care of you. To never turn from your side."

Anne smiled up at him. This man. He was beyond what she'd ever thought to dream of. All those years of lonely longing, when nothing else had felt right, she'd been waiting for him.

He was worth the waiting.

Anne twined her arms about his neck, sifting her fingers through the silken hair at his nape. "I should like above all things," she said, "if we were to take care of one another."

"As my lady wishes," he said, and bent for another kiss.

ABOUT THE AUTHOR

Misty Urban fell in love with stories at an early age and has spent her life among books as a teacher, scholar, editor, writer, and bookseller. Her favorite stories take you new places, teach you new things, and end with a win. She especially likes romances about unconventional heroines who defy the odds and the unexpected heroes who woo them, so that's mostly what she writes. When she puts down the book she likes to take long walks, drag her family to new places, or hang out around water, dreaming up new stories.

Visit her at mistyurban.com
Join author's newsletter

www.ingramcontent.com/pod-product-compliance
Lightning Source LLC
Chambersburg PA
CBHW050509110726
47899CB00005B/1389